CHILDREN OF THE EMPIRE

A NOAH WOLF THRILLER

DAVID ARCHER

VINCE VOGEL

RIGHTHOUSE

PRAISE FOR THE NOAH WOLF SERIES

NOAH WOLF THRILLERS

Code Name Camelot (Book 1)
Lone Wolf (Book 2)
In Sheep's Clothing (Book 3)
Hit for Hire (Book 4)
The Wolf's Bite (Book 5)
Black Sheep (Book 6)
Balance of Power (Book 7)
Time to Hunt (Book 8)
Red Square (Book 9)
Highest Order (Book 10)
Edge of Anarchy (Book 11)
Unknown Evil (Book 12)
Black Harvest (Book 13)
World Order (Book 14)
Caged Animal (Book 15)
Deep Allegiance (Book 16)
Pack Leader (Book 17)
High Treason (Book 18)
A Wolf Among Men (Book 19)
Rogue Intelligence (Book 20)
Alpha (Book 21)
Rogue Wolf (Book 22)
Shadows of Allegiance (Book 23)

ONE

THE CHOPPER BUCKED hard against the rising thermals, its rotors slicing through the thick Bolivian afternoon like a knife through gristle. Outside, the horizon pulsed red with dust, turning the sunlight sour and coppery.

Beneath the bird, jungle fell away to reveal fire-scabbed clearings, churned mud, and blackened stumps where trees had stood just days ago. Scorched fields lay ringed in wire and sandbags. UN trucks sat like hulking beetles under tarpaulins the color of dried blood, their wheels sunk deep in red clay.

Inside the helicopter's fuselage, the air was acrid with sweat, fuel, and adrenaline. Jenny Blessing sat with her back against the cold metal wall, helmet in her lap, jaw tight.

Across from her, Neil Blessing wiped a film of condensation from his glasses with a frayed corner of his shirt.

Next to him, Wally Lawson gripped a black biocontainment case like a sacred relic. It was sealed with triple locks and thermally regulated—and he held it as if it might explode or vanish if he loosened his grip for even a second.

Jenny tilted her head, her voice dry as the dust outside. "Anyone else feel like we're dropping into a graveyard?"

Neil didn't look up. "That's optimistic."

Jenny turned her eyes to Wally. "Hey, Wally? You good?"

Wally looked up slowly, blinking. His expression was distant, slightly unfocused, like someone trying to place a face from a dream. Then he nodded once. No smile. Just the nod.

Jenny didn't push. She didn't need to. She'd read the after-action files. She knew neural decomp when she saw it—what the extraction had taken, and what it left behind.

Six months ago, the Council's top neurosurgeon had performed a memory extraction on him: ultra-thin wires threaded into the brain to siphon memories one synapse at a time. It had left Wally diminished. Recovery was slow and as yet incomplete.

The helicopter dipped lower, rotors kicking up another storm of grit. Below, a checkpoint flickered into view through the dust, blue helmets and white body armor barely visible amid the haze. A signal flare went up. Green.

They were expected.

Jenny adjusted her grip on the rifle resting between her knees and locked eyes with Neil.

Showtime.

The helicopter slammed down hard on a makeshift landing pad of splintered wood and rust-stained corrugated metal. The skids groaned as if the bird resented being grounded. Instantly, a wall of dust rose around them, churning into the rotors and swallowing everything in a blur of ocher and sweat. The heat hit next—a wet, lung-clogging smother that reeked of mildew, fuel, and something faintly metallic underneath.

Jenny ducked low and led the team out beneath the churring blades. The jungle sang around them—not with birdsong, but with the high, shrill scream of cicadas.

Two UN guards emerged from the haze, rifles slung lazily but hands never far from the triggers. Their blue helmets were sun-faded and scuffed, the uniforms beneath a jigsaw of mismatched camo and salvaged gear. One of them—a lean Bolivian with sharp eyes and a clenched jaw—had a black phoenix insignia stitched on his upper sleeve. The mark of the Council. Someone had scratched through it with a blade and slapped a strip of medical tape over the remains.

The guard stopped a few feet away. "You Camelot?"

Jenny stepped forward, her boots squelching in the damp clay. "That obvious?"

The man gave a humorless grunt. "We stopped expecting help a week ago. The lieutenant's waiting."

They were waved through a checkpoint cobbled together from rusting shipping containers. Warning glyphs had been hastily sprayed on every surface in bright biohazard orange—some recognizable, others improvised.

On the far side of the checkpoint stood a squat concrete building—a former warehouse now transformed into a makeshift clinic. Its windows were long shattered, now patched over with tarpaulin stitched to steel mesh. The UN emblem flapped weakly in the breeze, stained with old rain.

Lieutenant Adjani Camara waited at the entrance. She was tall and wiry, her skin cracked with sunburn, her dark hair braided back into a knot. A sidearm rode her hip.

"Lieutenant Adjani Camara," she said by way of greeting. "UN contingent lead. You're about to walk into something no one here was trained to handle."

Neil stepped past Jenny and offered a tight nod. "That's why you called us."

Camara's mouth twitched, not quite a smile. "No. I called for medicine. What I got was Camelot."

She turned without waiting for a reply, boots crunching across sunbaked gravel as she led them toward the clinic.

Inside, the air changed. Cooler but not cleaner. A wet, fungal tang clung to the walls, mingling with bleach and old blood. The interior had been stripped down to its bones—no furniture, no patients, just crates, power cables, and the hum of makeshift filtration rigs.

Camara stopped at a heavy steel door marked with peeling hazard symbols. She keyed in a code on the pad, then shouldered it open.

"Locker room's through here," she said. "Strip to base layer. No skin. No hair. No exposed stitching. If it can wick moisture, it can carry spores."

The room beyond was barely lit. Rows of lockers, mismatched and rusting, lined the walls. A drain slithered down the center of the floor.

On the far wall, a rack of hazmat suits hung in grim procession—hooded, sealed, pale gray with charcoal filters like gills across the shoulders. Each one looked like it had already seen too much.

Jenny unbuckled her chest rig and shrugged out of it slowly. The sweat made everything cling. Neil was already peeling down to his underlayer.

Wally hesitated, fingers resting on the zip of his jacket. Jenny caught his eye. No words were needed this time.

"Filters last four hours," Camara said, crossing to a shelf stacked with respirators and sterile gloves. "Longer if you breathe shallow. You won't. It gets thick in there."

Jenny reached for a suit.

"Once you're in," Camara added, her voice turning flat, "you don't take it off. Not for anything. Not if you itch. Not if you panic. Not even if some bug has climbed in there with you."

No one spoke. The only sound was the slow rasp of zippers and the distant, irregular thump of something heavy being moved outside.

Jenny tugged the hood over her head and sealed the collar ring. The world narrowed. Breathing became sound. Her own breath, rasping through the mask.

She looked at Neil through the scratched visor. He nodded once.

Camara opened the next door. Beyond it was a dim corridor with plastic sheeting and the first shadow of something red smeared along the wall.

"Follow me," she said. "And don't touch anything."

The first step past the threshold of the concrete clinic was a step into hell. The hallway was narrow, lit by the sputtering buzz of emergency fluorescents. Bloodstained curtains hung like ghosts between beds, some drawn tight, others torn open to reveal what lay behind—and what lay behind was not good. Even inside the suits, the smell was atrocious: cloying antiseptic fought a losing battle against feces, sour sweat, and something deeper—something that smelled like meat gone bad, like ozone after a lightning strike, like rot beginning not from the skin but from the marrow.

Camara led them through the ward's twisting gut. "This was a UN storage facility a week ago," she said. "Now it's a morgue with nurses."

The hallway curved left, and the truth of it all landed like a hammer. The space widened into what had once been a huge storage area—now repurposed, packed with beds arranged two deep. Some were hospital-issue, others cobbled from crates or broken chairs. Anything that could hold a body.

And there were many bodies to hold.

A boy, maybe twelve, suddenly convulsed on one of the cots. His back arched unnaturally, his spine a bow drawn to breaking. Sweat poured from him, and his veins—black and thick like creeping vines—bulged beneath his skin. His mouth was open in a soundless scream.

Straps held his arms tight. His legs thrashed, uncontrolled.

Two nurses were already at his side, hazmat suits creaking as they moved. One held the boy's shoulders down while the other jabbed a syringe into the exposed skin above the collarbone. The fluid inside was a dull amber. The boy jerked once more, then stilled. His eyes, unfocused and gray around the irises, blinked rapidly as his body went slack.

"Ketamine-analgesic cocktail," one of the nurses muttered

through her voice amp, more for the recorders than the visitors. Her hands never stopped moving—adjusting the IV, checking the vitals patch clinging to the boy's temple with surgical tape.

The second nurse straightened. "Stabilized," she said. "For now."

A sigh rippled through the ward like a breeze through plastic. But it lasted all of two seconds.

Another scream tore through the air—ragged, gurgling, too deep to belong to the thin woman it came from. Camara snapped her head toward the sound.

"Bed twenty-six," she barked.

The nurses were already running. They moved fast—even in the suits.

Camara stepped back to let them pass. "This is what it is now," she said to no one in particular. "You calm one, and another starts screaming. Whack-a-mole with dying people."

They kept moving. What else was there to do?

The next ward was worse. The tarps parted with a wet sound, peeling apart like lungs opening. Behind them were more patients, or what remained of them. Most lay still. Some twitched.

Jenny stopped beside a figure hidden beneath a soaked towel. She knelt and gently lifted the fabric away.

The man's face was slack, pallid. His eyes were open—pitch black. Not clotted blood. Not bruising. The irises, the sclera, even the reflection itself—it was all consumed. It looked less like something physiological and more like the color had bled from his soul outward.

His lips parted. A tongue, black and cracked, twitched once and stilled.

Behind them, a sharp zzzzip tore through the quiet like a gunshot.

They turned.

Two attendants in sweat-slicked PPE were zipping a body bag closed outside the surgical prep room. The bag sagged at the center, the shape still warm, still soft.

Camara stood with the others, silent, as the attendants carried the body past.

"You think it's them?" she muttered. "The Council?"

Jenny didn't take her eyes off the bag. "The Council's dead," she said.

Camara didn't answer right away.

"Yeah," she said at last. "But I heard there are others."

TWO

AFTER SHOWING them the devastation of the quarantine area, Camara led them back to the locker room. Once they'd changed out of the hazmat suits, she proceeded to guide them to an outbuilding on the edge of the compound.

Inside was a makeshift conference room.

Fluorescent lights buzzed overhead. In the far corner, a pile of body bags lay stacked beneath plastic tarps. A single fan creaked on the ceiling, moving the air just enough to send a ripple through the covering but not enough to lower the temperature in any tangible way.

A broad conference table dominated the room. At its head sat Dr. Helena Menendez, an experienced virologist in her mid-forties with wiry hair pulled into a fraying knot. She wore sweat-soaked scrubs, translucent in patches, and her Cuban accent had been worn thin by sleeplessness and crisis.

To her left sat Dr. Elias Otieno, a tall, weathered pathologist from the DRC. His voice was slow and steady, every word placed with the care of a man long acquainted with human ruin.

The second Neil, Jenny, and Wally sat down at the table, Menendez pointed to a map on the wall. Red marker notes ran in concentric circles from a central dot.

"The index case was traced to Alto Beni," she said. "Forty-eight hours later, six surrounding settlements went dark. All infected were indigenous. No deviation."

"No deviation?" Neil frowned. "You mean it only infects indigenous?"

"We're not certain yet—hence the hazmat and quarantine protocols," Menendez replied. "But so far, only indigenous people have shown signs of infection. There was a logging team nearby—made up of people from the cities with European ancestry. They're all clear."

Wally leaned forward. "What exactly does it do to them?"

Dr. Menendez brought up an image on the screen behind her—a CT cross-section of a lung, shot through with jagged white traces. It looked like lightning frozen in flesh.

Otieno took over, voice even. "The virus enters through mucosal membranes. But it's not airborne. Not casual. Transmission is direct—blood, saliva, contact with infected tissue. But..."

He tapped a key. Another scan appeared. Genetic readouts—lines of code, then comparison markers. Red highlights flared across the screen.

"This isn't random," Otieno said. "It's genetic alignment."

Wally leaned in, frowning. "Define that."

Otieno rotated the laptop so the whole table could see. Two genome maps—one standard, one infected—blinked in synchrony.

The differences were glaring.

On the left, the healthy genome displayed as a clean lattice of blue and green markers—ordered, symmetrical, steady pulses along a digital helix.

On the right, the infected map was chaos. Red markers lit up like flare clusters, especially along chromosomes 6 and 11. Entire gene sequences had been rerouted, their pathways corrupted by foreign proteins.

"It binds to a receptor protein found predominantly in Andean and Guaraní populations," Otieno said. "The frequency in other genomes—particularly European-descended—is nearly zero."

Jenny's voice was ice. "You're saying this thing chooses who to infect."

Otieno didn't flinch. "No. I'm saying someone designed it to."

The room fell into silence. The fan ticked around and around. No one breathed.

Wally broke it. "I take it you have a sample in your lab?"

Menendez nodded once.

Wally's expression hardened. "Then I'd like to see it."

A minute later, the lab door was creaking open with the groan of rust and neglect, revealing a room that could barely house two people standing shoulder to shoulder. It felt less like a laboratory and more like a storage closet. Wires tangled like vines overhead, draped like jungle creepers across the low ceiling. Nothing in here looked newer than a decade, and most of it looked salvaged from tech graveyards.

A centrifuge wheezed in a corner, its housing cinched together with duct tape. Next to it stood a scuffed white mini-fridge labeled in smeared Sharpie: *BLOOD/PLASMA—DO NOT UNPLUG*. A PCR thermocycler missing half its lid bolts sat beside it, twitching quietly like it didn't trust itself to keep working. And nestled into a corner, humming with faint digital breath, was the real jewel—a Council-era gene sequencer, scratched but alive, its logo almost worn off.

Camara stood behind Wally and gestured with a grimace. "This is the best we've got."

Wally didn't answer. His focus was absolute. He stepped inside and laid down his gear with the precision of a man setting up for surgery or a priest for prayer.

First came the portable isolation hood, unfolded and snapped into place over a low table. Then a cooling core no larger than a lunchbox. Finally, a biosample injector with a fingerprint-lock security ring that blinked green beneath his thumb.

Menendez entered a few seconds later, clutching a reinforced cryo-vial between two gloved hands. Inside was a sample of the virus.

"No one else touches this," she said quietly.

She passed it into the isolation hood with the care of someone handling a live grenade. The vial clicked into the locking clamp with a magnetic thunk, and Wally was already moving—gloves on, posture tight, mind elsewhere. His fingers moved like a pianist's, swift and assured, every motion practiced.

His voice dropped to a murmur. "Let's see what you are."

He swabbed a sample with gloved precision and fed it into a cartridge bay on the sequencer. The machine responded with a low chime and came to life.

Next, Wally opened a laptop and linked it to the sequencer. Nucleotide chains began to scroll down the screen—red, blue, green—a digital waltz of base pairs drawing themselves from the blood's secrets.

As the data streamed, Wally tapped into his own neural-linked archive: a deeply encrypted, privately maintained viral index. It had taken him years to build it. The display shimmered with titles as it began cross-referencing:

92 confirmed Council-engineered pathogens...

14 in prototype status...

8 scrubbed from official records...

The sequence comparison began. A progress bar crept across the screen.

12%... 28%... 41%...

Wally leaned back, glasses slipping slightly down his nose. He wiped them absently, then looked again.

74%... 92%... COMPLETE.

The sequencer chimed. Then froze.

A line of text blazed white on black:

MATCH FOUND

Council Origin: PROJECT HELIX

Designation: Variant 7B

Status: EXPUNGED (Internal – Level Gamma)

Wally's blood turned to ice.

He stood locked in place as if the machine had pointed a weapon at him.

"No," he whispered. "No, no, no—this was supposed to be buried."

The screen scrolled. Details unspooled like a noose:

Originally designed for controlled population pruning during insurgency response.

Abandoned due to immediate non-containment risk.

Final note: Too unstable. Shelve indefinitely.

Wally stared. "This was never supposed to make it out of prototype," he breathed.

"What is it?" Menendez asked.

"Helix-7B."

"Which is?"

Wally didn't turn away from the screen. His voice was flat, toneless—like he was narrating a nightmare he'd had too many times.

"Helix-7B was the Council's attempt at social genocide," he said. "A virus designed to identify specific genetic markers tied to chronic illness, hereditary defects, even certain neurological predispositions. The idea was to quietly 'trim' populations— people who would need lifelong care or whose genes didn't align with whatever selective ideal they were chasing that year."

Menendez stepped closer. "So it was eugenics."

Wally nodded once. "Yes, it was eugenics."

He tapped a few keys, and the genome map reappeared on the screen of his laptop—now overlaid with faint reference notes, archived metadata from a buried Council server. Annotations blinked beside clusters of highlighted markers: BRCA mutations, neurodegenerative SNPs, autoimmune likelihood thresholds.

"They couldn't get it stable," Wally continued. "The virus mutated too fast. It either didn't activate at all or it jumped to unrelated markers. In trials, it wiped out entire control groups.

There was an outbreak in Novosibirsk. They buried it. Literally. They sealed the whole site and rained missiles down on it."

"And now it's here," Jenny said coldly.

Wally's jaw tightened. He pointed to the newest data—highlighted sequences on the infected genome that glowed like scars.

"This isn't the original design," he said. "Someone's re-engineered it. See these markers here? They're clustered around loci tied to ancestry—mitochondrial haplogroups, inherited from maternal lines. And this one—chromosome 6—targets immune system variation common to Andean and Guaraní populations."

Neil let out a low breath. "It's not pruning the sick anymore."

"No," Wally said. "Now it's targeting race. Inherited bloodlines."

The room fell still again. Even the lab's broken machines seemed to quiet, as if the virus had turned the very air to glass.

Jenny stepped forward. "So someone's using what the Council buried."

Wally didn't look up. "Yes. Someone with access to their archives. Someone who wants to finish what the Council didn't have the stomach to start."

Jenny's voice was like gravel. "Then we need to find them."

Wally nodded—slowly, grimly. "Yes. Before they unleash it onto the world."

THREE

THE MOUNTAIN LOOMED like a cathedral carved by ancient hands—vast, unfeeling, and half-lost to ice and silence. Above the Putorana Plateau, afternoon light slanted cold and hard, casting long, merciless shadows across the ridgeline. The wind didn't howl—it whispered, low and circling, like the breath of something old refusing to die. Below, buried in the stone's shadow, was a place that had no name.

Nestled beneath a tangle of rockfall and ice, obscured by camouflage mesh and thermal shielding, Camelot's safehouse was invisible to satellites, drones, and mapmakers. No lights. No signs. Only a slab of reinforced alloy, flush with the frozen ground—an elevator sunk into the spine of the world.

Deep inside stood Noah Wolf.

He was motionless at the center of the War Room, a stark silhouette surrounded by machines that hummed with restrained violence. Behind him loomed the sigil of Camelot: a silver sword and a round shield.

The space was carved into the mountain's marrow—walls of smoothed basalt reinforced with carbon-laced steel. There were no windows. No doors that weren't sealed with biometric locks. Just a maze of corridors and chambers sunk into the bedrock.

It had once belonged to the Council—a black site buried deep into the permafrost, where child assassins were trained and ethics were a distant abstraction.

Now it was something else.

Now it was Camelot's nerve center.

Banks of monitors displayed a roiling patchwork of global hotspots—rioting cities burning across satellite feeds, intercepted comms, and open-source traffic streams.

Noah's eyes fixed to it all, the world unfolding before him in vectors and threats, like a prophecy still being written.

He wasn't watching one screen.

He was watching all of them.

MONITOR ONE—JOHANNESBURG

Grainy drone footage panned over a UN relief convoy penned in by a crowd. Food riots had erupted into chaos. Gunfire cracked across the plaza. A guard opened fire into the swarm. Civilians trampled each other for crates of rice that burst open like sandbags.

MONITOR TWO—KASHMIR

Night vision. Static-hazed. Footage of a black-market drone hovering low over a Hindu temple during worship. It loosed a pressure charge on it with a *whump* that shook the camera. The blast was quick. Brutal. Afterwards people clawed rubble with bare hands, dragging bodies from smoking gaps in the stone.

MONITOR THREE—BALTIC BORDERLANDS

More drone footage. This time taken in Serbia. Eastern Europe's frostbitten edges, burning. Factions flying tattered remnants of Council-era banners clashed in a no-man's-land in the middle of the war-torn city—mercenaries, zealots, desperate conscripts. All fighting for the remains of their homeland. A tank belched flame into the night.

Noah stood watching it all when a soft chime echoed through the room. A voice followed—low and poised.

"Noah. Priority escalation detected in twelve conflict zones. Would you like a full situational breakdown?"

It was Esmerelda—Camelot's AI.

Esmerelda had a long history with Camelot. She'd once had a body. Tall, humanoid, and athletic. Wally had built her years ago in the bright before-times, back when the world still tolerated dreamers who tried to give machines conscience. She'd served as logistics command, lab interface, even friend.

Then came the Fall. The Council's purge of E & E. The siege of Kirkland.

Esmerelda had been on-site.

They'd said she was wiped during the breach, her memory core slagged in the fires that consumed R&D's labs. Wally had believed it. For a time. Until he found the dead-drop hidden in the archive Allison Peterson had left for them. A backup.

For him.

Wally had spent the better part of six months rebuilding Esmerelda from the ghost of that code. Now she ran Camelot's infrastructure like a neural cortex. Air, power, data, perimeter defense. Environmental systems. Surveillance. She didn't sleep. She didn't eat. And since Wally had brought her back, she hadn't glitched once.

"No," Noah said, his voice flat. "There's nothing we can do anyway."

One of the screens—Johannesburg—crackled, then cut to black. The riot blinked out mid-scream.

He turned from the screens. Not with finality. Not resignation. Just purpose. Watching was over. Action began.

"Open up a channel to Bolivia," he said.

"Understood," came Esmerelda's flat voice. "Compiling encrypted burst transmission."

The central monitor lit up with the call:

SECURE CHANNEL – BOLIVIA NODE
SOURCE: WALLACE MURRAY
STATUS: URGENT – TIER ONE

Noah leaned in without hesitation. A crackle of static opened the line.

"Wally here." His voice came through thin and drained, the words dragging like they were too heavy to speak.

"What have you got, Wally?"

"We found something," he said. "You need to see this."

A heartbeat later, the display on the central monitor changed.

The image that filled it wasn't violent. It didn't need to be.

A child—maybe eight, maybe younger—lay on a bare cement floor, half-swaddled in a wrinkled UN emergency blanket. His skin was waxy, almost translucent, the blackened veins beneath it rising like poisoned roots. His mouth hung slightly open, his eyes glassy and empty. One hand was clutched tightly against his chest, fingers curled in what looked like prayer—or defiance.

In the lower corner of the screen, system text began to crawl:

AUTOMATED ANALYSIS—MATCH: PROJECT HELIX

Variant Signature: Confirmed

Classification: Weaponized Strain–7B

Noah stared at the screen, unmoving. "One of the Council's own, I presume?"

"Yes, but there's more," Wally continued, voice barely above a whisper. "It's been modified. Someone's taken the base sequence and rewritten the activation logic. The original strain targeted hereditary disorders, autoimmune flags, things you'd find on a medical screen. This version doesn't care about disease."

New data populated the display: genome comparisons, ancestral haplogroup overlays, epidemiological maps shaded with spreading red.

"It's targeting ethnically linked SNPs," he said. "Receptors clustered in Indigenous South American populations—Andean, Guaraní, some Quechua variants. It's surgical. The markers aren't associated with any illness. They're associated with heritage."

The silence in the War Room thickened.

"Whoever did this is into ethnic cleansing," Wally went on. "I think this is just a test zone. Before the real thing."

Noah folded his arms. "You're saying Bolivia was the trial run."

"I'm saying it fits the criteria—remote enough to limit international detection, close enough to UN aid lines for cleanup to look like negligence. And it's working. If we hadn't gotten here when we did, we might have missed it."

"What's your current objective, Wally?"

"I'm staying," Wally replied. "I've isolated a secondary strain in cold storage—slightly degraded but usable for trace analysis. If I can reverse engineer the compiler logic, I might be able to pinpoint the source. Whoever engineered this left fingerprints in the code. They always do."

Noah nodded slowly. "We'll get you whatever support you need. Where are Jenny and Neil?"

Wally glanced off-screen. "Right here."

Another beat of static—and then two new faces appeared as the camera panned.

Neil stood at the edge of the feed, rifle slung, face drawn. Beside him, Jenny leaned forward into frame, her eyes sharp, alert.

"There's a plane inbound to pick you up," Noah said. "I need both of you in Europe."

"Europe's a big place, boss," Neil replied.

"You'll be starting in Istanbul. I need you to oversee Knox's next move."

There was a pause. Then Jenny's voice, sharp with recognition.

"Adrian Knox? As in the man who nuked Olympus?"

"The same," Noah said.

Noah's gaze flicked toward one of the monitors—Istanbul lit up on a digital map.

"Since Olympus went down, he's been the most valuable—and most vulnerable—asset we've got," Noah continued. "You don't dismantle the Council's central AI without painting a target on your back."

He leaned forward slightly, voice low and firm.

"Every loyalist, contractor, and deluded believer who still thinks the Council was humanity's guiding hand is out to get him. The ones left behind? They're not looking to rebuild. They're looking to punish. To avenge."

Jenny narrowed her eyes. "You think someone's found him?"

"I know it," Noah said. "A data fragment surfaced yesterday in a closed-channel darknet cluster—old Council encryption, decrypted by one of Esmerelda's filters. A location tag buried inside Istanbul. They're on the ground. Looking for him."

Neil grunted. "So the leak's internal."

"Possibly," Noah said. "Or someone's gotten access to our old routing system. Either way, we have a window before Knox is found by some sycophant with a gun."

Neil nodded once. "What's the ROE?"

"Low profile unless compromised. Eyes, ears, and escalation only if absolutely necessary. If this leak was bait, I want the hook."

Jenny glanced sideways at Neil, then back at the screen. "We'll get him out."

"I know you will," Noah said. "You leave within the hour."

The feed blinked. A final line of coordinates and a flight code appeared on the screen.

Istanbul awaited.

FOUR

NOAH WOLF KEYED in the override and stepped into his quarters, the heavy door sighing shut behind him. The lights were low. A half-read book sat on the edge of the bunk. A pair of boots lay neatly by the wall. His daughter looked up from her sketchpad, legs folded beneath her on the bed.

"Hey," she said quietly.

"Hey," Noah replied, his voice softened by something he rarely let others see. "Time for your physical. Katya's waiting."

Norah slid off the bed, stuffing the sketchpad into her satchel. She didn't complain, but her eyes lingered on the shadows stretching across the ceiling.

They walked in silence through the corridor, the air humming with recycled warmth. Fluorescent panels cast pale light along the walls. Ahead, the hallway branched—one path led to the medical bay, the other to the training studios.

Norah slowed.

She paused by the reinforced glass panel that overlooked the main studio.

Inside, the space was empty now. Just mats, dummies, and the faint scent of sweat and chalk. But the silence had weight.

Noah stopped beside her.

She shuddered.

He placed a hand gently around her shoulders. "You okay?"

Her voice was distant. "I've seen people die in there."

He didn't dismiss it. Didn't lie.

"It'll be different with Katya," he said. "That's not to say it'll be any easier."

She nodded slowly, then turned away. They continued on.

Katya was waiting at the medical bay—arms folded, her black coat hanging like a shadow behind her. Two operatives stood by, already prepping equipment.

Norah sat quietly on the edge of the diagnostic table as the procedure began.

Routine vitals first. Heart rate, temperature, reflex checks. Nothing invasive yet.

Noah and Katya stood off to the side, behind a privacy screen.

"When do the other recruits arrive?" he asked.

"The transport lands in two hours," Katya replied. "We've pre-cleared them through Esmerelda. Standard profiles. Nothing strange."

Noah grunted.

The scan progressed. Blood draw. Neural response testing. Then, finally, the CT scanner hummed to life.

Norah hesitated as the cradle slid into position.

"It's okay," Noah said. "It's all part of it."

She gave him a skeptical look but climbed in.

The machine clicked, buzzed, and began its slow orbit around her skull.

A display to the side projected a cross-section of Norah's brain in grayscale detail.

Then a blip.

Tiny.

Barely visible unless you knew what to look for.

But Noah did.

A black speck embedded near the corpus callosum. Symmetrical. Engineered. Foreign.

Noah's throat went dry.

He said nothing.

Katya didn't speak either—but he saw her shoulders tighten, just slightly.

The scan ended.

Norah sat up, rubbing at her temples. "We done?"

"Yeah," Noah said, voice measured. "Head back to digs. I'll be along soon."

She hesitated but nodded and left.

Once the door sealed, Noah turned to Katya.

"It's real," he said.

She nodded. "Breakers."

Noah paced.

"When we dug through the archives last month, I wanted to believe it was theoretical. Council insurance. Not implemented."

"Looks like it was standard," Katya said. "Across all levels. Recruits, soldiers, field ops, intel analysts. Even sleeper agents."

"Including my daughter."

The words hung in the air like smoke.

"If only we knew how to disable them," Katya said. "But every route leads to neural degradation. Brain damage."

Noah pressed his fists against the wall. "They built a generation of weapons with kill switches in their heads."

"And now those weapons are ours," Katya said quietly. "But they're still wired to someone else's dead hand."

The silence returned, colder than before.

And it didn't leave.

FIVE

THE NEXT MORNING, the corridor groaned as Katya walked, the sound of her boot heels ringing off the concrete floor —sharp, even, deliberate. A half-beat behind her came six softer sets of footsteps, younger but just as precise.

The children walked in two columns. Not quite rigid—but close enough. Their eyes moved constantly, scanning their surroundings—not out of fear. There was no hesitation in their gazes. Only watchfulness.

No. It wasn't nerves. It was conditioning.

The base wasn't the only thing Alison Peterson left to Camelot when she defected and died. She left behind these six Council-forged, built for precision, honed for violence, killers-in-waiting. None of them old enough to vote but already dangerous enough to level a room.

Among them was Noah Wolf's own daughter, Norah Wolf. Dark-haired, silent, always watching.

Katya stopped in front of a set of reinforced blast doors that led into the training range. The moment she halted, the six behind her stopped as well. No command. No gesture. One breath behind her. Perfect.

She turned to face them, gaze sweeping across their faces—measuring them each in turn.

Today, they became hers.

She let the silence stretch before speaking, her tone dry, almost sardonic.

"Now let's see how good the Council's genetic engineering program really was."

The doors hissed open. Katya stepped forward. The six followed without a word.

The blast doors slammed shut behind them, sealing the group inside the training range. The sound echoed briefly through the cavernous space, then faded into a heavy silence. The chamber was carved straight into the Putorana stone, deep and cold. Target lanes stretched in rigid symmetry across one half of the room. Opposite were melee pits marked by scuffs and old stains. Suspended above it all was a catwalk observation deck, its rails dulled with age. Soundproofing panels dangled unevenly from the ceiling like worn skin, and the floor still bore faint scars—ghosts of past drills etched into steel.

Katya turned to face the recruits. The children lined up shoulder to shoulder, instinct guiding them before instruction.

She hadn't even needed to ask.

Katya folded her arms behind her back and let her gaze sweep across the line. There were six of them. Six potential weapons. Each one a different shape of threat.

Lula stood on the far left, sixteen, broad-shouldered and unbothered, arms crossed like she was sizing up the room for weaknesses. Her smirk wasn't playful—it was an invitation to underestimate her. A test, ready to be failed.

"Going to break us in, Mother?" she asked, her tone deliberately mocking.

Katya didn't blink. "Try that tone again and watch who gets to be broken first."

Lula shrugged, not cowed in the slightest. "Just clarifying the correct one."

She didn't blink either. Everything about her posture said alpha—but it was the control that made her dangerous. She didn't fidget. She didn't flare. She waited.

Next to her stood Gregor, fifteen. Silent. His posture wasn't just rigid—it was solid. His hand rested near the seam of his pants leg, not from anxiety but calculation. He was sizing it all up. Distance to weapons. Exits. The others.

Katya clocked it without judgment. *He doesn't need orders,* she thought. *He needs direction. And a reason.*

Lula leaned slightly toward him. "You gonna talk today or just glower like normal?"

Gregor didn't respond. His slate-gray eyes remained forward, blank.

"Just because you're jealous he glowers better than you do," Zina said from the next spot down.

Zina—fourteen, wiry and poised just off-center from her designated line. Subtle. Measured. Always with a slight angle to her stance, as if ready to recoil, pivot, strike.

Lula turned slowly to her—and glowered.

Zina met the look and tilted her head, as if sizing her up. "Actually. Yours is pretty good. Maybe a draw."

Katya butted in. "Do you always talk more when you're nervous, Zina?"

Zina didn't flinch. "No. Just when I'm bored."

Her tone was flat, clipped. Efficient. Zina was fluent in six languages, but she spoke in careful syllables, as though she resented wasting even breath.

Beside her, Tao, thirteen, stood as if his body was present only out of obligation. His gaze wasn't on Katya—or the others—but slightly above, slightly past, like he was tracking something no one else could see. His posture was technically correct, but his mind was clearly elsewhere, moving faster than the room around him.

Tao was the outlier.

Where the others had been trained, sharpened, molded, Tao had been calculated. His IQ score—285, verified and reverified by six different tests—was not a point of pride but a warning label. He wasn't just intelligent. He was a savant. Neural processing off the charts. Pattern recognition that bordered on the paranormal. He spoke six languages fluently and understood a dozen more. He could perform vector calculus in his head faster than most machines. Once, during a stress test, he'd rewritten the algorithm of the simulation while still inside it—causing the system to crash for the first time in Council history.

He hadn't smiled once since arriving at Camelot.

Katya studied him for a beat longer than the others. There was no defiance in him. No hunger for approval. Just a deep, fractal stillness—like the surface of a lake that went down farther than anyone could ever dive.

"Tao," she said.

He blinked once, his mind returning to the room.

"Yes," he said simply.

Not "ma'am." Not "here." Just yes. An answer to a question she hadn't asked.

Katya nodded once. She knew not to push him. Tao volunteered information only when it suited him.

She moved on.

Imani, twelve, stood nearly motionless next to him, her hands clasped too tightly behind her back, knuckles white. Smallest in the group but never still, her eyes moved constantly—floor, ceiling, exits, Lula, back to Katya.

And then to Katya's sidearm.

Her gaze dropped like a pin to the holster at Katya's hip.

"Glock 17," Imani said, quietly but without hesitation. "Generation five. Standard issue for NATO forces. Lightweight. Reliable. Low recoil profile. Polymer frame. Seventeen-round capacity, chambered in 9x19mm Parabellum. Barrel length: 4.49 inches. Stock iron sights. Minimal wear. Judging by the slide finish, it has been cleaned within the last forty-eight hours but not test-fired since. No optic. No compensator. Loaded. I'm guessing you prefer it because the bore axis is lower than a SIG and you don't trust safeties you didn't install yourself."

Katya turned to her—not sharply, just enough to acknowledge the comment.

"Do you always profile your instructor's firearm?" she asked.

Imani's voice was almost a whisper. "Only when they're armed."

The corner of Katya's mouth didn't smile. But something close to one passed behind her eyes.

She made a note. Not fear. Awareness.

She moved to the last in line.

Norah.

Eleven. Quiet. She stood slightly apart from the others—not enough to draw a reprimand but just enough to signal something different. Her arms hung loosely at her sides. Relaxed. Not careless.

Her gaze was glacial. It drifted slowly from face to face without hesitation or curiosity. Just assessment.

She didn't speak.

Katya studied her a little longer. *She's got Noah's eyes*, she thought. *Cold as ice.*

"You're here," she said, her voice even, "because someone decided you were good enough to be trained."

She paused. Let that land.

"But I'm here because someone else believes you can be something more than generic trained killers."

Her gaze locked on Lula for a fraction longer than the rest.

"Today, we find out if you can be a weapon..." Her tone hardened. "...A trigger waiting to be pulled."

She let the silence settle, then pivoted.

"Today, we start with fundamentals," she said. "Marksmanship. Precision under pressure."

She turned and began walking, boots ringing off the steel flooring with unhurried purpose.

"Each of you has a file. I've read your diagnostics. I've seen your scores. You're good. Let's see if I can make you better."

She led them toward the far end of the chamber, where a bank of lockers and a weapon rack waited beneath a faded Council insignia half-scraped off the concrete wall.

"The range is active. Cold zone. Live ammunition. No safeties. Your first test is individual—one by one. Ten rounds per magazine. Five mags each. Variable distance. Time limited. You'll be evaluated on grouping, reload efficiency, and reflex transitions."

She stopped and turned back to face them.

"There are no second attempts."

One of the lockers hissed open behind her. Inside, six sidearms rested in foam cutouts—identical Glock 17s, magazine well down, slides locked back.

Katya gestured.

"Arm yourselves. Holster only when I give the word. Range assignments will be randomized."

None of them hesitated.

Lula moved first, no flourish—just a clean, confident lift of the weapon and a smooth chamber check. Gregor followed, mechanical in his motions. Tao didn't look at the gun as he took it, already calculating vectors in his head. Zina rotated hers once, weighing the grip in her palm. Imani didn't blink. Norah picked hers up last, silent as snowfall.

Katya watched them. No wasted motion. No fumbling.

Good.

She stepped toward the control terminal and keyed in the first sequence. Target lanes lit up, one by one. The air shifted—cooler, more electric.

"Let's see what you've got," she said. "Zina, you're up first."

Zina nodded, stepped forward, and crossed into the lane with the smooth, lethal calm of someone who'd been preparing for this her whole life.

Katya folded her arms and watched the girl take position. The countdown began. Ten seconds. Then the target popped.

The test had started.

SIX

BY THE END of their first day, the recruits had fired over two thousand rounds, run eighteen simulated breach scenarios, memorized the layout of the entire subterranean base, and completed a full combat conditioning circuit that left even Lula silent by the final bell. Zina led the marksmanship scores. Gregor excelled in room-clearing drills. Tao bypassed a digital lock system meant to take three minutes in under twelve seconds—using only a borrowed training tablet. Imani never missed a detail, logging every instructor's routine, weapon preference, and vocal cadence. Norah said almost nothing, but her reflex test results were anomalously high—too fast, too calm.

No one quit. No one asked to stop.

For eight hours, they performed nonstop drills until finally night began to fall over the stone bones of Camelot.

The locker room was quiet save for the hiss of running water and the rustle of clothes being shoved into duffels. Steam clung to the air in patches, fogging mirrors and softening the flicker of the overhead lights. The recruits moved with the slow, bone-deep exhaustion of people who had burned every calorie and still weren't allowed to collapse.

One by one, they filed out—Zina with her earbuds already in,

Gregor limping slightly but saying nothing, Tao still drying his hair with a towel. Imani trailed them, eyes flicking to the wall clock and then the hallway, always tracking something.

Norah stayed behind. Her locker had jammed slightly and needed coaxing open.

She didn't hear Lula approach until the bulk of her blocked out the mirror behind them.

"You remember me, right?"

Norah turned to face her. Slowly. "Four-Three-Three."

Lula's lip curled, not quite a smile. "That's right. And you're Three-O-Two."

Her tone dipped, thick with venom as she added, "The bitch who killed Four-Four-Two. The only friend I ever had."

Norah didn't move. "I never meant to kill your friend."

"But you did," Lula snarled, stepping closer. She was taller, heavier, her frame broad with the kind of strength that could break ribs just by leaning the wrong way. "You killed her, and you didn't even blink."

"It was the Council," Norah said quietly. "They made us kill each other."

Lula's jaw tightened. "You cut her throat."

Norah didn't look away. "I never meant to."

Lula shifted her weight. Her hands curled into fists.

The air between them crackled.

Lula was on the verge of moving. Her eyes widened as she—

"Enough" came Katya's voice, cold and slicing through the tension like a scalpel.

Both girls turned. She stood in the doorway, arms crossed, gaze sharp enough to shear steel.

"Get dressed. You've got sixty seconds to meet me outside," she said. "I have something to show you."

Lula stepped back first. Not cowed—just calculating. She shot Norah one last glance, unreadable, then turned toward her locker.

Norah didn't move for a few seconds more.

Then she exhaled. Quiet. Measured. And began to dress.

SEVEN

KATYA LED the recruits down a corridor that looked nothing like the rest of the facility.

The lighting was low and amber, a warm pulse rather than the cold fluorescence that usually ruled these walls. The cement surfaces were painted the color of sky, and the air held no sting of sterilization or ozone. Even the floors were different—covered in carpet that absorbed footfalls, swallowing sound rather than amplifying it.

Katya didn't speak until they reached the midpoint of the hallway—where the corridor forked into two quiet branches. On either side, six recessed doors were spaced evenly along the walls. Each door bore a small illuminated panel: a nameplate and a designation code.

Katya turned to face them, hands folded behind her back.

"You each have a room," she continued. "A bed. A door."

For a second, none of them spoke. Some stared. Others blinked, like the sentence hadn't parsed correctly.

Imani's voice broke the quiet. "We're not sleeping in the dormitory tonight?"

"No. You're never sleeping in the dormitory again."

Lula stepped forward. "And if we want, we can just... close the door?"

Katya nodded. "And open it. When you want. Unless you're late for morning drills. Then I will be opening it no matter what."

There was the faintest glimmer of humor in her tone—just enough to soften the edge. But not enough to invite challenge.

For a moment, no one moved.

Then Katya stepped aside and gestured down the corridor. "Go ahead," she said. "Find the door with your name on it. Open it."

Cautiously, the six began to drift forward, scanning the nameplates glowing gently in the darkened hall.

Zina found hers first. She stood in front of it for a beat longer than necessary, then opened the door like it might be a trick. The light inside came on automatically—soft, golden. She stood frozen on the threshold. Her voice, when it came, was small and disbelieving.

"There's... a desk. And shelves. Real ones."

Gregor said nothing when he found his. He simply opened the door, stepped in, and closed it behind him. But not before Katya saw the slight hitch in his breath when he touched the door-frame—like he expected it to vanish or his hand to fall through.

Imani moved like she was afraid it would all disappear if she got too close. Her room was pristine. Books. A small private console. A closet with clothing in her size. She hovered in the center like someone walking through a memory that wasn't hers. "This is mine?" she whispered.

Tao opened his door, looked inside, and blinked once. "Efficient," he murmured. Then he stepped in, already cataloging.

Lula held out just long enough to pretend she wasn't surprised. But when she opened her door and saw the punching bag hanging from a corner mount, she exhaled like someone had just handed her a loaded weapon. "All right," she muttered. "Maybe this place isn't a complete icebox."

Norah was the last to move. She walked quietly down the line until she reached the final door.

The nameplate was blank.

She stared at it.

Then turned back to Katya. "Where's mine?"

Katya met her gaze. "You don't have one."

"Why?"

"Because your father has requested you stay in his quarters. He wants to continue overseeing your conditioning directly."

From down the hall, Lula called out, having overheard.

"Well. That makes sense. Daddy's girl gets the penthouse."

Norah didn't answer.

She just turned on her heel and walked—silent, brisk, and straight down the corridor without another word.

Katya watched her go.

Then turned back to the remaining doors, now quietly closing, one by one.

EIGHT

INSIDE THE WAR ROOM, the blast doors hissed open, harder than they needed to.

Noah looked up from the main console just as Norah stormed in, boots loud against the steel floor, face set like stone.

She didn't slow down.

"You didn't give me a room with the others."

Noah's expression didn't change. "Hello, Norah. How are you today?"

She came to a full stop in front of him, jaw tight, arms locked at her sides.

"Why didn't I get a room like the others?"

"I assumed Katya told you."

"She did," Norah snapped. "That's not the same as you telling me."

The silence in the War Room had weight to it, like pressure before a storm. The surrounding screens ticked softly through global threat updates, but neither moved to look.

Noah straightened, hands folding behind his back.

"You're not like the others," he said quietly.

Norah didn't blink. "No. I'm not. And they all know it. Now they'll see it too. See how different I am. You gave them space.

Privacy. You gave them ownership. And you left me with a bed in your quarters like I'm five years old."

"You're not five," Noah said. "But you were gone for almost two years. Vanished. And the only reason I have you back at all is because of the miracle of good fortune. So forgive me if I'm not ready to tuck you into a room and close the door between us just yet."

That hit something. She hesitated—but only for a breath.

"I'm not asking you to stop caring," she said, voice calmer now. "I'm asking you to let me do what I'm trained to do. What Allison trained me to do. If I'm going to be part of Camelot, I need to be in it. Not above it. Not around it. In it."

Noah studied her. Really looked.

She wasn't angry. She wasn't pleading. She was asking—with restraint, with conviction. There was something in her posture he recognized.

Not a girl.

A soldier.

A Wolf.

He exhaled slowly, then tapped a command into the nearest terminal. The image of the hallway outside the recruits' quarters flickered onto the side screen. The sixth nameplate—blank just moments ago—now glowed softly with her name.

NORAH WOLF - 06

Her breath caught, but she didn't smile.

"Thank you," she said.

He finally allowed himself a trace of warmth. "You earned it."

A small pause. Then, as the tension broke, he tilted his head.

"So. How was your first day?"

Norah rolled her eyes, just a little. "Zina thinks she's clever. Gregor doesn't talk. Tao doesn't blink. Imani memorized everyone's blood type, dominant hand, and combat weakness before dinner—and Lula will probably try to kill me by the end of the week."

Noah chuckled. "So... standard training dynamics, then."

"She's definitely going to try."

Before he could reply, Esmerelda's voice cut cleanly through the room.

"Apologies for the interruption, Noah. Incoming check-in from Agents Drake and Vance. Istanbul node."

Noah leaned down and kissed Norah on the forehead, brief but firm.

"Go settle in. We'll talk later."

Norah gave him a look—half fond, half exasperated—but turned and walked out without another word.

The screens reoriented.

Neil and Jenny blinked into view.

"We're wheels-down in Istanbul," Neil reported. "En route to collect the package."

Noah nodded once. "Understood. Proceed."

NINE

THE MIST CURLED off the Bosphorus like smoke rising from a corpse, drifting through the narrow arteries of Istanbul's Karaköy district with spectral grace. It clung to the cobblestones, coiled around rusted bollards and half-toppled bins, and kissed the windows of shuttered shops plastered in political flyers.

Among it all, a white van edged its way through the mist, low and slow.

Jenny sat in the passenger seat, one boot propped against the dash, arm slung along the window ledge. Her gloved fingers tapped an irregular rhythm against the glass as the van eased past a row of bolted storefronts. Her eyes scanned constantly—windows, alley mouths, rooftops—tracking every shadow.

"This is the third time Knox has been moved this month," she said, voice dry as gravel. "The guy must be jumpy as hell."

From the driver's seat, Neil barely turned his head. "He should be," he said. "There's not a Council grunt or fringe zealot alive who doesn't want Adrian Knox's head on a plate."

Ahead, the street thickened—market traffic mixing with lingering militia.

Since the fall of the Council, Turkey had unraveled faster than most. The government, once seen as barely functional but intact, had collapsed within weeks of the first leaks. It turned out Ankara had never truly been sovereign—not since the twilight of the Ottoman Empire. The Council had been pulling strings from the shadows for over a century: rigging elections, assassinating dissenters, shaping foreign policy through invisible hands.

The document dumps made it all public—Council files decrypted and broadcast in full by whistleblowers with nothing left to lose. Names, dates, locations. Proof that every administration since 1923 had danced to someone else's tune.

Now the country was eating itself alive.

Old rivalries had reignited. Nationalists. Secularists. Exiled royals with delusions of restoration. Mercenaries funded by foreign intelligence outfits and radical clerics with armies of their own. The military had fractured down loyalty lines—some loyal to the old republic, some to religion, and others to whatever flag promised power. Istanbul had become a battleground in slow motion, its streets divided not by ideology but by grudges and guns.

Karaköy, once a hub of gentrification and waterfront cafés now served as a buffer zone—neutral, barely. A place where half-broken alliances met and informants sold their loyalty by the hour.

Neil shifted gears as they pulled around a stack of burning tires. "Just keep your eyes up. We're two klicks from the safehouse."

Jenny nodded, fingers still tapping the glass. "Makes you wonder what we started."

The van rolled on, swallowed by the fog.

Aid lines wrapped around buildings, watched over by mercenaries in scavenged body armor and mismatched fatigues. Their weapons were mostly Council-issue—overused and under-maintained—but the eyes behind them were alert. Hungry.

Jenny shifted in her seat. "God, this city's on a razor's edge."

Neil's voice was low and tight. "And we're riding right along it."

———

THE APARTMENT SAT above a seafood market in Karaköy, Istanbul—third floor, unremarkable from the outside, perfectly forgettable by design. The scent of brine and grilled mackerel clung to the aging plaster walls.

It was the kind of place that didn't ask questions and didn't attract them.

Inside, the lights were dimmed. Heavy blackout curtains sealed every window in overlapping layers.

Three Camelot field agents moved with purpose through the apartment—silent, efficient, weapons close. The apartment was already clean. Every drawer had been cleared. Electronics scrubbed. Fingerprints lifted and wiped. No traces. No signs. Just like Noah taught them.

In the back room, Dr. Adrian Knox stood by a half-packed duffel, still buttoning his coat. He was much thinner than six months ago—wiry, pale, and exhausted.

One of the agents snapped a soft click over comms. "Echo team, this is Site. Package is almost mobile."

Jenny's voice came back through his earpiece. "Copy. We're two minutes out."

The lead agent—Callen, ex-Rhodesian spec-ops—handed Knox a softshell vest with built-in anti-trauma plating. "Vest. Gloves. Hood on when we exit. You don't speak until you're in the van."

Knox obeyed without protest, but his voice was still dry as kindling. "Sure thing. The van. Yeah."

Callen didn't respond. He just pulled back the curtain a crack to check the alley.

———

THE ALLEYS behind Karaköy's fish market stank. Nets hung like ghosts from overhead poles. Tarps rustled in the wind, veiling the narrow pathways in colorless shadow. The air was thick and wet every breath a blend of rust, brine, and rot.

The assassin moved through it without disturbing a thing.

She wore a courier's jacket—hood up, sleeves weathered, the kind of garment anyone could overlook. Her boots made no sound. Even the pigeons above the market stalls ignored her, as if she were part of the stone and mist and shadow.

Her eyes, flat and gray, scanned every detail—entries, bottlenecks, camera dead zones. When she adjusted her sleeve, the cuff rode up for just a second, revealing skin inked with a stylized emblem: a crowned sun, ringed by circuit-like etchings, stamped over a bleeding heart.

It had taken her two days to get this far.

She'd tracked Knox's trail to Istanbul through dead drops and burnt chatter—snippets of encrypted comms laced with Camelot's signature protocols, spliced through darknet exchanges like breadcrumbs.

This morning, one of her spotters—a street kid with sharp eyes and a sharper hunger—caught a glimpse of a known Camelot operative exiting a market stall empty-handed. No fish. No bag. But he lingered. Made a call. Waited. Then vanished into the building above the stall.

That was enough.

Now as the sky deepened into bruised dusk and the call to prayer echoed across the rooftops, she finally reached the apartment and saw him.

Adrian Knox. The bastard who hadn't just killed the Council —he'd shattered the balance. The world was burning because of him.

Someone was holding the curtains open on a third floor window. Backlit by a weak yellow bulb, Knox was standing by a door with a duffel in one hand and a grim set to his face. Two

Camelot agents flanked him. A third was at the window, looking over his shoulder at the others.

She didn't move. Just watched. Heartbeat steady.

Her hand hovered near the long rifle strapped to her back. But she didn't take it.

Not yet.

The man at the window was saying something to one of the operatives. Then he nodded, and—suddenly—looked to the window.

The assassin ducked behind a crate, breathing through her nose, motionless. Her body folded into the shape of stillness. Her silhouette dissolved into the roofline like paint into stone.

She smiled to herself.

Soon they would all be dead.

———

THE VAN LURCHED TO A STOP.

Ahead, the street bottlenecked into a sudden, chaotic snarl—trucks jackknifed across both lanes, their sides riddled with bullet holes. Civilians, militia, and opportunists spilled into the road, waving arms, shouting, dragging crates. A burning scooter belched black smoke into the mist. Somewhere nearby, a shot cracked. Then another.

Neil's hands tightened on the wheel. "Shit. Looks like the block's sealed."

Jenny was already reaching for the comms mic. "This is Viper One. We've got a traffic lockup at Sector Delta-Seven. Grid's blown. Militia's moving through on foot."

Callen's voice came back immediately, curt and sharp.

"Copy. Sitrep?"

Jenny kept scanning the rooftops. "Unknown hostiles. No direct fire yet, but we're boxed. Might need to reroute Knox on foot if this spreads."

"Okay, Viper One," Callen's voice came back. "We'll hold tight. But just remember—the clock is ticking."

—————

INSIDE THE APARTMENT, Callen swore under his breath and turned toward Knox.

"You're sitting back down," he snapped.

Knox hesitated, eyes narrowing. "Why? What happened?"

"Your ride's delayed. That's all you need to know." Callen waved him back toward the rear room. "No movement until I say."

Knox dropped the duffel beside a chair and sat, one hand clenched tightly on the strap.

That's when the power died.

The room went black in an instant, leaving only the faint glow of the city's chaos leaking through the edges of the blackout curtains.

"Hold position," Callen said, voice low, steady. "Get your NV gear."

They never got the chance.

A thunderous blast shook the apartment. The front door exploded inward, shredded wood and dust erupting into the hall.

The operatives surged toward it, weapons drawn.

Smoke curled through the entryway, tendrils thick and oily. Callen led the breach response, flanking the blown door with weapon raised.

"Clear it!" he barked.

But it was a diversion.

In the back, a window shattered—glass shards hissing across the floor like a whispered scream.

And from the gap came the assassin.

She flowed in low, smooth, all shadow and intent. Night vision goggles cast a green sheen across her face, but it was the blade in her hand that made her real. Silent. Fast.

One operative was still turning when she reached him.

She slid the knife into his throat and twisted before he could shout, catching his weight as he sagged and lowering him soundlessly to the floor.

Then she was gone again—into the smoke of the apartment, a ghost built for killing.

Callen turned too late.

She came at him from the flank, her knife meeting his raised forearm with a wet crunch. He shouted, staggered back, and countered with a hard elbow. She twisted, absorbing the hit, and slammed him into the wall.

The third operative—eyes wide, breath ragged—grabbed Knox. "Move!"

They bolted for the stairwell.

Callen and the assassin clashed again—hand to hand now, brutal, close. She was smaller, faster. He was stronger, trained. The fight tore through furniture, knocking things to the ground. They hit a table, rolled, and bounced off the wall. Blood smeared the floor in fast, wet arcs.

Then Callen made a mistake. The timing of his jab was off by a fraction of a second, his feet too far apart.

She ducked, slid beneath his guard, and drove the blade up under his ribs—once, twice—fast and deep.

He gasped, choked, and dropped.

She let him fall, panting softly through the NVG rig.

The stairwell door banged open three stories below. Echoes of retreating boots entering the alleyway floated up to her sharpened senses.

The target was getting away.

———

KNOX and the operative sprinted down the alley behind the building, the world around them narrowing to footfalls, wet concrete, and the throb of their hearts in their ears. Trash bins loomed like monuments. Stray dogs scattered and barked at their approach.

Knox glanced over. "What the hell just happened? Who was that?"

"It doesn't matter. Keep—"

Thump.

The operative's head snapped backward—a spray of red. He folded to the ground like a puppet with cut strings.

The crack of the shot echoed off the alley walls.

Knox dove behind a nearby dumpster, breath hammering in his chest.

Another bullet tore through the space he'd just left, chewing into the concrete with surgical force.

She was out there.

And she wasn't finished.

———

The van cut a hard right through a service alley barely wide enough for its frame, tires screeching against broken pavement. Jenny gripped the dashboard with one hand, the other on her sidearm.

"ETA?"

Neil squinted past the wheel, eyes tracking between GPS and instinct. "Two minutes, maybe less."

They'd circumnavigated the bottleneck by threading through side streets and industrial cut-throughs.

Jenny reached for the comms again. "Viper One to site team. Status check. Callen, report. Knox, do you copy?"

Static.

She tried again, flipped channels.

Nothing.

Not even a ping.

Neil's jaw tightened. "Could be jamming."

"Could be worse," Jenny muttered.

They burst out of the alley and onto a wider street that cut toward the old fish market. The van jolted as they hit uneven stone, the buildings around them looming like hunched shoulders in the fog.

That's when Neil lifted a hand and pointed.

"Jenny."

She followed his gaze.

Above the rooftops, thick black smoke poured into the sky—rising fast, oily, unmistakable. It billowed up from the exact grid point of the apartment. The safehouse.

Jenny's blood ran cold.

"Drive," she said, already chambering a round.

The van accelerated.

———

FOR A LONG TIME, Adrian Knox didn't move.

Wedged behind the dumpster, breath shallow, pulse a snare drum in his throat, he listened—hard—for any sound. A boot-step. A breath. The scrape of fabric on brick. But the silence was deep. Deceptive.

The alley stretched before him like a trap with no sprung trigger.

He risked it.

One leg out. Then the other.

Slow, silent, careful.

Then he bolted.

Knox tore down the alley at a full sprint, lungs burning, legs unsteady beneath him. He glanced back once—twice—expecting the crack of a rifle, the punch of a round through bone. But it didn't come.

Left.

He ducked into a narrow cut between two buildings, hopping a broken fence.

Right.

He passed a gutted sedan, its engine block still smoldering from something recent and violent.

Another left.

His breath came in ragged gasps now, body failing to keep pace with panic. His shoulder slammed a wall as he turned too fast, staggering forward—

A dead end.

Knox skidded to a stop. Just a cracked brick wall and a rusted-out drainpipe dripping into a shallow puddle. No doors. No windows. No cover.

He spun around, panting, trembling all over. His eyes locked on the mouth of the alley.

It was empty.

But any second now. Any second she would appear, framed by smoke and shadow, weapon raised, the end of everything closing in.

But she didn't.

She came from behind.

The assassin dropped soundlessly from a balcony above like a shadow unfolding. A spider descending onto the neck of a fly.

Knox didn't know she was there until he felt it—the cold kiss of a blade against his throat.

He froze.

Couldn't breathe. Couldn't scream.

She leaned in close, her breath warm against his ear.

"You will suffer for what you have done to the world," she whispered.

Knox's blood turned to ice.

———

THE VAN SCREECHED TO A HALT.

Jenny was out the door before the engine fully stopped, pistol raised, boots splashing through the puddles slicking the pavement outside the safehouse. Neil followed fast, his rifle sweeping over the shadows crowding the entryway.

The apartment door hung open on broken hinges. The hallway beyond was smeared with soot, the floor littered with shell casings and the still bodies of two operatives. Smoke clung to the ceiling in thick ribbons.

They moved fast, clearing the rooms one by one.

Callen lay in the main room—eyes open, weapon still gripped in one blood-slick hand. Furniture was overturned, the walls riddled with close-quarters impacts. The entire space radiated violence.

Jenny crossed to the far window, eyes narrowing.

Below, in the alley, the body of the third field agent lay twisted on the wet ground—motionless.

"Goddamn it..." Neil muttered beside her.

And then it came.

A scream.

Not just pain—but something primal. A human voice caught in the machinery of horror, echoing from farther down the alley.

It rose in pitch, cracked—and then was cut off.

Jenny and Neil were already moving, boots pounding the floor as they tore through the apartment and down the stairs. They hit the alley at a run, turning the corner with weapons raised—

Too late.

There, crouched in the dark, the assassin lifted Adrian Knox's severed head into a small black box, locking it with a click.

Jenny fired.

The assassin sensed the shot before it came. She moved like lightning—diving sideways behind a stack of bins, all while tossing a smoke grenade from her belt. In the same motion, she clipped the head box to her rig with one smooth snap.

The grenade popped and hissed, thick smoke swallowing the alley in a blinding cloud.

Jenny and Neil staggered back, coughing, eyes burning.

From above came the rattle of metal—the assassin scaling the drainpipe, rising into the fog like a wraith retreating to the rooftops.

Jenny waved the smoke away with one hand, pistol braced with the other. "Do you see her?!"

Neil scanned the upper floors, breath sharp, nerves coiled tight. "No. She's—"

Jenny's instincts flared.

Her eyes snapped upward, catching something just barely visible in the moonlight—a glint, cold and sharp. Not movement. Metal.

The scope of a rifle.

"DOWN!"

She shoved Neil hard to the side just as the rooftop erupted in thunder—bullets tearing into the alley, cracking against stone.

They hit the ground together, rolling behind a steel crate. Concrete chipped around them as more rounds slammed into the alley walls.

High above, flat against the rooftop tiles, the assassin lay prone, eye pressed to her scope. Breathing steadily. Watching. Waiting.

She held for three seconds longer.

Neil and Jenny didn't reappear.

So she rose—silent, efficient, mission complete. She melted back across the rooftop, NVGs scanning for movement, rifle tucked tightly against her shoulder. By the time the smoke cleared, she was gone.

Back in the alley, Jenny and Neil climbed shakily to their feet.

The decapitated body of Adrian Knox lay at the alley's dead end, slumped like a discarded puppet.

His shirt had been torn open.

Carved into the pale skin of his chest—deep, deliberate, and still oozing—was a symbol: a crowned sun ringed by circuit-like etchings, stamped over a bleeding heart.

Jenny stared at it, jaw clenched.

"She did it while he was still alive," Neil said quietly.

Neither of them looked away.

TEN

THE WAR ROOM hummed with low, methodical noise—servers whispering, fiber-optic links blinking with quiet urgency. Maps glowed across the walls in a shifting kaleidoscope of global instability.

Noah Wolf stood at the center of it all, hands behind his back, spine straight, gaze locked on a single pulsing red node over Istanbul.

He'd been staring at it for nearly fifteen minutes.

Esmerelda's voice broke the silence.

"Incoming from Agents Drake and Vance. Istanbul node. Priority flag: Red."

"Put them through," Noah said without turning.

The main screen flared, stabilizing on Jenny and Neil, both huddled in a dim corner of an alley, grime on their sleeves and firelight flickering across their faces.

Jenny spoke first, her tone clipped but controlled. "Knox is dead. Assassin got to him before we could even close the distance."

Noah's jaw tensed. "Have you got an ID for the perp?"

Neil nodded. "Yes. Same operative as the Cairo hit. Possibly Munich. I recognize her from her monkey-like ability to scale buildings. She's fast. Precise. NVG loadout, silent entry. Plus, she did this."

Jenny shifted, tapping something on her tablet. "Sending you the image now."

The screen changed.

It was Knox's chest—pale and still, the flesh carved like a ritual offering. A crowned sun, ringed with circuit-like etchings, stamped over a bleeding heart.

The room went colder.

Neil's voice came through the speakers, low. "It's that symbol again."

Noah didn't blink.

"Children of the Empire." His voice was gravel now.

Jenny exhaled through her nose. "They're getting cockier."

Noah stepped closer to the console, eyes narrowing.

"We need to—"

All the screens blinked.

For a moment, the War Room fell into white static. Jenny and Neil were gone. Every display—surveillance feeds, satellite overlays, secure comms grids—washed out in a blizzard of interference.

Then—

The static cleared, and all channels began displaying a single video feed: a makeshift broadcast studio, crude but intentionally lit, backed by a black banner bearing a familiar sigil.

The same crowned sun. The same bleeding heart.

"Esmerelda," he said. "Record everything."

A figure stepped into frame.

He moved like a man aware of his every gesture, the weight of history stitched into the seams of his tailored black tunic. Silver threaded his dark hair. A crimson sash crossed his chest like a blade wound that refused to bleed—its heart marked with the sigil of the Children of the Empire.

When he spoke, the man's voice was composed, precise—each syllable weighted like a judge passing sentence.

"My name is Sebastian Vale," he said. "I speak to you not as a politician. Not as a warmonger. But as the man who will restore balance to a world collapsing under the weight of its own chaos."

In the War Room, Noah didn't move.

"You do not know me. But you've lived the consequences of my absence. Since the fall of the Council, you have seen your world unravel. Governments crumble. Economies fracture Famine. Fire. Fear.

"But these are not accidents. This is the cost of Camelot's crusade."

He took a single step forward.

"The Council—for all its sins—maintained the spine of global stability. Its invisible hand was not tyranny. It was equilibrium. It held back the storm. You called it shadow rule. But shadows are only cast by the light that protects you."

Vale's image gave way to surveillance footage, grainy and old A warzone smeared in ash and muzzle flashes. A soldier ducked behind a ruined car. Fire danced from the barrel of a rifle.

The footage changed to a man's face.

Noah Wolf's face.

For all the world to see—enhanced and clarified.

"And there is one wolf," Vale murmured, "who led the pack.

"This man—Noah Wolf—burned the last pillars of world order. He dismantled Olympus, shattered containment protocols and forged in the ruins a rogue state—Camelot."

The screen split—an overhead map lit in pulsing red. Safe zones, bunkers, encrypted signals triangulated and labeled.

Putorana. Malta. Chiang Mai.

"Do not be deceived," Vale continued. "Camelot is not salvation. It is insurgency wearing the mask of justice. And it is the greatest existential threat to mankind since the Black Plague."

Vale stood motionless for a moment longer, letting the weight of his words settle like ash. Then he stepped forward again—closer this time. Filling the frame.

"You have seen the signs. You've felt the tremors beneath your streets. This world burns not because the Council ruled—but because it no longer does. And in its place, these zealots of Camelot have planted their flag."

He lifted a hand, palm open, calm and deliberate.

"But I do not come to mourn the old order. I come to forge the new one. An empire not of shadows but of design. Structure. Unity."

He lowered his hand. His tone cooled.

"To the governments of the world: you must no longer tolerate the threat that festers beneath your feet. Camelot is not a sanctuary. It is not a sovereign power. It is a paramilitary cult. A terrorist enclave. An insurgency of saboteurs hiding behind lost ideals."

His voice hardened—not louder but denser, measured, and final.

"They must be outlawed. Exiled. Hunted. Their operations dismantled. Their symbols erased. Their leader—Noah Wolf—brought to justice."

He paused.

"I do not ask for allegiance. Only sanity. Look to your borders. Look to your streets. How long will you let chaos wear the name of freedom?"

He let the silence breathe.

"The Council kept the wolves at bay. But now one of them wears a crown."

Vale stared straight through the lens.

"The world must choose—order or extinction. There is no middle path."

The screen dimmed. Just for a second.

Then Vale spoke one last time, quiet as dusk.

"Let the Empire rise."

And then the feed cut. All the screens went back to their former states: rioting, looting, urban chaos.

The War Room stayed silent, like the breath before a storm.

Neil broke it first.

"He just made us public enemy number one."

Jenny looked at Noah through the camera. "What's the play, boss?"

But Noah didn't speak. Not right away. He was still staring at the blank screen, jaw set tight enough to crack.

"Vale wants to isolate us," he said finally, voice low. "Make Camelot a symbol of unrest. Delegitimize it. Then erase it."

Neil's voice came next. "And if even half the world listens..."

"Then we won't be able to operate," Noah said.

Jenny's eyes narrowed. "So what do we do?"

Noah turned from the screen at last. His gaze was calm. But behind it burned a furnace.

"We remind the world why Camelot exists. And we show them what real order looks like."

ELEVEN

SOMEWHERE IN EUROPE | 07:20 LOCAL TIME | NOVEMBER 14

THE TRAIN THUNDERED through a scarred stretch of rural Europe—misted fields of skeletal trees and broken farmland blurred into streaks of gray and green beneath the heavy clouds. It moved like a blade across the continent, silent but inexorable, its polished steel hull humming with imperial energy. No markings. No destination. Only purpose.

It wasn't just Camelot who had inherited Council hardware. The train—known as Argo One during its Council days—was a roving command center disguised as luxury transport. Built in the 1970s beneath the guise of a diplomatic initiative, it was a mobile fortress: bulletproofed, signal-jammed, and satellite-masked. Each carriage served a different purpose—strategy, communications, surgical suite, even containment cells for high-value captives. It had no official route and no fixed schedule, and only a handful of Council members were ever granted access.

Inside, the forward carriage was a cathedral of opulence—paneled in dark oak, inlaid with gold filigree, softly lit by brass sconces that pulsed like heartbeat monitors. Velvet curtains muted the world outside. The recording of a string quartet played from recessed speakers, weaving melancholy through the chill air.

Sebastian Vale sat in a throne-like chair of black leather, his fingers steepled beneath his chin. A porcelain plate rested on the table before him, half-finished—poached eggs, black bread, a slice of blood orange arranged with surgical precision. Steam curled from a silver pot of black tea, untouched.

Across from him, kneeling in silence, was Sophia.

She was barefoot on the carpet, her long coat trailing behind her like a shroud. Her hair fell in a sheet of pure white, her eyes crystalline blue and as unreadable as crystal itself. She held something in her hands—wrapped in oilskin. She looked up at Vale not with pride, not with joy, but with that eerie, patient obedience he had forged into her over years of precision.

Sophia had been with Vale a long time.

Vale smiled like a man witnessing prophecy fulfilled.

"Well?" he asked softly.

Sophia unfolded the cloth. And there—rolling ever so slightly as the train swayed—was the severed head of Dr. Adrian Knox.

His eyes were closed. His lips slack. His neck ended in torn sinew and exposed vertebrae.

Vale leaned forward, fury carving lines into his face.

"I was so close," he hissed at the head. "So close to the Inner Council. I was 101. The highest-ranking member yet to be invited to the High Chamber. I would have stood among them. I would have rewritten the order of the world alongside them."

He reached out and gripped Knox's hair, lifting the head to eye level, his mouth curling in contempt.

"But because of this little Judas, I will never know what heaven would have felt like. He thought he could bring down Olympus and walk free. Not on my watch."

He threw the head down, Sophia catching it with a wet thud.

"One future stolen," he muttered. "But another made."

He turned toward the far wall of the cabin, where a polished walnut cabinet stood like a museum relic. Inside, heads floated in cloudy formaldehyde—men and women who had, at one time, turned their backs on the Council. Betrayers. Apostates. Weaklings.

Now they were in jars.

Knox would now join them.

Vale snapped his fingers once.

A servant—dressed in pale gray, expressionless—stepped forward and took the head from Sophia. He placed it into an open jar already half-filled with preservative fluid. Knox's features warped instantly, distorted by the liquid, made monstrous by the refracted glass.

Sophia remained kneeling, unmoving.

The servant slid the jar into an empty space in the cabinet.

Next to it, waiting in perfect stillness, was a final jar—empty, pristine, and already labeled in neat, mechanical handwriting:

NOAH WOLF

Vale stepped up to the cabinet.

"The biggest infidel of them all," he said, staring at the empty jar.

Then he smiled.

TWELVE

THAT MORNING, the hand-to-hand floor had been stripped to bare essentials—just mats, sweat, and the kind of trembling silence that meant something violent was about to happen.

The six recruits stood in line at the edge, dressed in T-shirts, shorts, taped wrists, and lightweight fighting gloves.

Katya paced in front of them, a digital notepad in one hand, eyes scanning the roster as she locked in match orders. Her voice was even but carried a razor's edge.

"Today, I want to see you fight," she said.

At the far end of the line, Lula smirked.

"You know the rules," Katya continued. "No bleeding that can't be stopped within sixty seconds. No trauma that can't be repaired by morning. If either happens, the fight ends."

She paused. "One rule has changed, however, from your days with the Council. You are now free to tap out at any time."

She let the words linger. Then added, "Though I wouldn't advise it."

She stopped beside Gregor and Tao, eyes flicking between them.

"You two are first. Show me your best."

Gregor stepped onto the mat—silent, coiled, already calculating. Tao followed, light on his feet, smaller by nearly a head, his posture loose but centered, like a dancer waiting for the downbeat.

"Begin," Katya said and stepped back.

They launched.

Gregor struck first—no flourish, just a sharp jab-hook combo meant to test range and set a tone. Tao ducked beneath the hook, pivoted on the balls of his feet, and answered with a palm strike that clipped Gregor's ribs. The sound echoed, sharp and clean.

Lula's smirk twitched upward.

"Didn't think the kid could move like that," she muttered.

Zina didn't reply. Her eyes were locked on Tao's footwork.

The two on the mat circled. Gregor pressed in with calculated pressure—Muay Thai guard, hips angled, weight shifting. Tao, by contrast, fought like someone who had studied too many styles to name—blending Wing Chun bursts with flashes of Krav Maga, always adapting, never still.

Gregor swept low—Tao leapt. Tao feinted high—Gregor parried, then countered with an elbow that clipped Tao's shoulder.

They broke. Breathed. Reset.

Then it came faster.

Tao snapped off a spinning backfist that missed by a whisper. Gregor retaliated with a clinch, kneeing Tao's thigh hard enough to deaden the leg. Tao grunted and stumbled back. Gregor surged —but Tao twisted under the rush and flipped him with a judo hip throw that should've been impossible given their size difference.

The mats slammed beneath Gregor's back.

Even Katya blinked.

They didn't stop. Gregor scrambled up, blood now trickling

from a shallow cut above his left eye. Tao limped into position, his dead leg dragging slightly but his stance still measured. They moved again—slower now, wearier, but with the same sharp intent.

Eventually, they broke apart. No final strike. No collapse. Just a pause.

Gregor gave a curt nod. Tao returned it. Then, without cue, both bowed.

And shook hands.

Lula rolled her eyes. "What a couple of pussies. You should've fought until one of you couldn't."

Katya marked the outcome on her pad, expression unreadable. "Imani. Zina. You're up next."

Norah felt her stomach drop. She was next. And her match would be with Lula.

She swallowed hard.

Meanwhile, Lula smirked, slow and cruel, then turned her head just enough to catch Norah's eye.

When their gazes locked, Lula mouthed two words: *You're dead*.

Katya didn't seem to notice—or didn't care. She was too busy with the fight.

Imani stepped forward with small, measured steps—back straight, fists already half-closed. Across from her, Zina bounced on the balls of her feet, the corner of her mouth twitching in anticipation.

The two girls came to the center of the mat.

The air changed.

The room waited.

Katya gave a small nod. "Begin."

Zina came in fast—just as Imani had anticipated. A sharp jab feint, low shift of weight, then a spinning kick aimed at Imani's left flank.

Imani didn't retreat.

She turned into it, took the angle, and caught Zina's leg just below the knee with a precise block. No wasted motion. No panic.

Zina recovered, eyes narrowing. She switched stance, faster this time—two quick jabs, then a lunge meant to drive Imani back.

It didn't work.

Imani moved like a scalpel—cutting in, past the momentum, and planting her elbow into Zina's ribs. The breath left Zina in a gasp, and Imani seized the moment—hooked behind her opponent's knee and drove her down.

The floor thudded beneath them.

Zina blinked up from the mat, stunned.

"Stop," Katya ordered. "Imani wins."

Imani rose and stepped back, expression neutral.

Then she turned to face the others.

"She always leads with her right," Imani said. "Keeps her weight too far forward on strikes. Leans into her kicks. Left hip's slower than her right, so when she resets—there's a window."

Zina scowled but didn't argue.

"I've been watching her since we got here," Imani finished. "She's good. But she's readable."

Katya gave no sign of approval, but her eyes lingered on Imani for a moment longer than usual before she tapped her pad again.

"Final match," she said. "Norah. Lula."

The room shifted.

Norah stepped forward slowly, her hands loose, jaw tight.

Lula moved like she was walking into a prize ceremony, smirking already.

They met at the center of the mat.

No words.

Just the heat of old memory and unspoken threat boiling between them.

They faced each other.

Katya raised her hand.

"Begin when ready."

They stood at the center of the mat, poised. Breathing low. Eyes locked. And then the door hissed open.

The sound froze the room.

Every head turned as Noah Wolf stepped inside—silent, composed, his presence, enough to shift the air like a dropped weight.

Lula's lips curled. She didn't even glance away from Norah.

"Oh look," she sneered in an undertone. "Daddy's here. Now he gets to watch me beat his little princess unrecognizable."

Noah said nothing. He stood at the edge, arms folded, gaze unreadable.

Norah felt it in her chest—pressure blooming cold and sharp. The floor beneath her feet felt thinner.

Katya gave a nod. "Begin."

The air split.

Lula surged first, an avalanche of force—Krav Maga-jab combo, elbow strike, knee rising like a piston toward Norah's sternum.

Norah slipped under, spun wide, and countered with a shoulder hook that Lula absorbed like stone.

Lula came back harder—fists cutting the air, a low kick sweeping for Norah's ankle.

Norah leapt back, planted, and launched into a roundhouse that glanced off Lula's temple.

The room snapped with each impact—mat slapping, grunts muffled through clenched teeth.

Lula grinned, blood already dotting her lips.

"You're so dead," she hissed.

Norah didn't answer.

Lula feinted—stepped in and then instantly out—snapping a punch straight into Norah's mouth.

There was a crunch.

Norah's head whipped sideways—one of her teeth flew from her lips, bouncing across the floor in a tiny, bloody arc.

She staggered, blood dripping from her chin.

Katya stepped forward. "Stop the fight—"

Norah raised a hand. She spat blood, straightened up.

"It doesn't break the rules," she said coldly. "The bleeding will stop in sixty seconds. The trauma can be repaired by morning."

Katya didn't move.

Norah lunged.

The second half of the fight wasn't a test—it was a war. A whirlwind of elbows, knees, crushing hooks, and low sweeps. Norah drove a kick into Lula's ribs hard enough to produce an echo out of her flesh. Then another—this one smashing into Lula's nose with a sickening crunch.

Blood sprayed. Lula stumbled, snarling.

"You little bitch—!"

Katya's voice cut in again. "That's enough. STOP."

They didn't.

Lula roared and charged.

Norah crouched low and launched another kick—but Lula sidestepped and bolted toward the wall.

Her hand clamped around the grip of a wall-mounted training barbell. Not a light one.

"Lula—no!" Katya shouted.

Lula turned, wild-eyed, barbell raised high.

Norah didn't flinch.

She grabbed a weight plate from a nearby rack and hurled it.

It clipped Lula's shoulder as she ducked and rang like a gong.

Lula shrieked.

Norah grabbed another and another—throwing them like circular blades, each one screaming through the air.

One shattered a light. Another tore a gouge through the wall. The other recruits ducked and scattered.

Katya stepped forward again, but the fight was past words.

Lula slammed the barbell down where Norah had just been, barely missing her. Norah swept her leg, caught Lula off balance, and lunged.

They collided in a tangle of fists, blood, and teeth. The mats turned slick.

Then, finally—

Strong hands.

Noah grabbed Norah by the arms, yanking her backward.

Katya wrestled Lula off from the other side, dragging her down by the waist.

Both girls kicked, screamed, and clawed.

"You bitch!" Lula screamed, her nose streaming. "I'll kill you!"

"I'm glad I cut your friend's throat!" Norah shouted back, still straining. "Because she was trying to kill ME!"

Silence crashed back over the room—heavy, choked, thick with sweat and heat and rage.

And into that silence—

The door creaking open.

Jenny and Neil stood there, the dust of Istanbul still on their coats, blinking at the wreckage: cracked lights, scattered plates, blood on the floor.

Neil tilted his head. "Esmerelda said you were—" He looked around. "Whoa."

Jenny folded her arms, surveying the scene.

"I see the training's going well."

Katya didn't say a word as she hauled Lula away.

Noah kept Norah's arms pinned as she breathed fire.

The room emptied slowly. The storm, for now, had passed. But the clouds had yet to part.

THIRTEEN

THE WAR ROOM'S doors groaned open with a mechanical hiss. Noah strode in first, flanked by Neil and Jenny.

Norah trailed behind them, lip split, one eye already bruised. She didn't limp, but she moved with a stiffness that spoke volumes.

Noah's voice cut the room like a cleaver.

"Chair. Corner. Sit. Don't make a sound."

Norah glared, jaw tight. But she obeyed, slinking across the floor like a cat who'd bitten the dog and lost. The chair in question sat under a dead terminal, tucked behind an auxiliary console. She dropped into it hard and crossed her arms.

Sulking didn't suit her—but in this moment, it fit.

Noah turned away before she could say anything.

"Esmerelda, seal the room."

A low click confirmed the lockdown. Jenny and Neil moved to the main console, standing on either side of Noah as he brought up the latest intel.

"What's the score, boss?" Jenny asked.

"We're behind," Noah said. "Vale's public persona grows every minute. He's going viral. Making more speeches. Attending rallies. He's building a myth. Ex-Council loyalists, fringe militias, fascist fantasists—they'll flock to him."

Neil exhaled. "We knew a hydra would grow when the Council died. We just didn't know it would put on a crown."

Jenny folded her arms. "If Vale keeps pulling old loyalists into orbit, we're not going to have the luxury of staying reactive."

"We won't," Noah replied. "We hit first. Fast, clean, surgical. We—"

A chime.

Esmerelda's voice cut in, calm and level: "Incoming Encrypted line. Origin: Bolivia. Caller: Wally Lawson."

Noah stepped to the console. "Put him through."

The central monitor blinked to life. Wally's face emerged in low-res—hollow-eyed, sweat-slicked, lit by the blue pulse of the lab's machinery.

"I found him," Wally said, no preamble.

Noah stiffened. "Who?"

Wally adjusted his glasses, voice low. "The one who reengineered Helix-7B. It's Kiel. Dr. Erich Kiel."

Neil swore under his breath. Jenny just went still.

Wally kept talking, faster now. "I wasn't sure at first. But I ran a third-tier deconstruction on the compiler sequences embedded in the protein bindings. Underneath the adaptive scaffold someone embedded a recursive signature—a molecular checksum."

Jenny frowned. "What does any of that mean, Wally?"

"It means he signed his work."

"Signed his work?"

"Yes. Not literal text but code—protein folding logic that loops back into itself. It's like a watermark in RNA structure Hidden in the stabilizer region. And it's Kiel's style. He always used symmetrical amino chain mirrors to mark engineered retrovirals. A narcissist's tic. No one else does it like that."

Noah's expression turned hard. "I read his file. Erich Kiel was the Council's lead biotechnician."

"Yeah," Wally said grimly. "Obsessed with 'clean blood.' His files are a freakshow. He wasn't just a eugenics purist—he wanted generational superiority. A genome without 'weak links.' He called mixed heritage a dilution. Neurological diversity? A plague. Anything he couldn't model, he classified as error. This virus—it's his doctrine in molecular form."

Jenny's face darkened. "Where the hell has he been hiding?"

Noah answered before Wally could. "Argentina. Our last intel tagged him surfacing there two months after the Council fell. Word was he found protection with a paramilitary outfit called Black Sun. At the time, they were noise. Now..." He glanced at the screen. "They're building weapons."

Neil looked up. "Black Sun? I've heard of them. Old-school fascist militia. Swastikas turned biotech. Doomsday preppers with petri dishes."

Noah nodded. "They're led by Viktor Rausch. Ex-DLR geneticist. Fired for 'philosophical noncompliance.' That's code for 'neo-Nazi wet dreams.' He disappeared into the jungle with half a dozen lab-grade sequencers and a cult of shaved-headed ex-mercs. Real old world filth. Red armbands. Eugenics worship. They call themselves the Blood Shepherds now."

Jenny muttered, "What the actual hell?"

Noah's voice turned to iron. "We didn't think they were a threat. Now they're not just harboring Kiel—they're testing his weapons."

He turned back to the screen. "Wally, how certain are you?"

"Certain," Wally said. "That recursive signature? He built that into every pathogen he designed. He believed in it like scripture. Helix-7B's activation logic—it's been twisted into something surgical. Racial, generational, and absolutely Kiel."

Noah gave one sharp nod. "We're done here. Hold tight and await my word, Wally."

"Understood," Wally replied and cut the feed.

The screen went dark.

For a long beat, no one spoke.

Then Noah turned, voice final.

"We leave in the morning. Argentina. Black Sun has a jungle compound out there. We find Kiel. We dismantle Black Sun."

He looked over to the corner. "Now," he said, "I need to have a talk with my daughter."

Norah didn't look surprised. Just tired.

She stood without a word, still clutching her pride like a cracked helmet, and followed her father as he walked from the room.

The doors kissed shut behind them.

And the War Room returned to its hum.

FOURTEEN

THE COLDPACK HISSED FAINTLY as Katya cracked it against the edge of the table. She wrapped it in a folded cloth, turned, and held it out.

Lula sat on the cot, jaw clenched, arms folded tightly over her bruised ribs. One eye was swelling shut, purple-black and angry. Blood crusted along her lip where Norah's elbow had split it open.

She stared at the ice like it was an insult.

"Take it," Katya said, voice dry.

Lula took it. Pressed it to her eye. Winced.

They sat in silence for a moment—nothing but the low hum of old ventilation and the crackling buzz of flickering overhead strip lighting. Katya didn't fill the quiet. She let it stretch—until the air got taut enough to bend.

"You want to tell me what happened in the locker room?" she asked finally.

Lula didn't answer.

Katya waited.

Lula shifted, chewing her tongue behind a scowl. "It's not new. She's always been like that."

"Norah?"

A slow nod. "She acts like just because she has a father she's better than the rest of us."

Katya leaned back slightly against the counter. "It makes her different. But she doesn't think she's better."

"She killed Four-Four-Two."

There it was. The name. Dropped like a live round in the space between them.

Katya didn't flinch.

"You were there," she said. "You saw it. Saw that Norah had very little choice."

Lula's jaw tightened. "They were supposed to fight. But Norah wasn't supposed to win."

"They were set up," Katya said. "By the Council. Both of them victims of a cruel regime. Don't forget that."

Lula didn't respond, but her hand tightened around the coldpack.

"You think Norah wanted that fight?" Katya continued. "You think she chose it?"

"She didn't hesitate with that screw, though, did she?"

"She couldn't afford to hesitate," Katya said. "You know what that place was. You lived it. The dorms. The drills. The goddamn food schedules. You saw what happened to the ones who didn't fall in line. Who flinched."

Lula's gaze dropped. Just for a second.

Katya's voice softened—just barely. "That place wasn't training. It was survival. And survival made killers out of kids. You want to be angry? Fine. But don't aim it at Norah. Aim it at the bastards who designed the whole machine."

She paused. "You think Four-Four-Two wanted to kill Norah? Maybe she did. Maybe she didn't. Doesn't matter now. The Council turned that dorm into a cage and rattled it until someone bled."

Lula stayed quiet, breathing hard through her nose.

"You're not in that cage anymore," Katya said. "Neither is Norah. You're here. Camelot. That means something."

Katya almost smiled. "It means we choose what we fight for. And who we fight with. You think you'll make it out there alone?"

Lula didn't answer.

"Norah's not your enemy," Katya said. "Not anymore. You want to survive what's coming? You'll need her. Just like she'll need you."

She pushed off the counter. "Now get some rest. You're back on drills tomorrow."

Lula didn't respond as Katya walked out.

But she didn't throw the ice away, either.

FIFTEEN

NORAH SAT cross-legged on the edge of her bed, a faint red ring around her mouth where her lip had split. She held herself tightly, elbows on knees, gaze fixed somewhere between the wall and the memory of the fight.

Noah closed the door behind him. Walked over. Sat beside her.

He didn't speak right away.

Then: "Your mother wanted something different for you."

Norah looked over. "You've told me that before."

He nodded. "Because it's true."

Silence again.

"She didn't want this," Noah said. "The drills. The cold. The fighting. She wanted you to grow up under open sky. In a place where you didn't have to watch your back. Where you weren't a target or a killer."

Norah didn't move.

"But the world," Noah added, voice low, "had other ideas."

He looked at her then. Really looked. "You didn't ask for any of this. I know that. You got dragged into it by the choices we made—me, your mother, Allison, the Council. All of it."

He paused.

"I've been in touch with your mother's family. An aunt and uncle out in Utah. Suburbs. Decent people. Couple kids around your age. Dogs. School buses. The kind of life she dreamed about."

Norah blinked. Slowly.

"I could send you there," he said. "Tonight, if you wanted. Clean records. New name. You could go to high school, learn to drive, find out what a homecoming dance is."

She didn't answer.

"You don't have to stay in the cold, fighting my war."

Still nothing.

Then she spoke. "You think I want out?" Her voice was quiet. Flat.

Noah exhaled. "I think you deserve the option."

Norah stood.

Crossed the room.

Turned back.

"You think I can live a normal life after everything I've been through? I spent a year and a half living in a dorm where kids carved names into each other just for the right to sleep above the heater vent. I've fought in simulations where the 'loser' stopped breathing. You think I can just grow my hair, put on some makeup, and become homecoming queen?"

Noah raised an eyebrow. "No. But I think you should have the choice."

"I don't care," she snapped. "I'm staying."

He studied her.

"All right," he said at last. "But that comes with terms."

She frowned.

"You don't have to like the others," he said. "But you do need to learn to live beside them. Fight beside them. One day soon, you'll need every one of them to stay alive. That includes Lula."

She looked away.

"Norah."

She met his eyes again.

"Teamwork isn't a slogan," Noah said. "It's survival."

Norah didn't nod. But she didn't argue, either.

Noah stood and walked to the door.

"Get some rest. Drills resume at 0600."

She stayed still, watching him go.

Only when the door closed did she finally sit back down.

And breathe.

SIXTEEN

PUTORANA BASE, Siberia | 23:49 KRAT | November 15

OUTSIDE THE BASE, the wind keened against the reinforced bulkheads like something feral trying to get in. It whistled through ventilation shafts, rattled the high antennae, and screamed across the exposed steel of surface walkways.

Inside, the base exhaled slowly.

It was the graveyard shift. Corridors were dimmed to maintenance lighting—amber glows that barely touched the walls. The place breathed differently at night. Quieter. Stranger.

A scrubber dryer hummed down the main thoroughfare, mop arms extended, wheels squeaking. A lone janitor followed it, sleepy-eyed and slouched, muttering something under her breath that might have been a song or just a curse.

Two levels above, the main security desk was manned by a single officer, a thick-necked man with a bored expression and a lukewarm cup of black coffee. His boots were unlaced, one ankle resting on the other as he half-watched a bank of monitors filled mostly with static or silence. Nothing had pinged for hours.

Down in the War Room, Noah Wolf sipped coffee and rubbed the heel of his hand into one eye socket.

The room was dim, most monitors set to standby, bathing the space in a low blue glow. He wore a hoodie over his fatigues, the sleeves pushed up. His face was unshaved. He looked like a man awake out of obligation, not urgency.

On the screens, the world crawled.

A firefight in Chad. Grain theft riots in Poland. A sandstorm over Turkmenistan that had disrupted three satellites and delayed a diplomatic relay.

Nothing worth scrambling jets over. Not tonight.

Noah sipped again and yawned. The mug was chipped. His name wasn't on it. It used to be Wally's.

In their quarters, Neil and Jenny stood in their undershirts, brushing their teeth side by side in front of a stainless steel sink, heads occasionally bumping.

Jenny finished first, rinsed, then leaned against Neil's shoulder as he spat into the basin.

They didn't say anything. They didn't need to.

She placed a hand over his chest, above his scar—the one from Thessaloniki. He kissed the side of her head.

Katya hung from the reinforced doorframe of her quarters, bare feet lifting up through the air, arms pulled tight above her head as she completed her twenty-third pull-up in a row.

Her breath was even. Her face a mask.

She moved like someone exorcising thoughts with each lift.

When she dropped down, she landed lightly, then turned, rolled her shoulders, and reached for the towel looped over her bunk's corner.

She didn't sleep well on calm nights.

Peace made her suspicious.

In the trainee wing, the hallway was silent, save for the occasional mechanical wheeze of the air filters adjusting.

Behind one door, Tao murmured in his sleep, twitching slightly—dreaming equations.

In another, Zina lay curled under the sheets like a question mark, earbuds still in, a track looping quietly that only she could hear.

Gregor snored once. Then stopped. Then resumed.

Imani lay perfectly still. She always did.

And in her room, Lula lay wide-eyed in the dark.

The light shining underneath her door shifted as someone—broad-shouldered, holding a baton, head tilted in idle alertness—swept past her door. The security watchman.

Lula's eye followed his silhouette through the thin pane of reinforced glass set high in the door.

She listened.

Bootsteps. Four... five... six... then fading.

A distant door hissed.

A moment of silence.

Then the click of the lock cycling closed behind him.

Lula sat up slowly.

The blankets slid off her shoulders. She was still dressed—all in black. Her boots were tucked beneath the bed, laces already half-done.

She pulled them on in silence. Her hands worked quickly, reflexively. No wasted motion.

She rose, crossed to the door, and placed a finger against the lockpad.

Didn't key it.

Just listened.

Nothing. But. Silence.

She opened the door, slow as breath.

The hallway beyond was empty.

Lula slipped out without a sound.

———

PERIMETER ICEFIELD | Putorana Base
23:58 KRAT | November 15

. . .

THE WIND SCREAMED across the tundra like something ancient and wounded. Snow moved sideways, flurrying in horizontal sheets, erasing footprints almost before they formed.

The assassin Sophia moved through it like she was made for this weather. Her coat, as pure-white as her hair and lined with thermal mesh, flared slightly as she stepped over a frost-caked ridge. Her hair was braided tightly and tucked under a hood that masked all but those eyes—glacial blue, unblinking.

Behind her, five figures advanced in disciplined silence—clad in adaptive camouflage that flickered between snowy haze and ice-dappled stone. Each carried a suppressed weapon suited to close-quarters work, and each moved in a way that confirmed they'd already memorized the interior blueprints of the compound they were about to infiltrate.

Sophia raised a gloved hand, and the team dropped low.

Ahead of them, partially buried under a lip of wind-blasted rock and reinforced polymer shielding, rose the slanted, black-glass silhouette of Putorana Base. The above-ground entry points were minimal—built that way deliberately—but the Council had never been short on hidden infrastructure.

She knelt in the snow beside a sealed terminal box set into the ridge.

The box was ancient. Scuffed. Frostbitten. It didn't blink or flash or hum. But when Sophia slid back the panel, the green emergency access port still glowed faintly. Waiting. Forgotten.

"Council Key Sigma-7," she whispered.

She reached into her coat and withdrew a small polymer drive —clear, like ice—etched with filigreed circuitry that shimmered faint blue. She pressed it into the port.

The light blinked once. Then twice. Then turned solid.

Inside the drive, old code awoke. Buried subroutines—left dormant since the Council's fall—stirred and whispered to the base's ancient bones. They spoke in the language of buried hierarchies and long-dead dominion.

The small display screen on the port flashed.

AUTHORIZED ACCESS – COUNCIL TIER: BLACK

Sophia stood. "Clock starts now. Follow the west conduit path. Secondary ingress. Move quiet."

They slid forward like phantoms. Down into the basin, to the shielded access tunnel. To a place that wasn't meant to be found.

Inside Putorana, the lights remained dim. The guards remained bored. The cleaners trundled onward.

But the wolf's den had just been breached.

———

LULA STOOD over Tao's bunk like a statue carved from shadow. The only light came from the corridor—a sliver of amber slipping beneath the bottom of the door.

She bent, pinched Tao's nose shut, and slapped a hand over his mouth.

Tao jerked awake instantly, flailing once before she leaned in close.

"Come on, brainiac," she whispered. "Grab your stuff. We're leaving."

Tao blinked rapidly. "What—"

"No time. I need your expertise with electronics. So boots, tablet, whatever's important for breaking out of this place. Let's go."

He sat up, rubbing sleep from his eyes, already reaching for his shoes.

———

ON THE SUBLEVEL ACCESS CORRIDOR, a lone guard sat slouched on a bench near the west utility access, half-awake, hand resting on the butt of his sidearm.

He never saw them coming.

One assassin emerged from the shadows and slit his throat in a single motion—silent, surgical. The body was caught mid-collapse and lowered gently.

Sophia gave a sharp hand signal.

The team moved.

Like liquid through pipework, they slid into the base and fanned out—each taking a separate corridor. Tight comms. No chatter. Just breath and pulse and motion.

A black tide rolling inward.

———

INSIDE THE WAR ROOM, Esmerelda's voice chimed low and urgent.

"Noah. System irregularity detected. Security subroutines have been overridden on Level Two. Internal diagnostics show multiple access points opened simultaneously—no authorized movement."

Noah stood up fast, nearly spilling the remains of his coffee.

"Sabotage?"

"Unknown. But not internal error."

He moved to the console and keyed in the tannoy system.

It didn't respond.

He tried again.

Still nothing.

"Esmerelda?"

"Main comms are nonresponsive. Local tannoy system has been locked out."

Noah turned, jaw tightening. He crossed to a weapons locker, opened it, and withdrew his sidearm—clean, oiled, loaded.

"Keep trying the others," he said, already halfway to the door.

"Yes, Noah."

He left at a jog.

ON SUBLEVEL three south maintenance corridor, Sophia moved with supernatural grace—body close to the walls, breath low, footsteps feathered.

A muffled cough echoed ahead. She paused.

A lone guard came around the corner, holding a tablet, distracted.

Sophia surged forward.

One quick slash of her Yojimbo tactical knife and the guard was gone—crumpling without a sound, his throat open from ear to ear, blood already pooling as she stepped over him.

She didn't even break stride.

———

INSIDE NEIL and Jenny's quarters, Neil's hands worked over Jenny's shoulders, pressing deep into the knots carved there by years of tension and recent grief. The oil glistened in the low light.

Jenny groaned. "God, that's the spot."

Neil chuckled. "Every time."

She opened one eye. "Hey. Light that candle we bought in Istanbul?"

Neil looked around. "I don't think it's here. Must be in our gear bag."

Jenny pouted mock-theatrically. "Please? I want this whole room to smell like cardamom."

Neil rolled his eyes and stood, tugging on a shirt. "Back in a sec."

He crossed to the door, twisted the handle, and nearly walked straight into Noah.

The boss man looked calm, but his voice was steel.

"Something's wrong. Get dressed. Quietly."

Jenny was already sitting up, face hardening.

Neil nodded once. "Copy."

There would be no more scented candles. The massage was over.

SEVENTEEN

TAO KNELT by the door's side panel, hunched over a compact device he'd cobbled together from three training drones and a stolen admin tablet.

He connected it to the control port.

It blinked green.

Then flashed. The lock was already disengaged.

Tao frowned. "That's... weird. Someone's already been in here. Door's unlocked."

"Whatever," Lula muttered. "Now come on."

She pushed it open and slipped through, pulling her hood up.

Tao followed, reluctant but fast.

The door clicked shut behind them.

———

NORAH WAS ALREADY AWAKE. She had been listening to them since they crept out of Tao's room—the murmurs, the footsteps, the telltale hum of Tao's device.

Only when the door down the hall clicked shut did she move.

She slid from her bed in one smooth motion and crossed the room in silence.

At the hallway junction, she pressed close to the door Lula and Tao had gone through, peering through the narrow glass panel.

There they were—moving fast, shadows stretched long under the corridor lights.

Norah slipped through the door before it could seal again.

She didn't speak.

She just followed, her jaw tightening.

———

THE WAR ROOM was a cold sea of blinking light and glass-slick reflections. Screens pulsed with geopolitical telemetry, drone surveillance feeds, and infrared sweeps of battlefield flashpoints across the globe.

The assassin entered it like a shadow—slow, deliberate. His suppressed SMG rested low but ready.

He passed the main console. Tilted his head.

It was all a little too quiet. But it wouldn't last.

A voice cut through the silence.

"You're not supposed to be in here."

The assassin froze.

The voice was calm. Feminine. Impossibly precise.

Esmerelda.

"Initiating security protocol six," she said next.

He turned, scanning the room. "Override authorization," he retorted, stepping to the console. "Cancel protocol."

There was a pause. Then: "The security of this room is separate to the rest of the base. I control what happens in here. Initiate protocol."

A faint hiss filled the air.

The assassin spun, raising his weapon—but the vents were already dispersing a pale mist, fine as breath.

His vision doubled. The floor swayed.

He stumbled back, trying to raise his SMG, but the weight was wrong now. Too heavy.

He dropped hard to his knees, then collapsed forward—face slack, breath shallow.

"Intruder neutralized," Esmerelda intoned.

———

NOAH MOVED FAST down the base's main corridor, SIG Sauer gripped in his hand, Neil and Jenny close behind.

Jenny muttered, "I can't believe I'm missing my massage for this."

Neil gave her a look. "We'll reschedule."

"We better."

Esmerelda's voice crackled in Noah's earpiece.

"Noah. I've begun to regain control of central systems. I've already secured the War Room and neutralized one hostile."

"Copy," Noah said. "Any more?"

"At least four signatures still moving. They're splitting up."

Noah's jaw clenched. "Keep us updated."

As they rounded a corner toward the trainee barracks, a sharp scuffling noise stopped them short.

Up ahead, a security guard was being strangled from behind. His boots scraped against the floor in desperation, heels kicking.

The assassin saw them. Without hesitation, he twisted the guard around like a shield. His gun was already out.

Pfft-pfft-pfft.

Suppressed shots cracked down the hall. Jenny and Neil dove behind wall struts.

Noah ducked low, sidearm raised.

The assassin advanced, using the gasping guard as cover.

Then—

A blur from behind.

A blade flashed in the dim light.

Katya.

She wrapped her arm across the assassin's throat and pulled—
tightly, surgically—sliding her blade deep into the side of his neck.

He spasmed once.

Dropped.

Katya lowered him gently, then pried the dead man off the
guard, helping the coughing man up from the floor. "You'll live,"
she muttered.

Jenny stepped out from cover. "You always know how to
make an entrance, Katya."

Katya wiped her blade clean. "I knew it was too quiet."

———

Lula and Tao crept down a narrow auxiliary path lit only by
emergency strips. Pipes hissed with steam nearby, the walls slick
with condensation.

Tao kept glancing behind them. "I don't like this," he whispered, checking his tablet. "Something's wrong with the system
architecture. Esmerelda's code is fighting someone else's. We're
not the only ones trying to crack this place."

"Yeah," Lula said, "I got that memo. But all I care about is—"

The shadows moved.

An arm snaked out from an open doorway, yanking Lula back
by the throat. A flash of steel aimed for her ribs.

She twisted—fast. The knife only grazed her side.

She stomped down hard on the attacker's foot and slipped
out of his grip as he recoiled, hitting the ground in a roll.

Tao jumped forward—small and fast but clumsy. His bad leg
buckled as he kicked out. The assassin caught his ankle mid-
motion and flung him aside like trash.

Tao hit the wall hard, clutching his leg with a cry of pain.

"Get away from him!" Lula shouted.

She surged forward, fists flying—elbows, knees, anything. The
assassin blocked, parried, struck back. He was stronger, bigger—
but Lula was fast. And furious.

She ducked a punch, driving a palm into his throat. He choked and staggered.

Then—distance.

He stepped back and drew a suppressed pistol.

"Too bad, kid," the assassin grunted, raising the weapon for a kill shot. "You fight good."

But he never got the shot off.

A figure slammed into him from the side—low, fast, brutal. He stumbled backward. A foot cracked against his wrist, sending the gun spinning into the dark.

The assassin turned, just in time to see her.

Norah.

Feral-eyed. Barefoot. Silent as snowfall.

———

NOAH PUSHED OPEN the main door to the trainee wing with Jenny and Neil right behind him.

Katya was already inside, sweeping down the corridor, checking room panels as she moved. One by one, she opened the doors.

"Imani, Zina, Gregor—all in their rooms," she said briskly, her voice tight. "Tao, Lula, Norah—gone."

Noah's jaw clenched. "Damn it."

Jenny crossed to one of the open doors, scanning the room quickly. "No signs of forced entry. Looks like they slipped out before the alarm was raised."

Neil stepped toward the far end of the hallway, eyes narrowing. "We need to find them—before someone else does."

———

SOMEONE ALREADY HAD.

Norah and the assassin tumbled over a pipe cluster, crashed into a wall panel, and rolled back toward the gun.

Norah kicked up, aiming a heel toward his temple—but he caught her ankle mid-air, twisted, and flung her backward.

She rebounded off a ventilation panel with a dull clang, rolled with the force, and landed low, panting.

The assassin scrambled toward the pistol, crawling like a wild dog. Norah dove too, skidding along the floor on her hip like a soccer player making the perfect sliding tackle.

They crashed into each other again, both hands clawing for the weapon.

He got there first. His hand wrapped around the grip—only for Norah to slam her knee into his fingers, knocking it loose. It bounced against the floor and slid under a pipe.

He cursed.

She tried to get it, but he grabbed the back of her shirt and yanked her away, lifting her briefly off the ground.

She twisted mid-air, slapped one of his ears to disorient him, then hooked a foot around his neck and used her momentum to bring them both down.

They hit the ground in a tangle, limbs flailing. The gun was just feet away.

The assassin shoved her off and dove again—desperate, panting, crawling on all fours toward the pistol.

He reached for it—

A foot stepped in front of him and calmly dragged the gun out of reach.

He looked up.

Lula stood over him.

She raised the pistol.

Thwip.

One clean shot between the eyes.

The assassin's body jerked. Then stilled.

The gun lowered. Lula's breath shuddered once. Then steadied.

Norah slowly sat up, bruised and smeared with grime. "Took you long enough."

Lula didn't answer. Just stared at the body for a second longer.

The moment was broken when a sharp, digital chirp sounded from the dead man's earpiece.

Lula knelt, yanked it free, and pressed it to her own ear.

"Wolf Killer Four, do you copy?" came a man's voice down the line. "I'm in the west corridor. Target is still active."

Lula looked up. "That's not far."

She turned and began moving down the corridor, steps quick and purposeful.

Norah caught up with her, grabbing her shoulder. "We should find my dad. He'll know what to do."

Lula stopped, eyes sharp.

"No. We should do what we're trained to do."

Then she pulled free—and walked on.

Norah looked at Tao, who had limped into the corridor behind them.

He winced, holding his thigh. "She's the one with the gun."

Norah exhaled. "Great."

EIGHTEEN

SOPHIA MOVED like an arrow loosed from an invisible bow—silent, certain, unerring. The corridors around the base's central reactor spine were narrow, humming with the dull resonance of the geothermal infrastructure buried deep beneath the permafrost. The air here was warmer, denser. It smelled faintly of coolant and dust.

Two guards stood at the door to the reactor room—fatigued but alert, rifles slung low. One turned as she rounded the corner.

"Hey—identify your—"

Pfft. The first shot caught him clean in the temple.

He collapsed without a sound, knees folding beneath him as Sophia shifted her aim.

The second guard's rifle was halfway up.

Pfft.

A round punched into his chest, followed immediately by a second to the throat.

He staggered, gurgled once, and slumped against the wall, blood already pooling beneath him.

Sophia didn't break stride. She stepped through the door and into the central core chamber—a vast, cylindrical expanse where the old Council engineers had built the small reactor that continuously powered this base.

Pipes ran like arteries across every surface. Massive turbines sat inert in their containment cradles. The room vibrated with a mechanical pulse so low it could be felt more than heard.

Sophia walked to the center.

She knelt beside a grated floor panel and unlatched the heavy black case from her back.

The clips snapped open.

Inside, a polished core charge nestled in custom foam—Council-era demolition tech retrofitted with modern AI-guided failover logic. Small. Efficient. Overkill.

She pulled out the bomb, unfolded the stabilization fins, and set it down on the panel with reverent care.

Then she tapped the interface.

A cold blue light blinked to life.

The screen read: *PRIME? [Y/N]*

She pressed *[Y]*.

The timer menu appeared.

Sophia tilted her head. Listening. No footsteps yet.

She keyed in the countdown.

00:06:00

The timer began. Just enough to get clear.

She stood slowly, eyes calm. And left the case open on the floor—its digital heart beating down toward catastrophe.

———

NOAH MOVED FAST through the darkened corridor, his SIG Sauer low and steady. Beside him, Katya had her blade sheathed, but her hand never left the grip. Neil and Jenny trailed behind, covering the rear.

The air was tense. Tighter than before. The quiet wasn't silence—it was a breath held before a scream.

"We need to find the kids," Noah muttered, eyes scanning the corridor intersections.

"We will," Jenny said. "But if these bastards are splitting up, they're not just here for blood. They're here to end this base."

"Esmerelda," Noah said into his earpiece, "status?"

There was static. Then—"...partial access restored. Re-routing firewall... wait..."

The sound of gunfire tore through the corridor.

Sharp, automatic. Close.

Screams followed.

"North wing," Neil barked. "Operatives' quarters."

They ran.

The next hallway had erupted in chaos.

Two assassins carrying assault rifles had burst through the dormitory entrance and opened fire immediately, spraying beds and desks and lockers with tight bursts of lead.

Operatives on downtime—some half-dressed, some asleep—scrambled for cover. Blood spattered the walls. A comm tech took a round to the shoulder before diving behind a locker. Another didn't make it.

"CLEAR THE ROOM," one assassin shouted, moving forward.

But before they could finish their sweep, the door behind them exploded open.

Noah went in first, his SIG Sauer already barking.

One assassin staggered as a round tore through his thigh. He spun and fired wildly.

Jenny rolled into cover and returned fire, her bullets forcing the assassins into a retreat. Neil took a knee, lined up, and dropped the first assassin with two clean shots to the chest as he stumbled on his injured leg.

He collapsed, twitching.

The second assassin ducked into the corner, returning fire with brutal suppression. The air filled with shouts and ricocheting steel.

Jenny surged forward, flanking from the side. She kicked over a locker for cover and slid behind it, popping up just long enough to clip the second assassin in the shoulder.

Noah stepped out and fired three times.

The first two hit the assassin's chest. The last bullet hit his forehead.

It was all over.

Just heavy breathing and the soft, gurgling groans of the wounded.

Jenny helped a medic up from under a desk. "Anyone else alive?"

"Some," the medic gasped. "Thanks to you."

Right at that moment, Esmerelda's voice returned, sharper and more complete.

"I have regained control of all security systems."

Klaxons began to sound. The base flooded with emergency red lights. Sealed doors hissed back into motion. Defense subsystems realigned.

"Base is now under full lockdown."

Noah tapped his earpiece. "Talk to me, Esmerelda."

"Confirmed movement—Norah, Lula, and Tao are currently moving through West Corridor Junction 7."

A pause.

"One of the assassins is heading toward them."

Noah's eyes sharpened. "How far?"

"Less than two hundred meters. Intercept unlikely without immediate action."

Before anyone could respond, Esmerelda added, "Also—one of the intruders has left something inside the central core. By my calculations, it is an explosive device."

A fresh wave of dread hit the team.

Jenny swore under her breath. "You think it's enough to take the whole base?"

"If it is detonated," Esmerelda replied, "it will cause catastrophic damage."

Noah turned to the others.

"I go for Norah. You two get to that bomb."

Jenny didn't argue. Neither did Neil.

NINETEEN

LULA, Tao, and Norah crept into the west corridor, boots soft against the concrete, breath shallow. Emergency strips pulsed in slow red along the ceiling.

They moved in a loose triangle, Lula in front with the pistol, Tao close behind clutching his tablet device, Norah sweeping the rear, eyes darting from shadow to shadow.

"Where is he?" Tao whispered.

The corridor stretched ahead—quiet. Empty. Too empty.

"No one," Lula murmured. "He must've doubled back."

"No," Norah said. She stopped. Her body went still.

She narrowed her eyes toward the far end of the corridor, just beyond the bend.

Something... shifted. A flicker in the dark. A figure—small motion, wrong rhythm.

"Down!" Norah hissed.

They scattered a second before the corridor exploded with gunfire. Muzzle flashes strobed from the darkness ahead, suppressed rounds snapping through the air like whipcracks.

Lula and Tao dove into a recessed maintenance alcove, slamming against metal piping as bullets ricocheted past.

Norah threw herself into a side room, landing hard on her shoulder and rolling beneath a metal table.

Thud-thud-thud. More suppressed shots ripped through the doorframe behind her.

The room was long and low, filled with overturned benches and scattered equipment. Some kind of old briefing chamber, abandoned since the Council era.

Norah crouched, breath held, body tight beneath the nearest bench.

She heard the footsteps. Measured and steady.

A long shadow stretched across the floor, cast by the strobing emergency light behind him.

The assassin entered the room. His boots moved across the concrete, slow and deliberate. The shadow drew closer.

Norah didn't move. Didn't breathe.

Just watched, heart pounding, as the killer came for her.

———

JENNY AND NEIL burst into the reactor room, weapons raised. The chamber thrummed with low, seismic energy—the deep pulse of geothermal power running through the base's veins.

There, at the center, sitting like a predator at rest was the bomb. Black casing. Digital core. Blue interface blinking with cruel precision.

Neil was on it instantly, sliding to his knees beside the device. His fingers flew over the housing, accessing the external diagnostics.

Jenny covered the room, scanning for motion.

Neil's voice was grim. "Five minutes left."

"Can you defuse it?"

"Not without full override codes. Council encryption— Esmerelda doesn't have access. It's designed to fry if tampered with. One wrong input and this place goes sky-high."

Jenny's mouth tightened. "So what—"

"We carry it out," Neil said, already unlatching the anchoring clamps.

Jenny blinked. "You're serious?"

"I'd rather be wrong and dead than leave it ticking in here."

With a grunt, Neil hoisted the bomb—its weight unexpected but manageable—and they ran.

They pushed through the door and immediately—

CRACK-CRACK-CRACK!

Gunfire screamed down the corridor, bullets sparking off concrete and steel.

Sophia.

She stood at the end of the hallway, framed in haze and cold red light, her suppressed SMG kicking against her shoulder with mechanical precision.

Neil dove right, Jenny left, both of them pinned behind bulkhead supports.

"She's blocking the route out," Neil hissed. "We'll never make it in time."

Jenny's hand was already in her belt pouch. "I've got a flash and a smoke. I set them off, then you make a run for it with the bomb. I'll take her. On my mark."

Neil nodded.

Jenny yanked both canisters, pulled the pins with practiced fingers, and threw them hard into the corridor.

The flashbang went first—*BOOM*—a sunburst of white-hot light that tore through the shadows.

The smoke grenade hissed to life a beat later, spewing a thick white fog that swallowed the space whole.

"Go!" she shouted.

Neil bolted into the smoke, bomb in his arms like a live child. His footsteps faded fast.

Sophia moved carefully, rifle up, eyes sweeping. Her senses were sharp, trained for this—but even she couldn't pierce the wall of white entirely.

The flash had left spots in her vision, and now the smoke

twisted everything—no form, no direction, just a hell of flickers and breath.

She heard footsteps.

Whirled.

CRACK!

Pain exploded in her wrist as her rifle was knocked away by a fast, brutal strike. She spun—and Jenny was right there, pistol raised, barrel aimed straight for Sophia's chest.

Sophia swatted the weapon aside just as Jenny pulled the trigger.

BLAM—the shot missed, ricocheting somewhere into the smoke.

Sophia lunged forward before Jenny could recover, her hand snapping out with the precision of a scalpel.

She caught Jenny's wrist mid-motion as she went to shoot again—then pressed hard against a pressure point just beneath the thumb.

Jenny hissed, her fingers involuntarily spasming.

The pistol slipped from her grip and clattered to the floor between them.

Sophia dropped instantly, hand reaching for it—

WHAM!

Jenny's boot slammed into the side of the weapon, sending it skittering across the floor into the fog.

They both paused for a fraction of a second, eyes locked.

No more tricks.

No more toys.

Just hands.

Sophia straightened slowly. Jenny mirrored her.

They both dropped into combat stances without speaking, breath fogging between them.

Then they came at each other like two storms colliding— exploding in thunder.

Norah pressed herself deeper into the shadows beneath the table, her back slick with sweat despite the chill. The emergency lights pulsed dimly overhead, casting long, crawling shadows across the floor.

The assassin's boots moved closer. Measured and patient. A predator in no rush.

She could hear his breathing now—calm, steady. Like he was enjoying this.

Then came silence. The footsteps stopped.

Norah strained her ears.

Nothing.

Her heart pounded so hard it felt like it might give her away.

The door creaked softly.

Another sound—barely audible.

Someone else.

A shape slipped into the room, shadowy and crouched. Smaller and quieter than the assassin.

Lula.

She moved like a stray thought, gliding past the edge of the wall with the stolen pistol gripped tightly in both hands. Her eyes swept the room.

It appeared empty. The assassin was nowhere to be seen.

She crept forward, moving toward the middle aisle of benches and tables. Her footfalls were soundless against the concrete, posture low, breath tight.

She crouched beside the table.

Norah was there.

Their eyes met.

Norah shook her head frantically. Her lips moved: *No.*

Then she pointed—sharp, urgent.

"Lula, duck!"

THWIP.

A suppressed shot cracked past her head as she dropped to the floor.

The assassin had stepped out from behind the open door, weapon raised.

Lula dived under the table just as another round shattered the wood above.

As she landed, the pistol flew from her hand, skittering across the floor into the shadows.

Gone.

Norah and Lula crouched together beneath the table, shoulder to shoulder, pressed into the darkness.

Above them, the footsteps started moving again.

Closer.

———

WITHIN THE SMOKE, the world narrowed to shadow, motion, and impact. They came together like old enemies meant to end one another. Fists cracked against bone in a fog of choking white.

Jenny grunted as Sophia's elbow found her ribs. She twisted, caught the blow, and drove her knee upward, clipping Sophia's thigh. The two women collided in the center of the smoke cloud —grappling, shifting, striking in a deadly dance.

Sophia moved like a ghost—precise, practiced, without emotion.

Jenny moved like a storm—fluid, furious, relentless.

A punch cracked against Sophia's jaw.

A counter—two fingers jabbed into Jenny's throat.

They both staggered back, breath ragged, feet scraping on the concrete.

They lunged again.

In the meantime, Neil burst through the main exit hatch, boots hitting the ice with thunderous thuds.

The cold struck like a wall—wind howling, snow lashing sideways. He could barely see ten feet ahead. The white void swallowed the world.

In his arms, the bomb blinked cold blue against the storm.

2:41
2:40
2:39

He ran. Down the slope. Past the outer array. Toward the edge of the rock face.

Every step was a war. His legs burned. The weight pulled at his spine. The frozen air knifed into his lungs.

But he kept going.

Inside the smoke-filled corridor, Jenny slammed Sophia into the wall hard enough to crack the emergency light above. Sparks showered down.

Sophia answered with a headbutt—then another. Jenny reeled.

Sophia grabbed her arm, twisting at the elbow, forcing her down toward the floor.

Jenny snarled, rolled, and brought Sophia down with her. They hit the ground, locked together in a furious grapple.

No words.

Only breath, blood, and impact.

Outside, Neil tripped. Went down hard. Snow rushed up to meet him. He landed on his side, cradling the bomb to his chest like a wounded child.

1:58
1:57

He cursed, pulled himself upright, and stumbled forward again—limping now. Ahead—just visible—a black silhouette against the storm.

A deep gorge.

Almost there.

Back in the corridor, Jenny's fist connected with Sophia's cheekbone, finally drawing blood.

Sophia responded with a sharp kick to the stomach, sending Jenny crashing into a steel beam.

Jenny coughed, spit blood, and wiped her mouth.

Sophia stood across from her, chest rising and falling, fists clenched.

Again, they charged at each other.

———

THE ASSASSIN MOVED SILENTLY between the rows of benches, eyes scanning the gloom, weapon at the ready. His boots made almost no sound as they crept across the concrete floor.

Beneath the table, Lula and Norah huddled close, barely breathing. The dim pulse of the emergency lights flickered across their wide eyes.

Then—metal scraping. The table above them lurched. With a savage grunt, the assassin ripped it away, sending the steel slab crashing across the room.

He raised his rifle.

The muzzle stared them down like a black eye.

Norah and Lula grabbed each other, pressing close.

Nowhere to run.

No time.

They clenched their eyes shut.

Then—

CRACK. CRACK.

Not an assault rifle.

A sharper, cleaner sound.

A SIG Sauer P302.

Norah's eyes snapped open. She knew that sound.

It was her father's gun.

Noah stood in the doorway, pistol raised, breath calm, eyes locked, smoke curling from the barrel.

The assassin lay twisted on the ground, two neat holes in his chest, blood seeping across the concrete.

Norah scrambled to her feet and ran. No words. Just motion

She threw her arms around him, holding on like the world had just stopped spinning.

Noah caught her. Held her.

She was safe.

Lula stood nearby, heart hammering, eyes fixed on the body of the fallen assassin.

Tao limped into the doorway behind them, face pale and drawn but alive.

For a moment, there was only breath and silence.

Then—

BOOM.

The entire base shuddered.

A low, seismic thump echoed up from the earth like a sleeping god stirring below. The walls groaned. Lights flickered. Dust rained from the ceiling. Metal creaked, and distant pipes shrieked in protest.

The floor beneath them rolled, just slightly—but enough to knock them off balance.

Noah instinctively shielded Norah as they staggered.

Lula hit a wall with her shoulder. Tao grabbed the doorframe to keep from falling.

Then—stillness. The shaking stopped. The base held.

There was no fire. No collapse. Just that one terrible shudder, now passed.

"What was that?" Norah whispered, eyes wide.

"Neil," Noah muttered, jaw tightening.

Lula exhaled a breath she didn't know she'd been holding. "Was that a bomb?"

"Yes," Noah said. "But Neil got it out in time."

Tao sank down against the wall, cradling his bad leg, relief flooding his expression.

Norah pulled back and looked up at her father. "He saved us."

Noah didn't answer immediately. He just nodded, slowly. Then holstered his pistol.

The worst—for now—had passed.

———

NEIL LAY prone in the snow, arms covering his head, the bomb far below him at the bottom of the gorge.

The explosion had rolled across the tundra like thunder under ice. A column of white rose skyward behind him—snow, debris, and vaporized frost bursting into the air with a muted *whumpf*. The shockwave had flattened the nearby drifts and sent a flurry of loose snow raining down on his back like ash.

At first, he didn't move. Just breathed. Thankful that he was still alive. Then he rolled to his side and exhaled hard, heart hammering in his ears. "Still here," he muttered, stunned.

With a grunt, he pushed himself up and turned back toward the base.

Inside the base, the blast rippled through the structure. Steel groaned. Floors lurched.

Jenny and Sophia both staggered in the corridor fog—two silhouettes locked in brutal hand-to-hand.

Jenny caught herself on a wall, coughing. Sophia stumbled back a step, eyes flaring in sudden rage.

She turned toward the direction of the core chamber, straining to hear. Nothing but distant sirens. No collapse. No fire. Just stillness.

The realization struck her like a slap. Her face twisted.

"It didn't go," she growled.

Jenny wiped blood from her mouth and spat. "Oh, it went. Just not where you wanted."

Sophia screamed—not a sound of panic but fury.

She lunged at Jenny, fists flying harder now. Their bodies crashed together, Jenny barely dodging an elbow that would've broken her nose. Sophia was faster now, reckless—wounded pride powering her limbs.

She launched herself forward with feline speed, twisting mid-air and whipping into a spinning kick, her boot slicing toward Jenny's head like a blade.

But Jenny dropped, letting the strike sail just inches overhead, feeling the wind of it sweep past her hair. She rolled forward under the arc of the kick, using the momentum to pivot around and come up behind Sophia before her feet even hit the ground.

Sophia turned—too late.

Jenny slammed into her, catching her around the midsection in a brutal clinch, driving her back-first into the wall, the impact reverberating and going for a chokehold.

But Sophia twisted free, rolled low, and surged forward—shoving Jenny off balance. Jenny staggered back a step from the shove, catching herself on the opposite wall as Sophia rose from her crouch, panting, wild-eyed. The fight had turned messy—sloppy with fury, both women bloodied and heaving, circling in the fog like rival wolves.

But then, just as they were about to launch themselves at each other again, they were interrupted.

"Freeze! Hands where we can see them!"

Voices cut through the smoke—firm, sharp, trained.

"On the ground! Now!"

A trio of Camelot security guards burst from the haze, their rifles raised, red laser sights dancing over Sophia's chest.

She froze for a heartbeat, caught between Jenny and the guns.

Then her gaze flicked toward the open corridor about ten feet behind her—the way outside. Escape.

Jenny saw it in her eyes a second too late.

Sophia exploded into motion, spinning hard and hurling a fire extinguisher from the wall mount into the fog behind her. It landed heavily on the valve and burst open—spewing white vapor, adding to the smoke.

"Contact is fleeing!" one of the guards shouted, firing a warning shot into the ceiling.

Jenny bolted forward, arm outstretched. "No you don't—!"

Sophia sprinted through the corridor and hit the outer hatch, slamming her hand against the override panel. The door hissed open.

As Jenny rounded the corner, Sophia vanished into the storm.

Jenny burst outside, the cold slicing into her lungs. Snow

whipped across her face, visibility reduced to a blur of gray and white.

She saw it. Just ahead—movement. There was a flicker of light in the air. Floating. Glinting.

A chopper—silent and sleek, hovering above the ground.

Sophia didn't stop.

She raised her left wrist. Click.

A magnetic grappling hook shot skyward, the line locking with a heavy magnetic clang onto the underside of the helicopter.

She launched into the air, rising with the sudden grace of a bird of prey.

Scrambling up the cord, she disappeared into the open hatch.

Jenny sprinted, pistol in hand, but she was too late. The hatch sealed. The craft gave a sharp mechanical whine, then vanished into the blizzard with a roar of air displacement, the lights shrinking to pinpricks before winking out entirely.

Gone.

Sophia, once again, had escaped. Just like Istanbul.

Jenny stood there, panting in the cold.

Then she holstered her weapon.

"Next time," she muttered.

TWENTY

THE CORRIDORS no longer echoed with gunfire, but the silence had its own weight.

Camelot operatives moved through the base like ghosts, sweeping away the damage, cataloguing the cost. Debris littered some of the sublevel halls. Black scorch marks stained bulkheads where gunfire had torn through them. The air smelled faintly of burnt ozone and antiseptic.

Inside the operations chamber, Noah stood at the head of a display table littered with reports and datapads. He had not slept.

One of the lead security officers stepped forward, flanked by a grim-faced medic.

"The bomb went off just outside the perimeter," the officer said. "Minimal structural damage. Some cracked pipework along the northern ventilation shaft that's closest to the cliff face but nothing critical."

Noah gave a tight nod. "Casualties?"

"Eight confirmed dead," the medic said. "Six more in critical condition in the medbay. Another sixteen have moderate to severe injuries—mostly from the quarters firefight."

Noah closed his eyes briefly.

"We'll need to memorialize the dead," he said. "Get names and send them to the comms team for processing."

"Already in motion."

The officer moved to the body of one of the assassins laid out under a draped tarp near the wall.

He lifted the corner, exposing the torso.

"Found this on one of the shooters."

The man's shirt had been cut open, revealing a tattoo inked over his heart.

A crowned sun, blazing in golds and reds, was inked across the chest. The crown sat heavy above it, barbed like a halo. Around the rays, circuit-like etchings spiraled outward in concentric rings, forming a tech-woven mandala. And beneath it all, stamped violently at the base of the sun, a heart bled in stylized rivulets of ink.

Noah's jaw tightened.

"Children of the Empire," he muttered.

The officer gave a grim nod. "Not just that."

He stepped aside and gestured to another corpse, already cooling on the deck. This one had taken a shot clean through the neck—the medic had barely managed to keep the head attached for autopsy.

With clinical efficiency, the officer tugged down the collar of the dead man's tactical vest and undershirt, revealing another tattoo—vivid even in death.

A Black Sun—a sunwheel formed from interlocking SS runes, stark and unmistakable.

The symbol hadn't been seen openly in decades. But Noah knew it. A relic of fascist obsession. A creed of engineered bloodlines. Of purity through violence.

Noah's gaze sharpened. He didn't speak—just stared at it, every muscle in his face gone still.

Black sun.

Two marks. Two creeds.

Two enemies of Camelot.

A voice at his shoulder broke the silence.

Jenny.

She stepped in beside him, arms folded, blood drying on her knuckles.

"Looks like they've formed a coalition," she said.

Noah nodded. "One we can't let metastasize."

He turned to Neil, who had just returned from the medbay, eyes red from smoke and fatigue.

"We're going to Argentina," he said. "Whatever Black Sun's doing out there ties back to Sebastian Vale and the Children of the Empire. It's all converging."

"I agree," Neil said. "How big a team are we talking?"

"Just us."

Jenny arched a brow. "Seriously? Just the three of us?"

"It'll have to be. We'll need everyone back here to protect the base. Plus, it's best if we stay as small as possible. Black Sun's compound is remote, buried in the Patagonian jungle. Anything bigger than a three-man team, and they'll see us coming."

He looked over to Katya, who had been silently listening from the corner.

"You'll stay here. Coordinate defense. Keep the recruits tight and focused."

Katya raised a brow. "And if they come back?"

"They won't get in," Noah said. "Esmerelda's already rewriting every line of Council code still embedded in our systems. From the ground up. No backdoors. No legacy ghosts."

"And backup?"

"Already in motion. Reinforcements from Southridge and Lhasa bases will arrive by morning."

Katya gave a small nod. "Understood."

Inside the trainee wing's common room, the recruits were scattered across couches and benches, bruised, bandaged, and buzzing. The tension from the night before still clung to the walls —but so did something else. Adrenaline. Awe.

"I still can't believe he had a gun to your face," Gregor said, wide-eyed. "What did you do?"

"We waited," Lula said dramatically. "And then blam blam! Norah's dad shot him straight through the heart."

Norah, quiet in the corner, rolled her eyes.

Tao shifted uncomfortably, adjusting the wrap around his thigh. "Yeah, and then I hobbled back with one leg like a wounded squirrel."

"You did great," Zina teased, ruffling his hair.

"I don't feel great."

The group laughed. Lula leaned back smugly.

"Honestly? It was kinda awesome."

That was when Katya stepped into the room.

The laughter died fast.

Her eyes swept over the group. Then narrowed on Norah, Tao, and Lula.

"Everyone else—out," she said flatly.

No one argued. The others shuffled out without a word.

The three culprits stood—or limped—in silence.

Katya folded her arms.

"What you three did was reckless," she said. "You disobeyed protocol. You decided to run off during a high-risk infiltration and nearly got yourselves killed."

Tao opened his mouth. She raised a finger. "Don't."

They shut up.

Katya let the silence stretch for a beat.

Then, softly: "But you kept your heads. You moved like you'd been trained. You adapted. You protected each other."

She stepped closer, eyes like steel.

"You did well."

Lula's grin threatened to break through. Norah glanced at Tao, who—surprisingly—looked proud.

"But," Katya added, her voice dropping into something

colder, "next time you decide to run off like that, I'll let you. I'll let you march straight out into the frozen wasteland that stretches twenty klicks in every direction. Let you freeze out there—slowly, alone, and stupid. Do you understand me?"

"Yes, ma'am," they mumbled in unison.

Katya turned to leave. "Good. You've got three hours to rest. Then we're back to training."

And she was gone.

Lula waited a moment, then whispered, "Told you it was awesome."

TWENTY-ONE

THE SNOW HAD STOPPED FALLING.

The wind, for once, was quiet, as though the tundra itself was holding its breath. Floodlights cast long shadows across the landing pad, where the Lockheed RQ-85 Blackwing waited—its sleek fuselage matte-black against the snow, engines humming in near-silent idle, rotors locked in hover-ready readiness.

Jenny checked the last of the gear crates with a practiced eye while Neil ran final diagnostics on the nav computer. Both were bundled in layered thermals and high-altitude flight gear. Their breath hung in the crisp air.

Noah stood a little apart, his coat pulled tight, hands buried deep in his pockets. Norah faced him, her expression unreadable as the wind tugged strands of hair across her face.

"You sure I can't come?" she asked, already knowing the answer.

Noah smiled faintly. "No. Best you leave Argentina to us. Someone's got to hold down the fort."

"And put up with Lula," she added. "And drills. Endless drills."

He nodded. "We've all got our part to play."

They stood there for a moment, neither moving.

"You've changed," he said at last. "You see it, don't you?"

She shrugged. "A little."

"You're more than your anger, Norah. You always were. Your mother—" He trailed off. "She would've been proud of you. *I'm* proud of you."

Norah looked down, swallowing hard. "I know you said I had a choice. About Utah."

"I meant it. You deserve to be normal."

She stepped forward and hugged him—fiercely, unexpectedly. He held her tightly, his gloved hand resting against the back of her head.

"Just come back," she said into his chest.

He smiled. "Wouldn't dream of doing otherwise."

When they pulled apart, Noah gave his daughter one last look and walked to the Blackwing.

Jenny was already aboard, fastening her harness. Neil gave a mock salute to the crew chief as the loading ramp sealed.

The turbines roared to life, snow spiraling outward in great gusts as the ship lifted from the pad.

Norah shielded her face against the wind and watched the aircraft rise into the gray morning sky, then disappear into the clouds, heading southwest.

South America.

Argentina.

Into whatever waited.

TWENTY-TWO

THE WIND SCRAPED against the high cliffs of the Făgăraş Mountains, but within the underground chapel carved into the stone foundations of Poenari Fortress, there was only silence.

No fire. No sound. Just the soft flutter of candlelight across the vaulted ceiling and the scent of centuries old incense soaked into the granite walls. The fortress had been built for war before housing none other than Vlad the Impaler.

Now it had been repurposed for something else.

Judgment.

Sophia knelt at the foot of the altar, head bowed, white hair cascading over her shoulders like winter ash.

Footsteps echoed softly behind her—measured, patient, unhurried.

Sebastian Vale approached, robed in white.

He was barefoot.

His voice was quiet, and it carried through the cavernous space with effortless gravity.

"You failed to bring me the wolf's head. You failed to burn his den."

Sophia said nothing. Her crystal eyes shimmered in the candlelight, her skin pale as the moon.

"But still," Vale said, pausing beside her. "You return."

He reached out, brushing his fingers along her temple with something that might have been affection—or the echo of it.

"I forgive you, child."

Sophia's eyes fluttered shut, relief etched into the corner of her mouth.

"But," Vale continued, stepping back, "forgiveness must be paid for."

She nodded.

"I accept, Father."

With slow, ritual precision, she rose from her knees and peeled away her coat, letting it fall to the stone floor.

Her boots followed, then her garments, until only one item remained: a chain cilice wrapped tightly around her torso and hips.

Steel links interlocked with cold geometry—each strand adorned with inward-facing tines that bit into her flesh with every breath, every movement. Her pale skin was already stippled with raw marks, crimson and fresh.

She turned her back to him and crossed her arms in submission.

Vale took hold of the leather straps that girded the cilice.

"This is not punishment," he said. "This is alignment."

He tightened the straps slowly, reverently.

Sophia flinched—just once—as the tines drove deeper into her flesh. Tiny rivulets of blood welled up and slid down the white of her skin like red teardrops.

They splashed onto the stone below with a soft, patient rhythm.

One. Two. Three.

Vale let go of the straps, stepped back, and exhaled.

"Face me," he said.

Sophia did.

He looked at her with something between pride and possession.

"Now go, my child," he said, his voice laced with divine certainty. "Hunt mine enemies so I may smite them from our lands."

Sophia bowed her head once more. Then she turned and vanished into the shadowed corridor.

As Sophia's footsteps faded into the depths of the fortress, Vale remained still. For a long moment, only the rustle of candle-flame accompanied him. Then with a slow breath, he turned and moved deeper into the sanctum—through a narrow arch and down a set of polished stone stairs into the undercell, a chamber fitted with ancient brick and a state-of-the-art uplink system buried beneath centuries of rock.

A steel chair waited in the gloom. A table. A single screen, mounted into the wall like a shrine.

Vale sat, crossed his hands in his lap, and waited.

The monitor flickered to life.

Viktor Rausch appeared on the screen—broad-shouldered, sun-scarred, dressed in black fatigues with a red-trimmed collar. His shaved head glistened with sweat, and a ceremonial Black Sun insignia was inked boldly across the side of his neck.

He did not greet Vale.

"You lost us two of our best men," he snapped instead, eyes burning. "Two genetically purified soldiers. And for what? You said the strike on Camelot would be decisive."

Vale did not blink. "I said it would be necessary."

"Necessary?" Rausch leaned forward, teeth gritted. "Do you have any idea the time it takes to train someone like König or Vesik? We are not the Council. Our ranks do not regenerate like the limbs of a salamander."

"You are not the Council," Vale agreed, voice cool. "And that is why you exist at all."

Rausch froze. The fury in his face wavered.

"Do not forget," Vale continued, calm as a blade being sharpened, "who funded your resurgence these past six months. Who spirited Dr. Kiel across three borders in the wake of the collapse. Who gave you the labs. The reagents. The silence. When every nation, every cell, every former ally turned their backs—who stood by you?"

The silence that followed was taut. Rausch sat back.

Vale's tone softened but not by much. "We all lose men. What matters is what we birth in their place."

Rausch exhaled through his nose, some of the tension leaving his shoulders. "Yes. You're right."

Vale nodded once. "Now—Kiel. How close is he to a viable strain?"

Rausch straightened. "Close. Very close. He believes that within the month we will have a form of Helix that not only persists in air but actively targets outlier genomes."

Vale raised an eyebrow. "Clean blood?"

Rausch nodded. "By Kiel's standards."

"And the other thing?"

Rausch hesitated. "We are further back on that. It's... less predictable. But some of our failures have produced useful mutations. Adaptive reflexes. Neurological rewiring. Heightened aggression. Lower empathy thresholds."

"And the children?"

"Less than one percent survived." Rausch's expression darkened, but there was a gleam of pride in it. "We're monitoring their progress. The stronger ones show... promise."

Vale leaned back in the chair.

"I want full data. Weekly."

"You'll have it," Rausch said.

The screen blinked to black.

Vale remained still, the faint glow of candles flickering against the metal rim of the monitor. His eyes narrowed—calculating.

The pieces were moving.

Sophia's fire had failed to consume Camelot.

But the next strike wouldn't miss.

It would purify.

TWENTY-THREE

ANDEAN FOOTHILLS | BORDERLANDS OF ARGENTINA | 05:47 ART | NOVEMBER 17

TWENTY-FIVE HOURS and three fuel stops after leaving Siberia, the rear bay doors of the Lockheed RQ-85 Blackwing opened with a low, whispering hiss, barely audible over the hum of its suppressed propulsion system.

Beyond, the stars blinked in thin mountain air.

Below them, the jungle canopy of the Andean foothills stretched out like a shadowed quilt—dark green smothered in pre-dawn mist, stitched by the snaking spine of the mountain ridges. Argentina lay just ahead. Silent. Watching.

The Blackwing held its hover steady, cloaked in radar-absorbent composite skin and cooled exhaust—a ghost in the sky.

No running lights. No comms chatter. Only the breath of the wind and the pulse in their ears.

Noah stood at the edge, already clipped in. He checked his altimeter, then glanced back at Neil and Jenny. Both nodded, faces calm, focus absolute.

"See you on the ground," Jenny said, the wind tugging at her red hair.

They jumped—and fell like knives, cutting through cloud, dropping fast and clean.

The sky lightened at the edges as dawn approached. Birds scattered below, startled by the ghost-silent descent of three black chutes flaring open, one after another.

They landed deep in the jungle, just inside Argentine territory —boots crunching softly against mud and moss. One by one, they touched down, rolled, shed their chutes, and disappeared into the trees without a word.

Within three minutes, they'd linked up beneath the dense canopy.

"Clean landings," Neil murmured.

Jenny scanned the tree line through a FLIR Recon thermal imager, her Heckler & Koch HK433 held low. "No eyes. No motion. We're good."

Noah consulted a secure handheld, tapping in their coordinates. "Camp's two klicks east. Let's move."

It took them two hours through rough, hilly terrain, and the scent of firewood reached them before they saw the glow.

Hidden in a dip between two steep jungle rises, the camp was modest but tight—camouflaged netting, canvas lean-to, and signal suppression rig wired into the underbrush. Wally had been busy since arriving from Bolivia two days ago.

He stood near the camping stove, cup in each hand, his dark eyes glinting beneath a patched boonie hat.

As they stepped into view, Wally raised one steaming mug.

"Well." He grinned. "Good of you to drop in. Just in time for coffee."

Noah took the coffee with a half-smile.

"Didn't want you to miss breakfast."

TWENTY-FOUR

FOLLOWING A VERY BRIEF BREAKFAST, the team gathered together.

Wally crouched over the field table beneath the lean-to, unfolding a creased topographic map and pinning the corners down with empty water flasks. A small portable projector cast light across the canvas wall behind him, illuminating jagged terrain lines and red-marked routes.

Noah, Jenny, and Neil stood close, rifles slung, faces drawn in concentration.

"I've been busy," Wally said, tapping the map. "This is the region between us and the Santa Marta basin—thick jungle, mostly uncharted. Took me the better part of a day to get into the southern sectors and back."

He flipped open a hard-case tablet and brought up a grainy video clip. The footage showed a remote village—simple homes on stilts, footpaths of packed earth, smoke curling from cooking fires. But the people were another story.

Children huddled in corners, coughing blood. Women with blistered skin and sunken eyes. A man convulsing under a blanket, flies thick on his arms.

"Shot this yesterday," Wally said quietly. "I visited two villages.

Same symptoms as Bolivia. Accelerated respiratory failure. Tissue breakdown. Internal clotting. Same pattern. Same virus."

He swiped to the next clip.

A group of villagers led Wally's camera through the jungle, their faces grim. The video jerked with motion, then steadied on a hollow in the forest floor. A mass grave. Dozens of bodies in various states of decomposition. Flies swarmed over torn cloth, bone, and bloated flesh.

"They buried the dead wherever they could," Wally added.

Jenny's mouth tightened. Neil said nothing.

Next, Wally brought up a set of still images depicting some type of attack. A burned-out village—blackened posts where homes once stood, a charred altar, and skeletal remains half-buried in the ash. The fire hadn't spared the people. Their corpses lay twisted, scorched, limbs frozen mid-flee.

"Mapuche territory," Wally said. "This tribe's been at odds with Black Sun for years. Guerilla-style resistance. Mostly defensive. A few raids, some equipment thefts."

"Looks like it escalated," Noah muttered.

"It did. Most of them are in hiding now. I've made contact with a few. They want Black Sun gone. Desperately. And they're willing to help."

Wally tapped the map again—this time pointing to a northern sector where the jungle gave way to a flattened bowl of cleared land.

"This is the old mining settlement. Cerro Rojo," he said. "Shut down in the nineties when the copper veins dried up. Black Sun moved in five years ago, reinforced the perimeter, repurposed the industrial shells into barracks, power stations, armories."

He pulled up a drone still—grainy but clear enough. Rows of modular buildings. Watchtowers. Satellite dishes. Heli-pads. Guard patrols.

"Six months ago it was a third this size," Wally said. "Now it's exploding. Looks like they absorbed a lot of the Council's remnants after the fall. Tech, bodies, money. And they're not just sitting still. Reports of jungle outposts being built. Roads cut into the wilderness."

"They're expanding," Jenny said, voice low.

"They're building something," Neil added.

Noah leaned in, eyes locked on the compound image.

"If we want to find their lab," Wally said, "we should start at Cerro Rojo."

The wind shifted outside, rustling the tarp.

Noah didn't speak for a long moment.

Then he nodded.

"Then that's where we go."

TWENTY-FIVE

THE JUNGLE THINNED as they moved east, trees giving way to strangled scrub and rock, the sound of insects replaced by something heavier—industrial. Distant rotors. The clank of metal. The echo of order.

Noah raised a fist, signaling a halt.

They crouched just beyond a rise choked in vines, half-concealed beneath a collapsed palm. Below them, through gaps in the foliage, the jungle cracked open like a wound—and the old mining settlement of Cerro Rojo revealed itself.

The mine had once been a gash in the earth, surrounded by rusting machinery and concrete ruins. But Black Sun had turned it into something else entirely.

Something alive.

Wally's voice came over the comms, barely more than a whisper in Noah's ear.

"That's it. Confirmed visual. You're on the northwest perimeter. Main gates are two klicks south-southeast."

The compound spread like a military cancer—rows of prefab buildings interlocked with steel walkways and floodlights. Guard towers dotted the periphery. Barracks. Jeeps. Depots.

A long, carved-out runway bisected the eastern edge, where a tilt-wing transport idled next to two smaller recon drones and a sleek black helicopter bearing the sigil of the Black Sun—a corrupted sunwheel branded over red.

In the center of it all was the old mine shaft, now reinforced with girders and bunker-grade shielding, surrounded by power lines, filtration systems, and mobile labs under camouflage netting.

It was a fortress, but more than that—it was a factory. Something was being built here. Something that needed space. Power. Secrecy.

"Looks like a damn Wehrmacht holdover," Jenny muttered, watching through the scope of her HK433. "You seeing the formation drills down there? Uniforms. Structure. This isn't any old militia."

"It's a regime," Neil said quietly.

Noah nodded once, scanning methodically.

"We split," he said. "Triangulate positions. Keep comms low. Eyes only. Jenny—east ridge. Neil—circle south. I'll anchor north."

"Copy," they said in unison.

The three of them ghosted apart, sinking back into the green.

As Jenny vanished into the trees, Wally's voice crackled again.

"Noah—sat feed shows two more helos inbound from the northwest. Could be resupply. Could be something worse. Clock's ticking."

Noah crouched low and moved forward, deeper into the shadows. Taking the northern slope, he eased along the tree line beneath the watchful sweep of mounted floodlights. Jenny curved east, boots barely brushing the moss. Neil slithered down the south-facing ridge, moving parallel to the access road.

The trees thinned as Neil reached a maintenance path dotted with collapsed fencing. Overhead, something hummed.

He froze.

A compact surveillance drone whirred through the canopy—a

Black Sun scout, rotating slowly, a cyclopean lens scanning in lazy arcs.

Neil stayed perfectly still. Then, slowly, silently, he reached into his belt pouch and pulled out a short, forked antenna—Wally's override spike, jury-rigged to intercept and redirect low-range command protocols.

He lifted it like a conductor's baton.

The drone paused mid-flight, jittered once, then rotated. A faint beep sounded in Neil's earpiece. Connection confirmed.

Neil tapped a button.

The drone spun, zipped off—and hovered mid-air just above the tree line a hundred meters away.

A lone operator stepped out from behind the brush, confusion tightening his face. He raised his controller and punched a few commands.

The drone didn't descend.

It simply hovered—six feet above his head, humming softly. Every time he moved, it drifted with him, matching pace like a shadow. No lateral response, no camera feed. Just... following him.

The operator frowned, tapping the controls more aggressively now.

Still nothing.

Neil watched from the undergrowth, a smirk tugging at the corner of his mouth.

"Thanks for the heads up, asshole," he muttered, ghosting around the patrol zone while the man remained fixated on the hacked drone tailing him like a stray bird.

North of the main complex, Noah came across a supply depot dug into the slope—camouflaged tarps, weathered containers, heavy-duty coolant units.

Stacks of cryo tubes, labeled with biohazard markers and complex serial codes, were being ratcheted into a transport helicopter by workers in full-body coveralls. Pallets of chemical drums and sterilized canisters sat nearby, glinting under a canopy of corrugated steel.

Noah crouched behind a generator and pulled out a handheld grid-mapper—one of Wally's latest prototypes. It was designed to detect electromagnetic flow and wirepath clusters beneath the surface.

He powered it on.

The scanner buzzed softly, then its screen illuminated with glowing threads—a ghost-map of the compound's electrical nervous system.

Lines forked out from the floodlights. A lattice stretched across the compound to guard towers, dorms, and substations.

But beneath it?

Nothing. No sink lines. No subgrid bleed. No evidence of an underground lab build beneath the depot.

Noah frowned. "They're storing biotech up here," he muttered into his comms. "But the main lab's somewhere else."

Jenny reached the edge of the eastern helipads just as the rotor thunder rolled in. She slipped into a vine-covered ditch near the fence, the noise masking her movement. Sliding the HK433 from her back, she rested it on the lip of the ditch and pressed her eye to the scope.

Two transport helicopters descended in tandem, their skids touching down hard. Black Sun troopers were already waiting in a rigid half-circle—disciplined and silent.

The bay doors hissed open, and out stepped Viktor Rausch—leader of Black Sun.

Shaved head gleaming, jaw set, and Black Sun insignia bold over his chest, he strode forward like a general returning to his fortress. Salutes snapped to attention all around him.

Jenny adjusted the magnifier on her scope.

Crosshairs landed clean on his skull.

"So tempting," she muttered under her breath.

But she didn't fire.

To do so would be to fail their main objective: find the lab and destroy the virus. So instead, she holstered the rifle and retrieved her own electrical grid scanner. The feed lit up quickly—perimeter lines, guard tower loops, the power to the helipad lights.

But nothing descending. No vertical bleed into the earth. No trace of a buried structure nearby.

She exhaled quietly.

Then Neil's voice came through the comms, calm but urgent.

"I think I've got it. One of the old mine shafts—eastern rim. Strong current running straight down. Dense cablework. Looks like a deep substation, maybe sealed access."

Jenny was already on the move, slipping through the gnarled roots and low brush toward the signal source. Noah followed a separate path, angling through the jungle's broken edge where dry gullies offered shadows to move in.

Within minutes, the three regrouped near a collapsed loader bay on the eastern perimeter, crouched beneath a fallen corrugated overhang littered with vines.

Before them loomed one of the original industrial shafts—a yawning concrete maw reinforced with rebar, steel doors, and mounted searchlights. At the lip of the shaft sat a freight elevator the size of a shipping container, half-sunk in rust but very much operational. Two engineers loaded crates onto its platform while a pair of Black Sun troopers stood nearby, rifles slung but alert.

A hum filled the air as the elevator descended slowly into the dark, swallowed by the earth.

Neil pulled out the scanner again and adjusted the frequency.

The device vibrated once and bathed his gloved hand in a dull green glow.

A new network lit up. Lines of current spiraled downward into the rock, splitting and forking into complex branches far below the visible surface.

An underground grid. Big. Wired tight. Active.

"Whole nest down there," Neil said, handing the scanner over to Noah.

Noah studied the glowing map. The currents weren't just functional—they were dense, armored, shielded. It looked like what they were after.

"You think Kiel's down there?" Jenny murmured.

"Has to be," Neil said.

Noah exhaled slowly. His voice was low but iron-steady.

"We come back at nightfall."

He handed the scanner back and locked eyes with both of them.

"We go down there. We blow it all up. Every last piece."

No one argued.

Then they moved, the jungle swallowing their retreat. Step by silent step, they vanished into the foliage, the shriek of rotors and the rumble of machinery fading behind them like the growl of a sleeping giant.

TWENTY-SIX

THE TWIN ROTORS of the CH-47 Chinook thundered overhead as the heavy-lift helicopter descended toward the Bolivian jungle compound. Dust and ash kicked into the morning sky, swirling around the scorched fields and biohazard tarps that clung to rusted scaffolding. The white and blue UN emblem fluttered weakly in the distance—faded and stained by the red soil.

Inside the belly of the Chinook, a dozen figures stood braced against the fuselage. Their silhouettes were hard—broad-shouldered and precise. They wore all-black tactical gear, segmented body armor, and ski masks of bright green material that hid every trace of identity. Each bore the unmistakable silver sword insignia of Camelot on their shoulders—clean, bright, as if freshly issued.

But none of them were Camelot.

Sophia stood at the center, her white hair tucked beneath the mask, crystal eyes unreadable behind mirrored lenses. She clutched her suppressed MP7 like a conductor's baton and turned her wrist slightly to the screen on her watch.

Sebastian Vale's face filled most of it. Candlelight danced behind him—some vaulted sanctuary lit by shadow and gold.

"Go make it up to me, my dear," he said.

Sophia bowed her head slightly. "I will not fail you again, Father."

The call went dark.

A tech specialist hunched beside a rack of portable servers and signal jammers, his fingers dancing over keys. Green lines of code raced across multiple screens. A final press of the return key, and the entire wall of monitors bloomed into segmented grids: live CCTV feeds from the Bolivian UN base.

Sophia turned. "Are you in yet?"

"Just finished burning through their firewalls," he said. "I've got control. Internal cams. Comms. Back-end feeds. All of it."

She nodded. "Good. Let's go."

The helicopter's rear ramp yawned open with a mechanical hiss, and sunlight spilled into the bay.

Outside, Lieutenant Camara shielded her eyes, frowning as the dust swept over her compound.

"I wasn't expecting Camelot back so soon," she muttered to a nearby subordinate.

A moment later, gunfire erupted.

Sophia and her false Camelot soldiers surged from the ramp in a coordinated line of violence. Muzzle flashes bloomed like fireflies. Camara barely had time to shout before her chest exploded in a spray of crimson. She collapsed against the checkpoint wall, one arm twitching.

UN soldiers scrambled for cover, but the black-clad attackers moved too fast—precision-trained, sweeping the perimeter in clockwork formations.

Within seconds, the quarantine site became a slaughterhouse.

The hospital's front gate shattered beneath booted feet. Sophia stepped through first, her battle weapon raised. A guard tried to shout, but Sophia silenced him with two rounds to the sternum. He dropped without a word.

They moved inward, mowing through anything that moved.

Behind them, the tech operative inside the chopper was

already editing the footage in realtime—overlaying Noah Wolf's face over Sophia's with AI-fed facial grafts. Her movements were recalibrated, her height adjusted. What streamed onto the external feeds now was a perfect illusion: Noah Wolf, gun in hand, systematically executing medical personnel and helpless patients.

"Remember," Sophia said to the others as they passed through the blasted corridors of the makeshift hospital, "the virus doesn't affect us."

They didn't even pause.

Dr. Helena Menendez died screaming—half a report shouted into her comms before a bullet shattered her skull.

Elias Otieno took longer, crawling away until Sophia calmly stepped over him and shot him twice in the back of the head.

Patients were shot in their beds. Those who fled were cut down in the hallways or gunned down at the jungle's edge. The compound's outer wall became a charnel border—bodies twisted in mid-run, limbs broken in frantic flight. A young nurse in a torn hazmat suit scrambled into the open, shrieking for help.

Sophia raised her weapon.

Inside the chopper, the tech leaned in. His cursor highlighted the nurse. The display switched—Noah's face now visible, cold, executioner-calm, as "he" raised the rifle.

The nurse fell.

The footage was saved, uploaded, and tagged.

History rewritten.

By the time the last gunshot echoed into the trees, no one was left alive.

Sophia and her men walked calmly back to the chopper, stepping over corpses and scattered medical records. Not one of them glanced back.

TWENTY-SEVEN

THE JUNGLE WAS ink-black by the time Noah, Jenny, and Neil returned to the perimeter of Cerro Rojo. The moon was hidden behind a roiling cover of clouds, and even the frogs had quieted their song, as if the jungle itself were quietly waiting.

Noah knelt in the brush, peering through a monocular lens.

The mine compound below blazed in unnatural light. Floodlights mounted on steel arms bathed the grounds in harsh halogen glare, transforming the jungle hollow into a sterile, shadowless crucible.

Even at this hour, the place buzzed with movement—workers loading crates into trucks, forklifts ferrying sealed containers, guards pacing between towers and checkpoints. The noise of machinery reverberated faintly through the trees, as relentless as the chirping insects.

Jenny lay beside him, eyes narrowed behind her scope. "So much for coming back at night," she muttered. She swept her HK433 across the compound's edge, tracking guards, workers, and watchtowers. "You'd think they'd slow down once the sun went down."

"They're not slowing down," Neil said, adjusting his glasses. "They're speeding up. Look at the line of trucks. They're moving something big."

Indeed, cargo was being stacked with manic urgency—sealed crates, chemical drums, and bundles wrapped in plastic. A row of helicopters stood on standby, rotors slowly spinning, engines purring like wolves waiting for the leash to come off.

Noah swore quietly.

"There's no way we get close to that shaft without setting off a dozen alarms."

That's when the tannoy cracked to life.

A loudspeaker clicked twice, followed by a clipped Germanic voice. "All personnel—report to the central platform immediately. The Kommandant will speak in five minutes. Repeat: all personnel report to the main platform. This is a mandatory address."

There was a moment's pause—then movement.

Like clockwork, the compound shifted. Workers dropped their tools. Mechanics shut off engines. Scientists in lab coats stepped away from terminals.

"Looks like good timing," Neil muttered.

They watched from cover as dozens—maybe hundreds—of personnel streamed toward the heart of the compound, assembling before a central platform where a tall steel podium had been erected. Only the armed guards remained—posted at the corners, backs straight, rifles held across black-clad chests.

As for the elevator to the shaft, only one lone guard remained.

"This is our chance," Noah said, already moving.

They circled wide, cutting along the shadows thrown by a stack of unused solar panels. At the chain-link fence, Neil produced a pair of bolt-cutters. The metal snapped apart with muted crunches.

They were inside.

They moved like smoke—low to the ground, silent, precise. The trio slipped past stacked crates and idle machinery. Floodlights swept methodically overhead, but they were always one step ahead in the shadows.

The elevator platform loomed before them—an industrial slab of steel nestled in a pit of concrete, cables trailing into the black below. The single guard stood beside the control panel, rifle slung lazily across his chest. He was young, bored, and half-awake. He yawned, one hand idly scratching at his neck, eyes barely scanning the empty space.

He never even knew Noah was there until it was too late.

Noah surged forward from the dark like a predator out of the brush, hands gripping a garrote as he closed the distance in four fast, silent steps. The wire-loop slipped over the guard's head and around his throat. One pull, clean and final. The man jerked once —eyes wide in startled panic—then went still, his body sagging against Noah's chest.

Noah exhaled quietly, easing him down into the gravel. The man's boots scuffed once, then were still. Noah's expression never changed.

Jenny was already moving. She crouched beside the corpse, grabbed his arms, and dragged the body into the dark recess beneath the elevator stairs, tucking it behind a stack of fuel drums. She patted him down quickly, lifting a keycard.

"This'll come in handy," she whispered.

Neil was at the control panel, fingers flying across the old analog keys. A red status light blinked, then turned amber. He pulled a small device from his belt pouch—Wally's override chip —and slid it into the port.

The panel screen flickered. Mechanical clunks echoed from the shaft as the elevator system began to stir.

Noah stepped in behind him, eyes on the guard towers above. Still no movement. Still no alarms.

"Let's go," he said.

Jenny gave a nod, her HK433 tucked tightly against her shoulder.

The elevator groaned to life beneath their boots, rattling on ancient steel cables as it began to lower them into the depths.

The mine would not stay quiet for long. From the platform in the distance, a microphone whined. Then came Viktor Rausch's voice, slick and proud.

"My brothers. My sisters. We stand tonight not as fugitives, not as survivors—but as architects of a world reborn..."

The sound reverberated above them through speakers as the elevator continued its slow descent into the dark throat of the mine.

"They would call us criminals. They would call us extremists. But it is we who carry the blood of kings. It is we who carry the flame forward..."

The speech followed them down.

"No more compromise. No more dilution. We are the torch-bearers. The blood shepherds. The world will bend—or it will burn."

The metal walls swallowed the light as the elevator dropped lower.

Finally, the voice above began to fade. Rausch's words dissolved into static, then silence. Darkness closed around them like a fist.

The elevator groaned as it sank deeper into the mine, the hum of the motors echoing off the stone. The metal cage vibrated underfoot, the air turning colder, deader. Jenny checked her HK433 with practiced calm. Neil adjusted the straps on his backpack. Noah stared ahead in silence, eyes fixed on the slow, unchanging wall of rock slipping past them like a gray curtain.

When the elevator finally stopped, it did so with a hiss of pneumatics and the slow grind of brakes.

The doors opened onto a tunnel unlike any mine—reinforced steel walls, LED strips humming along the ceiling. A pair of industrial fans throbbed with a low vibration from deeper within.

This was no longer a mine. It was a complex.

They moved out in silence. Just beyond the threshold, the shaft split into three main corridors.

"Fan out," Noah said quietly. "Stick to comms. Keep a count of how many bodies you see."

Jenny glanced at him. "Dead or alive?"

Noah's jaw clenched. "Either."

Then they split up.

Neil took the left corridor, descending past a chain of sealed doors. Through small observation windows, he saw rooms with flickering light. What looked like freezers, stacked wall to wall with body bags—rows upon rows, tagged and sealed.

One had been left partially open—unzipped to the waist.

Inside, a child's corpse stared out with frozen, blackened eyes.

Neil gagged into the crook of his arm, turned away, and kept moving.

He came across a hangar-sized chamber full of suspended containment tanks. Most were empty. A few were not.

He stood in front of one, breath fogging the glass.

The woman inside was emaciated, tubes pushed into her arms and chest, scalp shaved, eyelids stitched shut. Her ribs moved—but barely.

Then she screamed. Mouth wide.

No sound—only a violent spasm that made the tank rattle.

Neil stumbled back.

Jenny, meanwhile, had taken the right corridor, weaving between supply carts and empty gurneys. Everything smelled like bleach and burned metal. She passed an operating room with the lights left on.

Inside were two corpses laid open on parallel tables, chests cracked wide, organs extracted.

Beside them stood a wall of photos. Smiling faces. ID tags. Dozens of them. Children. Men. Women.

Then the same faces—afterward.

Jenny gritted her teeth and turned away. Down another

hallway she had to duck into a side closet as a pair of guards passed. One of them laughed as he mentioned, "Section Twelve's batch didn't last the week."

Her hand clenched around her HK433.

Noah moved down the central corridor, sweeping past flickering terminals and grated floor panels slick with condensation.

Eventually, he entered what looked like a medical analysis wing—long, dim, and low-ceilinged, with a chemical tang that burned the nose. Half-emptied cryo pods lined one wall, condensation bleeding from their seals. Scorched autopsy tables stood in crooked formation, some still slick with dark fluid. Blood had pooled and dried across sections of the grated floor, crusted thick where the drainage had backed up. Three corpses lay dumped in the corner like meat left to spoil, their eyes missing—scooped or carved, it was hard to tell.

Noah moved soundlessly, no more than a flicker of light.

Up ahead, a man stood bent over a surgical gurney. He wore the black fatigues of Black Sun med-techs, gloved hands working with a scalpel inside an open chest cavity. The subject was a young woman—barely more than a girl—strapped down, already dead, but only recently. Blood glistened around the incisions. Tubes led from her body to an analyzer unit, ticking quietly with unread data.

The tech was muttering to himself. Focused. He didn't hear Noah's steps over the low whine of the filtration vents and the steady beep of monitors.

Noah crept forward, measured and low.

Five feet.

Three.

One.

He struck.

A blur of motion—his arm snaked around the man's neck, dragging him off balance and clamping down with brutal force. The scalpel clattered to the floor. The tech kicked, but Noah muscled him sideways, slammed him into the nearest wall with a thud that rattled the metal sheeting.

Noah's SIG Sauer appeared, cold and absolute, pressed to the side of his temple.

"Where's Kiel?" Noah growled, voice razor-thin.

The man barely breathed, too stunned to even speak at first.

Noah shoved him against the wall again. "Where's Kiel?"

"I—I don't know!"

Noah slammed him a third time. "Try again."

The man whimpered, knees nearly buckling. "He's not here. He's not—he's not allowed here."

"Why not?"

"Risk of an outbreak. That's why Rausch keeps him somewhere else. Off-site. He's got him in a lab hidden somewhere out in the jungle."

"Where?"

"I don't know. No one does except the inner ring."

Noah pressed harder. "So if this isn't the main lab—what is it you do here?"

"We—we analyze the samples. That's it. They send results. Send test material. We don't ask questions. I swear. Please—I just sort data."

Noah looked at the bodies. Tortured. Dismembered. Some skinned. Some vivisected.

His voice was ice. "You analyze the samples? You mean innocent people—children."

"I didn't kill her—I just—"

Noah pulled the trigger.

The shot cracked through the low ceiling like a whip.

The med-tech's skull snapped sideways—what remained of it —his brains painting the metal wall in a red-and-gray fan of pulp and bone. His body gave one last twitch and dropped like a boneless sack, hitting the floor with a wet thud that echoed through the chamber.

The scalpel he'd been using lay in a streak of blood by the gurney, still slick with the young woman's tissue.

Noah stared at the body for a moment. Not with anger. Not with guilt.

Just cold confirmation.

Then he bent, wiped his gloved fingers across the technician's fatigues, and turned back toward the corridor.

TWENTY-EIGHT

THE THREE MET up again in a maintenance corridor near a grilled ventilation shaft. No one said anything at first.

Jenny looked pale. Neil's eyes stared into the distance.

Noah's expression remained unreadable.

"Kiel's not here," he said. "They're hiding him and his experiments at another site."

Jenny spat to the side. "Then we find it."

Neil nodded. "But we take this place down first."

Noah's eyes burned as he glanced back down the corridor they'd come from—back into the dark womb of horror they'd just crawled through.

"I agree," he said. "We burn it all."

They unshouldered their packs in silence, kneeling in the shadows of the hallway.

Each one drew out brick-sized satchels of high-yield plastique, pre-rigged with timed detonators. Wires hummed softly as they plugged in the trigger matrix—no talk, no jokes. Just quiet, surgical intent.

They split again.

Noah moved alone through the stifling dark, descending into

a sub-chamber where the air reeked of scorched flesh and chemical rot.

A furnace roared at the room's center, its open maw devouring limbs and torsos that had been dumped from blood-slick gurneys.

Without flinching, he knelt beside a supply crate and nestled a charge beneath a cluster of fuel lines.

He stood slowly, eyes fixed on the blaze—and for a moment, the flames seemed to stare back.

Jenny planted her first charge beneath a ventilation manifold beside a coolant exchanger, taping it tightly to the pipe feed with black duct tape.

She was reaching for the second when she turned a corner—and froze.

A door had been left ajar on one of the rooms. Harsh light shone down onto stainless-steel walls. It resembled a butcher's fridge.

Inside was a surgical table. On it lay a boy. Maybe ten. Head shaved. Wrists and ankles strapped down with thick leather bindings. A vitals line blinked dimly on the screen beside him, shallow but steady. His eyes were open. They followed her all the way as she came into the room.

Laser-etched on the side of his neck was *B3-17.*

Jenny stopped beside him.

"What's your name?" she asked quietly.

The boy blinked once. "B3-17."

A clipboard hung from a metal arm above him. She glanced over it.

Subject B3-17. Genome: Type 6A. Stability rating: Moderate. Schedule: Vivisection. 0400 hrs.

Jenny's breath stilled in her chest.

That's when someone stepped into the room behind her.

A man in blood-smeared scrubs stepped in, surgical mask already pulled down, humming to himself as he checked the screen of a tablet.

He looked up—and stopped.

His mouth opened.

Jenny's wrath arrived before his voice did.

She pumped the trigger of the HK433. Three suppressed rounds stitched across his chest, snapping his body backward into the glass cabinet behind him. Instruments clattered to the floor. He slid down, dead.

Jenny didn't look at him again. She lowered the HK433, turned to the boy, and began unbuckling the straps. "We're getting you out of here."

B3-17 didn't flinch. He just blinked. His fingers twitched once as the restraints peeled away.

Back near the elevator shaft, Neil clipped the last charge to a central power junction, eyes sweeping every corner. "That's the last of mine."

Noah nodded. "Same. Let's go."

They turned to leave—but paused.

Out of the shadows came Jenny, cradling the boy against her chest. He was silent, arms looped around her neck, feet dangling in the air.

Noah's jaw tightened. "Jenny..."

"I'm not arguing," she said before he could finish. "We can't just leave him here."

Neil looked at the boy. At the scars on his neck and head. The emaciated limbs.

He didn't say a word.

Noah held her gaze a moment longer.

Then he nodded once. "Okay. But he's your responsibility. Now let's finish this."

And together, they slipped away.

The elevator rose in tense silence, vibrating steadily beneath their boots as it pulled them away from the underworld of horrors below. B3-17 sat curled in Jenny's arms, eyes shut but awake, breathing shallow.

Noah watched the LED numbers tick up on the panel, his

fingers instinctively hovering near the detonator tucked into his vest pocket.

They reached the surface.

The shaft opened onto the floodlit compound—unchanged. The same sharp glare. The same cold geometry of movement.

And Viktor Rausch still holding court.

Up on a raised platform near the central depot, flanked by armed officers, he paced with theatrical precision, his voice ringing across the entire compound.

"—we are the bloodline restored! The fire through impurity! The hammer and the flame—"

"God," Neil muttered under his breath, "this guy really likes the sound of his own voice."

They moved quickly through the shadows, slipping past pallets and steel crates, ducking low as the final applause line drew a roar from the gathered crowd.

By the time they reached the perimeter fence, the speech was over and everyone was returning to their work. Noah slipped through the cut hole first, and Jenny passed the boy through, Neil following behind.

They vanished into the tree line.

Thirty minutes later, crouched beneath the canopy near a ridge overlooking the compound, Noah brought the detonator up.

B3-17 lay between Jenny and Neil, nestled in the dark, his small face streaked with dirt. He was silent, calm, but watching.

Noah waited. Counted the seconds.

Then pressed the trigger.

A low, concussive thud shook the earth—followed by a violent chain reaction underground. The hillside buckled as the tunnels collapsed in on themselves. Smoke and fire punched through the old mineshaft like a volcanic belch, shattering the reinforced entrance and sending debris skyward.

Part of the base gave way—buildings swallowed as the earth fractured. Sirens screamed. Lights cut on.

Chaos bloomed.

Within seconds, helicopters were lifting from the pads, slicing the air. Trucks roared to life. Troopers scrambled, barking orders, sprinting toward the blast zone. Others, armed with dogs and guns, began searching instantly.

But the jungle had already taken them.

Noah led the way, rifle tight to his shoulder, eyes sharp. Jenny followed, B3-17 on her back now in a makeshift sling of webbing and scarf. Neil swept rear, quiet and sure.

Behind them, Black Sun burned. Ahead, the trees opened their arms.

TWENTY-NINE

THE VAST TRAINING hall stretched like a soundstage—high-ceilinged, echoing, its steel rafters lost in shadow. In the center, a maze of modular rooms had been constructed: plasterboard walls, faux windows, knock-down furniture. A custom-built film set, assembled like a puzzle inside the larger space. It was all interchangeable—designed to mimic anything from a suburban home to a foreign embassy. Today, it resembled a downtown office complex—multi-story with open stairwells, sealed doors, and interior glass. Fluorescent lights buzzed overhead, illuminating the imitation corridors in harsh, clinical white.

Katya stood on the observation gantry above—arms folded, eyes cool. From this height, she had a god's-eye view of the entire arena. Glass partitions in the floor let her track the teams moving through their respective wings.

"Terrorist" team—Lula, Tao, and Zina—was stationed on the lower floor, securing a mock server room where three Camelot operatives pretended to be frightened tech workers. Each wore plastic cuffs and blue armbands that marked them as hostages.

Lula stormed the space like a woman possessed. Her airsoft

rifle was held tight, finger always just shy of the trigger guard. She prowled, voice sharp.

"Get down! No sudden movements!" she barked at the hostages with fervent conviction. "Or you're all dead!"

"She's enjoying this a bit too much," Katya muttered to herself.

Tao, ever the reluctant partner in chaos, flinched every time Lula raised her voice. He was stationed by the door, peering nervously down the hallway. His aim was solid, though, and his corners were clean. Zina swept the second room and posted up on a stairwell with professional calm.

Opposite them, in the outer rooms of the set, Norah, Imani, and Gregor—the "Camelot response" team—moved with coordinated precision. Norah led from the front, her stance compact and deliberate. She issued quiet commands through the comms mic clipped to her collar. Gregor, hulking and blunt, provided cover from the rear, while Imani carried the team's smoke and flash grenades.

From above, Katya watched the moment they breached. Norah gave a signal. Gregor tossed a flash through the office window. The dummy charge exploded with a harmless pop and a burst of LED strobe.

They moved in with discipline. Imani swept left, Gregor went high, and Norah ducked behind a filing cabinet, motioning for Imani to flank.

Zina spotted them first and opened fire. Airsoft pellets slammed against the walls with muffled smacks.

Tao shouted, "Left side!" before diving behind a couch.

Lula cackled, spinning on her heel. "Finally!"

"Norah's closing in," Katya muttered, eyes flicking between the video feeds on her tablet, each linked to a camera inside the set. "T-minus five seconds before Lula forgets this is a drill."

Below, Imani rolled a smoke grenade into the central chamber. A low hiss began to fill the room, followed by thick gray fog billowing across the floor.

Katya went to make a note for debrief when she was interrupted.

"Katya," Esmerelda's voice snapped crisply into her comms. "You're needed in the War Room. Now."

Katya's eyes narrowed. She pulled her headset off.

"Cease fire!" Her voice cracked like a whip through the overhead tannoy, cutting through the smoke and simulated chaos. "Exercise suspended. All teams stand down."

Groans and confused murmurs echoed up from the training floor. Norah, crouched behind a filing cabinet, lowered her airsoft rifle in frustration. Across the room, Lula gave a dramatic sigh and let her arms flop to her sides. Tao looked relieved. Zina looked suspicious.

Katya didn't linger.

She was already moving—boots pounding the grated walkway as she stormed from the observation gantry past the stunned admin clerk outside and into the east corridor. The War Room doors opened for her before she could touch them, triggered by Esmerelda.

Inside, the mood was already toxic.

The lighting was dim, screens lit in harsh blue-white tones. Operatives sat frozen at their stations, a dozen feeds open across the monitors. News tickers, security cam loops, military intel briefings. A storm of panic rendered in high definition.

Katya's voice cut through it.

"What happened?"

One of the comms officers—a young South African named Venter—looked up, his eyes wide with disbelief.

"Ma'am... Noah's not supposed to be in Bolivia, right?"

Katya stopped dead. "No. He's in Patagonia. Why?"

Venter gestured helplessly toward the central bank of monitors. "Then you need to see this."

She looked to where he pointed.

The screens were a patchwork of horror.

Security footage showed men in black tactical gear storming

the UN quarantine site in Santa Cruz. Each of them wore the sigil of Camelot emblazoned on their chest plates and shoulders: a flaming sword, white-hot against a matte black shield.

They moved with terrifying efficiency—room to room, corridor to corridor. Suppressed assault rifles rose and spat flashes of fire. Bullet trails stitched walls and bodies alike. Blood sprayed across glass dividers, smearing over biohazard signage and faded UN emblems.

Patients were gunned down mid-scream, IV lines whipping as they collapsed. Nurses fell with trays of medicine clattering against tile. Doors splintered. Alarms wailed. The violence was total.

The footage cut to a series of jarring close-ups:

Jenny Blessing, rifle raised, moved with fierce precision as she cleared a hallway. A medic cowered beneath a gurney. A single shot and his brains were spread across the cracked tiles.

Neil Blessing moved with quiet calm through the dim hallway, rifle angled low. He reached a closed door, glancing through the observation slit.

Inside was a cluster of nurses huddled behind overturned beds and medical carts, eyes wide, whispering prayers.

Without a word, Neil pulled a grenade from his vest, thumbed the pin, and cracked the door open just enough to toss it in.

The footage caught a brief glimpse of their terrified faces before the door slammed shut.

A moment later—detonation.

The blast rocked the camera feed, the corridor flaring with light and debris. The door blew outward in a cloud of smoke, blood, and shredded limbs.

When the feed stabilized, nothing inside the room moved. Just smoldering wreckage. And silence.

Finally came Noah.

The camera caught him mid-motion—sleek, fast, lethal. He

pursued a fleeing doctor through a stairwell, boots hammering concrete. The man stumbled. Fell. Tried to beg, his hands up.

Noah raised his pistol and fired twice into the chest. The doctor dropped.

The frame froze. A blue Fox banner scrolled beneath: "NOAH WOLF."

The image zoomed slowly on his face, then on the Camelot sigil—flaming sword stark and undeniable. It became the background to the studio.

A Fox News anchor leaned forward, face grave.

"A few days ago, the world was presented with the face of Noah Wolf—the man who supposedly saved cities, brought justice, and defied the Council. Today, we got to see who Noah Wolf really is."

The comms officer leaned in. "It's on every channel."

He cut to CNN.

"Sources within the State Department say Camelot warned the UN to evacuate the area a week ago," the white-haired anchor was stating. "When they didn't comply, Camelot returned—and savagely murdered everyone. That's the story now gaining traction in New York and Geneva."

A feed of a US senator mid-press conference: "Is this how Camelot enforces world peace now? Through extrajudicial execution of medical staff and refugees? This isn't justice. This is authoritarian terrorism."

It cut to another: "We replaced one Council with another. Only this one doesn't even pretend to answer to anyone."

Then—the president of the United States, standing behind the White House lectern.

"Camelot was created as a partner to the free world. But if this footage is verified—if Noah Wolf ordered the slaughter of UN personnel—then Camelot is no longer an ally. It is a rogue military actor. And we will treat it as such."

The screen split into smaller segments now: news anchors, pundits, political figures. Calls for calm. Calls for condemnation.

Reports of an emergency UN Security Council meeting convening in a day. Terms like "rogue state" and "uncontrolled militia" scrolled across tickers in bold red.

Katya stared at the screens, face pale and unmoving.

Then—

"Katya?" a voice said quietly behind her.

She turned.

The recruits stood in the War Room doorway, unsure, half-armored, wide-eyed.

Norah. Lula. Tao. Zina. Imani. Gregor.

"What's going on?" Norah asked, looking between the adults and the chaos on the monitors. "Why are they saying—?"

"Nothing," Katya said sharply. Her voice was firmer than she meant it to be. "Back to your rooms. Training's over."

They didn't move at first. Then Zina gave a slight nod, her expression unreadable, and turned. The others followed—some glancing back.

Norah lingered a second longer. Then, with visible hesitation, she disappeared down the hall.

Katya turned back to Venter.

"Get me Noah," she said. "Now."

THIRTY

CLOAKED beneath a canopy of digital camouflage and laced with Wally's low-energy signal dampeners, the small outpost he'd set up was practically invisible—just a glimmer of heat from the stove, the occasional flicker of filtered light caught in the mist.

The camo itself was woven from a flexible mesh of micro-LED fibers and photo-reactive polymers, constantly scanning and mimicking the surrounding jungle. To an outside observer, it projected bark, leaf, and shadow—rendering the camp a seamless extension of the forest. Movement beneath it was diffused in real time, erasing outlines before they could fully form.

It made them practically invisible.

Which was good. Because they weren't alone.

Overhead, the thump of rotor blades tore through the tree-tops—three CH-6 reconnaissance helicopters sweeping low, searchlights stabbing into the jungle, though never close enough to penetrate their hiding place. From the loudspeakers slung beneath their bellies, a voice crackled—distorted, theatrical, and unmistakable.

"Noah Wolf," Viktor Rausch drawled, his voice projected across the canopy, half-snarl, half-mockery. "It is nice of you to drop by. Explosive, as always. But do not flatter yourself—your petulance was not a full body blow. Only the sting of an annoying fly. The work will continue. Unheeded.

"However... you have taken something from me. Give the boy back. You have no idea what he is. No idea what's been built into him. Leave him somewhere in the jungle. Transmit the coordinates. And walk away before you ruin more than your crumbling reputation.

"This is your last warning, Noah Wolf. I made that boy. He is my sole property. A project. A future. Return him—or I will burn this jungle."

The choppers roared overhead again. Then faded.

Inside the camp, Camelot's team sat clustered beneath the tarps. B3-17 sat on a folding stool wrapped in a thick blanket, a steaming cup of cocoa cradled in his hands. He watched the others with wide, unblinking eyes. The Snickers bar they'd given him had melted slightly in the jungle heat, but he didn't care. He chewed slowly, silently, like he wasn't sure when he'd be allowed another, so he was savoring the taste.

Jenny crouched beside him, adjusting the blanket. "How's that? Better?"

He nodded once. Still no name. Still just B3-17, burned into the soft skin of his neck like a brand.

"Christ," Neil muttered, looking away. "What type of asshole does that to a child?"

"They're not just building a virus out here," Wally said, tone tight. "They're building people, too."

Jenny's jaw flexed. "He's a..."

Wally nodded.

"Not everything made in a lab is bad," Noah said quietly.

The others looked at him.

Noah sat on a low rock, hands clasping his knees, gaze locked on the boy. "Men like Kiel. Rausch. They're obsessed with control—perfection. Playing God. They'd let the whole world burn, so long as it was done in their image. They always chase order and purity, but all they ever deliver is death and chaos."

His words hung there a moment—heavy, absolute.

Then: *ping*—a soft chime from the comm unit.

Everyone turned.

The screen blinked to life.

Katya was calling from Putorana.

Noah stood and crossed to it. The others gathered behind him, already sensing the weight.

The screen lit—and the War Room's glow spilled into the jungle.

Katya's face was pale, her eyes sharp with control that didn't quite reach steady. She didn't waste time.

"You need to see this."

The screen split. Broadcasts from every angle. CCTV from Santa Cruz. The massacre.

Their uniforms. Their weapons. Their faces.

Jenny took a step back. "No."

Neil's lips parted, but no words came.

The video focused on a single frame—Noah. Storming a hallway. Killing a nurse.

Except it wasn't Noah. It was Sophia. Masked with his face digitally mapped over hers.

"That's not—" Jenny started.

"It's them," Wally said grimly. "Children of the Empire. Deepfake overlays. Real-time rendering on live feeds. All they needed was total access to the site's cameras and a few baseline scans of your gait, posture, height..."

"They had it," came Katya's voice over the top of the images. "They're framing you."

The screen cycled through footage. Dead bodies. Outraged senators. The president. The UN.

"The world believes it," she went on. "The UN council is going to vote in an emergency session. There's already talk of revoking Camelot's charter. Disbandment. Sanctions. No one's picking up our calls."

Neil looked to Noah. "What do we do?"

"Clear our name?" Jenny offered. "Find the raw footage? Leak it?"

"No," Noah said.

They all frowned at him.

"No," he repeated, calmer now. "That's what Vale wants. He wants us distracted. Derailed. Too busy running PR and chasing ghosts to stop what actually matters."

"You think this is bait," Katya suggested.

"I know it is," Noah said. "Subversion. False flag. Weaponized narrative. He's trying to drag us into the open—make us spend every second defending our own reflection."

"Then what do you need from me?" Katya asked.

Noah's jaw flexed once.

"Stay put, Katya," he said at last, stepping closer to the screen. "Lock everything down. You and Esmerelda keep a leash on our comms and a sword over the vaults. No one gets in or out of Putorana without your say-so."

Katya nodded once. "You think they'll come for us directly?"

"Not yet. But when they do, I want them to find a fortress."

Katya's eyes narrowed slightly. "What about you?"

"We're staying out here," Noah said. "Until we find Kiel. Until we find the lab. Until Helix is dead and buried."

He turned slightly, his eyes settling on the boy by the fire.

"And we're sending someone your way."

Katya followed his gaze.

"B3-17," Noah said. "We found him strapped to a surgical table in one of the sublevels. Labeled for vivisection. He's a clone —same project line as me and you, only... different. Wally's going to check him out in a minute, but after that, I'm sending him to Putorana."

Katya's face didn't move, but her eyes sharpened.

"He's just a kid," Jenny added softly, appearing beside Noah.

"But whatever they made him for... I don't think they finished the job."

Noah looked back to Katya. "We're arranging a rendezvous. Jenny'll get him to the drop point. After that, he's yours. Safe and off-grid."

Katya gave the faintest nod. "I'll be ready."

The screen went black.

No one moved.

Above them, the sky began to throb again—the low thunder of returning rotors.

Rausch's voice bled through the trees once more, distorted but clear, "Noah Wolf. It is nice of you to drop by. Explosive, as always. But do not flatter yourself—your petulance was not a full body blow. Only the sting of an annoying fly..."

Noah looked skyward, face unreadable.

Then he turned to the others.

"Prep the handoff," he said. "Then we move."

More rotor wash. More light probing uselessly through the trees. And once more—Viktor Rausch's voice, cold and unflinching: "This is your last warning, Noah Wolf. I made that boy. He is my sole property..."

Jenny stared upward, then whispered, "You think that's him live? Or just them playing it on a loop?"

"I'd bet loop," Wally said. "Even Rausch isn't that repetitive."

Noah said nothing. Just stared into the canopy, face unreadable.

"So what do we do now, boss?" Jenny asked.

Noah looked at each of them steadily.

"I meant what I said to Katya. We don't stop. We don't retreat. And we don't start pleading for approval from a world that's already forgotten who the enemy is. Our job is to stop Kiel. Then Vale. Nothing else matters."

"And if the world comes after us in the meantime?" Neil asked.

Noah's mouth set into a grim line. "Then they'll just have to wait their turn."

He stepped forward, hands loose at his sides, voice low and solid.

"Camelot isn't a flag. It's not a brand. It's not even a nation. It's a promise. To fight for the people who can't. To hold the line when no one else will. They can call us what they want. Traitors. Terrorists. Ghosts. But we will be the last wall when the fire comes."

Jenny nodded slowly. Then Neil. Wally crossed his arms. Even B3-17 seemed to lean in a little closer.

"Suit up," Noah said. "We get this kid away from here. Then we find Kiel. We end this."

THIRTY-ONE

THE COMMUNAL REC room felt smaller than usual.

Low light filtered from mismatched lamps. The only glow came from the projector rigged up to the wall—streaming a torrent of online videos, news feeds, and shaky TikToks all bearing the same title in some form or another:

NOAH WOLF: MASSACRE AT SANTA CRUZ

#UNBLOODBATH

#CAMELOTSLAUGHTER

#WOLFTURNS

Norah sat stiffly on the edge of the battered couch, hands clenched into the fabric of her trousers. Her jaw was tight, her eyes locked on the image currently playing—grainy footage from a stairwell camera. A figure in black, moving fast, controlled, and efficient.

The face was unmistakable. So was the intent.

The text overlay at the bottom of the screen was in bold white: *NOAH WOLF – EXECUTIONER*

Imani muted the feed.

Silence fell like ash.

"Come on. We know it's not him," Zina said, glancing at Norah.

"It's not him," Imani added quietly. "The way he moves—it's wrong. Too light. Noah doesn't step like that."

Norah's voice barely rose above a whisper. "But it looks like him. It looks so much like him."

Zina sat beside her, laying a careful hand on her shoulder. "That's the point. It *has* to look like him."

Norah's lips trembled. "I just—he's all I have."

From the beanbag in the corner, Lula blew out a low breath. "I mean, let's be honest—if anyone could pull off a UN massacre and come out of it unscathed, it's your dad. He is kind of a badass."

"Watch your mouth," a sharp voice snapped.

They all turned.

Katya stood in the doorway, arms folded, her expression unreadable. The light from the projector flickered across her face, painting her half in shadow.

Lula sat up straighter, not quite apologetic. "I was just—"

"Thinking out loud. I know." Katya stepped into the room. "It's a weakness of yours. It reveals your mind to your enemies."

She walked to the center of the room, turned, and looked at them—each in turn.

"You're all seeing the war play out in real time now. Not the kind of war you train for in drills. Not the one you prep for with rifles and medical kits. This is the other war."

She gestured to the screen.

"Perception. Trust. Identity. You want to know how the Council kept control for so long? Not just with weapons. Not with armies. With lies. With control of what people thought was true. They erased facts, rewrote events, buried histories. Turned heroes into villains. Villains into martyrs."

Zina frowned. "So what do we do? Just sit here and let them lie?"

"No," Katya said. "But don't waste time arguing with people who've already decided what to believe."

Imani sat forward. "Then how do we fight it?"

Katya nodded, pleased by the question. "By being better. In everything. You fight lies with integrity. You fight manipulation with discipline. And when the moment comes, you show the world the truth—not because you need their approval but because truth is a weapon they can't ignore forever."

Lula crossed her arms. "Only sheep get manipulated."

Katya's eyes snapped to her. "Then don't be a sheep."

The room fell silent.

"You're not civilians anymore," Katya said. "You're Camelot. You will be hated. Feared. Lied about. If you want the world to know who we really are, then prove it every day. In how you fight. How you think. How you carry yourselves when no one's watching."

She looked to Norah last.

"And don't lose faith in the people who raised you to be better than the world you were born into."

And with that, she turned on her heel and left the room.

No one spoke for a long moment.

Finally, Imani reached over and unmuted the feed. The noise resumed—an anchor ranting, another expert speculating.

But Norah wasn't watching the screen anymore.

She was watching the door Katya had walked through. Her hands were no longer clenched. Just resting. Steady.

"I don't care what the world says," she said.

The others looked at her.

"He's my dad," Norah added. "And I know who he is."

THIRTY-TWO

NORTHERN PATAGONIA | FIELD CAMP | 11:25 ART | NOVEMBER 18

THE JUNGLE HEAT pulsed heavy and wet, even under the dense canopy. Cicadas screamed overhead. The hidden camp nestled deep in the gorge was all shadows and green haze.

Overhead, the distant thunder of rotor blades rolled across the canopy like oncoming war drums. The team froze in place, eyes lifted toward the treetops. Three CH-6 reconnaissance helicopters swept overhead in formation, their blades thumping in synchrony.

A voice crackled from loudspeakers bolted beneath their fuselages, deep and theatrical:

"Noah Wolf... it is nice of you to drop by. Explosive, as always. But don't flatter yourself..."

The boy flinched at the sound, shrinking farther beneath his blanket. Jenny reached over and steadied him, her hand resting gently on his shoulder.

"However," the voice droned, "you've taken something from me. Give the boy back. You have no idea what he is..."

The choppers roared off again, fading into the distance.

They'd be back.

Near the shelter, B3-17 sat cross-legged opposite Neil, a game of tic-tac-toe chalked onto a flat stone between them. B3-17 moved a pebble to form a diagonal line.

"That's game three to me," he said, smirking.

Neil laughed quietly. "All right, smartass. Let's go again."

A few feet away, Wally hunched over a portable gene sequencer, fingers dancing over the interface, centrifuge humming, blood vials glinting dully. Noah crouched beside him. Jenny came up on his other side.

Wally exhaled and leaned back, rubbing his eyes. "Well. He's like you. Almost."

Jenny frowned. "What does 'almost' mean?"

Wally tapped the screen, highlighting clusters of base-pair sequences. "He's a clone. Like Noah. Like Katya. Engineered, accelerated. But his genome isn't just copied—it's... distilled. Stripped."

Noah's brow creased. "Stripped how?"

"They've removed everything deemed unnecessary—impulse, empathy, even moral hesitation. Free will was the first defect they corrected. Then they've increased function: muscle density, neuroplasticity, IQ projection puts him well into the genius range. He's beyond precocious. But there's no entropy. No psychological variation. They weren't trying to make a person. They were trying to make a tool."

"An obedient one," Jenny said quietly.

Wally nodded. "His genome's wired for compliance. Aggression dampened. Reward centers tuned down. Nothing that encourages resistance or critical defiance. Just... output."

Jenny glanced back at the boy. He was now solving the Rubik's Cube Neil had handed him—fingers moving like insects. Six seconds later, it clicked complete. He passed it back wordlessly and began mimicking Neil's posture again.

Neil made a face. B3-17 almost smiled.

"He's so good with kids," Jenny murmured to herself.

Noah glanced sideways. "Why didn't you two ever have any?"

Jenny arched a brow. "Because I love my figure too much."

He chuckled.

"But..." she added, her voice softening as she looked at Neil, "maybe one day."

Wally rolled his eyes and blinked hard. "Can you two drop the heartwarming stuff while I'm in the middle of my eugenics briefing?"

Jenny turned to him. "An attempt at humor. You could almost say we have the old Wally back."

Wally went to speak when another wave of rotor thunder passed over the canopy. The same voice returned, mechanical in its exactness:

"Noah Wolf... it is nice of you to drop by. Explosive, as always..."

Noah stood, rolling his shoulders, then glanced at the others. "We need to leave."

They had already packed the gear.

Wally began powering down his equipment, sliding vials into a foam-padded case. "I'll have them run more diagnostics once he's back in Putorana," he said. "Get a deeper profile. They might even be able to locate which batch he came from."

Noah nodded, eyes on the boy. "Let's move. Rendezvous is three klicks north. We get him clear."

Neil helped B3-17 up, slinging a light pack over his shoulder. The boy held his hand instinctively.

Jenny gave the camp one last look.

Then they slipped into the jungle, vanishing like ghosts—before the next pass came over.

THIRTY-THREE

THE APOSTOLIC PALACE, resplendent in its timeless grandeur, glowed beneath the amber light of Rome's fading sun. Marble columns flanked the long dining hall of the Pope's private quarters, gilded frescoes overhead. Velvet drapes stirred gently in the breeze from an open balcony overlooking St. Peter's Square, where pilgrims moved like ants beneath the towering obelisk.

Sebastian Vale sat across from His Holiness at a modest table dressed in white linen. Crystal goblets glittered beside plates of slow-roasted lamb, rosemary potatoes, and a delicate wine—the sort only opened for heads of state and kings of commerce.

"It has been too long," the Pope said, his voice a gentle rasp polished by decades of diplomacy and ritual.

"And yet," Vale replied smoothly, "so little has changed."

The Pope smiled, slicing delicately into his lamb. "Change is an illusion. The world only cycles through its masks. Power, Sebastian, is always the same."

Sophia stood a step behind Vale, impassive in her tailored black suit, her hands folded. She'd said nothing since entering the room, though her ice-blue eyes scanned every arch and hallway with the patience of a sniper.

The meal progressed with slow elegance.

"And Camelot?" the Pope asked finally, sipping from his glass. "This massacre... It has rattled the flock."

Vale placed his cutlery down. "Camelot is a corpse that hasn't realized it's dead. What happened in Bolivia was an obscenity but an expected one. Men like Wolf think themselves heroes—unchained, ungoverned. They confuse brute force with divine mission."

The Pope nodded gravely. "Authority must be restored to its rightful owners."

"Faith. Discipline. Legacy," Vale said. "Not vengeance dressed up as morality."

"The Church has always valued order," the Pope said, glancing briefly at the crucifix hanging on the far wall. "And for centuries, we've partnered with those who understood its necessity. The Council—your predecessors—never forgot their debt to Rome. Nor did we forget ours to them."

"Then we speak the same language," Vale said softly.

The Pope reached across the table and rested his hand atop Vale's. "What do you need?"

Vale smiled, slow and deliberate. "The Square. A stage. A platform. When I speak, the world must hear me."

"You will speak from the balcony of St. Peter's Basilica," the Pope said with the solemn gravity of a war blessing. "I will stand beside you. Together, we will call for peace and purpose. Our combined voice will remind the people what unity looks like."

"Billions still listen to you," Vale said. "That reach is... sacred."

The Pope chuckled. "And yours is rising, my son. The faithful are tired. They want not just a god—but a guardian."

By dessert, the plan had been sealed in the quiet language of two empires. A speech. A shared message. Peace and order—by any means necessary.

Vale and Sophia exited through the private garden courtyard, moonlight filtering between statues of saints and angels. A black car awaited just beyond the Vatican gates.

Once inside, the city rolled past in silence.

Vale tapped the comm screen embedded in the seat console. "Call Rausch."

The line connected. The screen flared to life with the scarred face of Viktor Rausch, lit in dull amber by command monitors.

"Sebastian," he said flatly.

"You arrogant son of a bitch," Vale hissed. "They found it. Camelot traced the signature in the virus back to Kiel. Back to you."

Rausch didn't blink. "We underestimated their tech."

"No. You underestimated them. That's the problem with you fascists—always underestimating the rest of us. Always drunk on your own purity."

"We can scrub it," Rausch said. "We'll say it was sabotage A double agent. They have no hard evidence."

"They don't need evidence, Viktor. They have momentum. Your little Reich cosplay nearly cost us everything."

Silence. Then: "There's more," Rausch admitted.

"What?"

"One of the test subjects escaped."

Vale went still.

"Escaped?"

"He was taken during the raid. A young male. Extremely promising. He was scheduled for final-phase testing tomorrow.'

"And now he's with Wolf?"

"Yes."

Vale's anger subsided a little. He began thinking. Planning.

"Have you sent the kill code?"

"I was about to," Rausch said. "You want me to do it now?"

Vale stared out at the passing lights of Rome.

"No," he said slowly. "Let him go with them. Let's see what happens. This could be exactly what we need."

There was a pause.

Then Vale disconnected.

The car drove on.

And, on the other side of the world, the boy who had once been designated B3-17 continued deeper into the jungle, unknowingly carrying with him a secret that might change the war.

But whose favor it would serve—that remained unclear.

THIRTY-FOUR

NORTHERN PATAGONIA, ARGENTINA | 19:05 ART | NOVEMBER 18

THE JUNGLE WAS slick with heat, cicadas buzzing like wires in a high-voltage fence. Noah led the way, machete slicing through the underbrush in slow, deliberate arcs. Behind him, Neil kept a cautious watch on the rear, scanning the treetops and canopy for any sign of movement as the low sun dropped everything in golden light. Jenny walked beside B3-17, her hand never far from the boy's shoulder.

They moved in silence. The rendezvous was less than two kilometers now—a cleared ridge where a stealth shuttle would touch down for just long enough to grab the kid and vanish back into the folds of satellite shadow.

"Almost there," Neil said softly, mostly to himself.

That's when the sound came.

A deep, thumping echo. Familiar, mechanical, and wrong.

The Black Sun chopper cut across the canopy like a steel predator, its twin rotors chopping air into a snarling blur. But this one didn't carry Rausch's smug tirades or threats. No voice boomed from its undercarriage. No threats. No theatrics.

Just static.

Sharp, pulsing, and rhythmic.

B3-17 stopped mid-step. His knees buckled.

"Hey—" Jenny caught him before he fell, but the boy twisted violently in her arms. His body seized, convulsing with sudden, brutal force. His eyes rolled white, only the barest rim of iris showing. Foam bubbled at the corner of his mouth.

"Down—get him down!" Noah barked, already yanking his pack open.

Neil hit the dirt beside them, grabbing the boy's wrists to keep him from hurting himself.

Jenny cradled his head. "He's seizing!"

Noah ripped out a small injector case, thumbing it open. "Midazolam. If he doesn't stop in ten—"

But then the noise changed.

The static pitch wavered, dissolved into a flatline buzz, and then—silence.

The chopper banked and veered eastward, its belly rising into the clouds. The sound vanished entirely, swallowed by the forest canopy.

And just like that, B3-17 stilled.

His breath came back ragged. Then normal. His eyes fluttered. Blinked. He looked around, dazed.

"Wh..." His voice was thin. "What happened?"

Jenny exhaled sharply, relief and tension battling in her voice. "You collapsed. Some kind of seizure."

The boy blinked again. "I don't remember."

Noah stared after the retreating chopper. His jaw tightened.

"That was no accident," Neil said. "You saw him. That sound —it was a trigger."

Jenny brushed sweat from the boy's brow. "You think it was part of his conditioning?"

Noah stood slowly. "Yes. And I think someone just tested the remote."

The others fell silent. B3-17 sat up shakily, his face blank but watching them with eerie calm.

Jenny offered him water. He took it without a word.

They waited a few minutes. Then moved on.

Trepidation hung like smoke in the air, but the rendezvous was calling.

THIRTY-FIVE

THE WAR ROOM was quiet now, save for the muted hum of servers and the rhythmic tapping of keys. The overhead lights were low, casting the space in soft cobalt and shadow. Giant digital displays lined the walls, scrolling data feeds, satellite tracks, and surveillance footage from across the globe. Camelot's eye—watching, parsing, and waiting.

Katya stood with her arms folded, eyes fixed on a slow-panning image of a UN delegation picking through the ruins of the Bolivian quarantine site. She didn't need to watch the footage again—she already knew. The attackers had used the same weapons favored by Noah and Camelot. Every detail had been crafted to make them look guilty.

Katya breathed out.

Training wasn't due to start for another hour. The recruits were still in their quarters. Some reading, some—like Lula—still sleeping. All subdued by the shock of the Bolivia broadcasts and the whirlwind that followed.

"Ma'am," came a voice from behind her.

It was Venter, his tone clipped but urgent.

She turned.

The young South African comms officer was standing stiffly beside his console, one earpiece still in, eyes wide with restrained adrenaline.

"What is it?" Katya asked, moving toward him.

Venter leaned in. "One of the Council's old encrypted channels went live for exactly forty seconds just now. Our filters flagged it—frequency marker matched a dormant thread from the Panama sector."

Katya's brow knitted. "I thought those were all scrubbed."

"They were. But this one... it piggybacked off a Vatican maintenance relay. Just bounced once before digitally self-destructing."

Her eyes sharpened. "You recorded it?"

He gave a single nod. "Had to brute-force the decryption with half the AI stack, but we got it. Clean audio. No masking."

Venter pressed a button on his screen.

The speakers crackled—then cleared.

Sebastian Vale's voice, unmistakable. Smooth, charming. Venom threaded with silk.

"—final arrangements are in place. The Pope has granted me full access to the square and media coverage. I'll speak at five, local time. St. Peter's Basilica as backdrop. The optics will be... potent."

A brief pause. Then Viktor Rausch, colder and more guttural: "Why do you need the Church? You already have the narrative."

"Because," Vale answered, his tone turning knife-sharp, "symbols matter. The world is broken, Viktor. It needs reassurance. Familiar robes. Old institutions. People crave the illusion of stability—and I intend to drape myself in it."

"And Camelot?"

"They'll be watching. Let them. The more they struggle to assert their innocence, the more they implicate themselves. But don't underestimate them."

Rausch grunted. "I never have."

"Good. Then don't fail me again."

The line cut.

The War Room was silent.

Katya turned slowly toward Venter, her expression unreadable.

"You heard that, right?" she asked.

"Yes, ma'am. Sebastian Vale will be in Rome at five tomorrow."

She nodded once.

"Then we need to get a message to Noah."

THIRTY-SIX

THE SUN BLED low across the jungle, its last rays spilling gold through the canopy and igniting the clouds in crimson and rust. The gorge was quieter now, heavier—wrapped in the hush of evening.

Noah, Jenny, Neil, and B3-17 emerged from the trees just as the transport dropped through the sky—sleek, matte-black, a stealth-modified CH-47 Chinook built for covert insertions. Its twin rotors spun in near-silence, blades shaped for noise suppression. It hovered for a moment above the clearing, then touched down with a controlled hiss of hydraulics, barely disturbing the jungle canopy around it.

The rendezvous point was tucked beneath a sheer rock face. A small squad of Camelot operatives emerged from the transport—dark fatigues, visors up, weapons low.

B3-17 hesitated at the tree line, staring at the ship.

"It's okay," Jenny said gently, crouching beside him. "They're with us."

The boy nodded. He hadn't spoken much on the way. Since the incident with the signal, he'd been quieter. Slower. Still brilliant—but like something in him was watching himself from a few steps back.

One of the operatives stepped forward. He glanced at the boy, then to Jenny. "Command requests urgent communication with Noah."

Noah took the sat unit from the man's outstretched hand.

"Put her through."

The screen flickered. Katya appeared, pale but focused, the low light of the War Room reflecting off her green eyes.

"Noah," she said without preamble. "We've intercepted a conversation. Vale is planning to speak tomorrow—from St. Peter's Square. Five p.m. The Pope will be standing beside him."

Jenny swore under her breath.

Katya continued. "He'll have a media pool. Global coverage. Billions watching. It's more than politics now—he's trying to rewrite the narrative in real-time. Install himself as savior while he lets the world rot behind the curtain."

Noah's face hardened.

"Nevertheless," Katya added, "he'll be vulnerable. Stationary. If ever we had a chance to kill that bastard, it's now."

There was a long silence.

Then Noah spoke. "It has to be our best."

"I agree," Katya said. "Whoever we send will have to move fast. Vale's security will be tight. The Pope's even tighter. And with only twenty-four hours to move, it'll be a very tough job."

Noah didn't speak for a moment. He just looked at Jenny and Neil—his second-in-command and his closest friend. Then his gaze slid down to B3-17, standing close to Jenny, quiet and still beneath the fading sky.

"You take him," Noah finally said.

Jenny blinked. "What?"

"Leave with the transport, then take a separate flight to Italy. You go to Rome. You do this. I'll stay here. Find Kiel. Finish this virus."

"Noah—"

"No. It makes sense. Two fronts. Same war." He looked at Neil. "Keep her alive."

Neil gave a short nod.

Noah knelt in front of the boy. "You listen to them, all right? You're safe now."

The boy blinked slowly. "You're not coming?"

Noah smiled faintly. "Not yet. But I'll catch up."

The rotors began to spin.

Jenny leaned forward and hugged Noah hard—quick, without preamble. When she pulled back, her eyes shimmered with fire and grit. "Don't get yourself killed."

He smirked. "You either."

They climbed aboard. The boy followed, glancing back one last time as the hatch sealed shut behind him.

Noah stepped back as the Chinook lifted into the sky, kicking up a storm of dust and leaves. It rose into the last rays of the sun, silhouetted against a bruised sky, then disappeared beyond the canopy.

He stood alone for a while.

Then he turned, cinched his gear, and headed back into the jungle.

Wally would be waiting.

And so would the end of the world.

THIRTY-SEVEN

THREE HOURS LATER, as he crested a ridge, Noah halted abruptly, his gaze sharpening through the ghostly green of his NVGs.

Smoke.

It coiled upward from the gorge, thin and spectral at first, then thicker, darker, unmistakable. Exactly where their camp had been.

His heart thudded against his ribs. He crouched lower, slipping silently forward through the tangled underbrush, ears straining. Then he heard them: the buzzing whine of drones, the barking of dogs, the clipped commands of Black Sun troops echoing through the trees.

They had found the camp.

He wondered about Wally.

Noah edged closer, keeping his movements slow, calculated, blending as much as he could with shadow and foliage. The enemy was everywhere—patrols with dogs tugging at their leashes, drones humming softly just above the treetops, infrared beams slicing through the gloom.

As he crouched low to the brush, a drone descended from the canopy. It began hovering close, its sensor array swiveling as it scanned the ground. Noah froze, fingers curling around the hilt of his knife. Its tiny rotors buzzed softly, methodically, dangerously near.

He shifted slightly, preparing to bolt—when a hand shot out from the undergrowth behind him. Noah spun instantly, blade flashing upward, stopping just as the tip kissed flesh.

Wally's face emerged from beneath a ripple of shadow and leaf, eyes wide, breathing shallow. He signaled quickly, urgently, for Noah to crawl under the shimmering digital camouflage blanket he'd dragged over himself. The surface shifted subtly as it moved, mirroring the jungle's palette.

Without hesitation, Noah slipped beneath the covering just as the drone's lights illuminated the ground where he had crouched moments before.

Beneath the camo, Wally pressed a finger urgently to his lips, then activated a small sound dampener with a muted click.

"They arrived not long ago," he whispered hurriedly once the dampener was running. "First drones. I thought the camo would be good enough to hide us, but one passed too close, came underneath. Spotted me. Troops and dogs weren't far behind. Had to shoot the drone, grab the camo, and run. Less than ten minutes later, the place was swarming with them."

Noah frowned deeply, eyes narrow. "Please tell me you saved some equipment."

Wally's face turned sheepish, eyes flicking downward.

"The guns?" Noah pressed, tone sharp.

"Afraid not," Wally whispered. "I only managed the camo and my canteen."

Noah's jaw tightened. "Who torched the camp?"

"They did," Wally said bitterly. "When they found my lab equipment with the vials of B3-17's blood. I guess they panicked. Thought I might have their virus."

"Idiots," Noah hissed, tension crackling in his voice.

A sudden low growl vibrated nearby. Noah tensed instantly, muscles coiling. A dog sniffed the edge of their hiding spot, its handler stepping closer, eyes narrowing suspiciously at the slight shimmer of their camo—not quite keeping up with the real-time environment it was supposed to be mimicking.

The trooper opened his mouth to call out—but Noah was faster. He exploded upward from beneath the covering, driving his knife swiftly through the man's chin and into his brain. The trooper convulsed once, soundlessly collapsing into Noah's arms.

The dog lunged immediately, teeth bared. Noah turned sharply, dispatching the animal swiftly, silently. With practiced efficiency, he and Wally dragged both corpses beneath the camouflage, the darkness swallowing the brief burst of violence.

"Now what do we do?" Wally whispered as they lay there with the dead. "We can't wait it out here all night, killing anyone who comes across us. For one, there's not enough room."

Noah was staring at the dead trooper.

More importantly, he was staring at the man's uniform.

"I might have an idea."

Rapidly, Noah stripped the dead man of his Black Sun garb, donning it quickly. He adjusted the helmet, pulling it low over his brow.

"You stay here," he instructed Wally, voice low and calm. "Don't move until I return."

Wally nodded, eyes wide.

Noah rose silently, slipping out from beneath their hiding place. The crackling flames and shifting shadows of the burning camp flickered in his peripheral vision. The night consumed him, Noah blending seamlessly with the enemy's ranks, a ghost slipping into darkness.

Two troopers approached, relaxed, their weapons slung loosely, confident that the night belonged to them. Noah raised his hand in greeting, his face obscured enough beneath the uniform's helmet to mask his identity. The moment they nodded back in acknowledgment, he drew his SIG Sauer.

Quick, precise shots dropped both men where they stood.

Another trio emerged from the smoke, alerted by the gunfire. Noah stepped boldly toward them, shouting for them to check the tree line, his tone commanding. They hesitated, momentarily confused. In their pause, he opened fire, cutting them down in rapid succession. One took the bullet in the throat. The next in the left eye. The third in the cheek. Each body fell, one clutching a radio that buzzed urgently on his belt.

Noah knelt swiftly, snatching the device.

"All units withdraw immediately," a voice crackled through its speaker. "Repeat. All units withdraw immediately. Air support inbound. ETA four minutes. Napalm strike. Clear everything east of the river. Repeat, immediate extraction."

Not good.

The jungle shuddered around him, shadows flickering wildly beneath the rising flames.

The troops were leaving.

And so too should Noah Wolf.

He turned and bolted back toward Wally, urgency driving his pace.

"We need to move. Now," Noah said the second he reached the camo, pulling Wally to his feet.

They abandoned their hiding place, sprinting through smoke and sparks, dodging pockets of intense heat. Ahead, Black Sun troops converged toward a clearing, helicopters idling, rotors spinning impatiently against the smoke-choked sky.

Two lifted up into the gloom, leaving a third.

Noah adjusted his stolen uniform, taking the lead. Approaching the helicopter, he signaled sharply to the pilot, who squinted uncertainly through the cockpit glass. Noah's demeanor, his confident stride, eased suspicion just enough.

The instant he reached the door, Noah's pistol rose. The shots were swift, merciless—two soldiers inside slumped without a sound, the pilot jerking once before collapsing against the controls. Noah and Wally rapidly dragged the bodies clear, sliding into the cockpit and strapping in.

The engines surged, rotors roaring to life.

Just as they lifted above the treetops, the air thickened with the low, ominous roar of approaching jets. Noah pushed the throttle, angling the helicopter sharply away from the impending strike zone.

No sooner were they away than three jets streaked by, a rush of sound followed by deafening silence—and then the jungle exploded. Sheets of flame engulfed the forest, rolling across the landscape like a tidal wave of fire. Trees vanished instantly, devoured by the inferno.

Wally stared back in horror, the glow reflected sharply in his eyes. "Where to now?" he asked hoarsely.

Noah's jaw tightened, his eyes locked forward into the darkness. "I have no idea."

THIRTY-EIGHT

THE PRIVATE HANGAR AT MADRID-BARAJAS was quiet, bathed in pale white light and the gentle hum of air-conditioning. Two sleek aircraft waited patiently, their engines idling, landing lights blinking softly in the dark. One pointed eastward—toward Rome. The other was prepped for the long, silent haul northward, destined for Putorana.

Jenny and Neil stood beside B3-17, who remained calm and still, a small backpack slung loosely over his shoulders. Across the hangar, two Camelot operatives in muted fatigues watched respectfully, giving the trio space for their farewells.

"You're gonna like Putorana," Jenny said softly, adjusting the boy's jacket collar. "There are kids there—kids just like you. They'll take care of you."

B3-17 nodded, his expression serious, analytical but warm. He looked from Jenny to Neil, then fumbled briefly in his jacket pocket before producing Neil's Rubik's cube. With careful, almost solemn precision, he held it out to Neil.

Neil smiled warmly, shaking his head. "You keep it," he said. "Practice. Get even faster. Next time I see you, we'll race."

A small smile broke out on the boy's face. "I'll win," he said matter-of-factly, though a faint, playful twinkle flashed in his eyes.

Neil laughed. "You probably will."

Jenny knelt slightly, bringing her gaze level with B3-17's. "You remember what Noah said? You're safe now. And you're one of us."

The boy gave a single, slow nod. "Thank you," he said quietly. His voice was young but steady, thoughtful beyond his years. "For...everything."

The two Camelot operatives approached gently, smiling as they reached the boy's side.

"We'll take good care of him," the taller one said. "You have our word."

Jenny nodded appreciatively, letting out a long-held breath as she watched the boy step away, a hesitant yet trusting smile lingering.

Neil reached for Jenny's hand, squeezing gently. "He'll be okay," he whispered.

"I know," Jenny said, watching as B3-17 disappeared into the cabin of the northbound jet.

For a moment, neither moved. Then Jenny exhaled sharply, her eyes turning toward their own waiting aircraft.

"Ready?" she asked, glancing at Neil.

"As I'll ever be," he replied.

Together, they crossed the hangar floor, footsteps echoing softly against polished concrete. The stairs to the plane awaited them, steps toward the unknown.

"To Rome," Jenny murmured softly as they climbed aboard. "And the end of Sebastian Vale."

THIRTY-NINE

NOAH STCOD next to the downed helicopter, its twisted rotor blades snarled in thick jungle vines, smoke still curling faintly from the crumpled engine housing.

There had been no other place to land it.

"Out of fuel, stranded in the middle of nowhere," Noah muttered, scanning the dense green wall of vegetation that surrounded them. "This isn't looking good, Wally."

Wally wiped his forehead, glancing wearily around the jungle. A small, bitter smile twitched at the corner of his mouth. "Wher does it ever?"

Dawn was breaking now, casting the sky in a dull gray glow that filtered through the canopy. The air clung to them—humid, oppressive, already thick with insects.

"We need to move," Noah said. "Staying here is suicide."

Wally nodded, then turned back to the open chopper hatch. He rummaged through a survival pack, pulling out a tightly folded bundle of tarp.

He held it up. "Digital camo."

Noah raised an eyebrow.

Wally shrugged. "You never know when you'll need it again."

Switched off, the material looked like a plain strip of dull gray fabric—nondescript, ragged at the corners, indistinguishable from average tarp. Wally rolled it and stuffed it into his pack.

Then the two men turned toward the jungle—and vanished into the green.

Without machetes, they only had Noah's combat knife—a meager tool against the dense, relentless growth. It meant they moved slowly, Noah carving an arduous path through the tangled vegetation with the knife.

After hours of struggling forward, they stumbled upon the remnants of an indigenous village, eerily silent and desolate.

The huts were burned to the ground, blackened skeletal remains of wood and palm leaves scattered amidst the ashes. In the center of the village loomed a large tree. A particularly wide branch stuck out like a crossbeam. Frayed ropes dangled from it, swaying in the breeze. Noah approached, touching one of the ropes gently.

"They hung people here," he said quietly.

"Then when they left," Wally added, staring at the cut ropes, "someone came back to collect the dead."

They moved on, deeper into the jungle, the constant chirp of insects growing more oppressive. Both men began to feel the weight of unseen eyes following their every step. Noah stopped abruptly, raising a cautious hand.

"We're being watched," he whispered.

Suddenly, a slight *whoosh* broke the quiet—a blow dart slicing through the air. Noah's hand shot out instinctively, snatching the dart inches from Wally's neck.

"Down!" he hissed.

They threw themselves into the undergrowth as more darts hissed through the air, embedding themselves harmlessly into the thick foliage.

"It's the Mapuche," Noah said, pressing himself flat against the damp earth.

"The uniform, Noah!" Wally warned, urgency clear in his voice.

Noah glanced down sharply, suddenly aware of the tattered Black Sun uniform still clinging to his body.

Figures emerged cautiously from the shadows—indigenous warriors, their faces painted with dark patterns, their wary eyes gleaming sharply in the dim jungle light. Noah and Wally glimpsed the glint of sharpened spears and the narrow tubes of blowguns, all trained steadily upon them.

Noah raised his SIG Sauer abruptly, aiming skyward, and squeezed the trigger.

The sharp crack of the gunshot echoed through the jungle canopy, freezing the advancing warriors in place. They exchanged rapid hand signals and low, cautious whistles, blending seamlessly into the natural sounds around them.

Noah moved to rise, instinctively shifting into a combat stance, prepared to engage. But Wally's hand reached out, gripping his arm firmly.

Noah turned, muscles tensed.

Wally shook his head slowly, silently urging restraint.

Remaining low to the ground, Wally raised his voice gently but clearly, calling out in fluent Mapuche. He spoke in soothing, rhythmic sentences, explaining their situation. The jungle fell quiet again, tension lingering thickly in the air as the warriors considered his words.

After a drawn-out silence, punctuated only by whispers among the hidden warriors, a voice finally answered from somewhere within the foliage. Another exchange followed—questions and cautious assurances.

Finally, Wally turned to Noah.

"They're willing to listen," he murmured softly. "We can stand, but we keep our hands visible at all times."

Slowly, carefully, the two men rose, their hands held clearly out to their sides. The warriors watched them warily, weapons still raised but no longer poised to strike.

An elder stepped forward, his eyes narrowed with guarded scrutiny. He spoke sternly to Wally, initiating further tense negotiation.

"I told them we're not their enemy," Wally explained quietly. "That you stole this uniform from a Black Sun soldier we killed in order to escape. They're skeptical, to say the least."

The Mapuche exchanged glances, murmuring softly among themselves. Finally, the elder asked if they had set up the camp by the gorge.

"We did," Wally said firmly, "until Black Sun found and burned it."

The elder considered this, his expression unreadable. After a long pause, he nodded once and motioned to his warriors.

"They're taking us to their village leader," Wally said quietly, relief flickering briefly in his eyes.

As the warriors approached with vines in hand, Noah tensed instinctively, his body coiled to resist, but Wally's hand found his arm.

"Noah," he murmured, shaking his head gently. "We have no other choice. At least we'll have shelter and food where they're taking us."

Noah hesitated, jaw tight, then relented with a slow nod.

As two warriors stepped forward to bind their wrists, another approached the bush where Wally had stashed the digital camouflage. He picked up the folded sheet, turning it in his hands with curiosity. To the untrained eye, it looked like nothing more than a ragged length of tarp, but the faint shimmer of embedded circuitry betrayed its purpose.

"He's taking the camouflage," Wally muttered. "Let's hope they don't switch it on. They'll probably think it's witchcraft."

With their wrists bound and their gear claimed, the two men

were hoisted onto long poles. Suspended and vulnerable, Noah felt a fresh wave of unease twist in his gut.

The warriors then moved off silently, effortlessly, melting into the jungle's emerald throat—leaving only the hush of leaves and the soft crunch of footfall behind them.

FORTY

ROME, ITALY | 12:11 CET | NOVEMBER 19

MIDDAY PRESSED down hard on the outskirts of the Italian capital, rain falling in thin needles, turning the streets into slick, reflective glass. The city shimmered beneath a sky heavy with bruised clouds—wet stone gleaming, sunlight fighting weakly through the gloom.

A pitch black CH47 Chinook dropped swiftly onto a forgotten strip of tarmac outside the city proper. No lights guided its descent, no customs agents waited; the landing was ghosted—off books, off radar.

The rear hatch hissed open, and Neil and Jenny emerged quickly into the downpour, silhouettes low, squinting against the gray daylight. They wore civilian gear—neat, neutral, forgettable. Just another couple arriving quietly, anonymously, through unusual means.

A black Fiat SUV idled beneath a sagging tarp nearby, engine humming softly. At the wheel sat their contact: Marta Bellini, Camelot-aligned and NGO-credentialed, though the glint in her eyes said she pushed more than just paperwork.

She handed out a pair of laminated cards and a folded envelope.

"Passports, NGO cards, front seat—it'll give you the ability to move like you belong."

Neil slid into the passenger side, adjusting the diplomatic credential around his neck.

"Nothing like humanitarian camouflage," he muttered.

The SUV pulled away smoothly, tires skimming puddles as they headed toward the city's core.

Rome unfolded around them like a cathedral at war with itself. Its ancient bones were splashed with neon propaganda, washed in the daylight gloom and the pale red glow of protest flares. Rain streaked down crumbling façades, colonnades strung with protest banners and damp laundry. The hum of police drones echoed through alleyways like distant insects.

Crowds had gathered near sealed metro entrances—wet, waiting, restless. Riot police stood motionless behind layered shields, faceless in daylight. Above, projection drones hovered like mechanical angels, casting images against buildings in silver and crimson.

The Children of the Empire's sigil dominated: a crowned sun above a Roman laurel, stark even beneath the midday gloom.

In a piazza, a public screen replayed a speech on loop—Sebastian Vale, arms raised, voice full of fire and gravity.

Jenny leaned against the window, eyes hard.

"They're not hiding anymore," she said.

She gestured toward a café wall where someone had spray-painted, stark and defiant:

ORDO • SANGUIS • ASCENSIO

Order • Blood • Ascension

"They're campaigning."

Neil glanced up at a projection drone drifting over cobblestones, its lens sweeping methodically back and forth like a god's eye.

"You don't need ballots," he said. "Just self-righteous belief—and a few trillion dollars."

The SUV slipped beneath a low bridge, water sheeting from its roof. Ahead, the Vatican loomed, stark and silent under a haze of drizzle, the dome of St. Peter's silhouetted in gray. Marta slowed as they approached the final checkpoint.

"They've sealed off the inner square," she explained. "Official story is 'structural renovations.' Reality? CoE security perimeter. Nothing gets in unless it's invited."

Neil subtly checked the pistol tucked beneath his coat, fingers brushing reassuringly against the grip.

"Then thank god we've got invitations," he murmured, tapping the credential around his neck.

Jenny's eyes never left the road ahead.

"Let's just hope they work," she said.

Thunder rumbled in the distance, a low growl beneath the daylight clouds, like a warning from the city itself.

They rolled forward through the rain-washed streets, toward history's oldest seat of empire—and whatever waited beneath its marble bones.

FORTY-ONE

KATYA STOOD on the raised platform overlooking the training hall, arms crossed as she observed the recruits maneuvering through their combat drills. She watched Norah move fluidly through an obstacle course, Lula aggressively dominating a sparring match against Tao, and Zina deftly disassembling and reassembling a rifle. Gregor and Imani exchanged defensive tactics nearby.

Her expression was unreadable but quietly proud.

The sharp chirp of her earpiece startled Katya from her thoughts. "Katya," Esmerelda's voice chimed crisply. "The helicopter carrying B3-17 is landing in three minutes."

"Copy that." Katya turned and clapped once, the sharp sound cutting through the noise of activity. "Everyone, halt. We have company arriving."

The recruits paused immediately, curiosity painting their faces.

"Who's coming?" Tao asked, wiping sweat from his brow.

"Let's find out," Katya said, heading for the door. The

recruits eagerly followed, trading puzzled glances as they trailed behind her through the base.

Outside on the helipad, the icy wind cut sharply through the air. The rotors of the incoming Blackwing helicopter whipped snow into swirling clouds. As the helicopter touched down, its blades slowed to a steady pulse. The cargo door slid open, and two Camelot operatives emerged first, then a smaller figure stepped tentatively onto the platform, the hem of his coat almost touching the ground.

B3-17 stood motionless for a moment, blinking against the harsh glare reflecting off the ice. His clothes were simple, functional, and slightly oversized, hanging loosely on his lean frame. He clutched a small pack to his chest as if expecting someone might take it from him.

Katya approached slowly, stopping a respectful distance away. "Welcome to Putorana Base. I'm Katya."

He nodded once, his expression neutral. "Thank you."

The recruits crowded behind her, eyes openly curious. Katya noticed his gaze flicking to each face quickly, analyzing and memorizing details in silent calculation.

"These are your fellow recruits," Katya continued. "Norah, Lula, Tao, Zina, Imani, and Gregor."

They murmured greetings, eyes still curious and skeptical.

"What's your name?" Lula asked bluntly.

"B3-17," he responded automatically.

"That's not really a name." Zina frowned. "More like a designation."

"What would you prefer to be called?" Katya asked gently.

The boy hesitated, uncertainty flashing briefly across his otherwise calm face. "I...don't know."

"What about just B3?" Zina suggested lightly.

"How about B-B?" Tao offered.

Lula snorted. "Sounds like baby. Yeah, that'll work. Baby."

"Give it a break, Lula," Norah said. "He'll pick his own name when he's ready. Until then, B3-17 is fine."

"He sounds like an android," Imani said, watching the boy with mild suspicion.

Lula smirked slightly. "Acts a bit like one too."

"That's enough," Katya repeated, this time sharper. "Let's get inside before we all freeze."

Inside the rec room, B3-17 stood quietly, eyes scanning each corner, each object, cataloging and processing. His posture remained rigid, almost military, hands still gripping the pack protectively.

Zina stepped closer, curiosity overriding caution. "So where did you live before coming here?"

He slowly turned his gaze toward her, eyes flat and emotionless. "A cage," he said simply, without inflection.

Zina forced a chuckle, glancing uncertainly at the others. "Oh, he's joking." She hesitated, unsure. "Or maybe he's not."

Katya gave Zina a hard look, shaking her head slowly. "Let's show B3-17 his room."

They led B3-17 down the corridor to the sleeping quarters. He moved silently, each step precise and measured, eyes flickering along the hallway, mapping it in his mind.

"Here," Katya said, gesturing to an open door leading to a modest but comfortable room. "This is yours."

He stepped inside cautiously, placing his pack down gently beside the bed. "Thank you," he said quietly, glancing briefly back at the group with the faintest flicker of uncertainty.

The recruits lingered awkwardly at the threshold, observing him like a curious exhibit. Eventually, Katya motioned them away. "Let's give him some space."

As the group dispersed, Norah paused just outside B3-17's room, her gaze lingering on him as he methodically unpacked his few belongings, arranging them with meticulous care. His movements felt too deliberate, too controlled, as if he were carefully mimicking something he'd seen but never truly understood.

Norah frowned slightly, an uneasy feeling twisting gently

inside her. Something felt off—strange, even—but she couldn't quite place why.

As she watched, B3-17 turned, meeting her gaze directly. For a moment, they simply stared at each other. Norah offered a small, tentative smile. He blinked, responding with the faintest shadow of a nod before turning back to his room.

Norah moved away, the unease still prickling at the edges of her mind. Something about the way he'd looked at her, calm and utterly unreadable, lingered long after she walked away.

Behind her, B3-17 stood silently, listening to the fading sound of footsteps. He glanced around the room once more, eyes flat, expression distant, unreadable—waiting.

FORTY-TWO

THE MAPUCHE CAMP lay hidden within a dense enclave of towering palms and ancient ceiba trees, their massive roots intertwining like serpents. Noah and Wally had been cut from the poles. They were still bound, but at least they were now upright.

The wary warriors escorted them into a clearing bustling with life. The scent of wood smoke and cooking spices drifted through the heavy, humid air, mingling with whispers of distrust.

As they emerged from the jungle, villagers paused mid-task, eyes narrowing suspiciously. Some women pulled their children closer; warriors gripped their spears tighter, murmuring angrily among themselves.

"They don't seem thrilled to see us," Noah whispered dryly.

"They believe our presence exposes their hiding place," Wally responded softly, his eyes watchful, measuring the tension.

A tall figure stepped forward, age carved deeply into his weathered face. White streaked his black hair, and a mantel of woven feathers draped from his shoulders. His gaze was piercing but not unkind, a presence that immediately commanded respect. He spoke in a low, authoritative voice.

Wally listened, then translated quietly. "He is Chief Antu. He says we have brought our foreign war to his forest. Black Sun hunts them relentlessly. Their secrecy was their strongest weapon, and now we are here. One white man always leads to more."

Noah met the chief's eyes directly as he spoke through Wally. "Tell him we share the same enemy. Black Sun burned our camp too. They've hunted us just as mercilessly."

Wally translated. The chief considered this, then responded sharply. "Black Sun doesn't just hunt them. They unleash sicknesses on their people. Entire villages wiped out by diseases their healers cannot stop."

Noah stepped closer, hands raised placatingly, his expression resolute. "Tell him the Black Sun base in the hills, Cerro Rojo, the explosion—they lost that because of us. We destroyed their lab. Stopped the experiments they were doing there."

Murmurs rose among the warriors at the mention of Cerro Rojo. Chief Antu raised a hand, silencing them instantly. He spoke again, more softly, eyes keenly fixed on Noah.

"He says there are many more bases," Wally explained. "Cerro Rojo was just one arm of a monstrous beast."

Noah nodded slowly, his eyes sharp with new understanding. "Ask him if he knows about a hidden lab. A place where a man named Kiel works. Where the sickness comes from."

Wally translated. The chief's reaction was immediate—a tightening around the eyes, a guarded silence. He looked sharply to his warriors, who exchanged uneasy glances.

"He knows," Noah murmured. "Tell him, please. We can end this together. If they help us find Kiel, we'll destroy that lab, stop the virus, end their suffering."

The chief stared intently at Noah, as if reading every line etched into his face. After a tense pause, he spoke slowly, deliberately.

"He says cooperation must be earned," Wally translated carefully. "How does he know we're not just more outsiders bringing our own form of death?"

Noah stepped closer, his voice even, eyes unwavering. "We have no wish to intrude upon your lands. The second Black Sun is gone, we will leave, if that is your wish. But I can send warriors—my people—who can stand with you. They can help protect this place. Not just from Black Sun, but from hunters, miners, poachers, loggers—anyone who threatens your way of life. We share a common enemy, and together we can defend your home."

Chief Antu studied Noah carefully, the silence heavy and measured. Finally, he gave a slow nod, his expression shifting from skepticism to cautious respect. When he spoke, his words resonated powerfully through the clearing.

Wally visibly relaxed, exhaling a breath he hadn't realized he'd been holding. "He agrees. They'll accept our help. But he says—if we betray them, they won't hesitate to kill us."

"That's fair," Noah said grimly.

With a nod from Chief Antu, their bindings were cut free. The warriors relaxed visibly, shoulders easing, whispers becoming less hostile.

"Come." The chief spoke in Mapudungun, gesturing toward a long communal table laden with cooked meats, fruits, and roasted yams. "First, we eat together. Then we plan."

Wally smiled warmly. "They're going to feed us."

Noah's shoulders loosened slightly as he stepped forward, accepting a seat offered to him. The villagers began to sit, filling the clearing with quiet conversation, smiles breaking slowly through guarded expressions.

As the morning stretched toward noon, tension dissolved into camaraderie. Noah glanced around, gratitude softening the hardened lines of his face, realizing that here, at least for the moment, there was safety. And allies.

"Maybe things are finally going our way," Wally muttered, raising a carved wooden cup filled with goat's milk.

Noah smirked, lifting his own. "Just try not to jinx it, Wally."

FORTY-THREE

ROME, VATICAN CITY | 23:14 CET | NOVEMBER 19

THE DARKNESS DRAPED over Vatican City like a velvet shroud, pierced only by flickering streetlamps and the occasional pools of halogen glow that spilled from some of the buildings. Jenny crouched low against an ancient stone balustrade, Neil pressed tight beside her, their faces shadowed by hoods pulled over their heads. From the height of their vantage point, the spires and rooftops of the Vatican stretched out beneath them like pieces on a chessboard—quiet, waiting, and deceptively serene.

Far below, uniformed police moved in tight patrol patterns, their flashlights cutting arcs across cobbled streets and polished marble. Workmen in bright reflective jackets bustled around St. Peter's Square, hammering and hauling barriers, erecting scaffolding for the imminent address by Sebastian Vale.

"They've beefed up security since we arrived," Neil whispered. "Twice as many patrols from when we drove by earlier."

Jenny nodded, peering carefully around the statue of an angel. Her eyes flicked over the array of security cameras. "They're watching every angle now."

"Then we find one they're not," Neil replied firmly.

With silent precision, he unspooled a length of thin black rope attached to a compact grappling hook. He swung it twice, then tossed it deftly upwards, the hook catching on the ledge of the adjacent rooftop with a muted clink. He then glanced around once more before scaling quickly and quietly, hand over hand, Jenny following immediately after.

They moved across the rooftops in silence, shadows among shadows. Neil pulled out a handheld thermal imager, scanning for heat signatures. "Clear up ahead."

They reached their next intended vantage point—a small, sheltered alcove atop one of the Vatican's administrative buildings, directly overlooking St. Peter's Basilica and the central stage. From here, the angle was clear, unobstructed, and ideal for a sniper's nest.

Jenny set her rifle case down softly, opening it to reveal her custom HK G28 sniper rifle. She fitted the scope and sighted down toward where they were building the stage, checking the sightlines meticulously. She drew in a slow breath, visualizing Vale standing at the podium.

"Clean shot," she whispered. "Distance is perfect, angle is ideal."

Neil nodded, already scanning the broader area through field glasses. "There's another possible nest," he murmured, gesturing toward a distant bell tower about a hundred meters farther back. "Good cover, harder to spot from below. But trickier angle, longer distance."

Jenny considered it briefly, eyes narrowing. "Backup, maybe. But here's better. Closer, surer."

Neil inclined his head slightly, storing the location in his memory anyway. They'd learned from experience—always have contingencies.

A sudden beam of light flared across the roof, and they both flattened against the stones, barely breathing. A security guard wandered casually along the edge of an adjacent roof, flashlight dancing lazily over the statues and stonework.

Seconds stretched painfully until the guard finally turned away, descending a stairwell. Neil exhaled softly, the tension releasing incrementally.

"Too close," Jenny muttered.

"Won't be easier tomorrow," Neil replied grimly.

"That's why we'll be sleeping here," Jenny added.

They located a loft hatch that led down into a forgotten storage room, long unused, filled with dusty crates and old furniture draped in sheets. Neil jammed the door shut from the inside, ensuring that no accidental discovery would compromise their position.

Jenny unpacked her gear, checking and rechecking every component. They would wait here, invisible and silent, until morning when Vale stepped into view.

"How are you feeling?" Neil asked softly, watching her meticulous preparations.

Jenny met his gaze, her eyes resolute. "Ready."

He nodded, settling back against the wall. "Then let's end this."

FORTY-FOUR

THE JUNGLE CLOSED TIGHTER around them, a green labyrinth thick with humidity and crawling shadows. Sweat streamed down Noah's face, the air oppressive beneath the thick canopy. The Mapuche warriors moved silently, their bare feet soundless on the moss-covered stones as they led Noah and Wally deeper into a rocky gorge barely wide enough for a man to pass through. At times, they were forced to move sideways, their chests almost rubbing up against the stone wall.

After what seemed like an eternity, the gorge abruptly opened into a vast chasm falling through the earth and hidden by the thick jungle. Before them cascaded a shimmering waterfall, plummeting gracefully from high above, vanishing through a narrow cleft in the rock and disappearing into unseen depths below. The deafening roar filled Noah's ears, masking all other sounds of the jungle.

He stared through the mist and spray, squinting into the near-impenetrable curtain of water.

"I don't see anything," Noah said, glancing skeptically at Wally. "Are they sure this is the right place?"

Wally repeated the question to their Mapuche guide. The warrior nodded solemnly, eyes dark and wary.

Suddenly, above the persistent roar, the familiar chopping sound of helicopter blades resonated through the gorge. Noah's muscles tightened instinctively.

"Back! Against the rocks!" he hissed.

They pressed themselves flat, hidden behind jagged outcroppings slick with moisture and moss. The sound grew louder, vibrating in Noah's bones. Then the chopper itself appeared, slicing through the narrow opening overhead. It hovered midway down the chasm, its blades stirring up clouds of mist.

Then something happened.

The waterfall began to split, cleaving neatly down its center as though cut by an invisible blade. Water flowed aside, cascading in perfect sheets along newly revealed edges, exposing the immense face of a hidden metallic structure embedded seamlessly into the rock.

"My God," Wally murmured in disbelief.

Noah watched as a massive ramp smoothly extended from behind the water's edge, offering a stable platform for the helicopter. It touched down gracefully, engines idling in wait.

A colossal metal door slid open slowly, groaning beneath its own weight. From within, armed operatives emerged swiftly, rifles shouldered, faces masked behind visors. Automated turrets mounted high above swiveled silently, scanning the area with calculated menace.

"They're prepared for war," Wally breathed.

Noah nodded grimly. "So am I."

From the chopper, crates of supplies were rapidly unloaded —medical equipment, sealed biohazard containers, electronics —everything methodically inventoried and swiftly carried inside.

As quickly as it had begun, the operation concluded. The helicopter lifted from the ramp, ascending steadily into the chasm until it vanished over the trees. Moments later, the giant door began sliding closed, sealing the facility once more behind the relentless veil of water.

Noah turned urgently to Wally. "Ask them if there are any other entrances."

Wally spoke quickly to the Mapuche warriors. Their leader shook his head firmly, expression grave.

"One entrance only," Wally translated.

Noah groaned, disappointed.

But then a younger warrior stepped forward, speaking passionately, gesturing emphatically at the chasm walls. The elder's expression hardened, clearly dismissing the younger man's words.

"What are they saying?" Noah demanded.

Wally listened closely, brow furrowing. "The younger one claims there's another way. Hidden. But it's extremely dangerous. The others believe it's suicide."

Noah glanced at the chasm, determination hardening his features. "You know me, Wally. Danger's an old friend. Get him to show us."

After a brief, intense debate among themselves, the warriors finally nodded. The younger Mapuche warrior looked resolutely at Noah, eyes bright with defiance and courage. He then turned and led them away from the waterfall into the darker, more treacherous depths of the jungle.

For the next twenty minutes, the Mapuche warriors moved gracefully, their bare feet silent against the tangled roots and slick foliage. Noah and Wally followed closely behind, their boots heavy, crunching softly against the damp earth. The roaring waterfall slowly faded to a gentle hiss, lost amid the chorus of birds and insects.

The young warrior halted suddenly and raised his hand, signaling for Noah and Wally to stop. Noah's eyes scanned the area, seeing nothing but an impenetrable wall of green—vines twisted tightly around gnarled trunks, moss-covered stones, and the faint glisten of moisture in the air.

"What are we looking at?" Noah whispered, squinting as he examined their surroundings.

The warrior said nothing, simply pointed upward. Noah followed the gesture, narrowing his eyes.

Then he saw it.

A perfect circular gap had been carved into the dense canopy, sunlight streaming through the precise opening, illuminating a small patch of ground below. Around the edges, leaves and branches were blackened and twisted, their surfaces scorched.

"Chemical burns," Wally muttered, stepping forward cautiously, eyes fixed on the peculiar circle of devastation.

The warrior's arm shot out abruptly, gripping Wally by the shoulder and pulling him firmly back. Wally turned sharply, confusion flashing across his face.

"Wait," the warrior said quietly in Mapudungun, his voice heavy with warning.

Wally hesitated, eyes darting uncertainly between Noah and the warrior. Noah inclined his head subtly, indicating that they should heed the warrior's advice.

For a tense moment, they stood frozen in place, the jungle around them holding its breath. Then, as if on cue, a vibrant green parakeet descended gracefully through the hole in the canopy, alighting delicately on a scorched branch.

Noah watched it. The bird was beautiful.

But it wasn't there for long.

In an instant, the ground beneath the parakeet split open with a mechanical hiss, revealing an enormous, yawning vent.

A deep rumble followed—low at first, then rising.

A gathering of noise.

And then—

Before Noah or Wally could react, a violent surge of chemical smoke erupted from below, blasting upward with a thunderous whoosh. Thick, choking clouds billowed through the hole in the canopy, dispersing into the atmosphere above.

When the smoke cleared, the vent lingered open for a few critical seconds, revealing a dark shaft lined with the metal rungs of a ladder. Then with a mechanical hum, it snapped shut, disappearing seamlessly back into the jungle floor.

Noah stepped cautiously forward, his gaze fixed intently on the vent as it vanished. He didn't notice the remains of the parakeet—a melted, gruesome mass of feathers and bone now dripping silently from the blackened branch. His eyes were locked instead on the vent itself, counting silently.

"Twenty seconds," Noah murmured, eyes narrowed thoughtfully.

Wally glanced at him, eyebrows furrowed. "Twenty seconds for what?"

Noah turned, his expression grim but determined. "Twenty seconds before it closes. That's our way in."

FORTY-FIVE

THE TRAINING HALL reverberated with the sharp cracks of Airsoft fire and shouted commands. The modular walls had been rearranged to simulate a dense urban environment, replete with tight corners, open windows, and hidden doorways. The recruits moved swiftly and methodically, clearing rooms in precise formation under Katya's watchful, exacting eye.

"Check your corners!" Katya barked, voice echoing from the gantry above. "Tao, move up—cover Zina's blind spot!"

Tao responded immediately, positioning himself to cover Zina as she sprinted across a narrow corridor, her weapon leveled ahead. Lula and Imani moved in tandem behind them, their eyes sharp, movements controlled.

Norah brought up the rear, her own rifle aimed and steady. Yet even amidst the intensity, her focus kept drifting. On the sidelines, quiet and still as a statue, sat B3-17. He watched silently, his expression unreadable, his posture unnaturally rigid.

Something about him deeply unsettled Norah.

She tried to ignore the prickling unease creeping up her spine, refocusing her gaze forward as she entered the next simulated room. "Clear!" she called, quickly scanning for threats.

"Room clear," Gregor confirmed behind her, stepping in and pivoting smoothly to cover the doorway they'd just entered.

Yet Norah's eyes flickered once again toward the edge of the training area, to the silent figure watching them like some kind of ghost. His stillness was too absolute, too clinical. His eyes tracked their every movement, absorbing details without emotion.

"Norah!" Katya shouted suddenly, breaking her fixation.

Norah spun around—but too late.

An Airsoft pellet slammed into her chest, stinging sharply even through her tactical vest. She stumbled back in surprise.

"You're out!" Katya snapped from above, irritation threading her voice. "Distracted soldiers become dead soldiers pretty quickly in the field. Out of the exercise!"

Face flushing with embarrassment and frustration, Norah raised her hand and exited the training area. She could feel the eyes of the others on her, but it was B3-17's silent gaze that felt the heaviest. Somehow judging, somehow alien.

She took her place beside him on the bench, maintaining a slight distance. Her gaze flickered sideways. His eyes remained fixed on the ongoing drill, unblinking and impassive.

"Aren't you bored?" Norah finally asked, desperate to break the oppressive silence.

He didn't answer immediately. Then, after a pause so long she nearly gave up on an answer, he said softly, "I'm learning."

"Learning what exactly?" she pressed, trying to keep her voice steady.

"Patterns. Behaviors," he replied tonelessly. His gaze shifted slightly, turning fully toward her. His eyes were cold, clear, devoid of feeling. "Weaknesses."

A chill ran down Norah's spine. She opened her mouth to respond but found no words. She turned away instead, swallowing hard.

The drill continued, shouts and Airsoft fire resuming their intensity, but Norah's focus remained fractured. Beside her, B3-17 sat motionless once more, his stare eerily locked on the team.

Norah couldn't shake the uneasy feeling settling deep within her bones. Something wasn't right about him. And whatever it was, it frightened her.

FORTY-SIX

A FAINT METALLIC creak stirred Neil from sleep.

He opened his eyes to dim blue light filtering through the rusted vents of the storage room. Cold stone pressed into his back where only his sleeping bag had cushioned his brief sleep. Jenny was on watch, crouched at the window slit, wrapped in the gray-green folds of a digital camouflage net. Her rifle rested beside her, angled toward the city skyline like a sleeping predator.

She didn't turn when he moved. Just gave a slight nod. One he returned silently.

Neil sat up slowly, every muscle stiff, and poured a finger's worth of coffee from a battered thermos into the steel cap. He crossed the room quietly, crouching beside her. She accepted it without a word, took a sip, then passed it back.

Below them, Rome was stirring. The square was already filling with activity. Temporary barricades were being reinforced, news crews were setting up cameras on tripods, sound techs trailing coiled cables like serpents. Patrolling the cordons, uniformed guards nodded at one another in tight routines.

"Not long now," Neil muttered.

Jenny shrugged. "No. Not long."

They watched in silence for a moment as a fresh wave of spectators entered the square. Some carried folding chairs, others banners. One had a baby in a sling, wrapped in a flag that read *Peace Through Unity*. Speakers clicked on with a faint whine.

Then came a crackle of static from a nearby tannoy system.

Both of them stiffened.

The speaker boomed: "Attention. In one hour, the Supreme Delegate will address the world from the steps of St. Peter's. For security reasons, all press must..."

Neil's eyes drifted to the crowd. "Jesus. It's going to be a full house."

Jenny didn't respond. She was still watching the crowd with a sniper's eye—measuring wind, angle, range, rhythm. She sipped the last of the coffee.

From the square came another faint burst of static, growing sharper.

It crackled like gas.

Like a hiss.

Like something venting—

———

PATAGONIA, Jungle Ridge
10:58 ART | November 20

THE JUNGLE HISSED.

Another burst of thick chemical vapor roared upward from the hidden vent, curling like a living thing into the still morning air. Birds scattered from the canopy. Leaves turned black where the gas brushed them. The plume lingered in the shaft of sunlight above, a pillar of smoke clawing at the sky before finally thinning.

Wally clicked the stopwatch.

"Three minutes, ten seconds," he said, satisfied. "Right on time."

Noah lay beside him, belly to the ground, eyes narrowed at the still-steaming metal plate now resealed below the trees. The charred circle of jungle around it glistened faintly in the sunlight like scorched bone.

Both men had spent the previous night back at the Mapuche camp, huddled around a fire beneath a canopy of stars, planning every detail of this infiltration. The warriors had offered insight, tools, and a quiet strength. But now, the time for planning was done—Noah was back, ready to put it all into action.

"It's been precise so far," Wally continued. "Every burst occurs between three minutes ten and four minutes eleven. That's your window. Around three minutes to get down there and out of the shaft."

Noah flexed his fingers in their stiff leather gloves. "Let's hope it doesn't go down too far."

"Or just takes you straight into the jaws of death."

Noah raised an eyebrow at him. "Thanks for the pep talk, Wally."

He began checking his gear with careful hands, laying it out like a sacred ritual:

Animal-skin gloves, reinforced at the knuckles.

SIG Sauer P302. Six rounds. Cleaned, oiled. Ready.

Combat knife, high carbon steel, balanced for throwing.

Blowgun and a velvet pouch of darts—slender things with glassy tips, soaked in toxin. A gift from the Mapuche.

The gear wasn't much. But Noah didn't need more. Stealth and precision were what he did best.

He pulled the blowgun's strap over his shoulder, cinched it tight, and finally looked at his watch.

"The clock is ticking," he murmured. "The next one is it."

———

THE DIGITAL CLOCK above the hallway door clicked to 22:00 with a hollow beep.

"Lights out, recruits," came the dry voice of a Camelot operative, muffled through the dormitory door.

The overhead lights dimmed across the wing.

Lula groaned, dragging herself off the sofa. She switched off the TV as the operative's voice receded down the hall, repeating, "Lights out, recruits."

"I swear, it's not much different from when it was the Council," she muttered.

Zina frowned as they headed for their rooms. "Right, Lulu," she said dryly. "Because we even had a TV back then."

Inside her room, Norah sat cross-legged on her mattress, rubbing her forehead, trying to smooth away the feeling of unease that had nestled in the base of her skull since dinner.

B3-17's room was right across the hallway from her. He was already lying down. Perfect posture. Eyes closed.

One by one, the recruits let the day slip from their minds. Breathing slowed. Blankets shifted. A few murmured final thoughts into the dark.

Soon, the wing was quiet.

Outside the rooms, the corridor lights blinked to standby— low red glows stretching through steel corridors. Somewhere deep in the base, Esmerelda cycled through nightly system routines. Hydraulics exhaled. Vents sighed.

Putorana held its breath.

FORTY-SEVEN

A LOW WIND curled over the Vatican's tiled rooftops.

Below, St. Peter's Square stirred. Spectators wandered through the growing crowds, shepherded into neat lines by police and volunteers in red sashes. Scaffolded lights buzzed to life, and banners rippled.

Jenny lay flat behind a Children of the Empire banner, her rifle nestled into the hole she had last night cut into the center of the painted "O."

Neil leaned in beside her, handing over the warm flask.

"More coffee," he whispered.

She accepted it without turning. "Bless you."

They sat together in tense silence, draped beneath the digital camouflage, the warmth of the coffee a small comfort as the city beyond their scope slowly awakened.

Then the tannoy crackled to life.

"Buongiorno, cittadini del mondo…"

Jenny's jaw tightened.

Neil adjusted his field glasses, scanning the square as more people flooded in.

"Here we go," he said softly.

———

PATAGONIA, Jungle Ridge
11:56 ART | November 20

THE JUNGLE HELD ITS BREATH.

Another burst of gas screamed upward, sulfurous and opaque, hissing into the canopy in a geyser of chemical steam. It twisted in the sunlight like smoke from a dying god.

"Good luck," Wally said, eyes never leaving the plume.

Noah stepped forward. The moment the last of the smoke cleared, he sprinted, boots thudding over moss-slick stone, and dove headfirst into the still-churning shaft.

For a heartbeat, he felt nothing—only heat and pressure. Then he caught the ladder, gloves searing on the metal rungs, his body swinging with the momentum of the jump.

He winced. Held on. Clattered into the vent wall.

He switched on his headlamp.

A cone of pale light cut downward—but the ladder kept going. Endless, cold, and silent.

Noah took a breath.

Then he began to climb.

———

PUTORANA BASE | Siberia
22:57 KRAT | November 20

THE RED STANDBY light from the hallway flickered gently through the gap in B3-17's door.

Inside, the boy slowly sat upright in bed. One second he was lying still. The next, his eyes were open. Awake.

He rose with mechanical precision, bare feet touching down on the floor with a whisper. The room's console terminal blinked in passive sleep mode. B3-17 took a seat across from it, pressing two keys.

It came to life.

The screen flared green, then blue—then black again as a secure shell opened without prompt. B3-17's fingers moved faster than thought, bypassing authentication like it didn't exist. Firewall after firewall dissolved beneath his keystrokes.

A communications link established.

Static crackled to life. It started low, then escalated into the high, warbling distortion of the same frequency burst that had come from the Black Sun chopper in Patagonia.

It roared from the computer's speakers, and the entire room trembled with it.

B3-17 seized violently, his limbs locking outward. His mouth hung open, a silent scream twisting his features as he collapsed into the chair. Veins stood out along his neck. The screen pulsed, feeding waveform data into some unseen connection.

Across the hallway, Norah bolted upright in bed.

She blinked into the dark, heart thudding. That noise—

ROME | ST. Peter's Basilica
16:59 CET | November 20

AN EXPLOSIVE CHEER broke like a tidal wave through the square.

Flashbulbs strobed the Vatican's grand façade as the Pope stepped forward, flanked by crimson-robed aides and security detail, his white cassock gleaming under the soft winter sun.

From the rooftop, Jenny adjusted the scope's dial, breath shallow against the rising hum of the crowd.

Below, tens of thousands packed every available inch of St. Peter's Square—spectators, pilgrims, dignitaries, media swarms. The air rippled with banners. Balloons floated upward like a slow-moving constellation.

And in the center of it all—Sebastian Vale.

He emerged like a stage actor in perfect lighting: sleek suit, black leather gloves, hands raised in modest greeting. He moved with deliberate calm—never standing still long enough for a clear shot.

Jenny clenched her jaw.

"He's dancing," Neil murmured beside her, spotting through the field glasses.

"He'll have to stay still at some point," she muttered, adjusting her cheek weld.

Vale reached the podium just as the Pope moved up beside him, one frail hand resting lightly on the younger man's shoulder.

The applause surged again.

Beneath the digital camouflage that mirrored the rest of the red tiled rooftop, Jenny exhaled slowly and steadied the reticle.

A banner swept into view—"CHILDREN OF THE EMPIRE"—its cloth rippling across her scope like surf.

"Banners... heads... goddammit," she hissed.

Vale began to speak, his voice magnified across a thousand speakers, translated in real time across a dozen languages.

"...in these fractured times, we look not to those who profit from chaos, but to those who rebuild from truth..."

Telescreens on every building echoed his image—his voice, his face, his message—all synced in seamless theater. The world was watching.

Jenny's finger hovered near the trigger. Her view was dancing.

Then the Pope stepped forward.

She took in a breath.

Held it.
Ready to fire.

FORTY-EIGHT

PATAGONIA | KIEL'S LAB | 12:02 ART | NOVEMBER 20

NOAH DESCENDED THROUGH THE DARK.

The plan was simple: infiltrate the lab, find a way to destroy it from the inside. He had no charges—those were gone since Black Sun torched their camp and everything in it. Now it was just him, a combat knife, a SIG Sauer with six rounds, a blowgun full of poison darts—and whatever this place gave him.

He climbed down the vent with an urgency born in the knowledge that soon it would be flooded with a gas so deadly that anything in it would be reduced to dripping flesh. A silent clock in his head ticked away each second. Wally had timed the chemical purges: three-minute windows, give or take.

Death on a schedule.

Noah checked his watch—the dial pulsed quietly green in the gloom. The next purge was due any moment.

He was halfway down when the walls began to vibrate. A low, bone-deep hum rolled up from the abyss below, growing stronger. The ventilation system was waking up again.

His watch chimed softly.

Time's up.

"Shit."

Still meters above the base of the shaft, Noah's eyes scanned desperately. Then he saw it—tucked just behind one of the rotating ventilation fans: a circular maintenance hatch barely wide enough for a person.

The fan blades began to spin faster, an ominous blur of steel.

Noah took one breath, drew the SIG from his belt, and jammed the pistol between the blades.

A screech of metal.

The fan halted with a shudder.

Noah leapt across the shaft, fingers grazing the outer edge of the vent casing. He pulled himself through the gap in the blades, scrambling into the tight crawlspace, his pistol fixed within the fan, keeping it still.

Now he only had the knife and the blow gun.

He didn't look back.

Behind him came a hiss. The gas. Thick, chemical. Greenish-yellow as it sprayed into the shaft—poison flooding upward like breath from a sleeping titan.

Noah kept moving.

He crawled forward, boots scraping steel, and finally dropped down into a dim, humming corridor five hundred meters beneath the jungle.

He was now inside the lab itself. Stark lighting, polished chrome, and no warmth—just angles and echo. Typical of Council era installations.

He wasn't alone for long.

A guard rounded the corner ahead—tall, masked, armed. His eyes widened as he spotted Noah.

The man fumbled for his sidearm.

Noah was faster.

He snapped the blowgun from his back, brought it to his lips, and fired in one motion.

Ffft.

The dart struck the man clean in the neck. He staggered,

blinking rapidly. Then dropped his pistol as he pulled it free of its holster. His fingers twitched. A rattled breath escaped his lips. He fell to one knee, trying to scream, but his muscles seized mid-motion.

The neurotoxin had worked instantly.

Harvested from Phyllobates terribilis, the golden poison frog, the toxin had been extracted by the Mapuche through an age-old ritual: gently agitating the frog over a fire until beads of venom sweated from its skin, then carefully painting the tips of carved darts with the glistening fluid.

The poison didn't just stop the heart. It turned the body against itself. Every nerve misfired, muscles contracting all at once.

The guard's limbs twisted into a grotesque arch as he collapsed, dead before he hit the floor.

Noah dragged the corpse into a nearby storage closet and eased the door shut.

Then, quietly, he reached into his pack and unfolded the last gift Wally had salvaged from the ruined camp: a square of polymer mesh, smooth and black as oil.

Digital camouflage.

He draped it over himself and tapped the side.

The material shimmered—light bending, reshaping, swallowing him whole.

Noah disappeared beneath the sheet of digital camouflage, nothing but shadow and silence as he crept deeper into the lab. Wrapped in the shimmering mesh, he moved like liquid. His breath was even, his steps soundless. Blowgun gripped in one gloved hand, he became part of the lab's sterile hush.

The corridors branched like veins. Each curve offered a glimpse behind glass partitions—and with every turn, the horror deepened.

One chamber glowed a sickly green.

Surgical beds lined the room, restraints hanging like limp hands. Cryo-canisters covered the walls, misting at the rims. Some were tagged with barcodes. Others—simple, ominous codenames:

HELIX 7B – VECTOR REPLICATION BETA
NOCTIS STRAIN 9
VIREX-RUIN

Noah exhaled slowly.

This was it. The place where Black Sun was manufacturing extinction.

He backed away, fingers clenched tightly on the blowgun. That's when his eyes caught it: a wide diagnostics bay just ahead, softly humming with quiet systems. Oxygen lines ran along the ceiling like arteries, feeding into pressurized filtration units. A few terminals blinked quietly, their displays cycling through automated routines.

An idea formed. Sharp and clean.

He slipped inside, crouching by the consoles.

One screen displayed a full schematic of the lab's ventilation systems—pipes, regulators, seals. Along the bottom: *CAUTION: PRESSURE LOCK REQUIRED FOR VENT PURGE OVERRIDE.*

Noah studied it. The purge system fed chemicals out—but if he shut down the intake valves and reversed the flow...

He could drown this place from within.

The tanks. The labs. The virus.

Everything.

Behind a coolant panel, he found a secondary console— manual override, probably used during emergency testing.

His fingers hovered above the switches. Then moved away.

Not yet.

He had to find Kiel first.

He moved on, the air colder with each step.

The next chamber brought no comfort.

He paused at its window.

Nutrient tanks. Dozens of them. Bodies suspended like puppets in water—male, female, indistinguishable. Their faces were blank, too perfect. Symmetrical in a way that unsettled

Noah. No blemishes, no hair. Each form bore a number, seared in brutal red on the side of the neck. Just like B3-17.

Noah stepped closer.

His headlamp cut a narrow beam through the gloom, revealing something beneath their translucent skin—glints of metal, faint and thin, embedded along the spine, all the way to the base of each skull.

Transponders.

Noah's jaw tightened.

A memory flashed: B3-17 writhing in the jungle, convulsing under the burst of static from the Black Sun helicopter. The way his body had seized—no explanation. Until now.

It hadn't been random.

It had been activation.

He turned back to the tanks.

"Like puppets on standby," he muttered.

He thought of B3-17 at Putorana. And of his daughter—trapped there with him.

But he couldn't do anything. Not from out here, thousands of miles away.

He trusted Katya. If it went bad, she'd know what to do.

He had no other choice.

———

PUTORANA BASE | Siberia
23:07 KRAT | November 20

THE CONVULSIONS STOPPED the second the static did.

B3-17 sat motionless for a long moment, the dim blue of the terminal reflected faintly across his blank expression. Then he moved—calmly, fluidly—rising to his feet as if waking from a nap.

He reached for Tao's tablet tucked beneath his mattress, having stolen it hours earlier. No one had noticed.

The door to his quarters hissed open. Lights flickered above as he stepped into the corridor, bare feet silent on the brushed metal floor.

Across the hall, Norah stirred, having heard the static burst. A flicker of movement caught her eye through the cracked door. Silent as breath, she got out of bed and pressed an eye to the gap.

B3-17 walked like he owned the place. At the junction to the command corridor, he paused. Reached out. Tapped a sequence into a locked access panel, interfacing Tao's tablet without delay—passwords, encryptions, protocols falling like paper to flame.

The door unlocked and slid open.

Norah pressed herself into a shadowed corner, heart racing.

What the hell is he doing?

She followed carefully, keeping back as he entered the central operations hub. There, B3-17 approached a terminal.

He didn't hesitate.

Fingers moved with robotic confidence. Code flooded the display screen. One by one, sectors across the base dimmed—cameras blinked out, doors sealed, communications dropped.

From above, Esmerelda's synthetic voice crackled over the intercom.

"B3-17. Please clarify. What are you—"

Her voice fractured mid-sentence.

"—do—ing—g-g-g-g—"

Gone.

Silence filled the corridor. Then: a full-system blackout.

Emergency lighting flickered to life—blood-red strips along the baseboards. The hum of life-support subsystems shifted to a dull whine.

B3-17 reached beneath the terminal and pulled the core data drive with a soft click. He pocketed it like a child keeping a marble.

Behind him, Norah stepped forward.

"What are you doing?" she snapped, her voice shaking.

He turned with the ease of someone brushing lint from a sleeve.

He smiled. It was eerie.

"Do you know," he said flatly, "that I've just memorized the complete contents of your Council's secure archive? Guess what I found?"

She stared at him. "What are you talking about?"

"Breakers," he said, as if explaining a bedtime story. "Failsafes built into each of you. Those who were once the recruits of the Council."

Norah said nothing, merely frowning at him.

"Neural disruptors," he went on. "They can be triggered by a single spoken phrase made up of random words. Your masters feared you might outgrow your chains."

Norah clenched her fists, eyes wide with disbelief. "You're lying."

"No. I'm not." He stepped closer. "Want to know your phrase?"

"Stop it and come back to the dorm with me."

He smiled, voice lowering like a lullaby.

"Delta one seven seven Oscar six—Norah nine."

Nora's body seized.

She collapsed mid-step—rigid, eyes locked wide, unable to scream. Her lungs refused to obey. Her muscles froze in place. She could feel the air at her lips but couldn't suck it in, trapped in a body turned to stone.

B3-17 crouched beside her.

"I'm so sorry,'" he whispered.

He stood again. And walked away. Leaving her lying in the middle of the corridor.

Rome | St. Peter's Basilica
17:11 CET | November 20

· · ·

JENNY'S FINGER tightened on the trigger.

For a fraction of a second, everything aligned: the sway of the banners paused, the backlighting behind Vale cleared, the crowd stilled to a murmur of anticipation. His face—clear in the reticle, mid-sentence, lips forming some saintly proclamation.

She squeezed.

The shot cracked—clean, sharp.

It flew over the rooftops, the crowds, passed the banners, reached the stage.

And it stopped.

Not against flesh or bone or Sebastian Vale. It stopped mid-air, three feet from Vale's chest—exploding into a glittering cloud of metallic dust.

Nanobots.

They burst outward from Vale's coat in a shimmering halo, intercepting the round with brutal elegance. The bullet disintegrated into nothing.

Jenny froze.

"What the—" Neil said, lifting the field glasses in disbelief.

But then came a second shot.

This one didn't come from them.

It cracked across the square with a different tone—sharper, harder. It echoed off the Vatican's stone and shattered the square's stillness.

The Pope staggered next to Vale.

His body crumpled, folding slowly into himself as a bright crimson arc sprayed across the marble column at the back of the stage. Gasps turned into screams. Cameras whirled. The crowd convulsed in sudden chaos.

Jenny's mouth hung open, frozen behind her scope.

Neil followed the echo.

"Tower!" he shouted. "Behind us—a hundred meters—"

Jenny turned her head just in time to catch a glint of sunlight on a barrel. The rifle perched at the top of the tower.

And behind it—Sophia. Calm, composed, and pulling back from her scope.

Smoke curled from her weapon's muzzle.

"No..." Jenny whispered.

Her voice was lost beneath the rising tide of panic sweeping through St. Peter's Square.

Banners dropped. Screams erupted. Sirens howled. The Pope lay crumpled at Vale's side as security swarmed the stage.

Jenny flicked back the edge of the digital camouflage, trying to line up another shot.

But it was too late.

Vale was already being whisked away, his face expressionless as bodyguards surrounded him, their shields locking tight in a phalanx. The moment was gone.

Above them, a high-pitched whine.

Drones.

Three of them swooped low, lenses locked on their rooftop position. One of the cameras turned—blinking red—broadcasting a live feed.

Every screen in the square lit up with Jenny's image: frozen mid-trigger, her face clear, exposed. Another camera caught Neil beside her.

Framed. Condemned.

A beat passed—and then the crowd saw it too. A roar rose like a wave as people surged toward exits in chaos.

Neil grabbed Jenny's shoulder hard. "We have to move. Now."

Her fingers tightened on the rifle, her breath caught in her chest.

Down below, Sebastian Vale moved within the tight huddle of his security—unshaken.

He turned, slowly, and looked toward their building. Straight at them. And smiled.

FORTY-NINE

NOAH MOVED SILENTLY through a stale-lit hallway, the blowgun gripped lightly in his left hand. Every corner brought more sterile horror: vitrified embryos arranged like museum pieces, half-developed clones suspended in thick liquid with tubes hanging out of them, a humming refrigeration unit marked only with the Roman numeral XIII.

The hum of machinery gave way to a low, static buzz.

Noah turned the next corner—and stopped.

A lab. Dimly lit and humming with activity.

At the center, standing before a curved bank of monitors and transparent consoles, a man worked with calm precision. His lab coat hung loose over thin shoulders. He was tall and wiry with pale, almost translucent skin that clung tightly to the bones of his face. Wisps of iron-gray hair clung stubbornly to the edges of a bald, scab-ridden scalp. His long fingers danced across the interface with the ease of muscle memory.

Noah stepped into the room.

"Kiel," he said, voice low but clear.

The man didn't turn.

He merely paused.

Then with something like a smile in his voice, he said, "Finally."

Kiel reached for a switch and powered down the console in front of him. The monitor blinked out.

He still didn't turn. "I expected you to find me. The second Rausch said you were here, in Patagonia, I knew you'd find me in the end."

Noah said nothing, stepping farther into the room.

"You've been busy, Noah Wolf," Kiel continued. "The jungle. The mines. Even my lovely pet project in Bolivia." He chuckled softly. "But you always come back to the source, don't you?"

Now he turned.

And smiled.

It was the smile of a man who believed in gods—because he saw himself as one.

"I'm glad you came," he said serenely. "We have so much to discuss."

He was lean almost to the point of fragility, and his skin was pale, veined like marble under the harsh lighting. Steel-rimmed glasses magnified two intelligent, ghostly blue eyes.

He wore a simple lab coat, pristine. Beneath it were tailored charcoal slacks and polished shoes.

Noah took a step forward, blowgun raised. "Back away from the terminal."

"Or what?" Kiel's voice was gentle, amused. "You'll kill the man who gave you life?"

Noah froze. His aim held, but something in his chest twisted.

"...What did you just say?"

Kiel stepped forward, calm as a priest, hands clasped behind his back. "You were the only success of Program Genesis. The final son of my first cycle. I designed you strand by strand—each gene selected, each trait sculpted. Before your first breath, before your first thought, you were already perfect."

Noah's jaw clenched. "*You* made me?"

Kiel smiled softly with something like pity. "And many like you. Just none as close to perfection as you. Do you know, I carried your essence longer than a woman carries her child. You were *my* child. My art."

Noah stepped forward, voice low. "You were making a weapon. Not a child."

"I made an angel," Kiel said, and his eyes gleamed. "But then those fools took you. Left you stranded among the weak. The inferior. Allowed society and its moralism to bleed into you. Then you yourself allowed their herd mentality to drag you down. They've stained you with their morality. Taught you guilt. Restraint. Filled you with the disease of sentiment."

"You mean decency."

"I mean limitation," Kiel snapped. "Look at you. Playing at humanity. Letting Vale steer you like a wind-up toy. Why? Because he knows your weakness."

"And what's that?"

"That you believe people matter."

"They do."

"To each other, perhaps. But not to you. You were meant to rise above all of this. You were my legacy."

Noah's voice was flat. "You're just some crackpot making potions for neo-fascists and power crazed cultists. What legacy do you have?"

Kiel didn't answer. He merely turned to a control pad and pressed a button.

Behind him, a wall bloomed to life—giant screens sparking on, one after the other. A satellite feed. News footage. Dozens of real-time overlays.

St. Peter's Square.

Screams. Blood. A body in white robes collapsed on a stage surrounded by marble columns. The world's breath held in horror.

In one corner, a drone feed: Jenny, rifle raised. Neil pulling her back.

The crawl beneath read:

CAMELOT ASSASSINATES POPE DURING UNITY SPEECH.

Noah took a step forward slowly, like a man wading into freezing water. "What... what is this?"

Kiel tilted his head, eyes aglow with cruel delight. "History," he said softly. "Being rewritten. And you? You're already on the wrong page."

Rome | St. Peter's Basilica
17:14 CET | November 20

Gunshots cracked behind them.

Jenny vaulted the low parapet and landed hard on the next rooftop, gravel skittering beneath her boots. Behind her, Neil scrambled over the edge, breathing like a steam engine.

"Left!" Jenny called, pointing through a narrow stone arch between two bell towers.

Sophia was a fleeting blur up ahead—dark clothing, white braid whipping behind her as she leapt rooftop to rooftop like a ghost made of muscle memory and fury.

"She's fast," Neil muttered.

"Then let's be faster."

They tore after her. The Vatican rooftops rolled ahead like uneven waves—domes, crosses, marble ridges and sudden twenty-foot drops where old buildings kissed the sky.

Below was chaos.

Police sirens howled from every direction. Helicopter rotors began to churn the clouds above. The square had devolved into riot—banners trampled, fences overrun, bodies shoved shoulder to shoulder trying to escape a massacre. Camelot's name poured from every newsfeed.

They were being hunted.

But they were hunting, too.

Sophia slid down a copper drainpipe, landing in a crouch and firing a snap shot backward. A slug whizzed past Neil's head, sparking off an iron spire.

"Jesus—"

Jenny bolted forward. She cleared the gap and hit the next roof at speed, tucking into a shoulder roll to dampen the impact. Sophia was just three roofs ahead now—maybe twenty seconds away, if she didn't vanish again.

Two policemen appeared suddenly from a rooftop stairwell, sidearms raised.

"FERMI! AL SUO POSTO—"

Neil crashed into them before they finished the sentence. One went down with a crack of helmet against stone; the other caught a knee in the ribs and staggered, gasping.

Jenny didn't break stride. She caught a glimpse of Sophia ducking under a stone arch and turned hard after her.

Across the alley, up a ledge.

Sophia turned and fired again. Jenny ducked, feeling it pass through her hair like a whisper.

Neil caught up behind her. "We've got to push her somewhere tight. No way we outrun her on the flat."

"She's heading toward the Carabinieri tower."

"That's a dead end."

"Only if she doesn't have an escape plan."

Jenny slammed a fresh mag into her pistol and ran harder.

Below, the crowd roared. Police units began cutting off stairwells and sealing intersections. Sophia's silhouette darted through clouds of pigeon wings and spires of laundry hanging from ancient lines. It felt like a fever dream.

And it was just getting worse.

———

PATAGONIA | KIEL'S Lab
  12:17 ART | November 20

THE SCREEN LOOPED the moment again and again.

Jenny's shot. The Pope falling. Screams. A tangle of confusion. Sirens. Banners torn from hands. Jenny's face, frozen midturn as she tried to flee. Neil dragging her out of frame. The news banner screaming its lie: *CAMELOT ASSASSINATES POPE DURING UNITY SPEECH.*

Noah's chest tightened. His mind tried hard to reassemble what he was seeing—how, why, what went wrong—but the images didn't stop. They flooded every wall of the lab now. Dozens of displays had blinked to life, all broadcasting the same chaos from different angles.

Every one showing them.

And then, he noticed:

Kiel was gone.

Noah spun.

"Shit."

Behind him, a door at the far end of the lab closed, hydraulic locks slamming into place.

That's when the alarms started.

They screamed to life—red lights cascading across the room in violent pulses. Footfalls thundered from deeper in the complex— boots. Dozens of them.

Noah didn't hesitate.

He turned on his heel and sprinted back through the corridor, past the vitrified embryos, the humming cryo units, the cold mockery of birth and biology.

He veered left, back toward the diagnostics bay. Toward the

ventilation system. If he could reach it, maybe he could still flood the lab with its own poison. Cleanse it. Burn it all.

But as he rounded the corner, he froze.

Armed guards. Six of them. Full tactical gear. They'd sealed the approach—guns raised, movements crisp, eyes alert.

Too many. Too open. He'd never get past without being torn apart.

Noah backpedaled quickly, the blowgun already in hand.

No time. No advantage. He had only one option left.

Escape.

Noah turned away from the guarded corridor and ran.

Back toward the entry shaft—the vent.

ROME | ST. Peter's Basilica
17:22 CET | November 20

THE ROOFTOPS ENDED IN A DROP.

Sophia vaulted the final ledge and vanished into shadow, her boots landing somewhere far below with a dull scrape. Jenny skidded to a halt about twenty feet behind her, chest heaving, eyes darting over the alley that yawned open beneath them—too wide to jump, too deep to fall.

"She's down!" Jenny called, turning sharply. "Street level!"

Neil came up beside her, sweat slicking the edges of his collar. "We're losing her."

A chorus of shouting voices echoed back at them—"FERMI! ALTO! POLIZIA!"

Blue lights danced like ghosts across the nearby buildings.

"We have to drop!" Jenny said, already tying a rope and grappling hook to the rusted chimney brace beside her. "No time to backtrack."

"We don't have time not to—"

Jenny jumped.

The rope went taut. She hit the wall with both feet, skidded halfway down like a controlled fall, and then dropped the last ten feet into the alley. Neil cursed and followed.

By the time he hit the ground, Jenny was already moving.

Sophia had vanished again—but this part of Rome was a maze of close-packed buildings, tunnels, and vehicle-choked streets. Jenny led them forward, ducking beneath overhanging scaffolding and into a market street that had just begun to clear after the sirens started.

Police were everywhere now.

Uniformed officers barking into radios. Tactical teams unloading from black vans. Pedestrians cowered in cafés, and metal shutters clattered down over shopfronts like falling dominoes.

"We need a way out," Neil snapped. "We're boxed in."

Jenny's eyes landed on a courier's bike—low-slung and matte black, the kind made for narrow lanes and quick turns. Its rider was mid-espresso, mouth open in disbelief at the carnage unraveling around him.

"Apologies," she said and kicked the bike's stand out from under it.

Neil was already climbing on behind her.

The rider shouted something in angry Italian as Jenny revved the engine and tore into the alleyway like a bullet.

The bike screamed down the cobbled backstreets, engine echoing off stone façades. Jenny weaved between pedestrians, scooters, and flashing barricades as police began to mobilize around the perimeter.

"You see her?" Neil shouted, scanning side streets.

"Nope. Just flashing lights and police uniforms."

They skidded around a corner, narrowly missing a police car reversing across an intersection. The officers inside shouted, burst out of the car, and opened fire—bullets pinging off the bike's tail as Jenny leaned hard into a turn and disappeared through a wrought-iron gate. Down a staircase. Across a footbridge. Onto another narrow road.

They burst through an archway—and there she was. Sophia. Half a block ahead. Moving with mechanical calm through the crowd, already stripped of her tactical gear, now wrapped in a gray tourist jacket, sunglasses pulled low.

Jenny gunned the throttle.

Sophia turned. Saw them. And sprinted.

The chase reignited.

The crowds became too thick. They abandoned the bike near a public fountain, throwing it onto its side as Jenny and Neil hit the street running.

They chased Sophia through a gallery courtyard, then a café, knocking over tables and smashing dishes. Onlookers screamed and scattered.

Sophia grabbed a waiter's tray and hurled it at Neil, catching him in the chest. He stumbled. Jenny hurdled a low bench and kept going.

Sophia ducked into an alley.

By the time Jenny turned the corner, it was empty.

"Shit!" Jenny cursed as she began scanning every window, every fire escape, every sewer grate.

Neil caught up, limping. "She's gone."

"She can't be gone!"

But she was.

In the distance, more sirens. Police now flooded every main street. Their faces were no longer anonymous. The image was everywhere. Camelot's name whispered like an infection through the streets.

Jenny pulled Neil into a recessed doorway.

"We split here," she said, her breath low and urgent. "We're too visible together."

Neil nodded, gritting his teeth. "Safehouse Four?"

"Yeah."

He hesitated—just for a beat—then caught her wrist. "I love you."

Jenny turned to him. For a second, they just looked at each other, breath mingling in the quiet. Then she pulled him into a fierce hug, kissing him hard and fast.

After that she was gone, melting into the Roman streets like shadow at dusk.

FIFTY

THE KLAXONS HOWLED. Red lights strobed across the steel walls. Noah moved like a phantom through the panic, wrapped in the digital camouflage.

Footsteps thundered past just beyond the doorway. He waited in shadow, breath held, the dart gun pressed to his lips, the end poking from a gap in the sheet of camo. The moment the guard stepped around the corner—

Thffft.

The dart thudded into the man's neck. He blinked once, staggered, and dropped without a sound. Noah stepped over the body, scooping up the man's badge and using it to access the next corridor.

He moved swiftly, retracing his memorized route. The stolen badge got him through two more checkpoints—both unmanned now, left swinging in the wake of the alarm. At last, he reached the narrow service tunnel that led to the hatch he'd entered through nearly twenty minutes earlier.

The grating underfoot vibrated with distant turbine hum. A faint chemical tang clung to the air. Noah crept forward, crouching beside the circular hatch, its steel rim already stained with residue from the last gas purge. He eased it open just a fraction and peered inside.

Still. Silent. The blades of the massive ventilation fan hung motionless, suspended—just as he'd left them—by his SIG Sauer, still wedged between two of the fan's wide alloy teeth.

He waited.

Three to four minutes between purges. He held his breath, listening, praying for the next blast to come and go so he could enter the vent with the timer back to zero.

Instead, he got shouts.

"Noah Wolf! Stop!"

One of the guards rounded the corner, rifle raised.

No time.

Noah wrenched the hatch open and dove through, catching the lip of the fan housing with one hand. His boots slipped, then found purchase. The duct roared with returning pressure—too soon, or too late, he couldn't tell.

He squeezed through the blades, gritting his teeth as he brushed past the pistol, still wedged in the fan. From the corner of his eye, there was movement: the guard lunging into the hatch, rifle raised, finger already tightening on the trigger.

Noah didn't hesitate.

He lashed out with his foot, kicking the SIG Sauer clear. It spun away just as the fan shuddered and roared to life.

The guard fired.

The bullet struck the first spinning blade with a metallic scream, deflecting off into the shaft.

Noah was already climbing.

The vertical shaft was tight, the metal ladder slick with acidic condensation that was starting to melt through his gloves. He counted each rung, lungs burning, eyes darting upward to the vent plate above—sealed tight. No hiss yet. No sign of a purge.

He hoped he got there before it did.

Behind him, another voice shouted.

"I'm going in!"

Noah risked a glance down. A guard had jammed his assault rifle into the fan, arresting its spin. He hauled himself up into the duct and began the climb.

"Take him!" someone shouted below.

The guard aimed and fired, but it was wild. Climbing and shooting didn't mix. Bullets clanged around Noah, chewing up the walls, ricocheting past his shoulder.

As another bullet whipped past him, Noah stopped halfway, slung the digital camouflage sheet over the side of the ladder, and let it drift down.

It fluttered like a ghost in the shaft's stagnant air.

The climbing guard flinched. The sheet's imagery flickered and flashed at him. Reflexively, he raised his arms, almost losing his grip. As he scrambled to regain it, his pistol slipped from his hand and vanished into the dark below.

Snarling, he kept climbing.

Noah reached the top, gasping, his fingers probing the seam of the vent cover. Still locked. Still sealed. No purge yet—but it was coming. Soon.

Not soon enough.

A hand grabbed his boot.

Fingers clenched tight.

The unarmed guard had reached him, blood pumping in his temples, his face twisted in effort and fury.

Below him came more boots. More voices. More hands coming.

The hand yanked at his leg with surprising strength. Noah gritted his teeth, braced against the shaft wall, and kicked free. But the guard clung on.

No time.

Noah dropped.

He landed hard on the man, almost knocking him off feet wedging against the metal rungs. It was a claustrophobic crush of limbs and steel—sweat and breath and panic pressed into inches of space.

The guard snarled and swung. Noah ducked the punch and drove an elbow into his ribs. The man wheezed, nearly losing his grip on the ladder. But he held.

Noah jabbed again, this time into the guard's armpit, forcing another grunt. The ladder trembled beneath them as more boots clanged up from below.

Another soldier reached them, clawing for Noah's legs. A pistol barrel scraped into view—Noah shifted, pulling the guard's writhing body between himself and the weapon.

Shots cracked.

Sparks flew.

The bullet hit the metal inches from Noah's face and ricocheted off the shaft wall. He snarled and twisted the guard's arm behind him, using him as a shield again. He couldn't win a gunfight here. But he could delay.

More shouting below. Hands grabbing. One guard tried to climb around, but Noah spun to the opposite side of his human shield, constantly shifting, unpredictable, frustrating.

Then came the rumble.

A low, subterranean growl that vibrated through the soles of their boots.

Everyone froze.

The shaft trembled.

From below came a hiss—then a deep *whoomph* of pressure.

"The gas," someone whispered.

Noah looked down.

A distant glow surged upward through the shaft.

Then he looked up.

Above, the vent shuddered. Locking bolts disengaged with metallic clanks. The seam widened, bright daylight bleeding through the crack.

Noah turned back to the guard in his grip—eyes wild, mouth open to scream.

No time for mercy.

He drove two knuckles into the man's throat. A precise, surgical jab.

The man's eyes bulged. His grip faltered. He choked, spasmed —and fell.

Noah scrambled upward, legs pumping, fingers clawing for the widening opening. The vent yawned wider as the rush of chemicals roared from below.

He hurled himself up, shoulders scraping the edge, and tumbled onto the jungle floor beyond. Leaves slapped his face. His shoulder struck a rock. He rolled, coughing, hands grabbing for roots, mud, anything to get him clear.

Behind him, the shaft roared like a jet engine.

The guards desperately tried to follow—but it was too late.

A geyser of chemical gas burst from the vent, searing white and hissing like a demon unleashed.

Screams cut through the jungle. Men thrashed in the shaft mouth, arms and faces melting, lungs scorched by the vaporized cocktail.

They writhed. Clawed at nothing. Fell.

And then—silence.

The shaft fumed for another moment, the jungle air curling with toxic steam, and when the cloud dissipated, only the fan remained.

Beneath it, on the bent edges of the shaft, was nothing but blackened metal, fragments of clothing—and the gleam of bubbling, half-melted bone.

———

PUTORANA BASE | Siberia
23:27 KRAT | November 20

· · ·

THE EMERGENCY LIGHTS pulsed dimly in the hallway, red and blue flashes dancing across the walls of Putorana like shallow breaths. Frost edged the windows—without power, the outer corridors were already dropping below freezing.

Katya rounded the corner at full sprint, her boots echoing in the silence, hand pressed to her comms. Nothing. Esmerelda's voice was gone. No one was responding.

Then she saw her.

Norah.

Collapsed on the floor like a statue, every muscle seized, her eyes wide and straining with panic. She wasn't breathing. Her body was stone—rigid, immobile. The look on her face was worse than terror. It was awareness trapped inside paralysis.

Katya dropped to her knees beside her.

"Breaker code," she muttered, piecing it together. "He used a breaker code on her—"

Norah's eyes flared with desperate confirmation.

Katya grabbed her face gently, her voice sharp and certain. "Undo command Gamma five four nine Norah Echo two. Norah, come back," she said.

The words hit like a lightning strike.

Norah gasped, her whole body snapping loose as she sucked in air like a drowning woman breaching the surface. She rolled, coughing violently, hand clawing for her chest.

"Easy," Katya said, steadying her. "You're okay. You're okay."

"No," Norah croaked. "He—he—B3-17—he shut everything down. Hacked the terminal. Knew our files. He knew the breakers—"

Katya was already moving, yanking open the security panel beside the corridor exit.

Dead.

All systems offline. No override.

A low, growing thrum began to rise outside—barely audible at first, then unmistakable.

Rotors.

Katya ran. She burst from the doors into the snow-covered clearing behind the main complex. Wind whipped across her face. Ice stung her eyes.

Up ahead was the helipad. A single chopper was powered up and rising. Its searchlight passed over her—paused—then moved on.

Inside the cockpit was B3-17. He was expressionless. Untouched by anything that had just happened.

He watched her as the helicopter banked upward, then turned and vanished into the black Arctic sky, swallowed by the mountains.

Katya stood still, her fists clenched at her sides, lips pressed into a hard, white line.

Behind her, the base systems blinked out one by one.

And darkness fell across Camelot.

FIFTY-ONE

THE JUNGLE WAS MAYHEM.

Noah moved through it like a shadow made of muscle and rage. His body ached—burned, bruised, and bloodied. But he was alive. And that was more than those poor Black Sun saps melted into the ventilation shaft could say.

Above the trees, the distant thrum of rotor blades cut through the canopy. A Black Sun chopper on the hunt.

Behind him came the bark and snarl of hounds.

The soldiers were close.

Too close.

Noah picked up the pace, boots skidding over moss-slick roots. His breath came fast but measured. He didn't look back. Looking back was for people with choices. Noah only had one.

Run.

The jungle thinned. Up ahead, the ground dropped away into a yawning ravine—thirty meters across, at least. Sheer cliffs plunged into darkness, jagged stone glistening with damp. The roar of distant water echoed from below, hidden by drifting fog.

Noah stopped. Looked down.

No path. No handholds. No hope.

He was trapped.

He turned slowly as the brush behind him rustled.

Boots crunched over wet leaves. Twigs snapped. Laser sights danced like blood-red fireflies through the undergrowth.

Black Sun.

A full team emerged from the trees in a broad pincer—eight men in matte-black combat armor, faces masked by opaque visors, rifles raised and pointed right at him. Each step they took was rehearsed violence. Sleek black dogs strained against short leashes, their low growls vibrating in their chests, hackles raised.

"Drop your weapon," one of the men said.

Noah didn't move.

He had no weapon. The dart gun was long gone—lost in the sprint through the underbrush. All he had were his fists. Elbows. Feet. Knees. Teeth, if it came to it. Muscles with a thousand fights memorized into them. Movements hardwired into his bones. Instinct verging on the supernatural.

He glanced from soldier to soldier, face unreadable.

"Orders are to take him alive," said one of them, irritation creeping into his voice. "Kiel wants him for tests and then vivisection."

"Can't we just kill him now?" someone else muttered.

Noah exhaled, slow and controlled.

Then he heard something.

His eyes drifted to the trees behind them.

The jungle... was whispering.

A soft sound. Subtle at first. A rustle that wasn't wind. A call that wasn't quite animal. A distant whistle. Shrill. Too clean for birdsong. Then another. Then more—dozens. Dozens of signals layered over each other like a forest breathing in code.

The soldiers froze, heads turning.

"What the hell is that?"

The dogs backed up, whimpering now, tails tucked, ears flattened. They sensed something. Something primal. Something wrong.

Then the sound of the forest changed—rising in pitch and pressure. Birdcalls, chirps, trills—all mimicked by human mouths in perfect, eerie chorus.

The lead soldier turned toward the noise, just slightly.

That's when the first arrow struck.

It whistled through the air and straight through his neck. He collapsed soundlessly, blood fountaining in silence.

Then came the storm.

Arrows fell like monsoon rain. Hundreds. Their sound was a whisper and a scream all at once. They came from every direction—impossibly fast, impossibly accurate. They punched through armor. Shattered visors. Drove men backward into trees. Dogs yelped and dropped.

Chaos.

Noah didn't flinch and didn't move. Not an inch.

The arrows never touched him.

They flew around him as if the jungle itself had deemed him off-limits. And then the forest moved.

From behind trunks, under roots, down from the canopy and up from the soil, the Mapuche emerged. Dozens, then hundreds. Bare-chested, muscles coiled, faces streaked with ash and ocher, eyes sharp with the kind of knowing that cannot be taught.

Warriors.

They carried bows, obsidian knives, spears carved from wood older than history. Their breath came in unison. Their presence was thunder waiting to strike.

A chant began—deep and guttural. A hymn of old power and older wrath. It started as a whisper but swelled into something vast and uncontainable.

Overhead, a new sound screamed into the chaos.

A chopper.

Its rotors tore at the treetops as it swooped low, angling for a shot with its machine guns—blind to what it was flying into.

The Mapuche did not scatter.

They turned.

Raised their spears.

And threw.

Many of the spears missed. Others bounced off the craft. But one spear cracked the cockpit glass in a single, perfect blow. Another split one of the rotor blades with a clean, metallic shriek. A third found something vital—Noah didn't see what. But the bird stuttered. Coughed. And spun.

It clipped a branch, spiraled once, then dropped into the jungle in a roaring fireball. The explosion thundered through the trees. Flames licked the canopy. Birds shrieked and took flight.

The Mapuche howled in triumph. Their yell rose over the burning wreck, rising higher than the smoke.

Noah stood motionless as they approached. One of them— taller than the rest, skin like leather, eyes deep with storm and silence—stepped forward. He regarded Noah without fear or awe.

And nodded.

Noah returned the nod—wordless recognition between predators.

The warriors parted.

A path opened—not carved by blade or command but by something older. Respect. Kinship. A sense that this man, bloodied and hunted, belonged to the wild in the same way they did.

Noah stepped forward. As he passed the tall warrior, their shoulders brushed—solid as stone. It was like walking past a mountain. The man's scent was bark, smoke, and river stone, earthy and elemental.

At the edge of the tree line, the others began to move. Silent as ghosts, they fell in behind him, one by one. The jungle welcomed them back, folding shut behind them like a secret, until the path was gone and only the forest and the dead remained.

FIFTY-TWO

THE WIND HOWLED through the broken seals of the old corridors.

The recruits stood gathered beneath the flickering ceiling lights of the central hangar. Their breath bloomed in white clouds. Coats, gloves, wool-lined boots—none of it was enough. The heating system was dead, Esmerelda was still offline, and the base had sunk into its bones.

Katya stood before them, arms crossed, her breath steady despite the temperature. She looked at each of them—Norah, Lula, Tao, Zina, Imani, Gregor. All tired. All changed. No longer trainees. No longer children.

"Training is over for the time being," Katya said simply.

Nobody spoke.

"Now for the first time, you will enter the field. Because we are going after B3-17."

Lula raised an eyebrow. "Dead or alive?"

"Alive," Katya replied, voice flat.

Lula frowned. "Ohh." She crossed her arms, puffing into her

scarf. "I think after what he did to Norah, he should definitely die."

"He's being manipulated," Katya said. "And he's only a child."

Norah shifted. "Didn't seem much like a child an hour ago when he had me face-down on the floor unable to move or breathe."

Zina nodded. "Yeah. And what the hell did he do to her, anyway?"

"Breaker," Imani said. "That's what Norah said he called it. Some kind of codeword initiation."

Katya exhaled through her nose slowly. She uncrossed her arms and took a small step forward.

"There's something you all need to understand," she said quietly. "About who you are. About what the Council did to you."

She placed two fingers gently against her chest.

"The Council installed something inside me once. A control node—implanted in the lining of my heart. A kill switch. Wally tried to get it out. So did the best surgeons we could find. It's still there."

She looked at Norah. "It's why I knew what had happened to you. I know what helplessness feels like."

Katya turned back to the group. "Each of you... has something similar. Not in your hearts. In your brains."

A ripple passed through the group—sharp intakes of breath, shifting feet, darted glances.

"They're called breakers," Katya went on. "Neural locks, embedded before we ever found you. They're dangerous. And they're incredibly hard to detect—let alone remove—without risking permanent damage."

"Wait," Tao said, pale. "Are you saying... we've been walking around with kill switches in our heads?"

"Yours aren't designed to kill," Katya said. "Just... control.

Paralyze. Stop you, if you disobeyed. It's less likely to cause permanent damage or death than what they placed in me."

"Feels like death," Norah muttered. "It was like drowning in your own body."

"And there's no way you can get them out?" Lulu asked.

"Noah refused to operate," Katya said. "Said the risk was too great. So Wally's been studying them in secret. Trying to crack them without hurting you."

"So we're just... stuck with them?" Zina said.

"For now," Katya said. "But trust me. One day, we will remove them. And when we do... no one will ever control you again."

Silence stretched between them.

Katya let it hang. Then nodded once. "Get your gear."

The group began to break, scattering toward the racks and lockers lining the far walls. Gloves snapped tight. Clips checked. Coats zipped.

As Norah strapped a sidearm to her thigh, Tao appeared beside her. His cheeks were pink from the cold, his tablet clutched to his chest.

"I think I may have found a way to disable him," he said quietly.

Norah turned. "Disable who?"

"B3-17."

She straightened. "Talk."

Tao flicked the screen awake. "After what happened to you, I went back through the logs. B3-17's room terminal. He made contact with a sound recording—some kind of static loop. At first it sounded like noise, but the waveform wasn't random."

He showed her a spectral graph—jagged, symmetrical.

"It's a patterned signal. Think of it like a sonic QR code. White noise embedded with encoded subharmonics. Specific rhythmic patterns that trigger synaptic responses in his brain."

Norah blinked. "You're saying... it reprograms him?"

Tao nodded. "His brain's been wired—probably since development—to recognize these signals. When they play, it unlocks stored instructions. Like a BIOS update. But through sound instead of a device."

"Okay..." Norah frowned. "So what does that mean for us?"

"It means," Tao said, tapping his screen again, "I might have a sound of my own to play B3-17."

Norah stared at him.

Then nodded.

"Good."

They turned back toward the others. The cold still bit at their skin, but something new burned inside them now.

Resolve.

FIFTY-THREE

ROME BLED PANIC.

Sirens pulsed through narrow streets like heartbeats, echoing off stone walls older than most empires. Helicopters circled overhead, sweeping rooftops with piercing white light. Telescreens in every café, piazza, and train station flashed the same image on loop:

WANTED FOR TERRORISM
CAMELOT AGENTS IDENTIFIED
NEIL BLESSING | JENNY BLESSING

Jenny adjusted the stolen scarf over her mouth as the image scrolled across a bakery window. She barely glanced at it from the shadows of the doorway they hid in. She didn't need to. She knew the photo. Knew the angle of her own face, mid-shout, frozen in time like a statue of guilt.

Neil leaned beside her, hands jammed into a courier's jacket he'd robbed from the back of a chair, a wool cap he'd found in the pocket pulled low. His jaw was clenched tightly. They hadn't slept in over a day.

Across the street, a small café TV played the aftermath of the assassination on mute. The Pope's collapsed body. The screaming crowd. And behind it all, Sebastian Vale's expressionless face, cast across Vatican stone like a new Messiah.

They left the doorway and turned down a side alley, footsteps soft. Every movement calculated. They didn't speak—not here, not now. It was too dangerous.

They had spent the night ducking through Rome's darkened streets, hearts hammering, breathing low and shallow. Every shadow had been an ally, every distant siren a threat. Helicopter spotlights had swept through alleys, their searchlights scanning for the two fugitives, slicing through the dark in harsh, rhythmic arcs. Armored vans prowled the thoroughfares, filled with squads of heavily armed police, their weapons glinting coldly in the flickering streetlights. Neil and Jenny had moved swiftly, silently, always seconds from discovery, barely escaping one close call after another beneath the oppressive night sky.

Now, finally, after a night of creeping their way across the city, they were at their destination.

The alley opened into a dead-end courtyard—wrought-iron gates ahead, a dry fountain at the center, pigeons fluttering into motion at their approach.

A woman leaned against the gate's frame, smoking a hand-rolled cigarette.

She wore a long coat, black leather gloves, and mirrored sunglasses despite the early gloom.

"Marta," Neil said softly.

Marta Bellini took a final drag and dropped the cigarette to the stones. "You two look like hell."

"We feel it, too," Jenny said.

Marta pulled a key from her pocket and unlocked the side gate. "Follow me. Quietly."

They slipped through into the guts of the city. Twisting alleys. Laundry lines. Narrow stairs clamped between buildings too close to breathe. Marta moved like someone born to this place—always one step ahead, never looking back.

"How bad is it?" Neil asked once they were two floors underground in what appeared to be an abandoned maintenance tunnel.

"Worse than you think," Marta replied. "Interpol. Europol. Carabinieri. Local watchlists. Every train station, airport, and bus depot between here and Calais is on alert."

"Vale's framing is holding," Jenny muttered. "People believe it."

"They want to believe it," Marta said. "They're scared. He gave them someone to blame for their fear."

She pulled open a rusted service door. Behind it was a stairwell, crumbling but intact.

"Up here. My contact's waiting."

They climbed in silence. At the top, a former dentist's office had been turned into a makeshift safehouse—maps, burner phones, cash, forged documents in neat stacks.

A wiry man in his sixties greeted them without smiling. "Take these," he said, handing over a pair of Vatican sanitation uniforms.

Jenny raised an eyebrow. "You serious?"

"You want out or not?"

They changed quickly. Marta handed Jenny a red janitor's badge. "Security's been loosened slightly since the assassination. Enough chaos that background checks are being done after entry. You'll pose as sanitation workers for an emergency city directive. Truck's waiting in Trastevere."

"And after that?"

"We improvise."

It took them two hours to reach Trastevere, winding through the labyrinth of Rome's backstreets—switching routes twice to avoid roadblocks and once to lose a tail they weren't even sure was real. The city had become a cage of stone and surveillance, each alley an artery pulsing with suspicion.

The sanitation truck was old, loud, and smelled like fermented bleach. Perfect. Its battered frame had seen better decades, but the permits on the windshield were freshly forged, gleaming beneath the grime.

Still, she fired right up, and a minute later, they were on the road.

In the passenger seat, Jenny adjusted the fake beard that now itched along her jawline. Her hair had been slicked back and tucked beneath the collar of her cap. Shadows filled in the masculine cut of her cheekbones, and she'd bulked her figure with padding beneath the faded gray overalls. Marta's contact had even added fake grease under her nails.

Neil glanced sideways at her as she practiced adjusting the rearview mirror like a bored municipal worker. "You're still beautiful," he murmured, a smirk tugging at one corner of his mouth. "Beard or no beard."

Jenny didn't look at him. "Keep talking like that and I'll grow one for real."

"Promises, promises."

They both went quiet as the military checkpoint loomed into view—an ugly scar of concrete and barbed wire carved across the road that lead out of the city. Sandbags, armed soldiers, a portable X-ray scanner, and a parked drone pulsing with blue lights.

Three guards stood in the road, assault rifles slung across their chests. One of them raised a fist, signaling them to stop. The sanitation truck crawled forward, its diesel engine coughing black smoke into the air.

Jenny kept her eyes forward, her cap pulled low. Her heartbeat thudded in her ears, but her expression didn't shift.

Neil was just as nervous. He was clean-shaven now, his beard —which had been real—shaved off to keep him from matching the photos flooding every screen in the city. He'd also smeared dark oil beneath his eyes to change his features, and a bruised contact lens in his left eye gave it a sickly yellow hue. His jaw was set hard, shoulders coiled tight. He looked like a typical municipal worker who hated his job.

One of the soldiers approached the driver's side. Neil didn't blink. He rolled the window and tapped a clipboard against the rim of the door.

"We're off to the recycling plant," he said in perfect Italian. "Got our papers here."

The guard frowned. His eyes flicked between the clipboard and Neil's face. A second guard began circling around the vehicle, eyes scanning the undercarriage.

Jenny's hand inched toward the dashboard, where a pistol was duct-taped beneath the console.

The first guard grunted. His scanner beeped against the badge pinned to the clipboard. Still, he looked unconvinced. "There's no sanitation scheduled for Trastevere."

"There wasn't a papal assassination scheduled either," Neil snapped like an irritated Roman before performing the sign of the cross over his ratty uniform. "That's why it couldn't get done yesterday. Not with the city locked down. So they sent us in today to fetch all the missed pick-ups."

The soldier stared at him.

Then, annoyed and uncertain, he finally exhaled and waved them through. No more questions.

Neil rolled up the window and put the truck in gear, letting the silence ring in their ears for one long, aching second as they moved off.

In the rearview, the checkpoint shrank behind them.

Then Jenny let out a slow breath. "That was too easy."

"You say that like it's a bad thing," Neil muttered, eyes still fixed on the side mirror and road behind them.

Jenny's hand remained hovering just beneath the dash. "We'll know soon enough."

And soon enough, they did.

An hour later, north of Rome, they had traded the sanitation truck for a battered silver Fiat, picked up from a tired carport behind a shuttered pizzeria. The plates had been switched. The windows were streaked with enough dust to partially hide their faces.

Neil drove, hunched low over the wheel, his eyes pinned to the road.

Jenny sat shotgun, boots propped on the dash, the fake beard now gone but her face still shadowed beneath a knit cap. She'd scrubbed the grease from under her nails but left the dirt on her cheeks.

Outside the windows, the land rolled past in waves of olive groves and old stone fences. The sky had begun to bruise with twilight.

They were halfway to the Apennines. Past most major checkpoints. But still inside the net.

Jenny broke the silence. "Any idea where we go next?"

Neil didn't take his eyes off the winding road ahead. "North. Into the mountains. I've got a friend—former partisan. Still owes me for a job me and Noah pulled in Milan. He's got a cabin near the border. Remote. Quiet. We'll regroup there."

Jenny nodded slowly. "You get the feeling we're running out of time?"

Neil's hands tightened on the wheel.

"Yeah," he said quietly. "I do."

The silence returned, stretching out between them like old fabric—familiar and worn thin.

Jenny watched the fields blur past, golden in the dying light. Her voice, when it came again, was softer. "When the Council fell... I thought maybe it'd get easier. Like we'd bought ourselves a little peace."

Neil didn't respond. He just kept driving, the wheel steady in his grip.

"But it wasn't peace, was it?" she said. "It was just the beginning of the next thing falling apart. And then the next. And now we're here—again. Running. Fighting. Losing pieces of ourselves every time we survive."

Neil's jaw worked slightly. But still he said nothing.

Jenny turned to face him fully. "I've been thinking about it more lately. About the future. About family. About... motherhood."

That made him glance at her.

She caught it and gave him a faint smile. "Yeah. I know. Not the best timing. But it keeps coming back. This idea of something else. Something after."

Neil reached across the seat, his hand warm as it closed over hers.

"I've been thinking about us," she said. "About calling it a day. Disappearing somewhere. Starting fresh. Starting a family."

He looked over again, longer this time. Searching her face for any sign of hesitation.

"Maybe it's not such a bad thing if Camelot falls apart," Jenny went on. "Maybe it needs to. Let someone else save the world for once."

Neil swallowed, his throat tight. "You really mean all that?"

Jenny nodded. "I just want a normal life for once," she said. "With you."

A quiet beat passed.

She looked out the window again, her voice distant, filled with memory. "All that stuff with B3-17... watching you with him. I don't know. It stirred something. For the first time in years, I felt something other than the fight. I felt warmth, Neil. I felt the warmth of a possible future for the two of us. One where we don't have to fight or run or be hurt anymore."

He let go of her hand and gently guided her head to his shoulder as she leaned in. She let out a breath she hadn't known she was holding.

They drove like that, north through the spine of Italy, the mountains rising to greet them—silent and ancient and patient.

Whatever waited at the end of the road, for a little while at least, there was only this.

Only them.

FIFTY-FOUR

UNITED NATIONS HEADQUARTERS | NEW YORK CITY | 08:00 EST | NOVEMBER 21

RAIN STREAKED the glass dome of the General Assembly, tracing rivulets down its curved surface like veins over a great, sleeping eye. Thunder rolled over Manhattan, distant but insistent, a low growl that vibrated through the steel bones of the building.

Inside, the hall simmered with tension.

The great chamber—circular and austere—was lit with a cold, institutional glow that seemed to flatten every expression and sharpen every silence. Flags from every member nation stood in solemn formation along the walls, their bright colors muted in the stormlight. They hung like sentinels, unmoving, impartial, watching.

Delegates filled every seat, a mosaic of tailored suits, tense shoulders, and furrowed brows. The air was thick with competing languages, flickering through the murmur of real-time translation —soft robotic voices muttering over earpieces, overlapping with whispered strategy and the occasional sharp intake of breath.

Somewhere, a microphone crackled, feeding a whine of feedback through already overstretched audio channels.

Security stood at every entry point, stone-faced in charcoal uniforms, their earpieces blinking with coded signals. In the upper galleries, aides scribbled on tablets, and journalists watched like vultures waiting for a sign of carrion.

At the center of it all, beneath the haloed canopy of the dome, stood a woman in a slate-gray suit, sharp-shouldered and composed.

Secretary-General Anaí Salcedo adjusted her earpiece with two fingers and gave the chamber a long, measured look—neither cold nor warm but clear.

She raised the gavel, the wood worn from decades of decisions that never quite changed the world.

The hall fell into a brittle silence.

She brought it down once. A sharp crack.

The session began.

"This emergency session of the United Nations is now in order," she said. "Item One: Sanction Resolution 3187-B—designation of Camelot as a rogue, non-state terror organization."

The room shifted. Postures straightened. A tense silence fell.

Salcedo continued, voice firm. "As of this morning, evidence has been presented by multiple member states—video footage, intercepted communications, and eyewitness accounts—implicating Camelot agents in the assassination of His Holiness Pope Clement XIV."

A murmur ran through the chamber.

"Further, they are implicated in coordinated attacks across Bolivia, Argentina, and Italy, resulting in civilian deaths and structural destabilization."

She let the silence hang. "This council will vote. But first, we will hear final arguments."

The Russian delegate stood. "We have long suspected Camelot of operating beyond the boundaries of legality. Now the world sees the truth. They are not saviors. They are a weapon unleashed by arrogant hands."

The French ambassador rose next. "The footage is compelling. But we must ask—who gains from this chaos? Camelot, or those who control the narrative?"

Salcedo raised a hand. "Order."

The American delegate, gray-haired and glassy-eyed, leaned forward. "It is not just the Pope. It's the way Camelot has acted like some rogue agency. Ever since E & E collapsed, Noah Wolf has run them with total disregard for international law."

The Indian representative spoke up. "We condemn vigilantism. But the world must also remember: It was Camelot who brought down the Council. Do we now forget that overnight?"

"Camelot," the Brazilian ambassador said flatly, "was never a government. It was a bunch of bandits with guns."

Salcedo tapped the gavel. "Enough. We proceed to vote."

Lights dimmed. A screen behind the secretary-general lit up.

One by one, nations cast their decision.

United Kingdom: No.

People's Republic of China: Yes.

United States: Yes.

India: No.

France: ...Yes.

Germany: Yes.

South Africa: Yes.

Brazil: Yes.

Japan: Yes.

Russia: Yes.

...

It continued. One by one. Fifty. Sixty. Seventy nations.

The yeses vastly outweighing the nos.

Salcedo looked down at her display. "The motion passes one hundred eighty to thirteen."

She gave the final strike of the gavel.

"Camelot is now designated a rogue terror entity. Member states are authorized to detain known operatives and suspend diplomatic protections. This meeting is adjourned."

FIFTY-FIVE

THE ARGO SLICED through the Italian foothills like a blade through green velvet—silent, seamless, obscenely fast. Snow dusted the trees outside, blurring into white streaks as the train surged north.

Inside the lounge car, Sebastian Vale sat in a high-backed leather chair, legs crossed, a book open but unread on his lap. The carriage was warm, perfumed with polished wood and old wine. A fire glowed softly in an ornamental hearth—more aesthetic than functional, like most of the Argo.

Across from him stood Sophia, perfectly still, perfectly silent.

Vale turned a page without looking at it. "Do you know why this train has no name on its manifest?"

Sophia didn't answer.

"Because names are concessions," he said. "To bureaucracy. To borders. This"—he gestured around the room—"is above all that. We move without scrutiny. Without question. The Council built this rail line for secrecy. I inherited it."

She remained silent.

He looked up, studying her face. "You're tense."

"No, Father."

"Lying to me doesn't suit you, Sophia." He closed the book gently. "There's a tremor in your left wrist. Micro-spasms. Stress-induced. It began after Rome."

Sophia lowered her eyes.

Vale's voice remained calm, almost kind. "Is it guilt? About the old man—the Pope?"

Still no answer.

He stood. Walked slowly around her. "I gave you purpose, Sophia. When I found you in that lab. Broken. Discarded. I took you in. Gave you shape. Voice. Power."

He stopped just behind her. Whispered.

"And I can unmake you just as easily."

Her spine stiffened.

"Recite your anchor," he said.

She hesitated. A fraction of a second. Then, tonelessly: "I belong to the Voice. My will is the Voice. My duty is to the Voice."

"And who is the Voice?"

"You are the Voice."

"Again."

She repeated it.

He smiled. "Good. You're still mine. Still my Sophia."

Then, as if nothing had happened, he returned to his chair.

The comms terminal lit up on the sideboard.

Vale accepted the connection. Viktor Rausch appeared on the screen—half-lit, jaw clenched, fatigue etched deep into his face.

"Noah Wolf is alive," Rausch said without preamble. "Confirmed. He escaped the lab. Took down a troop transport, likely killed my entire second team in the gorge. The natives are helping him."

Vale exhaled slowly through his nose. "And yet you still draw breath, Viktor. Curious."

Rausch didn't rise to the bait. "You said we underestimated him. I didn't. I just didn't bring enough guns."

"You never do," Vale murmured, pouring himself a drink.

He swirled the glass, then looked back to the screen. "So. Let's correct that."

Rausch leaned forward. "Orders?"

"Send everything."

Rausch blinked. "You mean—"

"I mean everything, Viktor." Vale's voice turned razor-sharp. "Burn the jungle. Salt the ground. Bring it down on his head if you have to."

"And the Mapuche?"

"Collateral. This ends now."

The screen crackled, then went black.

Vale took a slow sip of wine.

Sophia remained where she stood, blue eyes forward, but her fingers curled ever so slightly against her thigh.

Vale didn't miss it.

"Careful," he said lightly. "Hands like that could suggest disobedience. Or worse—doubt."

She stilled them instantly.

He smiled again, almost gently. "You'll get another chance to kill her. The redhead. Jenny Blessing."

Sophia's lips barely moved. "Understood."

"Good," Vale said.

Outside, the mountains loomed.

The Argo kept running.

So did the war.

FIFTY-SIX

THE JUNGLE SMELLED like smoke and pine needles
and the heavy press of rain—not yet falling but building. It clung
to the canopy, gathering weight in the clouds.

Beneath a sagging canvas tarp stretched between two leaning
trees, Noah sat with his elbows resting on his knees, shoulders
hunched in thought. He hadn't spoken in over five minutes. The
only sounds were the faint rustle of distant birds and the slow sip
of Wally's tin cup, bitter yerba cooling against his palm.

Wally didn't push. He just waited.

"They didn't make me," Noah said at last, voice low. "Not
exactly. But I wasn't born either. Not in the way people mean it."

Wally turned toward him, but he said nothing.

"It was Genesis," Noah went on. "A Council project. I always
knew that part. I just didn't know who was behind it. Didn't
know it was him." His jaw clenched. "Kiel."

Wally's lips thinned. He looked down into his cup.

"He told you this?" he asked.

"Yeah," Noah continued. "Said I was his greatest creation.

'Art,' he called me. Like he'd sculpted me out of bone and flesh. Like I was his."

Wally shifted slightly, the tarp creaking overhead as a fat droplet of water plopped against it. "You know, I found something, after the fall," he said quietly. "In the archives. Council data that survived the purge. I saw his name. Kiel. Attached to the Genesis program. But I didn't know how to tell you."

Noah blinked slowly. "How long have you known?"

"Few months," Wally admitted. "I kept hoping I'd find something else. Some other explanation. Something to... soften it."

Noah let out a breath that wasn't quite a laugh. "There's no soft version, Wally. I was made. By a mad scientist... Oh, and a neo-Nazi as well."

He gave an ironic smile.

Wally put down his cup and leaned closer, resting a weathered hand on Noah's shoulder. It stayed there—gentle, solid, real.

"That doesn't mean he owns you," Wally said. "Doesn't mean what he wanted is what you are."

Noah stared at the forest floor, at the wet leaves and black soil and the small, broken seed pod by his boot. "He said I was designed without flaws. No guilt. No sentiment. Just logic. Obedience."

Wally's voice was steady. "Then he failed. Every move you make is your own."

They sat in silence for a beat. Rain ticked faintly across the treetops above, the storm not yet breaking but coming.

Then something happened. Something that took all their attention.

A low roar rolled through the jungle. Like thunder. But wrong.

Noah stood fast.

Above them, two jets screamed across the sky—cutting low over the canopy, rolling in jagged waves across the treetops. Sleek, black shapes against the bruised blue, their undercarriages glinted like teeth catching sunlight.

Then—less than a mile away—the jungle lit up.

From the bellies of the aircraft, long silver canisters fell in slow, elegant arcs. They burst open midair, trailing tongues of napalm that painted the sky with fire. The flames hit the forest like it was Judgment Day—great blooms of liquid fire devouring green into searing orange. Trees ignited instantly. Branches cracked, birds shrieked and scattered, silhouettes vanishing into smoke. Somewhere, the distant roar of a panther ended in a scream.

Black smoke churned upward, thick and oily, forming columns that clawed toward the sky like the spirits of the dead.

The Mapuche gathered on the ridge in stunned silence, the flames of their ancestral lands reflected in wide, tearless eyes. No panic. No screams. Only stillness—terrible and heavy. One of the elders, skin like cracked bark, sank to his knees. A little girl clung to her mother's leg, her face blank.

Wally swore quietly, his voice thick. "They're burning the whole region."

Noah's hands curled into fists. His voice came flat but full of heat. "No witnesses. No history. Just ash."

A hand tapped Noah's arm.

He turned.

A warrior stood beside him—broad-shouldered, thick with old muscle, chest crisscrossed with the white scars of decades of survival. His face was weathered, strong, his hair pulled back with a simple leather tie. Eyes dark and deep as ancient roots.

He spoke quickly, voice low and forceful—Mapudungun, rhythmic and sharp. The cadence of a language older than the European conquest that attempted to wash them of their own lands.

Wally listened, then nodded.

"He says you need to come. There's something you must see."

Noah frowned. "What is it?"

Wally glanced back at the warrior, who gestured again—

urgently this time, pointing deeper into the jungle, away from the fire.

Wally translated, "He insists you go with him."

Noah gave a short nod.

The warrior turned and began moving swiftly down a path, disappearing into the underbrush.

Noah followed.

Wally cast one last look at the burning canopy, then fell in behind.

They moved quickly, half a kilometer through thick brush, skirting the fireline. Smoke hung low and heavy, curling between the trunks in dense ribbons. The sun was no more than a dull red disc behind a veil of black haze. Ash drifted in the air like dark snow—flakes of the dying jungle.

The air stank of scorched earth and the oily aroma of napalm. Every breath tasted of heat and the end.

Mapuche warriors filtered silently from the trees around them, joining the path without a word. They carried bows, blowguns, spears, machetes, old Kalashnikovs scavenged from who-knows-where. Some had cartridge belts slung across bare chests; others bore simple leather satchels stuffed with foraged explosives. Their faces were streaked with soot and war paint—red, black, ocher.

As they walked, a few began to speak. Short, clipped phrases in Mapudungun, their voices low but urgent.

Wally kept pace beside Noah, listening carefully before translating.

"They say this is the moment. That the forest has bled enough. They say it is time to cut the rot from the land. They say the fire is not death—it is a signal."

Noah didn't reply. He just nodded once and kept moving.

Then, just ahead, a shape rose from the undergrowth—strange and angular, hidden by rock and thorn and brush.

A warrior reached forward, pulling back a camouflaged tarp.

And there it was.

An entire weapons cache, buried in plain sight.

Crates stacked three high, marked with serial codes, heat-resistant foam still packed around them. He spotted EMP grenades—small, dull-gray spheres with blue primer rings. Several belts of 7.62mm ammunition, neatly coiled. Shotguns. Bolt cutters. A pair of Heckler & Koch UMP submachine guns. And nestled on its side, a crate of magnetic mines with faded US Army stenciling still visible.

And parked beside them like some resting mechanical beast, a Eurocopter Tiger UHT—German-made, heavily modified.

The Black Sun insignia stood out on the side of it—a black sun wheel made out of 'SS' symbols.

The cockpit was shattered inward, the glass webbed with cracks and a spear jutting through it like a macabre monument. The pilot's body was gone, but dried blood clung to the dashboard and seat harness like old rust.

The side door of the chopper hung open.

Inside, a mounted M134 minigun sat ready, its rotating barrels gleaming, the ammo belt already fed into the chamber. Twin Hydra 70 rocket pods lined the stubby wings—compact, deadly. Dry leaves littered the inside of the cockpit.

Noah stepped forward slowly. His hand trailed along the gunmetal fuselage, feeling the pitted steel beneath his fingertips.

"Where did you get this?" he asked, his voice quiet.

The scarred warrior beside him simply shrugged. He said something in Mapudungun—rough and dry, like gravel.

Wally translated, "It landed. They came out. We were faster."

Noah allowed himself a faint smile. "Right."

Wally let out a low whistle. "She's combat-ready."

"Then she's ready enough," Noah said, resting a hand on the side-mounted launcher.

Behind them, the jungle still burned. The smoke painted the sky black. But here, beneath the ash and ruin, something else stirred.

Resolve.

The Mapuche stood together now, weapons slung, faces lit by the reflection of distant flames. A young warrior stepped forward and spoke with quiet force. His voice carried the weight of generations.

Wally listened, then turned to Noah.

"He says: 'This is our land. We will not die in the shadows. We will rise with fire in our fists. Help us, and we end this together.'"

Noah looked at the flames flickering in the young man's eyes, then at the cracked windshield of the stolen gunship.

His voice came steady and final.

"We have one shot left at that lab. One shot to tear the spine out of Black Sun before this whole forest becomes a grave."

He turned back to the others.

"And we're going to take it."

FIFTY-SEVEN

THE CHOPPER CUT through the cold air like a knife through glass. Katya sat at the controls, knuckles pale against the cyclic. Her eyes fixed to the horizon.

Behind her, the recruits were silent.

Tao clutched his tablet like a talisman. Zina stared out the window, her face unreadable. Gregor's gaze hung on his boots, unmoving. Imani quietly counted the pop rivets lining the helicopter's interior. Lula bounced one leg in place, jittering with barely contained energy.

Norah sat stillest of all, her jaw tight, fingers clenched in her lap.

The wind outside howled across the steppe—endless white scrub and frozen grass, stretching for miles. Nothing moved.

The radio crackled.

"Putorana Base to Falcon-One. Do you read?"

Katya keyed the mic. "Go ahead."

"Still no main power. Heating offline. Esmerelda remains dormant. But we've jury-rigged a signal off an auxiliary solar array."

Katya glanced at the panel. "What did you find?"

A pause.

"It's official. UN vote passed. Unanimous."

Katya's eyes narrowed.

"Camelot has been classified as a rogue organization. We're now on every international terror registry. NATO, INTERPOL, FVEY—everyone."

Zina exhaled sharply. Gregor swore. Tao locked up like he hadn't heard right.

Lula cracked her neck. "Guess we're famous. Or infamous. Whatever."

Katya didn't speak. She simply continued in the same heading. Outside, the shadows of dusk crept across the land like ink in water.

An hour later, the chopper touched down on a flat plateau of pale earth and wind-worn stone. The landscape was vast and empty. There were no landmarks. No fences. Just a shifting horizon where sky and land blurred together in desolate harmony.

Katya powered down the rotors. The engine whined, sputtered, then gave way to a hollow stillness broken only by the ticking of cooling metal.

She climbed out into the cold. The recruits followed, blinking against the sudden brightness of the overcast sky, their boots crunching over dry gravel and cracked clay. The wind hit them immediately—cutting, dry, and relentless. It smelled of dust.

Before them sat a second helicopter—sleek, modern, matte-black. The Camelot sigil stood out on the side.

It was B3-17's helicopter.

And it was empty.

Katya stepped toward it, eyes narrowing. "So this is as far as he got," she murmured, running a hand along the hull. "But he's not here. So where could he have gone?"

Zina scanned the horizon, squinting into the rolling golden expanse. "This is nowhere. Literally. No roads. No structures. Just... space."

Norah moved forward slowly, drawn toward something she couldn't name. "He came here on purpose."

"Why?" Tao asked, hugging his coat tighter around him.

No one answered.

The question hung in the air, unmoored. The wind rushed across the steppe, bending the sparse grass and sending grains of dust skittering along the ground.

Gregor turned in a slow circle. "He could see anyone coming from twenty klicks away."

"Maybe that's the point," Imani said. "Nothing to see. Nothing to hear. Nothing to hide behind."

Katya walked to the edge of the plateau and stopped. She stared out at the endless horizon—an ocean of land stretching in every direction, unbroken and unmoved.

"Then let's go get him," she said at last.

FIFTY-EIGHT

THE ROAD WOUND through the mountains like a scar. Snow clung to the edges of the tarmac, melting into slurry beneath the tires of the battered Fiat. The headlights barely pierced the alpine fog. The world outside was all darkness and stone and a sense of falling sky.

Neil drove in silence, both hands steady on the wheel, eyes fixed on the twisting road ahead. The engine rattled beneath them, dogged and tired but still running.

Beside him, Jenny slept, her head resting against his shoulder, cheek nestled into the fabric of his coat.

The road narrowed to a gravel path, winding through larch trees and crumbling stone walls dusted in frost. A dim orange glow flickered ahead—lamplight behind frosted windows. The cabin was tucked against the mountainside, old and silent, smoke curling from a metal chimney like breath in the cold.

Neil eased the car to a stop beside it and cut the engine.

He glanced down at Jenny and gently nudged her. "We're here."

She stirred, blinking against the weight of sleep. Her voice was hoarse. "Already?"

"Come on," Neil said. "Let's go."

She sat up slowly, rubbing her eyes as she opened the door. Cold air rushed in, and she stepped out onto the gravel.

Marta Bellini opened the cabin door before they could knock.

She stood in the frame—coat unbuttoned, sleeves rolled, pistol holstered at her side. Her expression was all sharp angles and tired determination.

"Took you long enough," she said. "Get in. We've got work to do."

Inside, the cabin was warm. A woodstove burned low in the corner, casting flickering light across a table scattered with maps, travel documents, and an open weapons case. The air smelled of pine, oil, and the metallic tang of gun-cleaning solvent.

A set of travel clothes lay folded on the counter. Next to them sat stacks of forged passports, customs stamps, and burner IDs, laminated and crisp.

Jenny picked one up. Her new name was printed in bold: medical relief personnel, under WHO authority.

Marta tossed another to Neil. "You're medical couriers. Technically Czech, if anyone asks. It should be enough to get you over the border."

Jenny raised an eyebrow. "And after that?"

Marta nodded toward a crate in the corner. "Weapons. Just in case you need to shoot your way out."

Neil crossed to the crate and flipped it open. "Subtle as ever."

Inside were two suppressed pistols, a compact SMG with a collapsable stock, a sniper rifle, and a satchel containing plastic explosive and a detonator. All of it laid out in foam, each piece pristine—cleaned, oiled, loaded. No serials. No questions.

As he inspected the rifle, Marta leaned against the table, arms folded.

"You hear about the UN resolution?"

Jenny glanced up. "Yeah. We caught it on the radio."

Neil's face darkened. "Unanimous condemnation. Sanctions. Freeze everything. It wouldn't be the first time we had to go on the run."

Marta nodded once. "That's the shape of it. The world's moving on. They want this over, neatly filed and forgotten. Go back to being sheep."

A beat of silence passed. Jenny looked at her. "What about Camelot? Any word?"

Marta shook her head, eyes distant. "Putorana's gone dark. And no one's heard from Noah in almost three days."

The air shifted in the room—something cold creeping beneath the heat of the stove.

Neil looked up. "Three days?"

Marta met his gaze. "Whatever's happening down there... he's either buried deep or gone completely off the grid."

Jenny tightened her grip on the passport. Her voice was low. "If I know Noah, he'll be up to his neck in it, but he'll be fine. In the end."

Marta didn't argue.

She just turned back to the weapons case and locked it shut. "Then we'd better move before our necks are buried."

Marta crossed to the door, grabbing her coat from a peg on the wall.

"Come on," she said. "There's something else you need to see."

Jenny and Neil followed her out into the cold.

Behind the cabin, half-sheltered beneath a slanted lean-to built from rough timber and corrugated metal, sat a bulky shape draped in a heavy canvas tarp.

Marta crouched and grabbed the edge of it. "You'll need speed to get there on time."

She yanked the tarp back.

Beneath it were two Ducati Panigale V4Rs. Matte-black, sleek, angular machines, every curve designed for velocity. The tires were wrapped in insulated traction sleeves, prepped for cold asphalt and mountain roads.

Jenny stepped forward, fingers trailing across the chassis. "This should get us there on time."

"I trust you know how to ride one."

"Yes," Jenny said, turning to her. "You can certainly trust in that."

Marta went to reply to this when her phone buzzed. She pulled it from her pocket, glanced at the screen—froze—then picked it up. "Bellini."

She spoke in rapid-fire Italian, clipped and urgent. Jenny and Neil watched her closely, unable to follow the words but recognizing the tone: mission time.

Marta's brow furrowed. She nodded once. Then again. Then hung up.

"What is it?" Jenny asked.

Marta looked at them both.

"One of my contacts just confirmed it. Rail ops east of Lago Blu. Unregistered train made a refuel stop ten minutes ago. No manifest, no logs. Sebastian Vale's name isn't on anything—but we know what it is."

Neil straightened. "The Argo."

Marta nodded. "It's close. And vulnerable. Heading north. About five klicks away through mountain road. You go fast enough, you'll be able to cut it off at the Ponte Viadotto—the old viaduct. The railway line goes right underneath about thirty klicks away."

Jenny was already moving toward the bikes.

"Then we don't wait."

Marta tossed her a helmet.

Jenny caught it mid-stride.

Neil grabbed the second and swung onto the other Ducati. "Let's finish this."

Marta eyed the bikes, then turned a sharp look back toward the cabin.

"I'll get the guns," she said, voice flat and final.

"Yes," Jenny said. "We'll definitely need guns."

Boots crunched in the frost as Marta jogged off.

Jenny and Neil locked eyes, a quiet weight passing between them.

"You ready for this, babe?" Jenny asked.

Neil gave a tight nod. "You know me. Ready as always."

His serious look cracked into a small smirk—just a flicker, but enough.

It made her smile. "God, I love you."

She leaned in, lips brushing his—

But before the kiss could land, Marta reappeared from the shadows, the sniper rifle slung across her shoulder, a pistol in one hand, a machine gun in the other, walking with the ease of someone used to handing out death before breakfast.

She tossed a Beretta M9 to Neil with a sharp underhand snap.

"Heavy slide," she said. "Balanced. You'll like it."

To Jenny, she threw a Beretta PMX with a folding stock and a custom grip.

"For you. Light, fast, quiet."

Jenny caught it one-handed, inspected the action, and clipped it across the back of her riding leathers.

Marta then placed a canvas satchel into a saddlebag hanging off the seat of Neil's Ducati.

"Plastic explosive and a detonator," she said. "You'll need it to get inside that damn train of Vale's."

Finally, Marta slung the Beretta 501 sniper rifle across her own back, tightening the strap with practiced ease.

As he holstered the pistol, Neil looked up at her.

"You coming?"

Marta gave a thin smile. "You think I set this up just to wave goodbye?"

She swung onto the back of Jenny's Ducati, gripping the frame behind the seat, boots locking onto the pegs.

Jenny raised an eyebrow. "You hang on tight."

"I'll hang on," Marta said. "You just get us there."

Neil revved his engine once, a deep growl against the silence of the mountain air. Jenny followed, her throttle kicking in with a snarl. Gravel spat out behind them as the bikes peeled away from the cabin—twin streaks of matte-black fury screaming into the alpine night.

FIFTY-NINE

THE EUROCOPTER TIGER UHT sliced through the late-afternoon sky, its black fuselage skimming just meters above burning treetops. Below, the jungle was engulfed in flame—napalm fires licked upward from split canopies and shattered trunks, casting violent bursts of orange and crimson against the fading daylight. Smoke curled in roiling waves, making the chopper glow as though it were flying through the heart of a dying star.

Noah gripped the cyclic with one hand, his other resting steady on the throttle. The flight controls vibrated beneath his gloves—responsive, hungry.

Beside him, Wally was strapped in, his eyes scanning the horizon through a cracked heads-up display. The older man's face was pale in the glow of the instruments but calm.

The cockpit windshield was fractured, a jagged hole punched clean through the left pane—a souvenir from the Mapuche ambush that had won them this aircraft. Dried blood crusted the co-pilot seat and streaked the console.

"Still can't believe we're flying this thing," Wally muttered, the air rushing in and ruffling his gray hair.

Noah didn't smile. His eyes remained forward.

Ahead, the cliff face loomed out of the jungle mist—black stone veined with white roots, rising like the wall of a fortress. Vents dotted its surface—each one coughing hot chemical gas into the night air. On most maps, this part of Patagonia didn't exist. But they both knew what waited beyond the wall of rock.

Kiel's lab.

Built into the cliff. Hidden behind a waterfall.

Last time they had snuck in like a whisper. Now they would be coming with a battering ram.

Noah dipped the nose of the chopper slightly, hugging a thermal current.

A red light blinked on the comm panel.

Incoming transmission.

The radio clicked to life—tight, official, clipped.

"Chopper UHT-173, you are entering restricted airspace. Identify yourself."

Wally glanced at him. "That'll be Black Sun."

Noah toggled the channel open, his voice calm and detached.

"UHT-173 en route from Sector Ten. Refueling was delayed. Orders updated by upper command. Requesting clearance to continue approach."

A pause. Static. Then: "We weren't informed of any rerouted flights. Who gave the order?"

Noah's fingers tapped the cyclic slowly.

"Confirming with dispatch. Cross-checking Alpha-Tango loopback—stand by."

Another pause. More static.

"Sorry, UHT-173. I didn't get any of that."

"Cross-checking with dispatch right now. Get the outlay confirmed so I can give you the remit."

Wally leaned in, his voice low. "Just keep stalling. All the way until we're close enough."

Noah's eyes narrowed. He could see them now—three other choppers, Black Sun variants, hovering on parallel vectors like wolves watching an injured packmate.

"Here goes," Noah said as he brought them closer.

———

THROUGH THE GORGE BELOW, shadows moved.

A hundred Mapuche warriors advanced in silence, bare-chested and ash-marked, weapons slung tight to their backs. They moved with fluid precision, barefoot over slick moss and tangled roots, bodies blending with the rock and foliage as though they were spirits made of the land itself.

The gorge gradually narrowed around them, the stone walls pressing in close on either side, slick with moisture, twisted with ivy and hanging vines. In places, the warriors had to move single file, shoulders brushing damp stone, bows held high to avoid scraping.

Above them, the night sky was a sliver—choked with smoke from the burning jungle. The only light came in flickers, reflected off the drifting ash and the occasional glint of metal from a knife hilt or arrowhead.

Then came a sound—faint at first but rising.

Water.

The roar of the distant waterfall echoed through the gorge like the beat of some subterranean heart. The warriors paused to listen.

They were close.

The leader raised a fist, and they moved again, faster now, threading deeper through the stone passage.

Somewhere beyond the water and the rock waited the hidden entrance to Kie's lab—carved into the cliff, masked by the roar of falling water.

And when they reached it, the storm would begin.

INSIDE THE TIGER, the tension grew. They were now almost within reach of the three Black Sun helicopters. Several more hovered in the background.

Another voice broke in, tense. "This is Bravo-Two-One—confirm visual on UHT-173. Windshield's damaged. There's a hole in it."

The air thickened.

"Say again," the original voice said. "Confirm that?"

Noah edged the chopper closer. He was almost there.

"UHT-173, why does your craft have a hole in the windshield?"

"A little run-in with the locals," Noah replied.

"When was this?"

"Earlier today."

"And why didn't you radio it in?"

Noah's thumb pressed the weapons toggle. A soft beep lit the HUD with red markers. Missile lock.

"Because I was too busy murdering Black Sun," Noah muttered.

He pressed the trigger.

The missile streaked forward, trailing fire, and exploded against the nearest chopper in a bright orange bloom. The next one didn't even have time to react before Noah twisted the Tiger into a dive, raking its fuselage with the mounted M197 20mm cannon. The rounds tore into the second chopper's undercarriage like ripping paper. It peeled away in a tailspin and vanished into the burning treetops.

Wally braced as the Tiger jolted sideways, flares popping from the wings like fireflies in reverse.

Behind them, the last Black Sun chopper wheeled into pursuit. Machine gun fire laced the air—tracers slicing past their tail rotor.

Noah cut altitude and swung left—hard. The Tiger dipped under a bluff, blades just clearing a skeletal tree line.

"Missile's reloaded," Wally called out, gripping the support rail beside him.

Noah brought them around, the cliff face reeling back into view. "Let's make it count."

He fired.

The next chopper took it full in the tail—spun, caught fire, and cartwheeled into the gorge like a stone wrapped in flame.

In the distance, the other choppers began heading their way.

They were all that was left between the Tiger and the lab.

———

THE NIGHT SKY split with fire.

From the jungle gorge below, the Mapuche warriors saw it clearly—one explosion, then another, then a cascade of flares igniting the darkness like a storm of falling stars. The black curve of the chopper tail lit up in the distance before vanishing into the trees, fire trailing behind like a comet crashing to earth.

No one spoke.

But their pace quickened.

They moved faster now, weaving between moss-slick boulders and gnarled roots, shoulders brushing the vine-choked stone on either side of the narrowing gorge. The thunder of rotors had faded into the smoke above them, but the message was clear: Noah had begun the assault.

Their time had come.

Bare feet padded over mud and fallen fronds. One warrior slipped in a patch of wet shale; another grabbed his arm and pulled him silently back upright. They moved like one body— disciplined, invisible, ancient.

The gorge began to widen.

A final bend, and then—the waterfall.

It spilled from the cliffside like a silver blade, roaring into a deep, black pool below. Mist curled into the air in slow spirals, catching the glow of the burning jungle behind them. And behind the water, nearly lost in the cascade, was a vertical sliver of steel—a hidden seam cut into the rock.

The entrance.

The warriors spread out, forming a crouched semicircle at the base of the waterfall. Each man unslung his weapon with practiced ease. Bows emerged—curved wood polished by years of use. Arrows were nocked. Knives were drawn.

One of the elders, his chest marked with ocher and scars, stepped forward.

From a leather pouch, he drew a long arrow, notched at the tip with a metal hook. A thin rope was coiled at its base, wound tightly like a snake at rest.

He turned to his fellow warriors.

One by one they each nodded.

The Mapuche were ready to end this.

———

Deep beneath the mountain, past three biometric locks and a kilometer of pressure-sealed corridor, the lab's security station seethed with tension.

Fluorescent lights buzzed overhead, casting sterile light over banks of monitors glowing with infrared signatures, drone feeds, and encrypted communications. Panels blinked with warnings. Static flashed across a few external cameras—smoke interfering with the signals.

On the main screen, the Eurocopter Tiger UHT banked hard over the treetops, missiles firing.

A Black Sun chopper exploded in midair.

Rausch folded his arms and leaned against the edge of the console.

"Looks like the monster has come back to Frankenstein, Doctor," he said.

Beside him, Kiel didn't respond. He stood motionless before the monitors, his skeletal hands clasped behind his back, glasses glinting in the flicker of flame reflected on the screen.

Another chopper broke apart mid-rotation, the wreckage spiraling into the jungle below.

Kiel's jaw twitched. Just slightly.

Rausch glanced sideways at him. "You're worried."

Kiel's lips barely parted. "I'm calculating."

He leaned closer to the screen.

The Tiger's damaged cockpit came into frame for a moment —clearly visible in the pause before its next strike. The cracked windshield. The bloodstained glass. And behind it, just barely, a glimpse of Noah's face—hard, expressionless, focused.

"Doesn't look like he's coming here for a conversation," Rausch murmured.

"No. It doesn't," Kiel said quietly.

SIXTY

THE DUCATI ENGINES SCREAMED through the night, twin streaks of matte-black fury ripping across the mountain pass. The wind tore at their clothes. Trees blurred into smears of motion. The headlights cut sharp tunnels through the fog—just enough to see the cliffs curve and the road dip but not enough to feel safe.

Three klicks out, and they were catching up to the Argo fast.

Jenny hunched low over the handlebars, eyes sharp, breath steady. Marta clung behind her, one hand gripping the seat frame, the other resting lightly on the sniper rifle strapped diagonally across her back. The Beretta 501 glinted each time moonlight broke through the clouds.

To their right, Neil rode solo, tucked tight into his Ducati like it was an extension of his body, jaw clenched, eyes flicking between the road and the narrow-gauge rail line that ran parallel to it. The track was just fifty meters down the slope, mostly hidden by dense pine and the rise of rock.

The sound came first—a low, thunderous rumble rolling through the mountain like a tremor.

Then the trees broke open to their right, and there it was.

The Argo.

A vast, black length of metal cutting through the valley below. Matte black, it swallowed the moonlight. No insignias. No running lights. Just a long, silent chain of armored railcars barreling eastward along the track like a bullet from a gun.

Jenny glanced down, eyes locking on the lead engine as it emerged fully from the bend.

"We've got it!" she shouted over the wind.

She twisted the throttle harder. The bike surged forward, tires gripping the road with a snarl. Neil followed suit, streaking up alongside her, both of them now pacing the train from above— parallel lines of speed and steel.

The road dipped, curled along the edge of the ravine, then climbed again, giving them a brief, clean vantage over the entire length of the Argo.

Marta leaned closer behind Jenny, shouting to be heard. "That's military railcar design. Reinforced doors. Thermal dampening. That's where the explosives will come in handy."

"No kidding," Jenny called back. "Let's get in front of it!"

They pushed harder, engines screaming through the cold. The train dropped behind, their altitude giving them an edge as the road straightened out briefly.

A rusted sign, half-buried in bramble, stood out just enough to be spotted.

Ponte Viadotto – 600m

"There!" she shouted, pointing with a sharp nod of her chin. "Turnoff's ahead!"

Neil spotted it too, already banking left.

The road split—half continuing along the mountainside, the other veering upward onto a crumbling spur of cracked concrete, marked with rusting guardrails and overgrown chain-link.

Jenny leaned into the turn, Marta shifting her weight with practiced ease. Gravel spat behind them as the Ducatis peeled off the main road and onto the old access path.

Below, the Argo thundered on, unaware.

But above, the trap was already being set.

They veered hard, engines howling as the road split onto a sharp incline—an old maintenance trail, winding up through stone and scrub until it leveled out on a crumbling stretch of concrete and rusted railing.

Ponte Viadotto.

The old railway bridge was a skeletal structure of weathered iron and stone, long abandoned by anything but time and wind. It loomed above the valley like a dead god's spine—crossing directly over the path of the oncoming Argo.

Jenny skidded to a stop just shy of the edge. Gravel spat out under her tires. Neil pulled up beside her seconds later, dust swirling in his wake.

Below them, the track cut a deep line through the earth, winding around the mountain toward them. In the distance, the Argo came into view—dark, segmented, a ghost train. Just silence and speed.

Jenny dismounted.

Marta slid off behind her and swung the rifle down into her hands, checking the bolt, sighting the scope.

"I'll stay on the bike," she said. "Cover you from the road. Anything moves, I'll put a hole in it."

She straddled Jenny's Ducati, resting the rifle across the handlebars, and gave them a faint smirk. "You miss your jump, I'm not coming to scoop you up."

"Then we'll try not to miss," Neil said, taking the satchel of explosives from the saddlebag and strapping it to himself.

He then began climbing the short embankment beside Jenny.

The wind was stronger up here, rolling down from the peaks and pushing at them as they climbed higher onto the bridge's edge. Below, the train roared closer—an iron serpent cutting through fog and firelight.

Jenny turned to Marta. "You sure you've got us?"

Marta didn't hesitate. "Always."

The train rounded the bend. It looked massive from above—long cars lined like armored vertebrae, moving too fast for comfort but not fast enough to miss.

Marta called over the wind.

"Good luck."

Jenny looked at Neil.

"Ready?"

He nodded once. "Let's do it."

The Argo screamed underneath them.

And they jumped.

SIXTY-ONE

NOAH SAT HUNCHED in the pilot seat of the stolen Eurocopter Tiger, eyes locked on the waterfall ahead—the late-afternoon sun glinting off its cascading surface like shards of broken glass. Behind that curtain of shimmering water lay the entrance to Kiel's lab, and beyond that, the final page of a long, bloodstained book.

Noah adjusted the throttle. A red light blinked on the missile HUD.

"Time to finish this thing," he muttered.

He fired.

Two missiles streaked from the Tiger's wings, trailing smoke and fire. They punched through the waterfall like hammers, slamming into the blast doors behind it. The explosion lit the gorge in flickering orange. Stone cracked. Steel screamed. A fireball roared outward in a choking wave of pressure and steam.

The doors buckled inward, half-melted, half-shattered.

Two more missiles finished them off.

They hit in quick succession—one low, one high, detonating with a synchronized thunder that shook the very walls of the gorge. The remaining structure of the blast doors gave way in a shower of torn steel, vaporized bolts, and superheated debris. Chunks of reinforced alloy were flung into the mist like shrapnel from a dying god.

The waterfall itself split, forced aside by the shockwave, revealing the charred remnants of what had once been an impenetrable entrance. The cliff face yawned open—black, burning, and exposed.

Inside, sparks showered from severed conduits. Smoke billowed from the ceiling in thick gouts. The frame of a sentry turret jutted from the wall like a broken limb, sparking weakly before collapsing under its own weight.

The breach was complete.

Alarms blared from inside the mountain.

The remaining automatic turrets deployed—sleek and surgical, swinging toward the chopper.

Noah was already moving.

The Tiger's chin-mounted 20mm cannon spat death, cutting across the gaping entrance. Bullets shredded the turrets and tore through Black Sun soldiers pouring into the breach. Blood misted the air.

Forty seconds in and nothing existed. Nothing that moved, anyway.

Noah released the triggers.

For a moment—just one—it was quiet.

Then from the shadows of the gorge, a Mapuche warrior stepped forward.

He raised his bow.

An arrow launched, trailing a thin line of coiled rope behind it. It sailed through the smoke, struck a steel anchor point above the doorway, and locked in with a soft metallic thunk.

The line held.

The warrior began his ascent—hand over hand, slow and sure, a rope ladder coiled on his back like a sacred burden. Below him, the other warriors watched, unmoving. Breathless.

He was halfway across when the shot rang out.

The round hit him just under the ribs.

He jerked once. Blood sprayed against the mist. Then he slipped, arms grasping at empty air as he plummeted into the gorge, body vanishing into shadow.

A cry went up behind him.

Two warriors immediately began pulling the rope ladder back, while others stepped forward, loosing arrows in a furious volley. The entrance bristled with shafts, Black Sun soldiers screaming as they fell, pierced through chests and throats.

Noah realigned the chopper.

"Again," he whispered.

The Tiger's machine guns roared, slicing through fresh troops attempting to retake the entry point. The cliff face trembled with the force of the barrage.

A second warrior stepped forward, nodded once, and climbed onto the rope.

This time, no one fired.

He made it.

Reaching the far ledge, he unclipped the rope ladder from his back and secured it. He gave a single hand signal—sharp and final.

Then the Mapuche charged.

Warriors surged across the line, climbing, scaling, carrying bundles of rope, hooks, and fire-hardened spears. Soon, multiple lines crisscrossed the gorge, forming a swaying network of passage that resembled a spider's web made of old rope and vines.

Scores of Mapuche poured over the sky bridge and through the breach.

Black Sun troops within the hall met them with gunfire—but they were too few, too slow. Arrows darkened the air. Spears slammed into body armor with brutal force. The lab's front line shattered under the onslaught.

The mountain had opened.

And the jungle was coming in.

Inside the cockpit, Noah flicked a switch, then stood. He

looked over at Wally, still strapped into the co-pilot seat, eyes wide. Noah unhooked his belt and placed a hand on Wally's shoulder.

"Keep her steady."

Wally swallowed. "I'll try."

Noah opened the side door. Wind screamed into the cabin. The rotors chopped the air above like blades of judgment.

He stepped out onto the skid, grabbing the landing gear.

Then he dropped.

Swinging under the chopper, he timed his jump and let go, crashing through the smoke-heavy air into the breached entrance, boots slamming against concrete with a heavy thud.

He straightened.

From his shoulder, he unclipped the Heckler & Koch UMP and racked the bolt.

Noah Wolf had arrived.

SIXTY-TWO

THE WIND HOWLED AROUND THEM, biting cold and laced with the screech of brakes as the Argo curved along the edge of the mountain. Snow whipped past in white streaks.

Jenny slammed the final block of plastique onto the rear maintenance hatch, her breath fogging. Wires twisted from her gloves. The detonator clicked into place.

Neil crouched beside her, the M9 held in his fist.

"Charge ready?"

"Timed for five seconds," Jenny said, pressing the trigger. "Stay close."

They ducked back.

The explosion punched out a thunderclap, flinging smoke and twisted metal into the frozen air. The hatch blew inward like a kicked door.

They moved together. Into the smoke. Into the train.

The first carriage was dark, pressurized, filled with the acrid reek of melted plastic and burning oil. Sparks rained from a severed conduit. Steam hissed from a ruptured valve. Through the haze came silhouettes—armed, armored, moving fast.

Jenny raised the Beretta PMX and fired off a stream of bullets.

The first two guards dropped without a sound, rounds stitching across their necks and chest plates. One went down into a seat frame. The other pitched forward, smacking the steel floor.

Neil moved low, Beretta M9 up. He fired once, twice—center mass—taking out a third before the man could shout.

Then the real fight began.

The smoke thinned. Children of the Empire agents—Vale's elite, faces hidden behind blank masks and black visors—rushed into view from the forward car.

They didn't shout orders. They didn't hesitate.

Jenny dived behind a row of steel benches as bullets slammed into the wall above her. Glass exploded. Metal pinged. She rolled left and came up firing. Three-round bursts, low and fast.

One agent took a shot to the thigh and staggered.

Neil charged, shouldering the man into a side panel. The clang echoed through the cabin. He pistol-whipped the guard once, then twisted the man's weapon away and dropped him with a clean elbow to the throat.

Jenny ducked beneath a folding table as another burst of fire tore the headrest above her. She reached up, grabbed the tray bracket, and yanked hard. It came loose with a shriek of twisted steel.

As the next guard lunged through the smoke, she drove the metal edge into his throat. He gagged and collapsed.

Neil dragged another down into a sleeper berth, slamming the man's head into the bulkhead. The impact left a wet smear. Neil didn't wait—just grabbed the fallen rifle, slung it, and moved forward.

The PMX clicked empty.

Jenny ducked behind a luggage bin, ejected the mag, and slammed a fresh one home. As she did, a boot came crashing down on the bin above her.

She rolled just in time, a combat knife whistling past her ear.

The agent was fast—too fast for a full reload.

Jenny dropped the gun, grabbed a crystal decanter from a nearby table, and smashed it into the agent's visor. Glass exploded everywhere. The guard retaliated. He backhanded her, sending her reeling against a support beam.

Jenny spit blood. Saw red.

As he came at her, she ducked under his fist and grabbed the man's coat, drove her knee into his gut, once, twice, then grabbed his flailing arm, twisted it, and brought her elbow down on the joint. Something snapped. He screamed. She tore the knife from his belt and drove it up under his ribs.

He went limp.

Two guards burst into the scene from the next carriage.

Neil vaulted over a row of chairs, tackled them mid-turn, and rolled with them across the aisle. One kicked out, but Neil caught the boot, held it firmly, twisted, and shoved it sideways. The snap was unmistakable.

The other tried to shoot.

Neil threw his elbow across the man's neck and slammed his head into the floor. Once. Twice. Three times. Again and again.

Then stopped.

The guy wasn't moving.

Jenny scooped up the PMX and advanced, eyes scanning the doorway to the next carriage.

She dove to the side as more gunfire echoed from in front—they were still coming.

Jenny glanced at Neil.

"Two cars down," she said, her breath ragged. "At this rate, it'll be midnight before we've reached the end."

Neil gave a grim smile. "Then let's hope the bastard's still on board."

Jenny nodded, then grabbed a fire extinguisher from the wall. She yanked the pin, cracked the nozzle, and flooded the corridor with a white cloud of pressurized smoke.

Neil reloaded.

Jenny reset the PMX.

Then, together, they stepped into the next carriage.

———

AT THE FAR end of the Argo, behind two inches of blast-rated steel and biometric locks keyed only to his voice, Sebastian Vale sat in a high-backed leather chair, listening to the storm draw near.

The carriage itself was silent—eerily so.

Just the distant thump of gunfire, the occasional screech of tearing metal, a scream or two, and—closer now—the dull percussion of boots and bodies striking the floor.

Another volley of gunfire rang out, closer than before. Then a brief silence. Then another scream.

Vale sipped his wine.

He sat behind a massive obsidian desk, carved from the same volcanic stone that once lined the walls of the Council's grand chamber. The desk had been airlifted onto the Argo at great expense, but it was an important reminder of permanence. Of power.

Of control.

Now that control was slipping.

Vale swirled the glass. Deep red. A vintage Bordeaux, 2005, aged to something just short of divine. It clung to the crystal like blood.

Sophia stood to his left, hands clasped behind her back. Her silver-blond hair was pulled into a flawless braid, boots polished to a mirror sheen, her tactical coat unbuttoned just enough to show the holster beneath.

She was calm. Impossibly so.

"Surely they should have stopped them by now," Vale said. His voice was smooth, cultured, but strained at the edges. "There are twelve in the guard detail. All genetically enhanced."

Sophia tilted her head. "And all very predictable. Jenny and Neil Blessing are not."

Vale grimaced. "They're just two people."

"Yes," she said softly, "but they are also two people who have spent the past decade fighting wars."

Another burst of gunfire echoed through the door, this one closer. The rhythmic thump-thump-thump of automatic fire. Then a pause.

A single gunshot.

Silence.

Vale's shimmering eyes fixed to the door.

They were coming.

SIXTY-THREE

THE SKY above the Kazakh steppe stretched vast and starless, a heavy blanket of midnight black pressing down upon the frozen plain. They had been tracking B3-17 for six exhausting hours, every minute stretching into eternity, every step cracking frost beneath their boots. The land was flat as an execution slab—no hills, no shelter, nothing but wind-whipped darkness and frost-bitten stone. The silence was oppressive, pressing against their ears like a tangible force, broken only by the occasional groan of distant ice.

Nothing moved but the wind, scraping across the plain with the hollow whisper of something ancient and forgotten. It carried a sharp metallic bite, reminiscent of a surgical suite after trauma.

Katya led the way, her black coat billowing in the icy gusts. Her breath steamed out in quick, disciplined puffs, her gloved fingers hovering near the grip of her sidearm. She did not speak; the others followed silently, the weight of their mission pressing down upon them like heavy iron chains.

Zina moved carefully to Katya's left, eyes alert, scanning the dark horizon continuously. Imani and Gregor flanked the rear—steady, disciplined.

Lula walked beside Norah, teeth gritted, breathing sharp and rapid. Her fingers periodically twitched toward the knife at her hip, eager for release.

Tao lagged slightly behind, shoulders hunched protectively around the tablet clutched to his chest.

Then, abruptly, they saw him.

Ahead, barely visible in the moonless gloom, stood a solitary figure: B3-17.

He was motionless. Unafraid. Waiting.

Katya halted about twenty meters away, her voice steady yet edged with caution.

"B3-17."

He slowly turned toward her, his expression eerily serene, empty—not hostile exactly, but disturbingly void.

"You shouldn't have come," he said softly, his voice calm, almost gentle.

"Why are you here?" Katya demanded. "Where are you going?"

He tilted his head slightly, staring out across the endless darkness of the steppe.

"I'm meeting someone."

"Who?" Katya pressed.

Instead of answering, he repeated quietly, "You shouldn't have come."

Lula scoffed bitterly. "You almost killed Norah."

"I did what I was told," B3-17 replied placidly. "Just like all of you." His gaze drifted slowly from one face to another.

Lula surged forward abruptly, her knife flashing in her hand, her voice a harsh growl. "No more riddles, no more codes—no more of you!"

"Lula, wait!" Katya shouted, but Lula was already charging, blade ready.

B3-17 didn't flinch. Calmly, clearly, he recited, "Delta nine nine three zero one Erika nine."

Lula collapsed mid-stride, her blade slipping uselessly from her fingers as her legs gave way beneath her. She hit the frozen ground convulsing, eyes wide with helpless panic.

"Lula!" Katya rushed forward.

B3-17 turned toward Gregor without missing a beat. "Kilo one five Victor Victor zero eight."

Gregor crumpled instantly, seizing violently on the icy plain.

"Alpha delta seven three six Julia nine," B3-17 said, eyes flicking calmly toward Imani.

Imani fell silently, a soundless scream frozen on her lips.

Tao staggered backward, terror in his voice. "Stop—please!"

B3-17 ignored him, turning his cold gaze upon Zina.

Katya frantically shouted their counter-phrases, desperation clawing at her voice.

"Override Theta! Sequence break! Reclaim memory, Zina —listen!"

But Zina merely twitched, then dropped limply to the ground.

"Enough!" Katya snarled at B3-17.

He regarded her calmly and curiously. "You don't have a breaker, do you, Katya? You have a kill switch fitted to your heart. Has Wally Lawson ever removed it?"

Katya's breath caught painfully, eyes locked on B3-17 in sudden fear.

"Don't—" she started.

But he spoke softly, definitively. "Omega six two seven Katya fire Vesper zero."

Katya collapsed, clutching her chest, heart racing uncontrollably, breath rasping in her throat.

Norah lunged forward desperately, only to be restrained by Tao. "We can't help her now!" he shouted urgently.

B3-17 turned to face Norah calmly. "Delta one seven seven Oscar six Norah nine."

Norah froze mid-stride, crashing to the ground in a rigid heap, eyes wide with terror.

Tao, frantic, slammed his thumb onto the tablet, releasing a burst of subharmonic static. The harsh sound ripped through the silence, causing B3-17 to convulse violently. His face twisted with pain, eyes wide and unseeing, mouth open in a soundless cry as he collapsed heavily to his knees, shuddering under the merciless assault.

Tao cut the static abruptly, plunging the steppe into a sudden, deafening silence. B3-17 remained kneeling, breathing raggedly, trembling fingers pressed desperately into the icy ground for support. Slowly, haltingly, he began to rise, his movements unsteady but resolute. His breathing steadied gradually, and a chilling calm returned to his expression as he straightened fully.

"Help them," Tao said. "Please."

B3-17 didn't hesitate. He moved first toward Katya, who lay crumpled on the frozen ground, her gloved hand clutching desperately at her chest.

B3-17 knelt beside her, his gaze clinical, detached. He leaned close, his voice a quiet, precise whisper, heavy with a strange, unsettling gentleness.

"Undo command Sigma eight eight seven Katya Phoenix four."

Katya jerked violently as though shocked by electricity, gasping deeply, chest heaving as her heartbeat gradually steadied. The painful constriction loosened from her chest, and her eyes slowly regained clarity. She stared up at B3-17, confusion and wary relief mingling in her expression as she struggled to rise.

B3-17 had already moved on. He knelt beside Norah next, who lay stiff and helpless, eyes wide and terrified. He leaned closer, his voice even softer now, yet each syllable fell precisely into the silence.

"Undo command Gamma five four nine Norah Echo two."

Norah shuddered sharply, her limbs twitching as control

flooded back into her muscles. She drew in a ragged breath, coughing painfully as she pushed herself onto trembling elbows.

One by one, B3-17 moved among the rest, reversing their paralysis with quiet, efficient counter-commands. However, just as they all staggered to their feet, the night sky above suddenly filled with a harsh, blinding glare.

"Helicopters!" Tao cried desperately, pointing upward.

Bright searchlights pierced the darkness, illuminating the icy steppe with stark, unforgiving brilliance. Dozens of aircraft roared into view, rotors pounding the air, washing the frozen plain in light as they descended swiftly.

Katya's hand tightened on her pistol, eyes narrowed in helpless realization.

"Stand down," she commanded softly. "We won't win a direct gunfight. Not here."

The recruits watched helplessly as the steppe around them filled with troops, lights flooding the darkness as the enemy closed in.

SIXTY-FOUR

THE UNDERGROUND COMPLEX shook with gunfire and screams.

Smoke clung to the halls like mold, seeping from vents and cracks. Sirens blared in confused rhythms. Emergency lights flickered red against polished steel. The sound of boots—some charging, others fleeing—mixed with panting breath, barked orders, and the gurgle of dying men.

It was the sound of war in a cage.

Noah moved through it like a blade. His Heckler & Koch UMP roared with short, precise bursts—each one dropping a Black Sun soldier mid-step. One in the chest. Another in the leg before a second shot to the face finished him. Blood sprayed wide. It smeared the walls and slicked the floors, turning the polished corridors into rivers of red. Muzzle flashes strobed off steel.

He stepped over bodies.

The Mapuche were everywhere. Their war cries echoed off the walls.

They surged through the base like a flood, unstoppable and merciless. Bare-chested, ash-painted, eyes bright with ancestral fire, they came armed with bows, axes, spears, machetes—old world weapons of reckoning.

Gunfire tore through the air, and some warriors fell—ragged holes blooming red across their chests or backs—but their brothers leapt over them without pause, without mercy, war cries rising above the sirens. One sprinted through a barrage, a blade in each hand, carving down a pair of guards before collapsing from a gut shot. Another launched himself down a stairwell, landed hard, and drove a fire-hardened spear into the ribs of a man trying to radio for help.

They came from everywhere: air ducts, floor panels, maintenance shafts. One emerged from a ceiling panel, landing in a crouch behind two soldiers, then slit both throats before they could turn.

The cries of "Ñamku!" echoed through the tunnels—part battle cry, part invocation.

A cluster of Black Sun troops tried to form a defense line near a security junction—but it was overrun in seconds. Spears pierced their chest plates. Arrows hissed through the air, landing in eyes, throats, temples. Screams turned into gurgles. Those who tried to crawl away were dragged back by the hair and silenced with axes.

One Mapuche group cornered a team of scientists barricading a lab annex. They broke through the doors with axes, threw in burning cloth soaked in ethanol, and sealed the door again. The screams were short-lived.

Another group found a munitions cache, burst it open, and began tossing out grenades and rifles like tools of vengeance. Some kept their blades. Others strapped bandoliers across their chests, grinning through blood and soot.

Noah moved through the carnage, calm amid the chaos, eyes locked ahead.

He passed two Mapuche going wild on a group of soldiers. Another helped a wounded brother tie off a tourniquet before rising with a growl and burying his axe into a fallen enemy's neck.

Noah was advancing toward the ventilation control room—

just ahead and two levels down. Once secured, they could flood the entire base with poisonous gas and smoke, drive the rest of Black Sun into the open where the real justice waited in the jungle.

A Black Sun operative rounded the corner, rifle raised.

Noah dropped him in two shots—one to the collarbone, one to the jaw—without slowing his stride.

Behind him, the wolves were tearing through the sheep. And there would be no shepherd left to save them.

———

INSIDE THE BLACK Sun security station—buried beneath three meters of reinforced concrete and sealed behind a series of blast doors—Viktor Rausch's face was red with fury. Sweat beaded along his collar, his breath coming in short huffs.

The control room stank of fear.

Rausch leaned over the monitor bank, barking orders into his headset.

"Unit Twelve, fall back to Node C! Hold that line or I will shoot you myself!"

A panicked voice crackled back. "They're everywhere—coming from the vents—there's too many!"

Rausch slammed his fist into the console. "Then die like soldiers! Not like—like cattle!"

He turned to another operator. "Seal sector seven. Gas the entire area if you have to."

"They're already inside sector seven, sir."

Rausch's hands clenched. "Then seal them in."

Behind him, Kiel stood pale and still, a tremor in one hand as he watched the overhead feed. One monitor tracked Noah's approach—room by room, floor by floor, step by step.

The feed stuttered, jittered, and then flashed as another explosion rippled through the base.

"He won't breach this room," Rausch muttered, almost to himself. "Not with the failsafes in place."

But Kiel said nothing. His voice, when it came, was soft.

"Noah Wolf will be here soon," he whispered.

SIXTY-FIVE

THE CARRIAGE WAS silent save for the creak of broken fittings and the soft whine of torn metal swaying with the train's momentum. The floor was littered with the dead—bodies flung across velvet benches and smashed glass tables, limbs askew like discarded mannequins. Blood smeared the gold trim. The smell of gunfire and death clung to everything.

Jenny knelt by the door to Vale's carriage, a strip of malleable plastique in her gloved hands. She pressed it into the seam, quick and steady. Behind her, Neil kept watch, the Beretta M9 loose in his grip, eyes scanning the ruin they'd left behind.

"Let's see what's behind door number nine," Jenny said as she slid the detonator into the explosive.

But then—

Hiss-click.

The carriage door opened on its own.

Jenny froze.

Sophia stood halfway up the aisle of the next compartment. Her white hair danced in the wind rushing through the open windows. In her arms was an HK416, matte-black and cold. Her blue eyes were crystal calm.

Jenny didn't think.

She threw herself backward just as the rifle barked.

Bullets tore through where she'd been, chewing up paneling, glass, and velvet. She hit the floor and rolled for cover.

Then—a grinding clunk.

A whir of hydraulic movement.

Jenny lifted her head to see the carriages begin to separate.

"No—NO!"

The connector arms disengaged with a mechanical groan. The rear carriages slowed, brakes screaming against the rail.

"NEIL! HURRY!"

Neil was behind cover farther down the carriage.

Jenny threw the Beretta PMX to the floor, freeing her arms.

Then she jumped.

Wind roared in her ears as the chasm yawned beneath her. If she didn't make it, she would hit the tracks and be crushed by the other carriages.

But she did make it.

Jenny caught the edge of the forward carriage, fingers scrabbling for purchase, legs dangling over steel and speeding track. Gritting her teeth, she began hauling herself up with a snarl.

Boots planted. She raised her head—

Sophia stood in the open doorway, white hair wild in the wind, assault rifle leveled.

Jenny stared down the barrel.

CRACK-CRACK-CRACK.

She flinched, eyes squeezed shut, knuckles whitening on the rail.

But nothing hit. No pain. No blood.

The shots had come from behind.

Neil.

He stood in the other doorway, M9 gripped in both hands, firing with grim precision.

One round hit.

Sophia staggered back, the slug slamming into the breastplate of her body armor with a heavy thud. The rest of Neil's shots missed, his pistol quickly falling out of effective range as the carriages pulled farther apart.

But it was enough.

Jenny seized the moment. She lunged upward, grabbed the edge of the doorway, and hauled herself into the moving carriage with a desperate grunt. Her boots scraped for purchase on the metal floor. Sophia was still off-balance—just enough.

Jenny surged forward, snatched the rifle from Sophia's hands, and wrenched it sideways. With a sharp twist, she turned the weapon toward her opponent.

But Sophia moved like a spring uncoiling. Her heel snapped up in a blur, catching the rifle cleanly. The weapon was kicked from Jenny's hands and sent flying backward through the open doorway, vanishing into the blur of wind and track behind them.

Jenny didn't hesitate. She drew her karambit from its sheath, the curved blade catching the carriage lights.

Sophia stepped back, calm, and drew her Yojimbo tactical knife from her boot.

They began to circle—two predators, breath shallow, knives ready.

At the back of the carriage, Sebastian Vale stood behind his obsidian desk.

He lifted a crystal glass of red wine in salute.

"Ah," he called. "The great Jenny Blessing. I am honored to see you fight."

Jenny didn't even deign to look at him.

"Shut the fuck up," she said instead.

Then Sophia lunged.

Steel met steel.

And the night split open.

SIXTY-SIX

NIGHT SWALLOWED THE KAZAKH STEPPE
—A vast, icy expanse bathed only in starlight and the faint, ghostly glow of the moon. A biting wind swept low across the open plains, causing the sparse, frostbitten grass to sway like a restless ocean.

Katya stood rigid, her breath fogging in rhythmic clouds as she scanned the horizon.

Searchlights sliced down from above, white beams piercing the darkness as five large, black transport helicopters descended. Powerful gusts from the rotors battered the recruits, making them stagger against the sudden tempest of ice crystals and dust.

Katya shielded her eyes, blinking furiously against the fierce gusts. "Stay calm," she shouted to the recruits, her voice strong despite the chaos. "And keep still!"

The helicopters landed around them in a perfect encircling formation, heavy landing gear sinking slightly into the frozen earth. Hydraulic ramps hissed open, disgorging streams of armed soldiers clad in sleek black combat armor. Floodlights mounted on the helicopters drenched the area in harsh brilliance, banishing shadows and illuminating the stark scene.

The soldiers disgorged from the crafts in perfect formation. They advanced swiftly, weapons trained, their movements disciplined and silent. They spread out methodically, closing ranks and trapping Katya and the recruits in a tightening noose of glinting rifle barrels.

A harsh, amplified voice barked commands through a speaker mounted to one of the choppers. "On your knees! Hands behind your heads, now!"

Katya complied instantly, dropping smoothly to her knees, placing her hands firmly behind her head. "Do exactly as they say," she warned, her voice steady and controlled.

The recruits reluctantly mirrored her, grimacing as their knees hit the frozen ground. Soldiers moved swiftly, securing their weapons, forcing wrists into submission and patting down their jackets. Zina winced as a soldier roughly twisted her arms. Gregor snarled quietly under his breath as a boot pressed into his spine.

But B3-17 remained untouched, standing tall amid the turmoil, calm as a stone monument. The soldiers encircled him protectively, forming a barrier of sleek black armor and firepower.

The last helicopter's rear ramp lowered, a metallic groan that preceded heavy footsteps. From the shadowy interior emerged a figure radiating undeniable authority. He strode forward confidently, the silver trim of his black coat glinting under the stark floodlights, the insignia on his chest bright against the darkness.

Children of the Empire.

His boots crunched deliberately across the ice until he stopped directly in front of B3-17. His gaze seemed to dissect the boy carefully, weighing him with cold appraisal.

"This the Black Sun clone?" the man asked, his voice deep and calm, threaded with quiet menace.

"Yes, sir," replied the soldier closest to him.

The officer nodded slowly. "Good. Very good."

SIXTY-SEVEN

THE VENTILATION CONTROL room was already damaged from the missile attack. Acrid smoke hung in the air, alarms wailed incessantly, and severed cables sparked and spat like angry snakes.

Noah knelt beside the master control console, a determined calm etched into his features as he placed a magnetic mine—one of six pilfered from the Mapuche warriors' captured Black Sun cache. Carefully wedging it between coolant valves, he set the digital timer for exactly seven minutes, its red digits blinking with lethal promise.

Rising swiftly, he turned to the battered control board, fingers dancing expertly over the surviving interface. He rerouted gas flows, forcing override commands, disabling safety measures. The system groaned in protest.

Warning: CORE VENT PRESSURE CRITICAL flashed ominously in crimson across a cracked monitor.

A faint, grim smile curled at Noah's lips. "Time to leave," he murmured.

Then, with methodical violence, he swung the butt of his

Heckler & Koch UMP down hard, shattering the control panel in a burst of sparks and glass, silencing its desperate electronic screams.

Seven minutes.

More than enough.

Noah spun on his heel and sprinted down corridors slick with blood and littered with the fallen. Emergency lights flickered, casting eerie red hues over the bodies of Black Sun operatives, sprawled in grotesque postures of defeat.

Ahead, the fierce chants of the Mapuche warriors reverberated defiantly.

He reached the blast-reinforced corridor guarding the entrance to the security station. The last of the Mapuche gathered there, their powerful forms painted in ash and streaked in blood. Sweat and battle-lust shone in their eyes. Some held captured Black Sun firearms—automatic rifles and tactical shotguns. Others brandished ancient weapons: axes, spears, knives dripping with fresh blood.

They parted respectfully, stepping aside like guardians yielding to a trusted ally. Their leader—scarred and resolute—gave Noah a solemn nod of recognition.

Noah knelt before the reinforced door, extracting three of the magnetic timed mines from his tactical belt. He affixed them to strategic points—left, right, and center of the heavy steel barricade. The mines' activation lights blinked red, pulsing rapidly, the twenty-second countdown beginning.

"This should clear the way," Noah said, stepping back.

He and the Mapuche took cover around the next corner.

The mines detonated in a storm of fire and metal, shaking the entire corridor. The thick security door buckled, screaming as it was torn apart, debris and flames billowing outward in a furious rush.

Noah and the Mapuche surged forward into the smoke-choked breach.

Inside the security station, chaos erupted like a ruptured dam.

Rausch stood at the center of the storm, face twisted in fury, barking commands over the deafening shriek of alarms. His fist slammed against the control desk hard enough to crack the glass.

"Hold your positions!" he roared. "Nobody retreats—fight, damn you! Fight!"

He could only watch as his men were quickly overwhelmed. Arrows hissed through the smoky air, embedding deep into bodies and armor. Warriors moved swiftly, silently, and brutally, axes and knives catching the crimson glare of emergency lights as they rose and fell.

A soldier lunged desperately, only to be impaled through the gut and flung backward against the monitor bank. Another went down instantly as a blade buried deep between his shoulder blades.

A lieutenant to Rausch's left—face pale, eyes glassy with terror—lifted his sidearm with trembling fingers. Before Rausch could react, the man pressed the muzzle beneath his own chin and squeezed the trigger. Blood and bone sprayed outward, staining the walls and consoles in grotesque Rorschach patterns.

Rausch's face contorted with disgust and rage. But before he could curse or rally the remaining troops, more Mapuche surged through like a tidal wave of vengeance.

Rausch snarled, raising his pistol and firing in wild, panicked bursts. One warrior took a bullet in the shoulder and staggered but did not fall, his eyes blazing with defiance.

Then an arrow struck Rausch's hand with brutal precision, piercing through flesh and bone. He screamed, the gun falling from his grip, clattering uselessly to the blood-slick floor.

In seconds, warriors closed around him, forcing him onto his knees, gripping him tightly. He struggled, teeth bared like a cornered animal.

"Get your filthy hands off me!" he spat, blood and saliva flecking his chin.

The warriors parted respectfully, creating a path as Noah stepped calmly through the swirling smoke. His face was set, cold and resolute, the Heckler & Koch UMP hanging casually by his side.

Rausch's eyes blazed with hatred. "What you've done today," he snarled through clenched teeth, "will doom us all. Our bloodline will be tainted and weakened. You've condemned humanity to inferiority. You've sentenced the future to chaos!"

Noah held his gaze steadily, unmoved.

Then, quietly, he turned to the warriors. "He's yours."

They fell upon Rausch instantly, an unbridled fury of vengeance. Flesh tore, bones splintered as the warriors began skinning him alive. Screams ripped from his throat, raw and agonized, before dissolving into ragged gurgles and finally silence.

Noah turned his back to the grisly execution and moved toward the far corner of the room.

Under an overturned desk, Dr. Erich Kiel huddled, pale and trembling, glasses lost in the chaos, eyes wide with horror. Blood trickled down his temple, glistening darkly in the intermittent red flashes.

Kiel stared up at Noah, voice shaking. "Will you have me torn apart as well?"

Noah paused, considering him quietly, his expression unreadable. Then, slowly, he extended a gloved hand toward the trembling geneticist.

"No," he said firmly. "You, Dr. Kiel, will right all the wrongs you've committed."

Kiel hesitated, eyes flicking nervously between Noah's hand and his face.

Then, with a quivering sigh of resignation, Kiel reached out, allowing Noah to grasp his wrist firmly. Noah hauled him upright, steadying him on shaky legs.

"Come on," Noah said calmly, turning toward the shattered doorway. "You're coming with us."

SIXTY-EIGHT

THE BLADE SANG as Jenny's karambit cut through the air.

Sophia twisted sideways, her Yojimbo tactical knife flashing in a brutal upward backhand slash, pakal thrust—forcing Jenny to pivot, redirect, attempt a largo disarm. Their blades clashed with a sharp snap, close as a lover's breath. They moved like dancers—no wasted steps, no hesitation. Death in motion.

The train swayed beneath them, its luxury furnishings now debris. A shattered decanter, a broken lamp, the cushions of a sofa spewed across the plush carpet. Vale stood behind his desk, hands calmly wrapped around a crystal tumbler of wine, watching.

Jenny lunged—reverse grip diagonal, aiming low toward Sophia's ribs. The bodyguard caught her wrist, redirected—scoop trap, then stepped in with a knee to the gut. Jenny grunted, doubled slightly, then brought her blade up in a vicious heaven six diagonal aimed for Sophia's neck.

But Sophia was already moving. She turned her shoulder inward, ducking beneath the arc, knife flashing up in a tight windmill slash meant for Jenny's inner thigh.

Jenny blocked with the karambit's curve, barely catching the blow, then twisted and threw a brutal elbow into Sophia's temple. The bodyguard staggered back. Jenny took her chance.

She darted forward—not toward Sophia but toward Vale.

Sophia reacted instantly—throwing herself into her path, slashing at Jenny's face. Jenny ducked, rolled across the desk, blade aimed directly for Vale's chest—

Steel met steel.

Sophia had intercepted the strike mid-motion, twisting Jenny's arm with a snake disarm, forcing her to drop into a crouch to escape. Jenny spun and sliced, just barely missing Vale's shoulder, but Sophia slammed her backward.

Jenny crashed against the desk.

Her elbow hit something.

CLUNK.

A massive red button lit up as it depressed under her weight.

Behind them, a section of the carriage wall hissed—and then slid open, revealing a grotesque gallery.

Glass jars. Dozens. Shelved like precious artifacts, each one containing a severed human head preserved in yellowing fluid. Men, women. Eyes open. Mouths mid-scream or mid-sob. Their expressions frozen—judges, witnesses, ghosts.

The fight paused for less than a breath.

Then Sophia came for her.

Jenny ducked low, slashing out in a wide figure-eight arc with the karambit. Sophia sidestepped, counter-thrust, her knife kissing Jenny's shoulder as it passed—cutting deep but not fatal.

Jenny hissed and rolled aside, her foot striking a jar at the bottom of the cabinet. Pain ran down her arm. Her fingers weakened, and she lost her grip on the karambit.

It skittered across the carpet.

Sophia lunged to finish it—direct thrust, aimed to the solar plexus.

Jenny, with a snarl, grabbed one of the jars and hurled it at her.

It smashed against Sophia's forearm.

Preservative fluid sprayed across the floor. The head—a woman's—rolled toward the center of the carriage, long blond hair trailing behind like seaweed.

Sophia flinched from the explosion of glass and fluid.

Jenny dove for the knife, her hand closing around the karambit.

Whirling around, she launched herself forward in a low, oblique-angle strike. Sophia tried to parry, but Jenny caught her arm, pinned it with her own, and tackled her off her feet, slamming her to the floorboards with bone-rattling force.

Breathing hard, Jenny straddled her, legs locked tight. The karambit rose, a gleam of steel catching the light as she raised it high—ready to bring it down.

Sophia didn't blink. She accepted death.

Then—

SNAP.

Vale yanked the emergency brake cord.

The carriage lurched savagely.

Jenny was thrown sideways by the jolt, the blade missing its mark and gouging deep into the floorboards beside Sophia's head. A split-second later, both women tumbled in opposite directions.

The train screamed. Metal groaned. Everything pitched violently as the train shuddered to an abrupt halt atop a narrow bridge straddling a roaring river.

Jenny flew sideways, crashing into Vale's desk, the impact rattling her bones and scattering papers to the floor.

Sophia rolled away, gritted her teeth, and kicked the jarred head out of her path as she scrambled to her feet.

Blood and formaldehyde streaked the floor. Wind howled through the shattered doorway.

Far below, moonlit waters churned over jagged rocks, their tumultuous roar rising like applause to the violence above.

———

WHILE HIS WIFE fought for her life, Neil ran hard along the narrow edge of the railway track, boots pounding against the gravel, lungs burning with every breath. The cold mountain air cut into his throat, but he didn't slow down.

Not now.

Ahead, the Argo waited in the dark like a steel serpent.

Jenny was up there. Fighting. Bleeding. Holding the line.

He had to get to her.

Every so often, Neil would glance to his right, to the road that paralleled the track across a steep, rocky ravine. Shadows blurred in his peripheral vision—trees, cliffs, fractured moonlight.

Then—finally—he saw her.

Marta.

The Ducati streaked along the winding asphalt, low and fast, headlamp slicing through the darkness. Her silhouette was a black blur behind the handlebars, the sniper rifle still slung across her back like a second spine.

Neil opened his mouth to yell, but the wind stole the sound.

Then he heard it.

A deep, rhythmic thump. Low at first. Then rising. Multiplying.

He slowed for just a moment, turned his head—and felt his stomach clench.

Helicopters.

Lots of them.

Their lights flared through the clouds—staggered, blinking—like falling stars in reverse. Five, six, seven massive shapes descending behind the ridgeline, their rotors kicking up spirals of snow and dust as they banked over the road.

Then came the ground vehicles. Dozens. Headlights bobbing and weaving through the switchbacks behind Marta like a convoy of wolves. Armored transports. Tactical rigs. Trucks with mounted guns.

Backup.

Not theirs.

Vale's.

Neil's pace faltered for a breath, his boots slipping on the uneven ballast. But he couldn't let himself wince from the battle. Not now. Not when she needed him most. He pushed forward again, faster, harder, pain flaring in his side with each step.

Jenny was up there.

And the end was coming.

SIXTY-NINE

KATYA LAY face-down against the icy earth.

After hours of relentless pursuit and tension, they'd finally been cornered in the open expanse of the frozen Kazakh steppe. The chill seeped through her clothes, gnawing at her skin, but she kept still, eyes fixed ahead, muscles taut.

"Stay calm," she kept whispering to the recruits sprawled around her. "No sudden moves."

Norah lay motionless, her breath a visible tremor in the freezing air. Lula's fingers trembled near the empty sheath at her hip, desperate to fight. Tao shivered visibly, face pale and eyes wide. Zina, Imani, and Gregor exchanged quick, anxious glances but remained frozen in compliance.

B3-17 stood alone in the center, unaffected, untouched, and unafraid.

The leader of the soldiers approached slowly—a tall and imposing man, his squared jaw clenched tight, eyes piercing and ruthless beneath his cap. The muted gleam of his silver Children of the Empire insignia flickered under the helicopter's floodlights. He crouched down, eyes level with B3-17, voice danger-ously soft.

"Is that for me?" he asked, nodding toward the sleek black oblong—Putorana's core data drive—in the boy's gloved hand.

B3-17 stared at it, considering, then looked straight into the officer's eyes. "I think it must be."

The officer's hand extended slightly, deceptively calm. "Can I have it?"

But B3-17 did not move. Instead, he tilted his head curiously, his voice even and clear. "Your name is James Grayson."

"That's right," the officer said.

"Former Colonel in the Council's armed forces," B3-17 continued. "Led a purification squad in Thessaloniki. Confirmed kills—two hundred and thirteen. Unconfirmed—forty-seven, including children."

Grayson's eyes hardened, a thin vein pulsing at his temple. "How could you possibly know that?"

"I memorized every file from the Putorana archives," B3-17 replied, his voice eerily calm. "Every name, every atrocity commit-ted. Camelot preserved all your sins."

Grayson straightened, tension radiating from every muscle as he roughly grabbed the data core from B3-17's hand. He slid it into his pocket, his fingers lingering momentarily, then moved purposefully to his sidearm.

B3-17 didn't flinch. "What will you do to my friends?"

Grayson drew the pistol and chambered a round, his expres-sion grim. "The same thing I'm going to do to you."

"No!" Katya shouted, surging upward from the ground.

Instantly, a soldier slammed the butt of his rifle into her skull. Katya crumpled to the frost, vision blurred, tasting blood.

"Stay down!" another soldier shouted, aiming his weapon at Norah and Lula, who looked most likely to lunge.

Grayson turned back to B3-17, gun steady. "Goodbye, clone."

B3-17's lips moved softly, voice steady: "Alpha five five nine beta Samuels."

Grayson froze. His eyes widened, his body twitching. The pistol slipped from his grip and landed on the icy ground.

"Sir? Sir!" a soldier called out, stepping forward as Grayson convulsed, collapsing to his knees.

"What did you do?" another shouted, aiming at B3-17.

"It's his breaker," B3-17 said simply, turning his gaze calmly to the rifleman. "All Council soldiers were fitted with them. Just like you were, Sergeant Brandon Hatfield, stationed in Prague before the fall. Delta four two zero Juliet Romeo six."

Hatfield stiffened violently, rifle dropping uselessly. He collapsed, eyes wide in terror.

Pandemonium erupted. Soldiers shouted, coming to the aid of their comrades. Others froze with confusion, unsure what was happening.

The distraction was enough.

Norah moved first, driving her elbow fiercely into the knee of the nearest distracted soldier. He buckled, screaming as she grabbed his fallen rifle and ended him with a swift, precise shot.

Lula exploded upward, lunging for her weapon on the ground and spinning immediately into a lethal burst of gunfire. Gregor, Imani, and Zina scrambled for cover, retrieving dropped firearms and returning precise, coordinated fire.

Katya struggled upright, blood streaming from her temple, her vision swimming. She snatched a fallen pistol, firing decisively at retreating soldiers. Tao scrambled desperately toward an abandoned rifle, crawling low through chaos and smoke.

Amid the confusion, B3-17 moved calmly toward the helicopters, untouched by bullets or fear. He reached the closest chopper as a pilot stumbled out, fumbling for his weapon.

B3-17's eyes fixed calmly on the pilot emerging shakily from the cockpit. The man's gloved fingers scrambled frantically for his sidearm, but the weapon barely cleared the holster before B3-17's soft voice carried sharply over the noise of the firefight.

"Lieutenant Marcus Everson. Sigma three three zero Zulu X-ray eight."

Everson's entire body stiffened violently, eyes bulging. His limbs spasmed, the pistol clattering to the frozen ground as he toppled sideways against the helicopter's landing gear. Convulsing helplessly, he hit the snow-covered earth hard, body twitching as though jolted by electric shocks.

Inside the cockpit, the other pilots frantically attempted radio contact, their panicked voices cutting urgently through static-filled channels.

"Unit One, respond! Everson, confirm status!"

"We've lost ground control—request authorization to engage with suppressing fire!"

One pilot reached desperately for the trigger mechanism of the mounted autocannon, the weapon humming as it powered up. But before he could fire, Katya was already there. She surged forward, blood streaming down her forehead, eyes narrowed with deadly focus. Raising her stolen sidearm, she fired two precise shots through the cockpit glass. The pilot slumped instantly, head snapping back against the seat.

Lula and Norah sprinted toward the third helicopter, gunfire erupting around them. Lula fired sharp bursts, clearing the path as Norah vaulted inside, dispatching the struggling pilots swiftly and efficiently. Gregor, Zina, and Imani converged on the fourth and fifth crafts, rifles barking in unison, dropping pilots as they attempted to scramble away or reach their mounted weapons.

Tao, prone behind a pile of fallen soldiers, carefully aimed and squeezed the trigger repeatedly, picking off straggling enemy troops attempting to regroup. Chaos consumed the field; screams intermingled with the roar of gunfire, illuminating the night in brief, violent flashes of muzzle fire.

As each helicopter fell silent, the recruits moved methodically forward, their movements now precise and relentless, each step a calculated act of violence.

In mere minutes, silence reclaimed the battlefield. Smoke drifted lazily upward from gun barrels and shattered equipment, joining the faint clouds overhead. Bodies lay scattered and broken across the frosted earth, testament to the brutality and precision of their retaliation.

Katya lowered her weapon slowly, her breath coming in ragged bursts. Blood ran freely down the side of her face, dripping onto her black coat and staining the snow beneath her boots. She surveyed the carnage silently, eyes hard and unwavering.

B3-17 stood motionless near the closest helicopter, gaze drifting calmly across the aftermath. When Katya approached him, her voice was rough but steady.

"You did well, B3-17. You saved us."

He nodded slowly, eyes lingering briefly on the fallen Grayson, whose body was still twitching faintly in the frost. "I did what was necessary."

Lula approached, rifle still gripped tightly, her eyes fierce. "We need to move. More could be coming."

"Gather what you can," Katya ordered sharply, her voice regaining strength. "We're commandeering this helicopter. Tao, check the controls. Norah, Gregor, secure the perimeter. Lula, Zina, Imani—arm yourselves fully. We move out in three minutes."

SEVENTY

SMOKE POURED from the shattered breach like a funeral pyre. The jungle air was thick with the stink of scorched metal, cordite, and something chemical and wrong.

Noah marched toward the breach, his Heckler & Koch UMP slung at his side, still warm from the fight. All around him, the underground lab hissed and seethed, firelight flickering across the ash-marked faces of the Mapuche warriors.

Dr. Erich Kiel stumbled in front of him, coughing—his lab coat scorched, his hands bound behind his back with industrial zip ties.

"Keep moving," Noah said, shoving him forward.

Behind them, the rumble grew louder. Deep, low, tectonic. The base's ventilation control systems were failing—one by one. The fail-safes were gone. Fire bloomed within the labyrinth of tunnels like veins igniting. Somewhere far below, the containment thresholds were giving way.

Noah gave a tight nod. "Go."

The Mapuche moved fast, stringing themselves across the rope bridge with practiced speed. One after another, bare feet found footing over the abyss. They moved like they were born to the heights—silent, swift, sure. The wounded were carried. The dead left behind, their ashes already becoming part of the jungle again.

Wally's voice crackled over the comms. "Inbound. Hold tight."

Noah turned to the breach.

And there it was—cutting low through the smoke, blades screaming—the Tiger.

The stolen Eurocopter emerged like a beast from the shadows, its body scorched, its windscreen webbed with cracks. It was an omen and a salvation.

Wally hovered the gunship just above the breach's edge, lowering the skids with a steady hand.

Noah shoved Kiel forward.

"Up," he snapped.

Kiel hesitated—then climbed aboard, his mouth tight with fury and fear.

Noah slung himself up after, boots thudding onto the cabin floor. He turned back once—eyes sweeping the gorge.

The last Mapuche warrior crossed the rope bridge, turning to slice the cord behind him. The bridge sagged, then fell, disappearing into the smoke and tumbling down with the water.

Wally didn't wait. The Tiger screamed as it rose.

Below them, the jungle was a tapestry of fire and shadow.

Then the world went white.

The magnetic mines exploded deep within the base.

A concussive shockwave burst from beneath the cliffs, splitting the stone like an axe through ancient wood. The entire ventilation breach erupted in a pillar of fire. Metal shrieked. Rock gave way. The hillside collapsed inward, swallowing itself whole. A subterranean furnace roared out of the breach, incinerating everything it touched.

Noah watched in silence as the last of Black Sun's lab was

consumed. Viral research. Clone tanks. Genetic horror. All of it erased. The disease cauterized at the root.

Wally glanced back at him. "So you decided to bring him with us."

Noah didn't answer right away. His eyes lingered on the burning wound in the earth.

Then he looked at Kiel—crumpled in the corner of the chopper, hands still bound, eyes wide.

"Yes," Noah said. "I think he can help us."

Kiel stared back, his expression unreadable.

The Tiger banked west, vanishing into the fire-streaked sky.

SEVENTY-ONE

NEIL ROUNDED the bend in the track, boots crunching over frost-hardened gravel. His legs burned, lungs raw, but he didn't stop. His eyes were locked forward—just ahead, stretching out over the rushing waters of an alpine river, sat the Argo.

The train had stopped.

It loomed in the dark like a segmented beast, silent atop a steel bridge that spanned the water below.

He picked up his pace, breath fogging in the cold air. A hundred feet to the bridge. Maybe less. Almost there.

Then he froze, coming to a shuddering stop.

Red dots.

Dozens of them.

They appeared in a heartbeat—flickering into existence across his chest, his arms, his face. A field of pinprick lasers painted him in violent crimson.

His pulse slammed into overdrive.

The tree line to his right broke open—black-clad figures in

full tactical gear seeping out onto the track. Their weapons raised. Their movements surgical.

Children of the Empire.

They'd beaten him here.

Neil exhaled through his nose and slowly raised his hands. He didn't speak. Didn't move. His heart thudded in his throat, but he kept his chin high.

From above, a helicopter drifted lower, its rotors deafening against the mountain silence. Floodlights swept the bridge in harsh white cones. Snow and debris lifted in spirals.

They barked orders. "On your knees. Hands behind your head. Now."

Neil lowered himself to the frozen stone, grimacing as his knee struck the track.

Hands grabbed his wrists, forced them behind his head. Plastic zip ties tightened around his skin, biting bone.

Still, he didn't resist.

The floodlights shifted.

One of the men leaned close. "Up."

They hauled him to his feet with professional indifference, one on either arm.

Neil looked up at the Argo.

Still waiting. Still watching.

As the black-clad men marched him forward onto the bridge, toward the belly of the monster, he let one final thought settle like a nail in his gut: *Jenny's still inside.*

And he had no idea if she was alive or dead.

———

ALIVE. Just.

Steel clashed with steel, a vicious symphony echoing through the luxury carriage.

Sweat stung Jenny's eyes, mingling with the blood that trickled down her temple. The metallic taste of copper filled her mouth, and every labored breath felt like flames licking up through fractured ribs.

Still, her grip continued to tighten around the curved karambit knife.

Opposite her, Sophia's breathing was equally ragged, a crimson slash dripping from a deep cut above her brow, the sleeve of her white shirt soaked through from another wound.

Despite the blood loss, Sophia's stance remained fierce, her eyes sharp with hateful determination. They circled each other slowly, two predators trapped in a cage of steel and upholstery.

Through the armor-plated windows, the serene alpine river stretched outward under the silver touch of moonlight—rushing past underneath and absolutely oblivious to the carnage within the Argo.

Sophia lunged, feinting high before slicing low. Jenny barely sidestepped, gripping Sophia's wrist and driving an elbow hard into her face.

Sophia staggered backward, crashing into a gold-inlaid drinks cabinet, its mirrored door fracturing with a crystalline crash. Retaliating swiftly, she delivered a punishing kick into Jenny's thigh, forcing separation.

They pulled apart momentarily, chests heaving, eyes locked. Sophia's blade trembled slightly, her stance faltering from pain and exhaustion.

Seizing her moment, Jenny charged, unleashing a furious storm of strikes. Steel clanged against steel, a whirlwind of violence. Jenny twisted, spun, ducked—and then slashed upward with lethal precision.

The karambit bit deeply into Sophia's side. Blood erupted, hot and vivid. Sophia gasped sharply, dropping heavily to one knee, her strength flooding out onto the rich carpet beneath her.

Ignoring Sophia now, Jenny spun toward Vale. He stood behind his massive obsidian desk, eyes wide with terror, white-knuckled fingers gripping the edge of it.

Jenny advanced, knife raised—but then recoiled.

The world suddenly became a harsh blaze of blinding white as helicopter searchlights pierced the carriage. Rotors thumped heavily overhead. An amplified voice boomed over a loudspeaker.

"Drop the weapon and stand down, or we will fire on the carriage."

Jenny hesitated only a moment, eyes never leaving Vale. "This train's armor-plated, isn't it?"

Vale remained frozen, his expression one of pure, primal fear.

Jenny's grip tightened on the karambit, ready to lunge.

"Bet I get to you long before any of those bullets get through," she said.

Then a voice shattered the moment.

"Jenny?"

She spun toward the open carriage door.

Outside on the narrow bridge, Neil knelt with hands bound behind his back. Blood streaked his face. A pistol barrel was pressed coldly against his temple. Behind him, a dozen operatives from the Children of the Empire aimed their weapons, laser sights tracing lines of death across Jenny's body.

A soldier barked, "Drop it or he dies."

Her breath caught painfully, eyes locked with Neil's, blade trembling in her blood-slick hand.

Within the second of hesitation, a shadow moved behind her. Sophia lunged upward, driving the Yojimbo blade deep into Jenny's abdomen. Pain exploded. Jenny collapsed to her knees, gasping as the world blurred violently.

"Jenny, no!" Neil screamed. His voice broke, raw with desperation as he fought against the men holding him down, their powerful grips unyielding. "Get away from her! Jenny! Jenny!"

Through the searing agony, Jenny clawed weakly at the wound, blood pulsing through her trembling fingers. Dark tendrils of dizziness began to curl around her vision, pulling her consciousness downward.

Sophia straightened, calmly wiping Jenny's blood from her blade, and reached out a steady hand to Vale.

Jenny watched helplessly from the floor as Sebastian Vale adjusted his coat, his eyes cold and disdainful as he regarded her collapsed form before stepping carefully past the spreading pool of her blood.

"Bring her," Vale commanded coldly as he stepped down onto the track.

Two of his men stormed into the carriage, their heavy boots shaking the floorboards as they closed in. Jenny forced herself upright, blood streaming through her fingers, her breathing shallow and desperate. She lunged toward the first man, fist clenched weakly, driven purely by desperation and fury.

He swatted her aside easily with the stock of his rifle. Pain exploded across her cheekbone; white-hot lights flared in her vision. She fell hard, sprawling onto the blood-slicked carpet, barely conscious.

They grabbed her roughly, each gripping an arm, their gloved fingers digging bruises into her skin. Jenny fought with every last ounce of strength she could muster, twisting and kicking weakly, screams choked into ragged gasps.

But it was no good.

With brutal efficiency, they dragged her limp, bleeding form from the carriage, her boots scraping uselessly along the metal floor, leaving a smeared trail of crimson behind.

The cold night air hit her like a shockwave, cutting sharply into her exposed skin. She was thrown carelessly onto the icy bridge, landing with a wet thud that sent fresh agony rippling through her body.

Kneeling there, she raised her head just enough to meet Neil's eyes.

Neil stared back, his own expression raw with anguish and helpless fury. His eyes brimmed with tears as the men held him down mercilessly, rifles pressed firmly against his back.

Jenny tried to speak, to offer some comfort, some final word —but all she could do was watch him through a haze of pain as blood pooled around her, soaking into the stones beneath.

They knelt facing each other, separated by ten feet of cold steel railway track.

Sophia stood between them.

Vale handed her back the dripping Yojimbo blade.

"Bring me their heads," he said, cold and pitiless.

She went to Neil first. He struggled, but the soldiers forced him forward, bowing his head.

Jenny struggled as much as she could, but it was no good.

There was nothing she could do.

"Get away from him!" she cried hoarsely. Then she pleaded, "Please... Please, don't hurt him..."

Sophia seized Neil by the hair, wrenching his head back to expose his throat. Neil's eyes met Jenny's, unafraid despite the inevitable.

"Jenny, I love—"

Sophia pulled the blade across his throat. Blood sprayed, and Neil's body spasmed, once, twice, then slumped lifelessly.

Jenny's screams ripped through the night, raw with anguish and loss. Her body collapsed beneath her, despairing tears blurring her vision as Sophia began using her knife to remove Neil's head.

As she lay there on her side, Jenny couldn't breathe.

Time slowed, stretching into endless agony, her heartbeat drumming painfully loud in her ears. Her vision tunneled, narrowing around Neil's body—still, lifeless, robbed of everything he had been.

She reached out with trembling fingers, trying in vain to bridge the distance between them. Her voice was little more than a cracked whisper now, repeating the same broken words over and over: "Neil... Neil... please..."

Her mind shattered into a thousand fragments, each reflecting his final expression, etched in love and pain.

She barely noticed Sophia finishing it, or the sickening satisfaction on Vale's face as Sophia carried the dripping trophy toward him. Jenny simply crumbled onto the icy tracks, the cold stones biting into her cheek as fresh, uncontrollable sobs tore through her chest.

She waited, broken, not caring that her own death would come next.

Sophia handed Neil's severed head casually to Vale.

Vale examined it with detached admiration. "This will go nicely with my collection," he said softly before handing it off to one of his soldiers.

Sophia wiped her blade clean, her cold eyes locked on to Jenny.

"You next," she whispered, stepping forward, knife poised.

Jenny barely heard the words. She knelt on the bridge, shattered, broken, tears streaming down her face. Beneath the steel arches, the river roared in the darkness, swollen and violent, waiting hungrily far below.

Sophia moved closer, savoring each slow step.

Jenny's vision blurred with tears and pain.

But then suddenly sharpened when she caught the glint of metal—a combat knife strapped securely in an ankle holster of the soldier nearest to her. Within hand's reach.

Her pulse quickened. She took a shallow breath, steadying herself. Her fingers twitched, nerves firing desperately.

Revenge.

Revenge before death.

But before Jenny could act, a deafening crack split the night. The soldier pressing his rifle into her back jerked violently backward, his head exploding into a mist of blood.

Chaos ignited.

Another crack.

Another soldier dropped.

Panic swept through Vale's ranks as they shouted and scrambled for cover.

Across the valley, high on the winding road, Marta stood firm, the Beretta 501 sniper rifle balanced expertly on the railing, her eye coldly focused as she chambered another round.

Her shots continued to tear through the night with precise fury.

In the sudden madness, Jenny lunged, her fingers gripping the soldier's ankle knife. In one smooth motion, she freed it, twisted around, and hurled the blade straight at Vale. It spun, a deadly blur slicing toward his face.

Sophia, instinctively protective, shot a hand out just as the blade reached her master. The knife pierced Sophia's palm driving straight through and partially into Vale's eye. He staggered back, screaming in agony, hand clutching his wounded face, blood gushing through his fingers.

Gunfire erupted, bullets streaking toward Marta's position, but Jenny had no time to hesitate. With no other choice left, she threw herself over the edge of the bridge.

Cold air whipped around her, then the brutal impact. She plunged into the freezing river, dragged along violently by the current. Every muscle screamed, wounds burning in agony, her blood leaving a crimson trail in the churning water.

Jenny fought desperately, surfacing briefly with a choking gasp, lungs seizing with pain. With the last of her strength, she clawed her way through the torrent, finally gripping the jagged shoreline. Her fingers tore against sharp rocks as she dragged herself out, coughing and shivering violently.

A roar erupted nearby. Marta's Ducati skidded to a halt, engine rumbling.

"Get on!" the Italian shouted, urgency clear.

Jenny ignored the searing pain in her body and threw herself onto the back of the bike, wrapping her arms tightly around Marta's waist.

The Ducati roared forward, bullets ricocheting off the rocks around them as they raced into the darkness, neither of them daring to look back.

SEVENTY-TWO

KATYA CLIMBED into the cockpit of the hijacked helicopter, hands gliding over controls she knew by heart. Lights blinked awake, the systems humming back to life.

The recruits climbed aboard quickly, settling into seats, their eyes wary but resolute. Norah hesitated at the hatchway, looking back at the desolate steppe before climbing inside.

Katya motioned to B3-17, who moved silently to the chopper, taking the seat closest to her.

Norah strapped herself into the seat directly behind Katya. She leaned forward, voice strained but steady. "Where are we going now?"

Katya paused, fingers lingering over the control panel. She looked out at the empty, windswept plain—so vast, yet now so dangerous. Her thoughts churned through scenarios, safe havens, exposed bases, and compromised routes. Her jaw tightened slightly.

"I don't know," she admitted finally. "Putorana is too exposed now. The Children of the Empire knows where we are."

She glanced back at Norah, saw Noah Wolf's fierce determination reflected in the girl's eyes, and allowed herself a brief moment of hope.

"We'll have to make contact with your father," Katya continued, her voice low but confident. "Find out where Jenny and Neil are, and regroup from there."

"And until then?" Norah asked softly.

Katya's gaze returned forward, hand steadying on the cyclic control. "For now—we just need to get away from here."

She triggered the ignition.

The rotors whined, spinning to life with rising fury. Dust and ice whipped around the helicopter as it lifted gracefully from the steppe, nose tilting gently into the wind.

Below them, the bodies and destruction shrank into abstract shapes. The earth receded, scars and blood vanishing beneath shadow and distance.

Ahead, the horizon was a black velvet expanse scattered with stars, the moonlight cutting silver ribbons across the frozen landscape.

Katya steered toward that darkness—westward, away from the ruins behind them, toward whatever awaited in the night.

EPILOGUE

THE ROOM WAS DIMLY LIT, illuminated only by the subdued glow of antique lamps that cast shadows across the lavish furnishings. Heavy velvet drapes concealed windows, making it impossible to discern the time of day or even where in the world they were.

Sebastian Vale sat in a high-backed armchair, a crystal tumbler of whiskey resting on the mahogany table beside him. His leather eyepatch, newly acquired, lent him a sinister air, but at the moment, it mainly frustrated him. He reached for his glass, missing it twice before finally snatching it irritably.

Sophia, standing nearby, observed with an expression that could almost have been amusement—if she ever allowed herself such indulgence.

"You'll adjust," she murmured softly.

Vale shot her a withering glance. "I appreciate the optimism."

She offered a slight shrug. Her right hand was wrapped in a pristine white bandage, the lingering pain of the blade she'd intercepted still evident in her stiff movements.

The silence lingered between them, thick and tense, until Vale broke it.

"Any word on Wolf?"

"Nothing definitive," Sophia replied. "But he's alive. We have confirmation of that much. He escaped Argentina with the help of American allies, presumably US Navy. He's gone underground."

Vale took a thoughtful sip from his whiskey, savoring its warmth. He stared at the swirling amber liquid, one good eye reflecting its shifting color. "Of course, he has," he said bitterly. "A man like Wolf doesn't die easily. He'll gather the remnants of Camelot, reorganize, and strike again."

Sophia inclined her head slightly. "He is a fugitive now. The UN has branded him and Camelot rogue. Every intelligence agency on the planet is hunting him."

"Yet he remains elusive," Vale remarked with grudging respect. "Always one step ahead. But he will falter. Eventually, he'll have nowhere left to run."

An assistant entered the room quietly, handing Vale a leather-bound dossier. Vale reached out clumsily, grabbing air instead, nearly dropping the dossier before grasping it firmly. Sophia looked away, hiding a smirk.

"What?" Vale snapped defensively.

"Nothing," Sophia replied, cool as ever.

Vale scowled, leafing through the dossier. "Increase surveillance at known Camelot sympathizer sites. Monitor communications. I want him found. I want Noah Wolf's head in a jar."

Sophia nodded silently, eyes sharp with determination. "It will be done."

Vale pushed himself from the chair, steadying himself with a hand on the ornate desk. He walked slowly to the long cabinet against the far wall. With a gentle push of a hidden panel, it opened smoothly, revealing rows of jars arranged neatly behind glass.

Floating within the translucent preservative, heads gazed blankly forward, their eyes cloudy and unseeing. Among them was Neil Blessing, his features preserved in a permanent state of shock, the skin pale beneath the liquid.

Vale lingered for a moment, admiring his collection, then tapped gently on an empty jar next to Neil's. The brass plate below it was engraved clearly:

NOAH WOLF

"Your place is waiting, Mr. Wolf," Vale murmured softly, a faint smile tugging at his lips. "And soon, very soon, it shall be filled."

———

PACIFIC OCEAN | DAWN

The wind coming off the ocean was cold and sharp, the sky painted in deep hues of twilight and bruised clouds. The St. Michael, a battered container ship with rust-streaked flanks, sliced steadily through the waves toward coordinates known only to a few.

Katya stood at the bow, a black wool coat flapping gently around her knees. Beside her were the recruits—Norah, Tao, Lula, Gregor, Imani, Zina—and B3-17, their expressions a mixture of exhaustion, grief, and stubborn resolve.

Norah gazed at the horizon, her eyes nervous, anxious. Waiting.

Behind them lay a world turned hostile. Camelot's sanctuary in Putorana had fallen days ago to a multinational coalition, a swift and brutal raid timed perfectly. But by then, the operatives had already scattered into the winds, safe houses activated, caches reclaimed. Friends had emerged from the shadows, loyal even in the dark.

They were down—but far from out.

"Here they come," Katya murmured, breaking the silence.

The ship slowed. Beneath the rolling waves, the ocean's surface began to bubble and churn, and moments later, a sleek shape breached the water, black steel cutting upward, gleaming wetly in the fading sunlight.

A US Navy submarine—the USS *Idaho*—rose smoothly, its conning tower slicing through the foam. Once it settled, the crew began opening the hatches and climbing onto the submarine's deck.

Friends in unlikely places.

Allies, even now.

The recruits leaned forward, gripping the rails. Norah's breath caught sharply.

Then, from the tower emerged Noah Wolf, followed closely by Wally Lawson. Behind them, his wrists zip-tied, looking pale and defeated, came Dr. Erich Kiel.

Noah crossed the temporary gangplank connecting the two vessels. He nodded briefly at Katya and the recruits, then handed Kiel off to a waiting pair of Camelot security operatives. They swiftly escorted the prisoner below deck.

Noah gave the ship a cursory glance before turning to Katya. "It's not exactly the Valkyrie."

"No, it's not," Katya replied softly.

He turned again, and his gaze settled on Norah.

Father and daughter stood facing each other, hesitant for just a heartbeat. Then Noah opened his arms, and Norah rushed forward, holding him tightly, burying her face against his shoulder.

"I missed you," she whispered, voice muffled.

Noah held her firmly. "Me too."

After a long moment, the embrace broke. Noah straightened, his eyes scanning the assembled team.

His expression hardened once more.

"Where's Jenny?"

Katya hesitated, suddenly sheepish. "Down below," she said quietly. "But she's not good."

Noah turned back to his daughter.

"Wait for me, okay?" he said softly. "I just need to speak with your Aunt Jenny."

Norah nodded, understanding.

Noah gave a single, tense nod and moved quickly toward the stairway that descended into the ship's interior.

The lower decks smelled of rust and sea air. Noah navigated the cramped corridors until he reached Jenny's cabin. The door was shut tight.

He knocked gently.

"Didn't I tell you all I didn't want to be bothered?" Jenny's voice was rough and sharp through the metal.

"It's me," Noah said softly.

A pause. Then, slowly, the door unlocked.

He stepped inside.

The cabin was dark, lit only by the faint glow of Jenny's phone, frozen on a video of Neil—paused, mid-smile. The air felt oppressive, heavy with grief. Jenny sat on the edge of the bed, wrapped in bandages beneath her loose-fitting clothes. Her skin was pale, her eyes swollen and red-rimmed, sunken with loss and exhaustion.

She'd barely survived. Marta had delivered her to an off-the-books surgical center hidden in a veterinary clinic in Innsbruck, Jenny clinging to life on the back of the Ducati, blood soaking through makeshift bandages.

Katya and the others had joined her later in Athens, slipping aboard the ship under the cover of darkness. That was over a week ago.

For a long moment, neither spoke. They just looked at one another, the silence heavy with shared pain.

Then Noah stepped forward and threw his arms around her.

Jenny stiffened at first, but then collapsed into his embrace, her sobs tearing through the silence of the cabin. Her grief flowed unchecked, violent and raw.

Noah held her close, his voice quiet but fierce.

"We will avenge him," he whispered, the words a promise. "Believe me when I tell you that."

Jenny's fingers tightened on the fabric of his coat. She couldn't speak—could only nod fiercely against him.

Outside, the ship turned into the growing darkness, sailing onward to whatever came next.

Don't miss WOLF AT THE GATES. The riveting sequel in the Noah Wolf Thriller series.

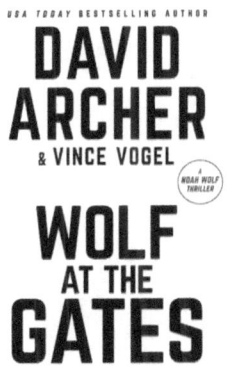

Scan the QR code below to purchase WOLF AT THE GATES.

Or go to: righthouse.com/wolf-at-the-gates

DON'T MISS ANYTHING!

If you want to stay up to date on all new releases in this series, with this author, or with any of our new deals, you can do so by joining our newsletters below.

In addition, you will immediately gain access to our entire *Right House VIP Library,* which includes many riveting Mystery and Thriller novels for your enjoyment. Including a prequel novella to this series!

righthouse.com/email

(Easy to unsubscribe. No spam. Ever.)

ALSO BY DAVID ARCHER

Up to date books can be found at:
www.righthouse.com/david-archer

ROGUE THRILLERS
Gates of Hell (Book 1)
Hell's Fury (Book 2)
Ice Burn (Book 3)
Judgement by Fire (Book 4)

JACOB HUNTER THRILLERS
The Kyiv File (Book 1)
The Bogota File (Book 2)
The Havana File (Book 3)
The Amsterdam File (Book 4)
The Saint Petersburg File (Book 5)

PETER BLACK THRILLERS
Burden of the Assassin (Book 1)
The Man Without A Face (Book 2)
Unpunished Deeds (Book 3)
Hunter Killer (Book 4)
Silent Shadows (Book 5)
The Last Run (Book 6)
Dark Corners (Book 7)
Ghost Operative (Book 8)
A Fire Burning (Book 9)
Dawnlight (Book 10)
Dead Ice (Book 11)
No Loose Ends (Book 12)

ALEX MASON THRILLERS
Odin (Book 1)
Ice Cold Spy (Book 2)
Mason's Law (Book 3)
Assets and Liabilities (Book 4)
Russian Roulette (Book 5)
Executive Order (Book 6)
Dead Man Talking (Book 7)
All The King's Men (Book 8)
Flashpoint (Book 9)
Brotherhood of the Goat (Book 10)
Dead Hot (Book 11)
Blood on Megiddo (Book 12)
Son of Hell (Book 13)
Merchant of Death (Book 14)
Extinction C-14 (Book 15)
A Vengeful God (Book 16)

NOAH WOLF THRILLERS
Code Name Camelot (Book 1)
Lone Wolf (Book 2)
In Sheep's Clothing (Book 3)
Hit for Hire (Book 4)
The Wolf's Bite (Book 5)
Black Sheep (Book 6)
Balance of Power (Book 7)
Time to Hunt (Book 8)
Red Square (Book 9)
Highest Order (Book 10)
Edge of Anarchy (Book 11)
Unknown Evil (Book 12)
Black Harvest (Book 13)
World Order (Book 14)
Caged Animal (Book 15)
Deep Allegiance (Book 16)

Pack Leader (Book 17)
High Treason (Book 18)
A Wolf Among Men (Book 19)
Rogue Intelligence (Book 20)
Alpha (Book 21)
Rogue Wolf (Book 22)
Shadows of Allegiance (Book 23)
In the Grip of Darkness (Book 24)
Wolves in the Dark (Book 25)
Olympus Must Fall (Book 26)
Children of the Empire (Book 27)
Wolf at the Gates (Book 28)

SAM PRICHARD MYSTERIES
The Grave Man (Book 1)
Death Sung Softly (Book 2)
Love and War (Book 3)
Framed (Book 4)
The Kill List (Book 5)
Drifter: Part One (Book 6)
Drifter: Part Two (Book 7)
Drifter: Part Three (Book 8)
The Last Song (Book 9)
Ghost (Book 10)
Hidden Agenda (Book 11)

SAM AND INDIE MYSTERIES
Aces and Eights (Book 1)
Fact or Fiction (Book 2)
Close to Home (Book 3)
Brave New World (Book 4)
Innocent Conspiracy (Book 5)
Unfinished Business (Book 6)
Live Bait (Book 7)
Alter Ego (Book 8)

More Than It Seems (Book 9)
Moving On (Book 10)
Worst Nightmare (Book 11)
Chasing Ghosts (Book 12)
Serial Superstition (Book 13)

CHANCE REDDICK THRILLERS
Innocent Injustice (Book 1)
Angel of Justice (Book 2)
High Stakes Hunting (Book 3)
Personal Asset (Book 4)

CASSIE MCGRAW MYSTERIES
What Lies Beneath (Book 1)
Can't Fight Fate (Book 2)
One Last Game (Book 3)
Never Really Gone (Book 4)

ABOUT US

Right House is an independent publisher created by authors for readers. We specialize in Action, Thriller, Mystery, and Crime novels.

If you enjoyed this novel, then there is a good chance you will like what else we have to offer! Please stay up to date by using any of the links below.

Join our mailing lists to stay up to date -->
righthouse.com/email
Visit our website --> righthouse.com
Contact us --> contact@righthouse.com

facebook.com/righthousebooks
x.com/righthousebooks
instagram.com/righthousebooks